Homer Hickam is the bestselling and award-winning author of many books, including the #1 *New York Times* memoir *Rocket Boys*, which was adapted into the popular film *October Sky*. A writer since grade school, he is also a Vietnam veteran, a former coal miner, a scuba instructor, an avid amateur paleontologist, and a retired engineer. He lives in Alabama and the Virgin Islands.

CARRYING

Albert

HOME

Homer Hickam

HARPER

Harper
An imprint of HarperCollins*Publishers*
The News Building
1 London Bridge Street
London SE1 9GF

www.harpercollins.co.uk

This paperback edition 2016

3

First published in the USA by HarperCollins*Publishers* 2015

Published by HarperCollins*Publishers* 2015

Copyright © Homer Hickam 2015

Homer Hickam asserts the moral right to be identified as the author of this work

A catalogue record for this book is available from the British Library

ISBN: 978-0-00-815424-0

Printed and bound in Great Britain by
Clays Ltd, St Ives plc

CARRYING ALBERT HOME

The somewhat True Story of a
MAN, HIS WIFE, and HER ALLIGATOR

AS TOLD BY

Homer Hickam
(THE YOUNGER)

STARRING

Elsie Lavender Hickam
(Who thought what she said caused the journey)

AND

Homer Hickam
(THE ELDER)
(Who thought what he did caused the journey)

AND FEATURING

Albert Hickam
(Who actually caused the journey)

AND

The Rooster
(Whose presence on the journey is not entirely understood)

THE PARTS OF THE JOURNEY

Introduction to the Journey

UNTIL MY MOTHER TOLD ME ABOUT ALBERT, I NEVER knew she and my father had undertaken an adventurous and dangerous journey to carry him home. I didn't know how they came to be married or what shaped them to become the people I knew. I also didn't know that my mother carried in her heart an unquenchable love for a man who became a famous Hollywood actor or that my father met that man after battling a mighty hurricane, not only in the tropics but in his soul. The story of Albert taught me these and many other things, not only about my parents but the life they gave me to live, and the lives we all live, even when we don't understand why.

The journey my parents took was in 1935, the sixth year of the Great Depression. At that time, a little more than one thousand people lived in Coalwood and, like my future parents, most of them were young marrieds who had grown up in the coalfields. Every day, as their fathers and grandfathers had done before them, the men got up and went to work in the mine where they tore at the raw coal with drills, explosives, picks, and shovels while the roof above them groaned and cracked and sometimes fell. Death happened often enough that a certain melancholy existed between the young men and women of the little West Virginia town when they made their daily farewells. Yet, for the company dollar and a company house, those farewells were made and the men trudged off to join the long line of miners, lunch buckets swinging and boots plodding, all heading for the deep, dark underground.

While their men toiled in the mine, the women of Coalwood were tasked with keeping their assigned company houses clean of the never-ending dust. Chuffing coal trains rumbled down tracks placed within feet of the houses, throwing up dense clouds of choking ebony powder that filtered inside no matter how tightly doors and windows were shut against it. Coalwood's people breathed dust with every breath and saw it rise in a gray mist when they walked the streets. It blossomed from their pillows when their tired heads were laid down and rose in a sparkling cloud when blankets were pushed aside after sleep. Each morning, the women got up and fought the dust, then got up the next day and fought it again after they'd sent their husbands to the mine to create more of it.

Raising the children was also left to the wives. This was at a time when scarlet fever, measles, influenza, typhus, and unidentified fevers routinely swept through the coalfields, killing weak and strong children alike. There were few families untouched by the loss of a child. The daily uncertainty for their husbands and children took its toll. Not too many years had to pass before the natural innocent sweetness of a young West Virginia girl was replaced by the tough, hard shell that characterized a woman of the coalfields.

This was the world as it was lived by Homer and Elsie Hickam, my parents before they were my parents. It was a world Homer accepted. It was a world Elsie hated.

But of course she did.

She had, after all, spent time in Florida.

→ ←

Long after my parents made the journey that is told by this book, my brother Jim and I came along. Our childhoods were spent in Coalwood during the 1940s and '50s, when the town was growing older and some comforts such as paved roads and telephones had crept in. There was even television and, without it, I might have never heard about Albert. On the day I first heard about him, I was lying on the rug in our living room watching a rerun of the Walt Disney series about Davy Crockett. The show had made the frontiersman just about the most popular man in the United States, even more popular than President Eisenhower. In fact, there was scarcely a boy in America who didn't want to get one of Davy's trademark coonskin caps, and that included me, although I never got one. Mom liked wild critters too much for that kind of cruel foolishness.

My mom walked in the living room when Davy and his pal Georgie Russell were riding horseback through the forest across our twenty-one-inch black-and-white screen. Georgie was singing about Davy and how he was the king of the wild frontier who'd killed hisself a b'ar when he was only three. It was a catchy tune and I, like millions of kids across the country, knew every word. After a moment of silent watching, Mom said, "I know him. He gave me Albert," and then turned and walked back into the kitchen.

I was focused on Davy and Georgie so it took a moment before Mom's comment sank into my boyhood brain. When a commercial came on, I got up to look for her and found her in the kitchen. "Mom? Did you say you knew somebody in the Davy Crockett show?"

"That fellow who was singing," she said while spooning a dollop of grease into a frying pan. Based on the lumpy slurry in a nearby bowl, I suspected we were having her famous fried potato cakes for supper.

"You mean Georgie Russell?" I asked.

"No, Buddy Ebsen."

"Who's Buddy Ebsen?"

He's the fellow who was singing on the television. He can dance better than he can sing and by a sight. I knew him in Florida when I lived with my rich Uncle Aubrey. When I married your father, Buddy sent me Albert as a wedding present."

I had never heard of Buddy or Albert but I had often heard of rich Uncle Aubrey. Mom always added the adjective *rich* to his name even though she said he'd lost all his money in the stock market crash of 1929. I'd seen a photograph of rich Uncle Aubrey. Round-faced, squinting into a bright sun while leaning on a golf club, rich Uncle Aubrey was wearing a newsboy "Great Gatsby" golf cap, a fancy sweater over an open-collared shirt, plus fours knickers, and brown and white saddle shoes. Behind him was a tiny aluminum trailer which apparently served as his home. It was my suspicion that rich Uncle Aubrey didn't need much money to be rich.

Seeking clarification, I asked, "So . . . you know Georgie Russell?"

"If Buddy Ebsen is Georgie Russell, I surely do."

I stood there, my mouth open. Giddiness was near. I couldn't wait to tell the other Coalwood boys that my mom knew Georgie Russell, just one step removed from knowing Davy Crockett himself. I would surely be envied!

"Albert stayed with us a couple of years," Mom went on. "When we lived in the other house up the street in front of the substation. Before you and your brother were born."

"Who's Albert?" I asked.

For a moment, my mother's eyes softened. "I never told you about Albert?"

"No, ma'am," I said, just as I heard the commercial end and the sound of flintlock muskets booming away. Davy Crockett was back in action. I cocked an ear in its direction.

Seeing the pull of the television, she waved me off. "I'll tell you about him later. It's kind of complicated. Your father and I . . . well, we carried him home. He was an alligator."

An alligator! I opened my mouth to ask more questions but she shook her head. "Later," she said and got back to her potato cakes and I got back to Davy Crockett.

Over the years, Mom would do as she promised and tell me about carrying Albert home. At her prodding, Dad would even occasionally tell his side of it, too. As the tales were told, usually out of order and sometimes different from the last time I'd heard them, they evolved into a lively but disconnected and surely mythical story of a young couple who, along with a special alligator (and for no apparent reason, a rooster), had the adventure of a lifetime while heading ever south beneath what I imagined was a landscape artist's golden sun and a poet's quicksilver moon.

After Dad went off to run heaven's coal mines and Mom followed to tell God how to manage the rest of His affairs, a quiet but persistent voice in my head kept telling me I should write the story of their journey down. When I heeded that whispering voice and began to put all the pieces of it together, I came to understand why. Like a beautiful flower unfurling to greet the dawn, an embedded truth was revealed. The story of how my parents carried Albert home was a bit more than their fanciful tales of youthful adventure. Put all together, it was their witness and testimony to what is heaven's greatest and perhaps only true gift, that strange and marvelous emotion we inadequately call love.

—HOMER HICKAM
(the younger)

xv

PART I

How the
Journey Began

1

WHEN ELSIE CAME OUTSIDE INTO THE BACKYARD TO SEE
why her husband was shouting her name, she saw Albert lying on his
back in the grass, his little legs splayed apart and his head thrust backward. She was sure something awful had happened to him but when her
alligator raised his head and smiled at her, she knew he was all right. The
relief she felt was palpable and nearly overwhelming. After all, she loved
Albert more than just about anything in the whole world. She knelt and
scratched his belly while he waved his paws in delight and grinned his
most toothsome grin.

At just a little over two years old, Albert was over four feet long,
which was big for his age according to a book Elsie had read about alligators. He was covered with a thick skin of exquisite olive-colored scales
with yellow bands on his sides that the book said would disappear over
time. Raised ridges rippled down his length, even to the tip of his tail,
and his belly was soft and creamy. His expressive eyes were the color of
gold but glowed a compelling red at night. His face was quite striking,
his nostrils perfectly placed atop the tip of his snout to allow him to breathe
while resting in the water, and an endearing overbite that presented

rows of brilliantly white teeth. He was, Elsie believed, about the handsomest alligator there ever was.

Of course, Albert was also smart, so smart he followed Elsie around the house like a dog and when she sat down, he crawled into her lap and let her pet him like a house cat. This was good because she was no longer able to have either a dog or a cat, due to Albert's tendency to ambush them from under the bed or out of the little concrete pond her father had built for him. Albert had never actually eaten either a dog or a cat but he'd come close, enough so that both species had declared the Hickam house and yard off-limits for at least the next century.

After smiling back at her "little boy," as she liked to call him, Elsie took note of her husband, who had ceased yelling and was just looking at her with an expression that she interpreted as somewhat peevish. She could not help but also note that he was dressed in a rather peculiar fashion, which led her to ask, "Homer, where are your pants?"

Homer did not answer her directly. Instead he said, "Me or that alligator." Then he said it again, this time low and slow. "Me . . . or . . . that . . . alligator."

Elsie sighed. "What happened?"

"I was sitting on the toilet doing my business when *your* alligator climbed out of the bathtub and grabbed my pants. If I hadn't climbed out of them and run out here, he'd have surely killed me."

"I guess if Albert wanted to kill you, he'd have done it a long time ago. So what do you want me to do?"

"Choose. Either me or him. That's it."

There it was. How long, she wondered, had this been coming at her, at them both, at them all? Yet, she had no answer other than the one she gave. "I'll think it over."

Homer was incredulous. "You're going to think it over when it's me or that alligator?"

"Yes, Homer, that is exactly what I'm going to do," Elsie said, then flipped Albert over and beckoned him to follow. "Come on, little boy. Mama's got some nice chicken for you in the kitchen."

Homer watched in disbelief as Elsie led Albert inside the house. At the fence, Jack Rose, neighbor and fellow coal miner, approached and coughed politely. "You gonna catch cold, son," he said. "Maybe you ought to go put on some pants."

Homer's face turned crimson. "Did you hear?"

"Everybody on this row likely heard."

Homer knew he was in for some terrible ribbing. Coal miners always liked to take a man down a notch and Homer being chased into the yard without his pants by Elsie's alligator was going to make it easy for them. "Help me out, Jack," he pleaded. "Don't tell anybody about this."

"Okay," Rose said, amiably, "but I can't guarantee the missus." He nodded over his shoulder to the window where Mrs. Rose stood with a big grin. Knowing he was doomed, Homer hung his head.

That night, over supper, Homer paused over his brown beans and cornbread. "Have you thought it over yet? About me and Albert?"

Elsie didn't look at him. "Not yet."

Homer was clearly miserable. "I'm going to catch heck from the other miners about being chased outside without my pants."

Elsie still did not look at him. She was staring at her beans as if they were sending her a message. "I have a solution," she said. "Quit the mine. Get out of that dirty old hole and let's go live somewhere clean."

"I'm a coal miner, Elsie. It's what I do."

She finally looked at him. "It's not what I do."

All night long, Elsie slept with her back turned to Homer and the next morning, after fixing him breakfast and handing him his lunch bucket, she provided no kiss, or a wish that he might return home safely. Homer was certain he was the only Coalwood miner who went to work that day without some sort of well-wishing from his wife and that knowledge was a heavy weight to carry. On top of that, a miner named Collier Johns gave him the business about his excursion in the yard without his pants. Johns thought himself sly by asking, "Did Elsie's alligator really scare you out of your pants, Homer?" This was followed by general laughing and slapping of the knees by the other miners on the shift. The correct and expected response from Homer should have been something funny or ribald but he said nothing, which took all the fun out of the ribbing and it subsided. The suspicion was that Homer had fallen ill, perhaps gravely so. Later, there was much discussion of this on the company store steps. The conclusion was that his illness was his wife, a peculiar girl who, though lovely, was the kind who could destroy a man by wanting more than he could provide.

Two more days went by until Elsie walked outside into the yard, where Homer was sitting on a rusty chair he'd scrounged from the company junkyard. She stood before him and, after taking a deep breath, announced, "I will let Albert go."

Relieved, Homer said, "Wonderful. Thank you. We'll put him in the creek. He'll be fine there. Lots of minnows to eat and the occasional dog or cat trying to get a drink."

Elsie pressed her lips together, an expression Homer knew all too well meant she was not pleased. "He would freeze in the creek during the winter," she said. "He has to go home to Orlando."

This was an astonishing proposal. "Orlando? Good Lord, woman! It must be eight hundred miles to Orlando!"

Elsie defiantly raised her chin. "I don't care if it's eight thousand."

"And if I refuse?"

Elsie took another deep breath. "I'll take him myself."

Homer could almost feel the earth shifting beneath his boots. "How would you do that?"

"I don't know but I'll figure out a way."

Instantly defeated, Homer asked, "Does he have to go all the way to Orlando? Could we not drop him off in one of the Carolinas? It's warm down there, so I hear."

"All the way," Elsie replied. "And when we get there, we have to find the perfect place."

"How will we know the perfect place?"

"Albert will know."

"Albert is a reptile. He doesn't know anything."

"Well, at least he has an excuse for that, doesn't he?"

"You're saying I don't know anything?"

"I'm saying none of us do. I'm saying everything we think is true is probably not true at all. If I said a million things and you said a million and one things back, none of our words might even come close to what the truth really is."

"That doesn't make any sense."

"It's the most honest answer I can give you."

After his wife had gone back inside the house, Homer sat brooding in his junkyard chair. For one of the first times in the entire history of his life, he felt scared. A week ago, the mine roof had cracked like a rifle shot and a giant slab of rock had missed him by inches but that hadn't scared him at all. He'd never told Elsie about that but he knew she knew. She seemed to know everything he tried to keep from her. In contrast, Homer confessed to himself he knew very little about the woman he'd married and had now put the fear of God in him with her threat to head off for Florida whether he went along or not.

There was, he realized, only one thing to do. He would seek the advice of the greatest man he knew, the incomparable William "Captain" Laird, World War I hero, graduate of the Stanford University engineering school, and lord and master of Coalwood.

And so, although he did not know it, the journey began.

2

AFTER A FULL SHIFT UNDERGROUND, HOMER SHOWERED at the company bathhouse, dressed in a fresh pair of coveralls and town boots, and asked the office clerk to see the Captain. The clerk waved him to the door and the Captain roared *"Enter!"* to Homer's knock. His hat held in his hands, Homer stepped up to the Captain's desk. The Captain, a huge man with ears like an African elephant, looked up and frowned. "What the devil is it, son?"

"It's my wife, Captain."

"Elsie? What's wrong with Elsie?"

"She wants me to take her and her alligator to Orlando."

The Captain sat back and considered Homer. "Does this have anything to do with you running around your yard without your pants?"

"Yes, sir, it does."

The Captain cocked his head. "Okay, son, I'm always up for a good story and I sense this might be a good one."

After taking an offered chair, Homer told the Captain about Albert chasing him outside and then what he said and what Elsie said. The Captain listened intently, his expression gradually changing from bemusement to squinty-eyed interest. When Homer was finished, the Captain said, "You know what I think this is, Homer? It's kismet or damn close."

Homer had heard of kismet but he wasn't sure what it was and said so. The Captain leaned forward, his bulk looming as if to smother Homer's doubts. "There are times that come to us to accomplish things that don't make sense but make all the sense there is in the universe. Does that make sense?"

"No, sir."

"Of course it doesn't. But that's what kismet is. It makes us career off in odd directions from which we learn not only what life is about but what it is *for*. This journey may be nothing less than your chance to discover these things."

"You're saying I should go?"

"I am, indeed. You are hereby granted your annual two weeks' vacation and you have my permission to draw one hundred dollars from the company to finance the trip."

"But that's so much money! I'll never be able to pay it back."

"Yes, you will. You're the kind of man who figures out how to pay a debt and then does it. Now, let us speak of Elsie. Have you made it clear to her that she is the most important person in your life?"

"I guess not, Captain," Homer answered, truthfully, "but she surely is." He scratched his head. "Trouble is I don't know if I'm the most important person in *her* life."

"Well, maybe that's another reason you've been given this journey, so that the two of you can figure out what kind of couple you are meant to be. When are you leaving?"

"I don't know. Until just now, I wasn't sure I was going."

"Go in the morning. A thing put off is a thing not done." The Captain's countenance turned gloomy. "Make no mistake. I'll miss you. You have those goons on Three West running good coal and likely they'll fall back into bad habits with you gone." He shrugged. "But I'll make do. A young man on his way to adventure in tropical climes! I wish I were you."

"I will tell you truly, Captain," Homer answered. "I sense this journey will be one of the most painful experiences of my life."

"It may very well be," the Captain agreed, "and perhaps that is all the more reason you should do it. That said, in two weeks, I want to see your bright and shiny face back on Three West."

Homer rose from the chair, thanked the Captain, received a farewell salute, and walked outside into the dusty air, oblivious to the line of evening shift men tromping past to the manlift. In the sequential manner he'd been taught by the Captain, he made some rapid decisions. Getting to Florida from West Virginia with a wife and an alligator was a daunting task. His first decision was to eliminate going by train or bus. Neither of those conveyances would likely accept an alligator as a passenger. No, to get there, they'd have to go by car. Luckily, he had a good one, a 1925 Buick four-door convertible touring car he'd recently purchased from the Captain.

Homer's next decision led him to walk to the company store, where he procured a large washtub on credit and then went to the pay window and got one hundred dollars in the form of two fifty-dollar bills. As he walked to his house, the tub hitched up on his shoulder, he caught the attention of several ladies sitting in chairs on their porches. Their husbands were evening shift miners and so they had a little time on their hands to sit and watch anyone and everyone who might walk by. Most of them spoke to him as he passed, and one, a new wife in town, even asked him if he might stop for some iced tea. Though he politely touched his forelock to all of the ladies in a gesture of respect, he kept walking. He was a handsome young man, Homer Hadley Hickam, nearly six feet tall, his straight black hair kept slicked back with Wildroot Creme Oil. He had the broad shoulders and muscles of a coal miner, and a lopsided smile and very blue eyes that many women found interesting. But he wasn't interested in them, not since he'd met and married Elsie Lavender.

Homer stowed the washtub in the back seat of the Buick, which was parked in front of the house, then went inside to apprise his wife of the decisions he had made. After peeking into the bedroom and not finding her, he discovered Elsie—her full married name was Elsie Gardner Lavender Hickam—sitting in the bathroom on its cracked linoleum floor. Her back was against the bathtub and she was holding her alligator, who was looking at her in rapt adoration. She was also crying.

Not counting sad movies and onions, Elsie had only seriously cried twice before, to Homer's recollection: once when she'd agreed to marry him, and again when she'd opened the box holding Albert and read the accompanying card from a fellow she'd known in Florida named Buddy Ebsen. In both cases, he still wasn't sure why. Uncertain what to say to this third bout of serious tears, Homer naturally said the wrong thing. "If you're not careful, that thing will yet bite off your arm."

Elsie raised her face and the sight of it hurt Homer's heart. Her usually bright hazel eyes were puffy and rimmed in pink and her high, prominent cheekbones—which she said came from the Cherokee in her blood—were wet with tears. "He will do no such thing," she said, "because Albert loves me. Sometimes, I think he is the only one in this old world who does."

Recalling the Captain's recommendation, Homer said, "You are the most important person in my life."

"No, I'm not," she shot back. "Not even close. First is the Captain. Second is the coal mine."

"The coal mine is not a person."

"In your case, it might as well be."

Homer did not want to argue, mainly because he knew he couldn't win. Instead, he said the thing he knew would either make her very happy or call the whole thing off. "We leave for Florida in the morning," he announced.

Elsie pushed a tear-soaked strand of hair from her cheek. "Are you joking?"

"The Captain gave me permission to go as long as I make it back in two weeks. I bought a galvanized washtub at the company store for Albert to ride in. It's in the back seat of the Buick. I also withdrew one hundred dollars from the company." He dug into his pocket and displayed the two fifties.

Her astonished face told Homer all that he needed to know. She believed him now. After all, a man didn't get two fifty-dollar bills from the company if he wasn't serious about using them. "If you still want to go, I think you should pack your things," he said.

Elsie pondered her husband, then stood up and put Albert in the bathtub. "All right," she said, "I will." She brushed past him heading for the bedroom.

When he heard her open the closet door followed by the rattle of coat hangers, Homer felt a little panic crawl up his back and perch on his shoulder. When he looked at Albert, the alligator seemed to be sizing him up. "This is all your fault," Homer said. "And, damn his hide, Buddy Ebsen's."

3

EVERY MORNING WHEN ELSIE BLINKED AWAKE, SHE WAS always a little surprised to find herself a coal miner's wife. After all, to avoid that very thing, she'd caught a bus to Orlando the week after she'd graduated from high school. As soon as she stepped off the bus, she knew she'd made the right decision. It was as if she'd entered a kind of beautiful and sunny wonderland. Her Uncle Aubrey was there at the bus station to meet her and regally placed her in the back seat of his Cadillac and drove her like she was some kind of queen to his house, as fine a house Elsie had ever seen even though there was a FOR SALE sign out front. Her uncle explained he had lost a lot of money in the Depression but was certain that, as long as Herbert Hoover was in charge, he'd be rolling in greenbacks again before long.

Elsie got a job waiting tables at a restaurant and enrolled in secretary's school, and started meeting young people who were vastly more interesting than anyone she had ever known. She especially liked one boy, a tall, lanky fellow named Christian "Buddy" Ebsen, whose parents owned a dance studio in downtown Orlando. From the start, Buddy took a special interest in her. Unlike some of the others, who made fun of her for her West Virginia accent, Buddy was always kind and polite, always listened to her attentively, and was just so much fun. He even had her over to meet his parents and taught her to dance all the latest dances.

But Elsie had learned that good things didn't always last and, sure enough, Buddy left with his sister to go to New York, there to make his fortune as an actor and a professional dancer. After a few months passed with not so much as a letter from him, Elsie had to admit to herself that Buddy probably wasn't going to come back anytime soon. She found herself lonely and homesick, and after graduating from secretary school, took the bus back to West Virginia. It wasn't to stay, she told Uncle Aubrey, but just for a visit, a visit that had now lasted three years and included, almost inexplicably, marrying a Gary High School classmate and coal miner named Homer Hickam.

The morning after Albert chased Homer into the yard, Elsie saw her husband off to work and then retreated to the bathroom, there to cuddle her alligator who mostly lived in the bathtub. Albert had been a surprise gift from Buddy, arriving a week after the wedding, inside a shoe box with holes punched in it and string holding it together. Besides a cute little alligator no more than five inches long, there was a note inside. *I hope you will always be happy. Something of Florida for you. Love, Buddy.*

So many times Elsie had dissected that message! She wondered if Buddy had hoped she would be happy because, without him, he thought she wouldn't be? And why send something of Florida that would live for years if he hadn't wanted her to think of him all the time? And, maybe more important, there it was in his looping cursive, that word: *Love*.

Absently, she petted Albert while she thought of the other man in her life, who happened now to be her husband. The first time she saw Homer, she was playing guard on the Gary High School girls' basketball team. They were in the Gary gymnasium and the opposing girls were from the high school in Welch, the county seat. During a lull in play, Elsie's eyes drifted to the top row of the bleachers and landed on a sharp-faced boy who was watching her in a way that made her feel a bit unsettled. A pass from her teammate bounced right off her and she had to scramble to get it. Then, without a thought, she threw the rules away and bounced the basketball between her legs, twirled about, threw an elbow into the girl guarding her, and dribbled in for a layup, every single move against the rules of girls' basketball. The referee blew the whistle and the Welch coach nearly fainted at the audacity of a girl actually touching another girl and working the ball. Elsie ignored the hysteria. She was looking for the boy for whom she had shown off but was disappointed to see that he was gone.

The next day he was waiting at her locker. He said, "My name is Homer Hickam. Would you go with me to the dance this Friday?"

That was when Elsie noticed his eyes. They were the bluest eyes she guessed she'd ever seen and there was a kind of cold fire in them. Before she knew what she was doing, she'd said yes, which meant she had to tell the captain of the football team that she'd changed her mind.

Outrageously, come Friday, Homer didn't show. Elsie went to the dance alone and was forced to dance with another dateless girl while watching the captain of the football team dancing with the head cheerleader. She was mortified. In the two months of school that followed, Elsie saw Homer in the school hallways and in a couple of classes but she ignored him. The worst part of that was he ignored her, too. Then three days before graduation, he stopped her in the school hallway. "Will you marry me?" he asked.

She drew herself up, clutching her books to her chest. "Why would I want to marry you, Homer Hickam? You didn't even come to the dance you asked me to!"

"I had to work. Daddy got his foot broke in the mine so it was up to me to go pick coal at the tipple to tide us over."

"Why didn't you tell me that?"

"I figured you'd hear about it."

Elsie shook her head in astonishment at his thickheadedness, then pivoted on her heel and walked away. "We will get married," he called after her. "It is meant to be." But Elsie kept her head up and didn't turn around. She didn't think *anything* was meant to be except that she was going to get out of the coalfields the very first chance she got, which was exactly what she'd done. For more than a year, she had lived the life she'd always dreamed about. She hung on a dandy fellow's arm, and breathed clear air, and soaked up sunshine. But then it had all somehow gone wrong, and she found herself back in West Virginia. Before she could escape again, her brother Robert informed her that the superintendent of the coal mine in Coalwood wished to entertain her in his office.

"Why does he want to see me?"

"Because he does. You shouldn't question a great man like Captain Laird."

Robert drove Elsie to the coal mine office and ushered her inside, leaving after the Captain gave him a wave of dismissal. "Please sit down," the Captain said politely.

Elsie sat before the massive oak desk and the majesty of the grand man behind it. She said nothing because she didn't know what to say. The Captain smiled at her. "I asked you to come today so that I might speak with you concerning a young man who works for me. He is a most enterprising man, bound to rise to the very pinnacle of the coal mining profession. I believe you know him well. Homer Hickam."

Elsie was only a little surprised. She knew, because her brother Robert had told her, that Homer worked for the Captain. "I know him," she confessed.

The Captain's smile did not waver. "You are a lovely young thing. It is perfectly clear to me why Homer desires you but I fear you have broken his heart. This makes him somewhat inefficient in his work. Can't you help him and me and this coal company by marrying the boy? It is a simple request. You have to marry someone."

"Sir . . ." Elsie began.

"Please call me Captain."

"All right. Well, Captain, I like Homer, I really do but there's this boy in Florida. . . . He's off chasing fame and fortune in New York right now but I think he wants me and he might come back."

The Captain reared back in his chair, looking contemplative, and said, "A man who'd decamp to New York instead of marrying you must be a very unserious man! In fact, I would imagine he is so unserious that he is up there enjoying himself. I've been to New York many times. There are women there, Elsie, women like you don't know. Some of them even have platinum hair." When Elsie's lips trembled and her eyes turned damp, the Captain gently asked, "Do you know how it is that I came to marry my wife?"

When Elsie confessed in a choked voice she didn't know, the Captain told her how he'd pursued the woman who was now the lovely Mrs. Laird, and how, after he'd asked her a dozen times, she said she'd marry him only if he had a plug of Brown Mule chewing tobacco in his pocket and, what do you know, he did!

"This is called kismet, Elsie. It is what made her say what she said and me have what I had. Do you understand?" He came from behind his desk and sat down beside her and patted her knee. "Let kismet be your guide for that is the will of the universe."

Elsie tried to wrap her mind around kismet but had trouble with it. She had always thought God made things happen. It had never occurred to her that there was something else floating around in the air that did, too.

"Look, daughter," the Captain rumbled on. "Why don't you at least agree to meet Homer in Welch this Saturday eve? Maybe you two could have some fun there. That wouldn't be so bad, would it?"

"I don't suppose so, sir," Elsie agreed.

"Fine. He will meet you in front of the Pocahontas Theater at seven o'clock Saturday evening. Can you make it?"

"Yes, sir. One of my brothers will drive me there."

And so it was settled and her brother Charlie drove her in his jalopy to Welch and dropped her off. Homer arrived on time and they went inside, with very little conversation beforehand, and watched the movie that was, as she recalled, one about Tarzan, the ape man. They did not hold hands. Afterward, she and Homer waited outside Murphy's Department Store for Charlie to pick her up. That was when, without preamble, Homer once more asked her to marry him.

"No," she said.

"Please," he replied. "The Captain said he'd give us a house and I shall soon be a foreman. We would have a good life."

Since she had talked to the Captain, Elsie had been feeling terribly blue about Buddy and had let her imagination get away from her. She saw him in New York going out with a lot of flashy women and just having the time of his life while she languished forlornly first in Florida and now back in the awful Appalachian hills. Impulsively, she decided to leave Homer's proposal to kismet, just as the Captain had said she should do. She heard herself say, almost as if in a dream, "If you have a plug of Brown Mule chewing tobacco in your pocket, I'll marry you."

Homer looked sad. "You know I don't chew tobacco."

Elsie felt a glimmer of relief.

Homer dug in his pocket and then held up a pouch on which there was a picture of a brown mule and was redolent of a sweet chaw. "But I just happened to pick this one up off the bathhouse floor. Thought it might belong to one of your brothers."

Elsie stared at the pouch, then at Homer's twinkling eyes, and for one of the only times in her life, she simply gave up. "I'll marry you," she said and instantly burst into tears. She supposed Homer took them as tears of joy but they were something very different. They were tears for herself, for who she was and now would be, a coal miner's wife. After that, the days ticked by until the wedding and then it came and went. She barely recalled saying the words in front of the preacher and slipping on the cheap ring that turned green within a week.

Afterward, she wrote Buddy to tell him that should he come home from New York at last, he would no longer find her in Orlando but instead married to a man in Coalwood, West Virginia. His response was Albert, whom Elsie raised in the kitchen sink until he got too big, whereupon she transferred him to the bathtub in the upstairs bathroom, the only bathroom in the house. While Homer was at work, which was nearly all the time, she sat with the little alligator and sang him songs. She also fed him bugs and, when he grew large enough, chicken parts donated by the company butcher in the company store. She took him outside and walked him around the yard on a leash like he was a puppy while miners on their way to work stopped long enough to tip up their helmets and watch in wonder. Her daddy came over and dug a hole in the backyard and lined it with concrete so that Albert could have a little pond to swim in during the summer. Because Homer was so busy digging coal, she spent more time with Albert during her newlywed year than with her husband and it seemed to her that Homer didn't really mind.

It wasn't long before Albert got so big he began to stroll around the house, sometimes crawling up on the couch, his tail flipping over the table lamps. He made a *yeah-yeah-yeah* sound when he was happy or excited. He flung himself into Elsie's lap and cuddled every chance he got, turning over so she could scratch his creamy belly. The only thing Albert was afraid of was thunder. One night, when the thunder was like somebody beating on a kettle drum, Albert climbed out of the bathtub, pushed open the bedroom door with his snout, and crawled into bed. When Homer turned over and looked into Albert's glowing red eyes, he jumped up and ran for his life, tripping down the steps and going right over the rail, his fall cushioned only by the cherrywood coffee table in the living room. Hearing the crash and subsequent groans, Elsie cuddled Albert for a few minutes before she got up to see how Homer was doing. From the floor of the living room, he said he was fine, save a bruised hip, but the coffee table wasn't and since it was company property, they would have to pay for it if it couldn't be fixed.

"I never liked that old coffee table, anyway," Elsie said and, when the thunder receded, escorted Albert to his bathtub, then went back to bed. As she lay there, listening to Homer trying to reassemble the coffee table, a thought occurred to her. "If I could only get Homer to Florida," she mused, "maybe he'd change into someone more like Buddy."

Now, with the astonishing journey Homer had proposed, she considered her closet and what to pack. She also realized that perhaps what the Captain called kismet was giving her a second chance to get out of the coalfields. She really hadn't thought Homer would agree to carry Albert home but now that he had, it would mean days on the road, time enough for her to perhaps sway him, for the sake of their marriage, not to return to West Virginia.

And, if that didn't work, maybe when he got a look at how beautiful Florida was, it would convince him those old Appalachian hills were nothing but ugly traps.

And if *that* didn't work?

Well, she would cross that plank over the creek when she came to it but she thought she already knew the answer.

Once she got out of the coalfields this time, no matter what her husband did, she was *never* coming back.

4

HOMER PLACED SOME BLANKETS IN THE ROOMY TRUNK OF
the Buick plus a wooden box that held an extra shirt, a pair of khaki
pants, a toothbrush and shaving mug, a razor, and cream. He then went
upstairs to the bedroom, where he found Elsie just as she closed a cardboard suitcase, an arm of a blouse hanging out. Silently, he tucked the
arm of the blouse in, then took the suitcase, the only one they owned, to
the car.

Before long, Elsie appeared with Albert on the rope that served as his
leash. Homer gestured toward the washtub. "Albert goes there."

Elsie inspected the tub and wrinkled her nose. "It's too small. His tail
will hang out."

"It's the biggest tub I could find. It will have to do."

Elsie had a quilt over her arm. She tossed it to Homer. "Put that in
the washtub so he'll at least have something soft to lie on."

Homer inspected the cloth and its intricate needlework. "My mother
made this. She worked two years on it."

"Albert likes it. Put it in the washtub."

Homer draped the quilt inside the washtub and turned back to his wife to find that Elsie had put her arms around Albert behind his front legs and had lifted him up. "Well?" she said. "Pick up his tail."

Homer picked up Albert's tail even though he'd read that an alligator could use his tail to knock a man down and be on him before anything could be done. But all Albert did was moon over Elsie while she eased him into the washtub. "He fits fine," Homer said, relieved.

"Sweet boy," Elsie said and patted Albert's knobby head. He grinned at her. "You go to sleep now."

"I have procured maps from the company gas station," Homer apprised. "I have Virginia, North Carolina, South Carolina, and Florida. They were out of Georgia."

"What happens when we get to Georgia?"

"We will keep heading south. The sun will rise on our left and set on our right. Eventually, we'll come across Florida."

"I want to see my folks," Elsie said.

Homer raised an eyebrow. "We don't have time to see your folks. We need to get back to Coalwood in two weeks or we could lose our house. I might even lose my job."

Elsie's laugh was harsh. "What a disaster that would be!"

"Look, Elsie . . ."

"No, you look, Homer. Mama and Daddy love Albert. Daddy built him a pond and Mama sends him birthday and Christmas cards. If we took him to Florida without letting them say goodbye, they'd never forgive us."

No matter how they had indulged their daughter's love of her alligator, Homer doubted Elsie's parents cared two cents about the reptile in the back seat but he held his peace. After a final look around at the mountains and the little town he loved, he steered the Buick out of Coalwood and aimed it in the direction Elsie wanted to go.

→ ←

The Lavenders lived in Thorpe, a typical little McDowell County coal camp with gray dust drifting about and houses coated with black grime. The Lavender house was positioned on the side of a steep hill well above the level of the mine tipple, which meant it sat in clear air. Although it belonged to the coal company that owned Thorpe, it had been assigned to Jim Lavender because he was a talented carpenter. Coal companies were always after him and the Thorpe mine had won out by offering him a house not only high on the mountain but with an adjoining barn and two acres of land. Jim's wife, Minnie, was a pleasant, kindly woman who had birthed nine children and raised seven to adulthood. Two sons had died, one at birth, the other when he was six. His name was Victor and Elsie said one day he'd played in the nasty creek that flowed from beneath the Thorpe tipple, caught some sort of disease, and died two days later. What he'd died of, nobody knew for sure. Elsie often talked about Victor, wondering what he might have become had he lived. Homer supposed he might have become a coal miner like all her other brothers but it was Elsie's opinion Victor would have become a writer. Where she got that, Homer surely didn't know but he left it alone. He supposed a dead brother could be anything Elsie wanted him to be.

When Homer pulled up in front of the Lavender house, Elsie got out and opened the back door. "Help me get Albert out," she said.

"You should just leave him in the car," Homer replied. "That way, your folks could come out and see him and then we'll be on our way."

Elsie petted the alligator's snout and was rewarded by him opening his jaws and showing her his fine white teeth. He made his *yeah-yeah-yeah* happy sound. "Your father is silly, Albert," Elsie said, "because with his planning and his money and his maps and all, he has failed to notice that we have no food."

Homer silently conceded this was good thinking on Elsie's part. Restaurants were expensive, even if one could be found on the open road, so it made sense to carry as much food as possible on an extended trip. If there was one thing the Lavenders had, it was food. Their hillside farm was well tended.

Homer and Elsie carried Albert in his washtub up the steps to the front porch, where they sat him down between two rocking chairs, one of which was full of Jim Lavender. Jim was wearing muddy boots and bib overalls and his left arm was in a sling. "What's wrong with your arm, Daddy?" Elsie asked. "Did you have a fall?"

"In a manner of speaking," Jim answered. He raised his eyebrows. "Why do you have Albert with you?"

"Because we're carrying him to Florida."

"Really? I figured you to keep him until he ate Homer."

Homer took off his hat. "Well, sir, he's already big enough for that, at least a mouthful at a time."

Jim smiled at Albert, who smiled back. "He is a handsome beast, ain't he?"

"Yes, he is, Daddy," Elsie agreed. "And sweet, too."

Elsie's mother appeared at the screen door. She was dressed in a faded frock, a grease-stained apron, and a frown. "Hidy, Elsie, Homer," she said without passion. "Is that Albert? He's growed."

"That's Albert, Mama," Elsie said. "You look like you've been crying. What's wrong?"

"Your daddy's arm is what's wrong," Minnie answered.

"Let's not talk about my ailments," Jim quickly said, then stood up. "Think I know why you've come. If you're going all the way to Florida, you need to stock up with some victuals. Well, you've come to the right place. For twenty dollars, we could supply you enough to go to Texas."

"Jim, we ain't charging these children nothing," Minnie scolded. "Now, you come on in, Elsie, so we can talk."

"Albert should come in, too," Elsie said. "I don't want the sun on him."

Minnie nodded. "Jim, you go on up to the pigpen, do what you have to do to get these children a ham."

Homer helped Elsie carry Albert inside, then went back out and followed Jim off the porch and past a chicken coop toward a copse of trees on the back edge of the property. There, he caught the odor of pigs.

"Got me a big old sow and a slew of piglets," Jim said. "A couple of boars, too. They're snuffling around in the woods."

"What happened to your arm?" Homer asked.

"I had me a fall. It was from Mrs. Trammel's bedroom window. A midnight visit, if you will."

"So you broke it," Homer said, unsurprised at his father-in-law's philandering. He had that reputation.

"Naw. Dilly Trammel shot me as I was climbing out." Jim winced, as if the memory made him get shot all over again. "Trudy and me heard him at the front door—an hour before he should've been home, by the way—but then he sneaked around and winged me with his pistola while I was doing my best to save the honor of his wife by not being caught. What kind of man would be so low as to shoot a man looking after the honor of his wife?"

"I'm sure I can't imagine," Homer said while frowning.

Jim smirked. "So tell me, Homer, why are you on this fool's errand? If I was you, I'd just toss that reptile in the nearest creek and take Elsie home."

"I'd like to but I just can't. It's what Elsie wants and I'm bound to do it."

Jim shook his head. "There's only one way to control a female. You let her know who's boss. Granted, that might be hard with Elsie but it's what you got to do."

Homer shrugged. "I love her, Jim."

"Love! Stuff of women's magazines. Anyway, Elsie's a special case. She always took a iron hand. I had to smack her more than once when she was a girl. It didn't do much good but she knew when she'd done wrong by my lights."

"Yet you came over to Coalwood and built a pond for Albert," Homer pointed out. "Why'd you do that?"

"I'm her father and she asked me to."

"Well, I'm her husband and she asked me to take her alligator to Florida."

Jim grinned. "A romantic coal miner! That's a rare breed!"

Homer searched for a retort but couldn't find one. "How about that ham?" was the best he could do.

Jim pointed toward a gigantic pig that stood just inside some low brush. "That's Bruiser, one of my boars. Man could eat off him for a year."

"He's some pig," Homer agreed. "But he looks kind of mean."

"Mean? He's downright vicious. Bet he'd eat Albert given half a chance."

Jim led Homer into a tool shed where he selected a knife, its sharp edge shimmering in the pale light, and showed it to his son-in-law. "String 'em up, slice 'em along their necks, end of their days. A sharp knife's the key."

"Pigs know when you're going to kill them," Homer said, turning from the knife. "They're smart and they know."

Jim shrugged. "They all know, Homer. You think a cow don't know?

You think a chicken don't know? I killed a bunch of 'em and I can tell you they all know and they don't like it one bit. But that's the way God designed us, to eat. And to eat, we have to kill."

Taking a loop of rope, Jim led the way out of the shed to a board nailed between two trees with thick nails protruding from it. "This is where I hang 'em," he said. "Tie up their back legs, then string 'em up, then stick 'em. You heard about somebody crying like a stuck pig? That's where that phrase came from."

Homer was unsettled by Jim's description of a dying pig and watched morosely as his father-in-law made a noose out of the rope and handed it over. "This is for Bruiser," he said, nodding toward the giant boar, which was carefully watching them through an opening in the surrounding brush. "Put this around his neck."

Homer looked at the thin rope and then at the boar. "You're joking. That pig's six times bigger than me."

"Look, boy, it's your ham."

It was indeed his ham so Homer took the rope and crept up on Bruiser. To his surprise, the boar didn't move although its serious oil-drop eyes watched him closely. "Just loop it around his neck?" Homer asked.

"Better than around his tail," Jim replied.

Homer edged around the boar. "Easy, pig," he said.

"His name is Bruiser," Jim reminded.

"Easy, Bruiser," Homer said, then lunged with the rope, successfully placing the loop over the boar's head.

Bruiser's response, after a moment of apparent contemplation, was a shriek and a massive flailing of his cloven hooves. Hanging on to the rope, it felt to Homer as if his arms were being pulled out of their sockets. Still, he gamely gripped the rope and tried to keep up with the pig but it was devilishly fast and, in seconds, Homer found himself on his stomach being dragged over the roots of trees and through various thorny bushes and stinging nettles. He twisted until he was on his back, then began to spin over and over until at last he could hold on no longer. Defeated, he let go, then lay draped over a protruding tree root, mentally searching his body for wounds and contusions and broken bones. Finding nothing disastrous, he got to his knees, then struggled to his feet.

Jim walked up with a big pink ham on his shoulder. He held up the knife. "Needed it to cut down one of the hams what was curing."

Homer sagged against the big oak. "Why did you want me to catch Bruiser?"

Jim looked back into the woods. Trees were waving from where the pig had barged through. "Didn't. Just wanted to see how long you'd hang on. You did pretty good."

Homer was not a man who much cared to cuss a man out but, in this case, he made an exception. It did not seem to bother his father-in-law. In fact, based on his laughter, it was a source of some amusement.

A little later, while Homer was trying to wash the blood off his arms at the water pump in the yard, Elsie marched up to him and said, "I want you to hit my daddy."

Homer shook his head. "I can't do that, Elsie."

"Did he tell you what he did?"

"Yes, but I still can't hit him. He's only got one arm so it wouldn't be fair. Besides, knocking down an old man just isn't in me to do."

Elsie stared at him hard, then wheeled away. Before long, he heard Jim give out a loud yelp. When he came inside the house, he saw Elsie holding a stick and Jim clutching his wounded arm, his face screwed up in pain. Nothing else was said after that, even at supper, where Jim kept a studied silence and both Minnie and Elsie wore enigmatic smiles. Homer just kept his head down.

→ ←

Even though he had multiple aches from being dragged through the woods by an enraged pig, Homer rose early and, with Elsie and her mother directing him, loaded the car with loaves of baked bread, the big smoked ham, gunnysacks of smoked chicken, a box of early summer tomatoes, multiple jars of green beans, and a basket of onions. Homer was gratified that the food was probably more than sufficient to carry them through two weeks on the road. With any luck, he would only need to spend his money on gasoline and, here and there, maybe a night in a motel. Otherwise, they'd just camp in a field somewhere.

Albert was also carted out in his washtub and placed in the back seat, where he snored softly, his stomach full from a big breakfast of fresh chicken.

Through the window, Homer shook his father-in-law's offered hand. "Hope you know what you're doing," Jim said.

"We'll be okay," Homer replied.

Jim's expression was doubtful. "I had my fun with you yesterday, Homer, with Bruiser and all, but I hope you know I care about you. You're a good man, maybe too good by a sight, so keep in mind there's a Depression out where you're going. We're mostly walled off from it here in the mountains. People you'll run across are going to be desperate. Stay on guard."

"I will, Jim. Thanks for the advice. And the bruises."

Jim grinned, then stepped back. Elsie kissed her mother, leaning in through the window. "I love you, daughter," Minnie said. "Say hello to brother Aubrey."

"I will, Mama. Wish we had room to take you with us."

Minnie straightened up, then leaned into Jim, who'd come over and put his good arm around her. "I have enough to do around here," she said. "Now, off you go."

Suddenly, a russet-colored rooster with a green tail launched itself inside the car and sat with a defiant expression atop the basket of onions. Homer looked over his shoulder at the creature. "You'd best get out of here, rooster," he said. "Albert's already giving you the eye."

"It ain't mine," Jim advised. "I don't know whose it is but I'd keep it if I were you. It might provide dinner somewhere along the road."

Homer made one last attempt to swat the rooster out of the car but it responded by hopping into the washtub and atop Albert's head. Albert rolled his eyes up, then grinned. "All right, you green-tailed thing, if that's the way you want it," Homer said and, with last waves to Jim and Minnie, steered ahead the Buick, loaded down with food, a husband and a wife, an alligator and a stowaway rooster, all bound for Florida.

5

ON THE DRIVE ACROSS THE FIRST OF THREE MOUNTAINS before reaching the Virginia border, Elsie sat silently, clearly chewing something over. To Homer's distress, she did not once pass the time with talk of the weather or the bumpiness of the road or anything else. All she did was stare straight ahead. Uneasy and lonely for her voice, he finally asked, while almost instantly regretting it, "Are you mad at me about something?"

She responded, "I'm mad at myself for asking you to hit my father. It's none of your business, after all. You're not part of my family."

Wounded, Homer answered, "You're my wife, Elsie, so your parents are my family, too."

"Then why didn't you hit him like I asked?"

"I was afraid I'd hurt him."

Elsie barked a laugh. "The only thing that could hurt my daddy is a direct hit by lightning."

"Well, just the same . . ."

"You're weak, Homer," Elsie interrupted, "weak in ways that often surprise me. But never mind, I'm done talking on this particular topic."

Homer was left feeling even lower than before and his mind batted imaginary conversations back and forth between Elsie and him that went nowhere. In the valley between the second and third mountain on the way to the Virginia border, the rooster hopped up and crouched companionably on Homer's shoulder. It smelled faintly of a barnyard. Startled, he tried to push it off but it dug its claws in and hung on.

"Are you going to let that rooster sit there?" Elsie asked.

"I think I am," Homer answered. "He seems to like me."

"Really? *Why would he like you?*"

Wounded anew, Homer replied, "I'm sure I wouldn't know."

After crossing the state line into Virginia, the roads got better and the mountains got farther apart until they turned into rolling hills that framed wide, green valleys. While Elsie dozed, Homer did his best to enjoy the scenery. Dairy cattle, grazing on the early summer grass, kept their heads down and horses gamboled in the meadows. Albert was quiet, except for an occasional long, contented sigh, and, before long, Homer relaxed. Despite Elsie's sharp tongue, he perceived it was going to be an easy trip. They'd get to Florida, drop Albert off, and get back well before the two weeks were up. After that, he imagined the years would pass and he and Elsie would recall the fast drive they'd made to Orlando and how they'd argued but everything had turned out okay. They'd laugh and laugh about it.

When they passed through a Virginia farm town, Elsie came awake. "What a tired old place," she said.

Homer agreed that the town looked tired. A few indolent men, dressed in faded coveralls, sat on the steps of the empty buildings and watched the Buick idle by, their eyes betraying little interest. At a stop sign, Homer took note of a man standing on the corner. He was wearing a suit and looked knowledgeable. "What town is this?" Homer asked him.

The man doffed his hat. "Tragedy. We're the county seat. You'll find us on the map halfway between Despair and Hopelessness." He paused, perhaps waiting for Homer and Elsie to laugh, but when they didn't, he said, "Hillsville's the actual name of our fair village."

"It looks nice," Homer said. "Except how come so many stores are boarded up?"

"That unhappy situation referred to in the press as the Great Depression. Farmers can't get a decent price on their crops and milk, so they don't have money to buy things."

"I'm sorry," Homer said.

"At least we're not starving and won't be as long as folks can stay on their farms. Problem is banks foreclose on a couple of missed payments, they have to hit the road. Is that why you're out and about?"

"No, sir. I'm in the coal business and fully employed. People still need coal to heat their homes and the steel mills to make their steel."

Elsie put in her two cents. "By coal business, he means he's a coal miner who works beneath about a billion tons of rocks, one of which might fall on him at any time."

"It's not that bad," Homer said.

Albert stuck his snout out the window and sniffed the air. The man took a step back. "Is that a crocodile?"

"An alligator," Homer said. "We're taking him home to Florida. By the way, are we on the right road?"

"Since it goes south, I would say so. Are you taking the rooster home, too?"

"We don't know why he's here," Homer admitted.

"Well, as the preacher in this town, I say blessings on you all. You've cheered up my day and given me something to talk about with the congregation other than the empty offering plate. Why, you're a regular Noah's Ark!"

Homer thanked the preacher for his blessings and drove on. After turning at the next corner, he beheld a courthouse with a statue of a Confederate soldier in front. "They fought a lot of Civil War battles around here," Homer said. "Brother against brother, so the history books say."

"Sister against sister, too," Elsie replied. "Women fought in the war, too."

"I didn't say they didn't," Homer replied, wondering why Elsie tried to make everything into an argument.

"Let's stop and have lunch here," Elsie proposed. "It looks pleasant enough and there are some benches."

Homer agreed and lunch was served, slices of ham, onions, hunks of homemade bread, and glasses of water from a jug Elsie had filled at her parents' house. Albert got some chicken and the rooster pecked a couple of worms out of the hard dirt. It was pleasant sitting around the courthouse and they had to stir themselves to get back into the car and keep going.

A few miles past the town, they came upon an overturned hay wagon that completely blocked the road. A skinny man in bib overalls and a team of horses were watching it as if they expected it to turn upright at any moment. "What happened?" Homer asked.

"Snake in the road shied my horses. They pulled me into the ditch. When I tried to get out, it turned over."

"Can I help?" Homer asked.

"Naw. The wife will miss me sooner or later and send my brothers and her brothers with enough new horses to get me going."

Homer got out and inspected the deep ditches that ran alongside the road. "I can't get across," he concluded.

"Where you headed?" the farmer asked.

"Florida."

"You're the first people I ever met who was going to Florida. What's it like?"

"Hot and full of bugs so I've read."

"That explains why I never met anybody going there. If you want to keep going south, go back up the road about five miles and turn right onto a dirt road. There's a big old maple tree at the turn and there's also a gas station in sight. Go about ten miles on it and I know for a fact it connects with a road that goes all the way to North Carolina."

Homer thanked the farmer and turned the Buick around. Five miles passed, then six, then another and another. A gas station was passed and then Elsie saw on her side of the road what she thought was a large maple tree. Behind it was a dirt road. "Is that it?" she asked.

Homer stopped and peered at the leaves on the tree. "Must be," he said.

"It looks like a dusty road," Elsie said. "It'll make Albert sneeze."

"I shall go slow," Homer replied, "so as not to disturb Albert in any way."

"You're being sarcastic."

"For which I am heartily sorry."

"You're still being—oh, go ahead."

Homer turned onto the road. It wasn't a bad road for a farm road, just a little dusty as Elsie had predicted, but Homer went slow as promised. After going for several miles, they discovered it was the wrong road, mainly because it was a dead end, arriving at an old house with acres of kudzu growing over it. As they drove up, they saw, despite the broken windows and peeling paint, that it had once been a grand mansion. Elsie said, "This must have looked like the plantation in *Rebel Love*."

"What's *Rebel Love*?"

"A novel I read. It's about this man and a woman who own a plantation somewhere in the old South. Then the Civil War comes and the man is killed and the woman has to run the plantation herself. Then this young rebel officer shows up awful wounded and she takes care of him and then they end up being together on a cotton bale."

"Being together?"

"Yes. You know."

Homer had to think to know but when he realized he knew, he said, "I didn't know you liked trashy novels."

"It wasn't trashy. I learned a lot about the Civil War. Anyway, it's none of your business what I read. You know what, Homer? You're irritating sometimes."

"I shall endeavor to become less irritating."

"Just you saying that is irritating." She peered at the old house. "I'd like to look around this place a bit."

"We don't have time to look around."

Elsie made a face at him, then got out of the Buick and opened the back door and coaxed Albert out of his tub onto the ground. Albert swished his tail in anticipation. "Come on, boy. You can take care of your business while I have myself a little adventure."

"Do you want me to go with you?" Homer asked.

"Suit yourself."

It did not suit himself but Homer still got out and followed his wife and her alligator in the hope he might keep them out of trouble. The rooster, as if he knew exactly where he was, hopped out of the car and ran ahead.

Mud, weeds, and scraggly hedges were all that remained of the grounds. When Homer and Elsie reached the back of the house, they saw that the entire roof of a wing had collapsed beneath the weight of the kudzu. "The old South," Elsie said. "Or what's left of it."

Homer studied the dilapidated house and the disheveled yard. "The Hickam family fielded a pair of twin brothers who rode in the cavalry with a Confederate captain named Mosby," he said. "They stole their horses, so my daddy said, and kept them after the war. What about the Lavenders?"

"Fought on both sides," Elsie answered. "My daddy said they likely shot at each other in the Wilderness Campaign."

Homer and Elsie took a moment to contemplate a past they hadn't experienced while also feeling sad for ancestors they didn't know. "I wonder where the slaves lived?" Elsie asked.

"Old shacks, probably long since rotted away."

"I'm glad I didn't live back then with slavery and the war and all."

"Not sure those people would care to live in our time. Everything they knew has been blown away by the winds of history."

Elsie studied Homer. "Sometimes you surprise me. You can be deep."

"Well, I'm a coal miner."

Elsie tried not to smile but she did, anyway. "You know what I'd like to do?"

"Honestly, Elsie, I can't imagine."

"Spend the night here."

"What? No. We need to keep going."

"Where? We're lost."

"I'll find the way."

"Oh, come on. It's getting dark. We'll have to stop soon, anyway. Don't you have any romance in your soul?"

"I have plenty but I don't see what this old house has to do with it."

"We could build a fire and cook and maybe even have some of that elderberry wine Daddy put in the trunk for me when you weren't looking. Come on, Homer. Let's have some fun for a change."

Homer looked to the west to see the sun settling down at the tops of the trees. It would be dark soon and he wasn't exactly certain where he was without a study of the maps. "Okay," he said, relenting, "we'll spend the night here but we have to be up at first light."

Elsie smiled. "For your reward, you may kiss me."

Her sudden change in demeanor filled Homer with cautious joy. He kissed her lightly on the lips while trying to ignore Albert, who had bitten the cuff of his pants and was pulling on it.

Elsie held on to Homer while Homer tried to shake off the alligator. "Don't take me back to that place," she said.

"What place? Albert! Stop it!"

"Coalwood. I'm begging you."

Albert finally let go and retreated, looking a little sheepish or, in his case, alligatorish. "But we have to go back to Coalwood," Homer said to Elsie. "It's where we live and I work."

"It's where you work *now* and where we live *now* but couldn't that change?"

"Elsie . . ."

She shook her head and pushed him away. "Build the fire and I'll get the wine. We're going to have a nice evening whether you like it or not."

"Look, if you want to talk about Coalwood, let me list sequentially all the reasons we have to go back."

"List sequentially my backside, mister," she growled and stomped off to the Buick.

➡ ⬅

By the time Elsie got back with a bottle of wine and two empty jelly jars, Homer had gathered some scrap lumber and sticks to make a fire. "I looked through those big glass doors over there and saw what looks like an old porch glider," he said. "This place has had people in it since the Civil War. Likely the Depression drove them out."

"Won't it be locked?"

Homer held up a rusty screwdriver. "Found it over there. I can open anything with one of these."

Elsie smiled. "You're more talented than I thought."

Homer jimmied the door and, with Elsie's help, carted the glider out and placed it beside the fire. "It's mildewed but if we put the blankets on it, it should work just fine," Elsie said. She held up the wine and the jelly jars. "Let's have some of this and then we can put one of the chickens on a spit."

Homer went after the blankets and also carried along Albert's tub. Soon, after roasting the chicken and eating a portion of it, they tried Jim's homemade wine. Albert and the rooster were asleep in the tub. Everything was warm and cozy.

"This is nice," Elsie said, snuggling into Homer's shoulder.

"It sure is," Homer said, knocking back some more of the wine.

After a few minutes of cuddling and wine sipping, Elsie was feeling warm and reckless. *They were on the road!* There was at least a chance for them to create a fine new life, if only she was clever enough. She allowed Homer to kiss her again, this time a long, deep kiss with a promissory note at the end. Relaxing, she sighed and said, "This reminds me of one time when I was in Florida. We made a fire on the beach and had wine and it wasn't homemade. It was real wine from Italy."

She felt Homer tense. "I can guess who you were with."

Elsie had meant to convey how wonderful Florida was but knew she'd made a mistake. She rushed to cover it up. "It wasn't like that. It was a whole bunch of us. They were just a swell gang. I never had so much fun. When we get to Florida, I'll introduce them to you."

"Will you introduce me to Buddy?"

She hesitated. "You know he's not there," she finally answered in a small voice. An image of Buddy dancing with platinum-haired women rose in her mind, which caused her to look sad.

"But I know where he is." Homer shrugged her head off his shoulder and stood up and pointed at her heart. "He's in there, isn't he? And I guess he always will be."

Elsie started to tell a lie she knew her husband wanted to hear. *I don't love Buddy. I love you.* To her astonishment, what came out was "I'm sorry." When she realized what she had said, she tried to tell her lie again but it still came out the same. "I'm sorry."

"So am I, Elsie," Homer said. "I guess we both are." His last words before he stalked off into the darkness were, "We're going back to Coalwood."

Elsie sat on the glider for how long she didn't know. She spent the time kicking herself for not being able to lie to her husband when she'd most needed to. She pulled a blanket about her and stretched out on the glider and watched the unblinking, unmoving stars in the celestial heaven. Her breathing was a little ragged. What was Homer going to do? He might even abandon her! But then she thought, no, Homer would never do that. He was too honorable. Still, he had said they were going back to Coalwood. All her hopes for the journey faded. She'd never be able to change Homer's mind now. The truth was, she confessed to herself, she wasn't sure she wanted to.

Elsie noticed a sweet, sugary smell and realized it was honeysuckle, the perfume of the old South she'd read about in *Rebel Love*. She sat up and drew the sweet air into her lungs as deeply as ever she could. The coal camps where she'd been raised always had an irritating petroleum odor and when the coke ovens were lit, the belching smoke gave her choking fits and left her throat as raw as an open wound. *Oh, I could breathe this forever,* she thought as the honeysuckle essence drifted softly by.

Relaxing, Elsie thought about how she might change things with Homer and decided, for the sake of the journey, she'd just have to get the lie out of her mouth. *Buddy is gone from my heart and you are my husband and that's all that matters.* It ought to be enough, she figured, to get him all the way to Florida, and time enough for her to convince him to never go back to Coalwood and maybe, just maybe, turn her dour husband into someone more like that long-legged and limber dancer she'd fallen for.

Elsie cast off the blanket and stood to look for Homer but he was gone. She supposed he was probably in the car sulking. Had Buddy ever sulked? Not that she could recall. He was always laughing, telling jokes, being so warm in the way he talked to her. Taking his shadow in her arms, she began to move according to the last dance she and Buddy had danced among the palm trees. Two steps forward, two back, one to the right, one to the left, then a twirl. Elsie took another drink of wine, then another and kept dancing, remembering, breathing in the honeysuckle air.

6

ELSIE CAME AWAKE WITH A START AND FOUND HERSELF looking skyward toward a blinding sky alleviated only by the face of her husband. "What's wrong?" she asked, before closing her eyes as tightly as she could lest they explode.

"Nothing's wrong except probably your hangover."

Some of the previous evening came back to her. She had danced and then . . . she supposed she had sat down on the glider and had herself more wine. After that, sleep had come and crazy dreams. She'd been back in Orlando and danced and danced with Buddy. "I'm sorry," she said, then put her arm across her eyes to further block the light. She had a terrible headache. "I'm sorry for . . . for telling you that story about being on the beach. I'm sorry for saying I was sorry. I meant to say . . ."

"It's okay," Homer said. "It doesn't matter."

"It does matter. And I feel bad for making fun of you when you said the rooster liked you. Of course he likes you. He likes you because you are good and you are kind even if you are a coal miner."

"Nothing like faint praise to start the morning," Homer said. "I've made coffee. Can I help you up?"

Elsie allowed him to help her up but she kept her eyes closed, lest the light sneak in and blow her brains out. He folded her hands around a cup and she greedily drank the bitter brew. "My head is killing me," she confessed.

"I have some aspirin in my kit," Homer said. "I'll bring you a couple."

"Thank you." After a few more swallows of coffee, she could feel her mind sorting itself out. Then she felt her hand being taken and two pills being placed in her palm. She gulped them down, then managed to get her eyes open to a squint. "Where did you sleep last night?"

"Right beside you. There."

"On the ground? Didn't you get cold?"

"It was my choice. But now, Miss Lavender, it's your turn to choose."

Elsie picked some coffee grounds off her tongue. "The choice is really yours," she said, dreading what he was going to say.

His answer was a surprise. "Okay. Here's what I choose. You stay here and take it easy while I take the Buick to get some gas at that station we passed. Then I'll come back for you and we'll keep going."

Elsie managed to get her eyes open enough to study his face. "Where are we going?"

"Why, to Florida, of course. Why else are we on the road?"

"But you said we were going back to Coalwood."

He peered at her. "We are. After Florida. What did you think I meant?"

"I don't know. The wine got to me, I guess."

"It surely did. When I came back, you were dancing."

She looked up and searched his eyes for anger but saw only hurt and disappointment. *I'm sorry* was on her lips but she forced the words away. "You know, you still owe me a dance from that time you stood me up in high school."

He shrugged. "I can't dance. That was another reason I chickened out and didn't take you."

"I bet you'd dance real good, Homer, if only you gave it a try."

Hurt once more welled in his eyes. "Somehow, I think I'd come in a distant second in that category."

Elsie stayed silent in the face of the truth.

"Well, I'm off to get some gasoline," Homer finally said in a cheerful voice that Elsie knew was forced. "I've already had my breakfast but I got out some bread and cheese for you. They're right there beside the fire."

"Where's Albert?" Elsie asked.

"I put him in the car for the night so he wouldn't get cold. This morning, I took him for a walk. Now he's asleep again in the back seat. Unless you want to get him up, I'll just leave him there."

"You took care of him last night? And walked him this morning?"

"He didn't even try to bite me."

"He never meant to bite you. He was just being playful."

Homer didn't reply. He just kept walking. After she'd heard the Buick start and rumble away, Elsie sat until her headache began to fade. Finishing the coffee, she shook off the blanket and stood up and walked away from the fire. She took a breath. The essence of honeysuckle was still there, made all the fresher by the cooler morning air. Breakfast could wait.

And once more, although this time very slowly lest her headache return, she danced. One step to the left, one right, two forward, two back, and twirl.

7

WHEN HOMER PURCHASED GASOLINE FROM THE STATION at the crossroads, the attendant, a young man wearing a paper cap, couldn't cash the fifty-dollar bill he offered. "You can get change at the bank," he said, nodding back toward town.

Homer thanked him, said he'd be right back, then drove to town, parking opposite the building marked FARMER'S BANK AND LOAN. The rooster, who'd been sitting atop Albert, jumped atop the seat, looked around, then fluttered out of the car. "You're a strange bird," Homer muttered as the rooster ran away as if on an urgent mission.

When Albert crawled out after the rooster, Homer quickly slipped the leash around the alligator's neck. Albert tugged hard against it in the direction of the rooster, his claws skittering on the boards of the sidewalk, all the while making the grunt that was his unhappy sound. To Homer's ears, it sounded a bit like he was saying *no-no-no*. "I'm sorry, Albert," Homer said. "He's too fast. You'll never catch him." Homer suddenly felt a bit lonely. "I'm going to miss him, too."

The door of the bank opened and the preacher from the day before walked outside. He tipped his hat. "Well, you didn't get far," he said. "Why is your alligator making that unhappy sound?"

"His rooster ran away."

"I'll pray that he returns."

"That rooster has a mind of its own," Homer said, more to himself than the preacher. "I don't even know why he's with us."

"Perhaps he's an angel who's decided to help you on your adventure. By the way, are you here to rob the bank?"

Homer was taken aback. "What do you mean?"

"Well, we heard bank robbers were in the area. You could use Albert like a gun."

"Oh. No, like I told you, I'm a coal miner. Bank robbing's not in my line of work. I'm just here to get change for a fifty-dollar bill."

The preacher touched his hat again. "Well, many blessings, young man. Tell your pretty wife I send her blessings, too."

"Thank you, sir," Homer said, touching his forehead in reply. "I will."

Before leaving, the preacher held the bank door open for Homer and Albert, who was still desperately clawing in the direction the rooster was last seen. "Come on, Albert," Homer said as he pulled him across the polished wooden floor of the bank. With a hiss and a whimper, Albert lowered his head, shaking it back and forth.

Behind the counter, an older fellow wearing a green eyeshade looked up from his ledger. "What do we have here?" he asked in a tone that indicated he'd seen nearly everything.

"I need change for a fifty-dollar bill," Homer said. He tugged at Albert to approach the teller's window. "Come on, boy."

The teller took it all in. "I've worked here for forty years and I believe this is the first time I've ever had a crocodile in my bank."

"He's an alligator."

"What's wrong with him? He looks agitated."

"He misses his rooster."

"I see," the teller said drily. "Did he eat it?"

"It ran away."

"I'm not surprised," the teller said, even more drily. "Now to your dilemma. Change for a fifty you say? I think I can help with that."

Albert crawled beneath a desk along the wall, splayed his paws out and dug in his claws and made his unhappy grunt. Homer gave a tug but the alligator was wedged tight. "All right, Albert," Homer sighed. "Go ahead and mope. I've got to take care of business."

Homer dropped the leash and took a step toward the teller but that was as far as he got before the doors suddenly burst open and two men barged inside, both of them carrying shotguns. "Hands up! This is a robbery!" one of them yelled.

Although shocked, Homer still could not help but note that the man who'd yelled was very short, no more than five feet tall. The other man, a huge black fellow, lumbered over toward Homer and waved a shotgun at him. "Don't move," he ordered.

The little man approached the teller, aiming a shotgun up at him. "All your money. *Now!*"

The teller blinked, although so slowly Homer thought he was going to take a nap, before advising, "That's just not going to happen."

The little robber was taken aback. "Why not?"

"All the money I have is in that safe—that *locked* safe—and it's made of case-hardened steel, which you couldn't open with three sticks of dynamite. Also, because I'm leaving." And with that, the teller turned and walked to the back door not two steps behind him, looked over his shoulder, shrugged, and went through it.

"Why didn't you shoot him?" the big man asked.

The little man pouted. "In case you didn't notice, Huddie, I couldn't get a bead on him from this angle. Now, get over here and help me over the counter."

The big man, apparently named Huddie, said, "Okay, Slick," to the little man, apparently named Slick.

Huddie helped Slick through the teller's window. Slick dropped behind the counter with a thud. Homer could hear him mumbling. "Dammit. It really *is* locked. What's wrong with people these days? Don't they trust anybody?"

"The teller said we could blow it with three sticks of dynamite," Huddie said.

"In case you aren't aware of it, you idiot, we don't have even one stick of dynamite."

"Then we should probably get some."

"The voice of a genius, ladies and gentlemen!"

Homer heard Slick rummaging around some more, then saw a shiny coin fly over the counter, bouncing once and landing beside Homer's shoe. It was a penny, heads up.

"That's all there is," Slick announced.

"What are we gonna do?" Huddie asked.

Slick nodded toward Homer. "See if that farmer's got anything on him."

"I'm not a farmer. I'm a coal miner," Homer said.

Huddie stuck the shotgun next to Homer's nose. "You gonna be a dead coal miner you don't empty your pockets."

That was when Huddie started screaming, mainly because his right leg just below the knee was at that moment inside an alligator's jaws. Huddie also pulled the trigger of the shotgun, which discharged, fortunately toward the ceiling. Plaster rained down while Homer hit the floor.

Huddie continued to scream as Homer sat up and dusted the plaster out of his hair before noticing that Huddie had dropped the shotgun. Homer picked it up and climbed to his feet. "Don't move," he said to the giant robber whose leg was still clamped within Albert's jaws.

Huddie glared at Homer. "You can just put that gun down, mister. Slick only gave me one shell and, as you might have noticed, I burned it. Help me get this thing off me. Please, I'm beggin' you."

Homer opened the shotgun, saw that Huddie was telling the truth, and laid it down. He also picked up the penny and put it in his pocket because miners considered a heads-up penny as good luck and he'd just had some. He looked behind the counter but there was no sign of Slick. He'd apparently gone through the same door as the teller. Homer turned to Huddie. "Albert, let the man go. You've done your job. That's a good alligator."

Two men came inside the bank, the teller and the preacher. "What do you know?" the teller said. "Caught us a robber."

"Get the police," Homer suggested, while working to pry Albert's jaws off the big man's leg. Albert finally got the idea and opened his mouth, then looked up and grinned at Homer. "Attaboy," Homer said.

"We don't have any police in town," the teller said, "but I called the state boys."

Outside, an old, dented, faded red pickup truck squealed to a stop. "Come on, Huddie!" the little man named Slick yelled.

Huddie crawled to his feet, pushed Homer away, and limped past the teller and preacher, who made no attempt to stop him. He flopped into the back of the truck and, wheels burning rubber, it sped away.

"Guess I'd best call the state boys and tell them to be on the lookout for an old red truck," the teller said. He put out his hand. "But thank you, mister."

Homer shook the teller's hand. "Thank Albert."

"Thank you, Albert."

"God bless you, Albert," the preacher added.

Albert looked up at them and made his *yeah-yeah-yeah* happy sound.

"I still need that change for a fifty," Homer said.

The teller beamed. "And you shall have it, sir."

With change for not just one but both his fifty-dollar bills, Homer walked Albert back to the car across the empty street, coaxed him into his washtub, and then sat beside him. Homer found himself in an odd mood. "You know, Albert," he said, "sometimes it takes a fright to realize something about others and about yourself, too. Well, we just had a fright and I realize maybe I was wrong about you. I want to apologize. You're a fine creature. It was low of me to not like you." He thought for a moment more, then said, "If you have to know, I've been jealous because Elsie sees Buddy Ebsen in you." He patted the alligator's head. "Forgive me, okay?"

Homer didn't expect Albert to reply and he didn't except for the low rumble of a snore as he began to doze. His heart warmed anyway, Homer climbed behind the Buick's wheel and headed back. After paying the attendant at the gas station, he turned toward the old plantation. Along the way, he found Elsie hiking along the dirt road. She waved him down. Her face was drawn with worry. "I thought you'd left me."

"Sorry. Got delayed."

She climbed inside. "What happened?"

"You might say Albert and I robbed a bank." He dug into his pocket and held up the shiny penny. "See?"

"Dammit, Homer, if you're going to lie to me, at least make up a good one." She studied him. "Why is there plaster in your hair?"

Homer, having escaped death, was feeling brash and even a bit puck-ish. He put the penny back in his pocket. "Snow," he said. "Freak storm." Elsie rolled her eyes.

They returned to the old plantation and loaded the food and blankets and the other things into the car, and then Homer drove back to the crossroads and stopped to look left and right. There was no traffic in sight. Before he could make the turn, there was a sudden fluttering of wings and the green-tailed rooster flew through the open window and landed on his shoulder.

Elsie frowned. "Where's *he* been?"

"I don't know but I'm glad he's back," Homer said.

In the back seat, Albert made his *yeah-yeah-yeah* happy sound. The rooster looked at him and crowed. Elsie put her hands over her ears and squeezed her eyes shut. "Shut up, you stupid rooster! I'm still feeling the wine!"

Chuckling, Homer made the turn and drove past the spot where the hay wagon had turned over. He was gratified to see it was no longer there. The road to Florida lay wide open. The rooster, its feathers warm, nestled in next to his ear. Elsie leaned back and closed her eyes. Albert crawled up to the window so he could grin at everything that passed by. The old Buick hummed along and Homer, the penny in his pocket giving him confidence that all would be well, whistled a happy tune.

I was forty-three and spending time in North Carolina researching a book about life and war along the Outer Banks during World War II. After a couple of weeks without checking in with my parents, I called and Mom answered the phone. "Where've you been, Sonny?" she asked.

"North Carolina, Mom. I told you I was writing about German U-boats off the coast."

U-boats didn't interest her but North Carolina clearly did. "Do you like it there? Are the people nice?"

After I told her I liked it fine and the people were very nice, she said, "You trust people too much. That's why you keep getting hurt. You need to be more careful."

I knew where that was coming from. I had recently been through a painful divorce and a mother tends to take up for her son, even when he's in the wrong. She lowered her voice, enough that I suspected she didn't want my dad to hear. "Your father and I drove across North Carolina one time. We didn't think we were ever going to get through it. We kept getting slowed down.

The first time was because of radicals. Your dad called them Communists. To tell you the truth, I was sort of attracted to them. Even thought about joining up."

"You wanted to be a Communist?"

"No, a radical. That was because I trusted them to do what they said they were going to do."

I made an informed guess. "Was this when you carried Albert home? Did he want to be a radical, too?"

"Don't make fun. Those were serious times. People were starving. They lived in camps along the road and they couldn't buy a job. That's how come the radicals were out there. They said they were going to change things, make the poor rich and the rich poor. That sounded good to me."

"What did Dad think?"

"Your dad . . . I'll tell you the story but you have to promise not to tell the police." She lowered her voice even more. "There might still be a John and Jane Doe warrant out on us."

"A John and Jane . . . Mom, what are you talking about?"

"I'm talking about sock mills, Sonny. And trust. And dynamite." ⤴

PART II

How Elsie
Became a Radical

8

WHEN THEY REACHED A SIGN THAT SAID *WELCOME TO NORTH CAROLINA, THE TAR HEEL STATE,* Homer said, "Elsie, we're officially in North Carolina. After that, we'll just have South Carolina and Georgia to go before running into Florida."

Elsie had been dozing but, at her husband's advisory, came awake. "How long until we get there?"

"Four days, I think, then maybe another day to Orlando. We can still make it back to Coalwood within our two-week allotment if we press steady on."

"Oh, what a splendid result that would be."

If Homer noticed her sarcasm, he didn't mention it. "How about lunch?"

Elsie agreed that she was ready for lunch and before long they spotted a picnic table alongside the road. "Don't tell the rooster," Homer said, "but I'd like a sandwich made from one of his former girlfriends."

"He's your rooster, not mine," Elsie replied. "I don't talk to him."

Elsie took sandwich makings from the car and set out a spread on the picnic table, then tossed a couple of chicken pieces to Albert, who had crawled out of the car on his own, doing a fine belly flop into the grass and rolling over to ask for a tummy rub, which Elsie, after she'd finished making the sandwiches, happily accomplished. The rooster also jumped out of the car and started pecking in the gravel, clearly unconcerned about his past gal pals now resting between slices of bread, tomatoes, onions, and cheese as well as in Albert's stomach.

When she heard the sound of snapping twigs, Elsie was surprised to see a dozen or more children filtering out of the trees. They were a pathetic, snot-nosed lot, their ragged clothes loose and hanging from their bony frames. They looked longingly at the food on the table.

"There must be a vagrant camp nearby," Homer said.

Elsie's heart instantly melted. "We have to give them something," she said.

Not waiting for charity, the kids suddenly raced in. Half of them cleared the picnic table while the other half threw open the car doors and tossed out the rest of the food. They were so fast and thorough and professional in their thievery, all Elsie and Homer could do was slap at them ineffectively and then watch with astonishment as the children disappeared into the woods, the last one with a feathery creature beneath his arm. "They got it all," Homer said in wonder, "even the rooster!"

"What'll we do?" Elsie asked.

"We're going to put Albert in the car and lock it. Then we're going to see if we can get our food back. And the rooster."

After seeing to Albert, Elsie and Homer emerged on the other side of the woods and beheld a dusty clearing that contained ragged tents and lean-tos made of old tarps. Wisps of smoke wafted from cooking fires where women stirred pots. "Our food is down there," Homer said.

They descended into the camp. "We need help," Homer said to anyone who would listen. "Our food was stolen by children who came from

here and we need it back. We aren't rich. We don't have much, either."
The camp people edged back, their hollow eyes watching carefully as the
couple walked between the tents and tarps, repeating their plea. There
were no children in sight.

A man's voice called out, "Did I hear someone asking for help?"

Elsie and Homer turned to see a man who'd emerged from one of the
tents. A thin fellow with soft eyes, a mustache, and a broad forehead, he
was dressed in a gray suit, vest, an open shirt, and wore what was obviously an expensive fedora. There was about him the air of a civilized,
cultured man. He was clearly no vagrant. "It was us," Elsie said. "A
bunch of kids from this camp cleaned us out." She pointed at the woods.
"We're parked over there. We just stopped for lunch."

The man provided a sympathetic shrug. "Circumstances have made
even the little ones into thieves. This much I know. Whatever they got
from you isn't coming back. These people are starving."

"But it was all the food we had," Elsie said.

"And they took our rooster, too," Homer added.

"What did it look like?"

"He was russet with a green tail. A big red comb. Kind of unique."

"I'm very sorry," the man replied. "I haven't seen it."

"Who are you?" Elsie bluntly asked.

"I'm a writer. These people are American nomads, forever on the move,
trying to feed themselves and their families. I'm thinking about writing a
book about them. My name is John Steinbeck. Perhaps you've heard of me."

After a moment of reflection, Elsie said, "No, sorry. What's it like to
be a writer?"

Steinbeck smiled. "It has its challenges."

"Well, Mr. Steinbeck, I am the wife of a coal miner," Elsie replied,
"which also has its challenges."

Steinbeck doffed his hat. "That I have no doubt about, madam. Is this your husband?"

Homer put out his hand. "I'm Homer Hickam, Mr. Steinbeck. This is my wife, Elsie. I've read two of your books, *Tortilla Flat* and *The Red Pony*. I found them excellent."

"He reads a lot of books," Elsie said, her voice betraying a subtle jealousy.

Steinbeck shook Homer's hand. "Might I ask what direction you're going?"

"South," Homer said.

"To Florida," Elsie added.

"Could you see your way to give me a ride? I want to take a look at the textile mills just south of here. They have labor problems there which interest me."

"We'd be pleased to give you a ride, Mr. Steinbeck," Elsie said.

"We'd better go before somebody steals our car," Homer said nervously.

"Thanks. Just give me a second to get my bag."

Homer led the way back through the woods with Elsie and Steinbeck following. At the Buick, Homer put Steinbeck's bag in the trunk, then opened the door to reveal Albert. "Is that a crocodile?" Steinbeck politely asked.

"Albert is an alligator," Elsie said. "Have you never seen one?"

"I grew up in California," Steinbeck answered. "Now I live in New York City. No alligators in either one of them."

"I have always wondered what it would be like to live in California or New York City," Elsie said.

"Living there is much like living anywhere, Mrs. Hickam."

Elsie was dubious. "Believe me, Mr. Steinbeck, I'm certain both places are very different from living in Coalwood, West Virginia."

Steinbeck nodded and said, "Tell me, why do you have an alligator?"

"We're carrying him home to Florida."

"Where's he been?"

"He's been living with us," Homer said, then switched topics. "What kind of labor problems are they having in the textile mills?"

"Strikes, lockouts, beatings, shootings, and murders. Some people say Communists are behind the whole thing and I want to find out if that's true."

"Labor unions came into the coalfields and the next thing you know there was a war," Homer said. "You ever hear of Mother Jones and the Pine Creek Mine War?"

"I have, indeed. Bloody mess. The army had to finally break it up."

"Before this Depression is over, I'm afraid the army might have to break a lot of things up," Homer said. "But we'd best get back on the road. Elsie and I are on a timetable to get to Florida and back as soon as we can."

"You may sit up front, Mr. Steinbeck," Elsie said. "I'll sit in the back with Albert."

"Thank you. And please call me John."

"That is very nice of you . . . John."

When Elsie settled in beside Albert, he looked up at her, then made his sad *no-no-no* grunt. "I think he misses the rooster," Elsie said.

"I do, too," Homer confessed, then steered the Buick out of the picnic area. Not more than a mile or so, he reached a crossroads, thought for a moment, then kept going straight. "I think this is southerly," he said.

"Why aren't you sure?" Elsie asked.

"The children also stole the gas station maps."

Even though the vagrant children had put the journey in a dire situation, Elsie could not keep from chuckling. "Kismet," she said.

9

AFTER SOME MILES PASSED, STEINBECK SAID, "SHOULD we reach a market, I'd be pleased to purchase you some food to make up for your loss."

"No, thank you," Homer said.

"Don't be so prideful, Homer," Elsie said. "Thank you, John. We would appreciate it."

Homer tamped down his pride, then said, "I'm curious, John. Why don't you have a car?"

"To meet folks, I just decided to thumb for rides. I've gotten around fine."

"Do you mind if we talk about writing?" Elsie asked.

"I'd like that very much. What exactly do you want to know?"

"Well, I'm thinking maybe I could write some. My brother Victor would have been a writer but he died too young."

"That's a shame. Was he talented?"

"He was only six when he passed but I think so. He liked to tell stories."

"That's very good. The trick is to turn a story into a book. Do you think you could do that?"

"Well, I went to secretary school when I lived in Orlando and my professor admired both my typing skills and my descriptive sentences."

Steinbeck chuckled. "Did he, by God! Once you have mastered typing and the descriptive sentence, you are more than halfway toward being a professional writer. What kind of books do you want to write?"

"Maybe I could write funny ones. I wrote a letter to my mother once about Albert and she said it made her laugh."

"Did you mean it to be funny?"

"No, but I guess it turned out that way."

"That's the best kind. Just tell your story and don't worry about if it's funny or not. If you try to write funny, it usually isn't. That's why comedians on the radio don't write novels. If they do, they just turn out to be a series of punch lines."

"You're teaching me so much!" Elsie enthused. "And, now that I think about it, I have a great idea for a novel. It would be about a young woman who grows up in the coalfields and then goes to live in a fancy house in Orlando where she meets lots of interesting people who make her laugh and feel good about herself."

"You could title it *When Elsie Met Buddy*," Homer groused.

Elsie made an unseen face at him. "It's fiction, Homer."

"Is it?"

When Elsie didn't reply and lapsed into wounded silence, Homer felt bad for attacking her. It was just that he was so blamed jealous. He tried to think of something to say that would rescue the situation and came up with, "Maybe you should just write about Albert."

"An excellent idea," Steinbeck said.

"I'm not going to write anything," Elsie grumped.

Homer knew better than to say anything else. He just clamped his mouth shut and drove on while hoping to come across a market or a roadside grill. When neither presented themselves, and the sun began to fade, he started looking for a cheap motel or a decent field in which to spend the night.

After topping a hill, Homer saw two sawhorses blocking the road ahead. He drove down to them, then stopped. Three men wearing suits and fedoras and a general air of authority stepped into his headlights. One of the men strolled over, deliberately moving aside his coat to reveal a holstered pistol on which he rested his hand. One of the other men moved to the passenger side and switched on a flashlight, Steinbeck blinking into the beam. The third man walked behind the Buick as the first one asked, "This the one, Claude?"

"West Virginia license plate. Yeah, got to be it."

The man closest to Homer leaned in. "Get out of the car."

"What's this all about?" Homer asked.

"It's about you getting out of the damned car!"

Elsie piped up from the back seat. "We're only passing through on the way to Florida."

The man look surprised. "You got a woman in there with you? Guess that's no surprise. Women can be red, too."

Homer was confused by the comment. "She's got some Cherokee in her but she's mostly white," he said.

The man was apparently not interested in Elsie's ancestry. "I told you to get out and I meant it, *comrade*." He pulled the pistol from its holster.

Homer had never been called comrade before. In fact, he'd never known anybody to be called that except in the newspapers, usually in stories about Russians and such. He was about to ask for an explanation when two cars pulled up, one on each side of the Buick.

The three men in suits regrouped behind the sawhorses while a fellow in a plaid shirt and a cloth cap leaned out from behind the wheel of the car on Homer's side. "What's this?" he asked. "You the law?"

"Citizen's committee," the apparent leader of the men replied. His associates' hands moved to their holstered pistols, their fingers nervously working on the butts. "You boys turn around and go back where you come from. We don't need your kind here."

"What kind is that? Men who want to work?"

"No, a buncha dirty reds. You boys turn around or you'll catch it."

"We're not gonna catch anything because the way I see it, we're Americans who have a right to be on a taxpayer paid-for road and we're going to go down it." Before the three men could react, the man wearing the cloth cap floored the Ford. It lurched forward, knocking down the sawhorses. The driver of the car on the other side laid on the horn and yelled at Homer, "Get going, you stupid sumbitch!"

Obediently, Homer pressed down on the gas pedal, steered around the remnants of the blockade, and kept going. The other car was close on his tail.

"What's happening?" Elsie asked in a small voice.

"This is the labor trouble I was telling you about," Steinbeck said.

A few miles down the road, Homer saw the Ford pulled off to the side of the road. The man with the cloth cap was out of it, waving Homer in. Homer started around but the chasing car cut him off and he had no choice but to stop. The man in the cloth cap came over and clicked on a flashlight, shining it in Homer's eyes, then Steinbeck's, then Elsie's, then Albert's, which flashed back red. "A crocodile?"

"He's an alligator," Elsie explained.

"You from the party, right?"

"Party?" Homer asked blankly.

"He's a coal miner," Elsie said.

"*The* coal miner?" The man put his hand inside. "Glad to see you, brother! We been waiting!"

Homer politely took the man's hand, then let it go. "Waiting for what?"

"We got the goods. You were told, right? My name's Malcolm. I know the drill. Just call you the coal miner, right? We were told that."

"Actually, my name is—"

"Hey, Grimes!" Malcolm yelled. "It's the coal miner!"

Malcolm grinned at Homer. "Follow me to the goods," he said, then got in the Ford and pulled out on the road.

When the fellow in the car behind blew its horn, Homer reluctantly started the Buick and fell in behind the Ford with the second car on his bumper. He glanced at the writer. "What do you think?"

"I think this is a lucky break. These are the kind of men I want to write about."

Homer was annoyed by the writer's joviality. "We'll leave you with them, then. Are you all right, Elsie?"

"I'm trying to decide if I should be scared," she replied.

"I'll protect you," Homer promised. He was disappointed when Elsie didn't reply with gratitude or make any response at all. Surely, she knew he meant it!

Malcolm turned off on a dirt road and went on a couple miles, finally stopping at a field containing about a dozen tents that glowed in the dark from the lanterns within. The silhouettes of a number of men could be seen around the tents.

"I'd like a word with you," Homer said to Malcolm after they'd parked their cars.

"First, let me show you the goods," Malcolm said. When Homer hesitated, he said, "Your woman will be all right. The boys will set her up in a tent."

"We don't need a tent," Homer said. "There's been a mistake about me. I'm not who you think I am."

The second driver walked up. "You're not the coal miner?"

"I'm *a* coal miner, not *the* coal miner."

The second driver put out his hand. "I'm Grimes," he said. "Glad to have you with us."

"Didn't you understand what I just said?" Homer demanded. "I'm not the coal miner, I'm—"

"I'd like to see your goods," Steinbeck interrupted. "I'm a writer and curious about the labor movement."

Grimes scowled. "*Movement?* We're not a movement, mister, we're the wave of the future. Someday, unions will be more powerful than companies. And we'll own *presidents*!"

Malcolm held up a kerosene lantern to get a better look at Homer and Steinbeck. To Homer, he said, "I know you have to be careful but we're in the party. Maybe not as far into the party as you but pretty much. Just take a look at the goods, that's all I'm asking. Your friend will need to stay behind. This ain't for everybody to see."

Homer studied Malcolm's face. It was not the face he thought someone mean and dangerous would have. Its chin a little weak, it was more the face of someone who was uncertain of himself and looking for approval. "Will you let us go if I look at whatever you've got?"

"Sure. But you'll be very impressed. I promise you."

"I will look at what you have," Homer said, "but then we will take our leave, understood?"

"Sure, sure," Malcolm said with an ingratiating grin. "After you see my goods, you still want to leave, I got no beef."

After motioning for Steinbeck to stay, Homer followed Malcolm to a large canvas tent. A brawny guard stood outside. Malcolm nodded to him, then threw open the flap and beckoned within. Homer stepped inside to find four unpainted pine boxes stamped TUG RIVER MINING COMPANY. One of them had the lid open and Homer was only a little surprised when he saw the red tubes inside. "Dynamite sticks," he said, "the kind that was used in the mines about a decade ago."

"Will they still work?" Malcolm asked, picking one of the sticks up.

"They may be a little shocky."

"What does that mean?"

"Drop one and it might go off."

Malcolm carefully placed the stick back in the box. "So how do we set it up?"

Homer felt a chill run up his back. "What did you have in mind?"

"See all those men out there? They worked for the Stroop Sock Mill before its damn lousy owner put them out on the street. It's time to show Stroop we're not going to take it lying down. It's time to do something that will tell the whole world how serious we are."

Just to be certain he was right about what Malcolm meant, Homer asked, "You want to blow up a sock mill?"

"That's right, coal miner. You ready to help me?"

"No! And I'm leaving. Right now!"

Homer hurriedly left the tent. When he got to the Buick, neither Elsie nor Steinbeck was there, nor was Albert. He turned around and nearly bumped into Malcolm, who'd obviously followed him. "Where's my wife?" Homer demanded.

"Take it easy," Malcolm replied. "I told you my boys were gonna escort your lady to a tent. It's that big one. See? You can join her. Look, just think about what I'm asking."

"I've already thought about it. The answer's no."

Malcolm shrugged and once more flashed his ingratiating smile. "Stay the night." This time Homer recognized it wasn't a request but an order.

Inside the tent, which contained two cots covered by thin blankets and a small folding table on which a kerosene lantern rested, Homer found Elsie sitting on one of the cots with Albert in the grass beside her. She looked up as Homer entered. "There's a couple ham sandwiches on the table. Albert ate one and seemed to like it."

Homer sat heavily on the other cot. "These fellows intend to blow up a sock mill."

"Why would they do that?"

"Because they've got a grievance. And because they're crazy." He grabbed a sandwich off the table and took a bite. "Malcolm said he's got guards watching us so we're stuck here for the night. Might as well get some sleep. Where's John?"

"Took him to another tent, I think."

A little over an hour later, Elsie was asleep but Homer was still awake, trying to think a way out of the situation. One thing was certain, he wasn't going to show these subversives how to explode their dynamite.

He heard a footstep at the tent entrance. "Could you come out, please?" Malcolm called.

Malcolm led Homer to a fire and nodded toward a crude wooden bench set before it. "Your woman comfy?"

Homer sat on the bench. "She's my wife and I guess she's okay. Look, Malcolm, let me try to explain one more time. I'm not who you think I am. I'm just a common fellow trying to drive to Florida with a wife and an alligator and, temporarily, a writer. That's all I am. Will you just let me go?"

"Do you know how to explode that dynamite?"

"Of course I do. I'm a coal miner. But I'm not going to show you how."

Malcolm took on the aspect of severe disappointment. "Never suspected you fellows would test me so much. Where's your piece?"

"Piece?"

"Your pistol. In your sock?"

"I don't have a pistol. Look, at sunup, we're leaving. That's it."

Malcolm took a deep breath. "The mill's bringing in strikebreakers every day. If we blow it up, it's gonna make a statement the party's got to like."

"What's this party you keep talking about?"

Malcolm shook his head in disbelief. "You still think I'm a cop, don't you?"

"No, I think you're an agitator and probably a Communist."

"Yeah, we're birds of a feather. Now, look, Stroop's locked the workers out, brought in some thugs and strikebreakers, so the only choice I got is to blow it up."

Homer tried to imagine what the Captain would say to Malcolm. "Let me try some logic on you," he said. "If you blow up the mill, there won't be any place for the workers to work."

"Ah, another test. Okay. By blowing up the Stroop mill, we'll show the other mill owners we mean business."

Homer tried again. "If you blow up the Stroop mill, the other owners might get afraid and shut down. Then everybody will be out of a job."

Malcolm studied Homer, then laughed. "Good God, man. Another test? Surely I've passed! By the by, will one stick of dynamite set off the others or do I need to run fuses to all of them?"

Homer was saved from replying by the arrival of several cars and trucks, their headlights sweeping across the little camp. "You boys put down your guns!" came a yell in the dark. Malcolm leapt up. "Follow me!" he yelled at Homer.

Homer didn't follow Malcolm. He ran to the tent and took Elsie, who had awakened and was standing in the doorway, by her hand. "Let's go!"

"Albert!" Elsie gasped. She ducked into the tent and quickly re-emerged dragging the alligator with her arms wrapped around his head. Homer picked up Albert's tail and they made a run to the Buick to hide behind it as men ran past them shouting, then disappeared into the darkness. There was a pistol shot and then more shouting followed by the sound of fists striking flesh. Then the attackers set some of the tents on fire and got into their cars and drove away.

Homer and Elsie waited for a while, just to be sure the invaders were gone, then put Albert in the car and went to see what had happened. They found Malcolm sitting Indian-style on the ground. His face, unhappy but unmarred, was lit by a burning tent. A man lay on the ground beside him.

Homer asked, "Who were those men?"

"Stroop's strikebreakers."

"I heard a shot."

"Winged one of my new volunteers. That's him stretched out on the ground. He just came in yesterday." Malcolm reached over and lifted the pants leg of the man, revealing a florid wound.

Homer thought he recognized both the man and the wound. When the man sat up and Homer got a better look at him, he was certain of it. "I don't know who he told you he was but his name's Huddie and that's an alligator bite, not a bullet wound. This fellow's a bank robber."

"Ain't none neither," Huddie growled.

Malcolm shrugged. "Bank robbers like John Dillinger are the heroes of our time."

"Huddie's no Dillinger. He's more like Fatty Arbuckle."

Malcolm shrugged, then beckoned Homer away and lowered his voice. "I was kind of expecting something like this. After you got your gander, my fellows hid the dynamite in a haystack so we're still in business. You in?"

"No!"

"You're good. I'll give you that. When do the tests end, coal miner?"

Homer shook his head, then walked with Elsie back to the car. "You sleep inside and I'll stand guard. We'll leave at sunrise, no matter what."

Elsie sleepily curled up on the front seat. It was Homer's firm intention to stay awake all night to stand guard but his eyes soon got too heavy. He sat down and put his back against the front wheel on the passenger side of the Buick and that was the last thing he recalled until the next morning, when he was awakened by Steinbeck crawling from under the car to sit beside him. "Rough night," the writer said, squinting at the pink spokes of sunlight emanating from the eastern edge of the pasture.

"You got your stuff? We're leaving in about ten minutes."

"You don't want to see how this ends?"

"I know how it ends. People get hurt. Sometimes, they even die. That's what always happens when Communists start causing trouble."

"Far as I can tell, these Communists, as you call them, were just sitting around their campfires and sleeping in their tents. It was a capitalist who sent rough men to beat them up."

"Don't try to confuse me," Homer griped.

Malcolm came over. He had a red-stained rag tied around his head although Homer didn't recall seeing any kind of head wound on him the night before. "I'm rallying the men this morning," Malcolm said. "You want to see my style?"

"No," Homer said.

"Yes," Steinbeck said.

Elsie and Albert got out of the Buick. "We're off to do our business," Elsie said, and, leading Albert on his leash, walked toward the outhouse behind the tents.

"Looks like your woman's not quite ready to go," Malcolm said. "She'll want some breakfast, too. Come on, let me show you what I do."

Steinbeck looked pleadingly at Homer. "Really like to see this for my book."

Suddenly curious, Malcolm asked, "You're a real author, published and all?"

"One or two," Steinbeck replied, a trifle smugly. "My novel *To a God Unknown* was recently brought out."

Malcolm blinked thoughtfully. "Never heard of it. But, before this is over, I'll write a book about poor men using dynamite to blow up capitalist sock mills."

Steinbeck frowned. "Blowing people up . . . not sure people would want to read about that."

"You kidding?" Malcolm laughed. "Fellow named Hemingway writes books about blood and guts and I bet he sells a helluva lot more than you do."

Steinbeck looked offended. "I don't know about that."

"Come on," Malcolm said. "Listen to me get these fellows stirred up."

Malcolm led them to a grassy rise in the meadow, where sat Huddie, flanked by a very short man Homer also recognized. They were sitting on a plank atop two old stumps. Malcolm's lieutenants were herding the other men around.

"You ready, Huddie?" Malcolm asked.

"He's ready," the short man said.

"I thought you'd still be running, Slick," Homer said.

"Hi there, stranger," Slick replied. "I think you've got me confused with somebody else."

"Slick's a party operative," Malcolm said, then smiled at Homer and shook his head. "Should have known you'd know each other. All that stuff about you not being in the party! Did I pass the test?"

"You pass for stupidity," Homer groused.

Malcolm grinned. "I'll keep trying to win your confidence." He addressed Huddie. "Roll up your pants leg. No, the other one."

When the big man complied, Malcolm put his hand on Huddie's shoulder and addressed the men who had gathered around. "Listen up, people. I want you to take a look at this fellow and the wound on his leg. Why is he wounded? For the same reason they beat us up and burned our tents last night. This fellow is a radical, get it? That's what they called him before they shot him, what they called all of us. *Radicals!* What's a radical? Somebody who wants fellas like you and me to have food on the table for our families and roofs over our heads. That's a radical! That's why those scabs knocked us around and wounded this poor fellow."

"At least he ain't dead!" somebody yelled from the crowd.

"Naw, he ain't dead," Malcolm agreed. "But they wanted to kill him. Why? Because he's dangerous! And you know what? Just by being here, you're dangerous, too. They wounded this man and busted us up last night. Next time, they'll murder all of us. You gonna put up with that?"

Grimes yelled out, "No, by thunder!"

"Are you a radical?"

"Hell, yes! We're all radicals!"

"You gonna let those scabs stop us?"

"No, no, no!"

Malcolm held up his hands for silence, not that anybody other than his lieutenant had said a word. That was when Homer noticed Elsie walk up with Albert in tow. Everyone moved back to give the alligator more room. Albert hissed at them and opened his jaws.

Undaunted by the reptile, Malcolm bowed his head. "Why don't we pray for justice?"

Grimes, his voice hoarse, brayed out, "We don't want to pray! We want to kick those scabs across the county line!"

"All right," Malcolm went on. "We'll march. When do you want to do it?"

"Right now!" It was Grimes again.

Malcolm smiled. "You inspire me. You truly do. All right, we'll march." When not even Grimes responded, he added, "But first we'll make some signs."

"What do you think?" Homer asked Steinbeck after the listless strikers were herded off.

"This is exciting," the writer answered.

Homer ran his hand through his hair. "John, I'm thinking you haven't seen too many bloody heads. Last night was just a taste. Where I come from, mine owners have used machine guns on strikers and strikers have turned it around and ambushed mine owners or murdered their families in the night. It was during a strike when I first saw hate on a man's face. Hate is an awful thing. It gets inside you and makes you do things you swear you'd never do. It's why I begged for a job in Coalwood and was happy to get it and now don't want to lose it. The owner there—Mr. Carter—and his superintendent—Captain Laird—give their men a living wage, decent houses to live in, and a company store that doesn't gouge. He even provides money for the local schools. They built a playground with all new equipment. Even stocked the library with books. Probably included a few of yours, for all I know. Owners do that, the unions can't get a toehold and neither does hate."

Steinbeck absorbed Homer's little speech. "The mills around here don't seem to agree with the philosophy of your Mr. Carter."

"No, I suspect they don't."

Steinbeck studied Homer. "How'd you like to see the mill from the inside and maybe meet this Stroop fellow? There's a phone line leading to that farmhouse. I'm a bit of a celebrity, you know. I bet I can make some calls and get us an invitation."

Homer thought it over. "Okay," he concluded. "Maybe I can tell the owner about how it is in Coalwood and he'll change his tune and stop all this nonsense. Malcolm's got it in his head to blow up that mill. The owner—this Mr. Stroop—has got it in his head to beat up people. You reap what you sow, the Bible says."

"You sure about this, Homer? Maybe I could distract Malcolm, let you and Elsie make a run for it."

Homer shook his head. "The way I see it, if everybody ran from bad things instead of trying to stop them, bad things would be all there is."

"That's a good line. Maybe I'll steal it."

Homer shrugged. "Make your call," he said.

10

ELSIE WAS UNEASY. AFTER APPRISING MALCOLM OF THEIR intentions, Homer and Steinbeck were gone to the mill and she was left behind as something of a hostage. Her stomach reminded her that she hadn't eaten breakfast about the same time that Malcolm walked up bearing a paper sack and a cup of coffee. "Breakfast," he said.

Elsie didn't like the way Malcolm looked at her. It was like she was a piece of meat. Wordlessly, she accepted his offering and, to escape him, went into her tent, one of only a couple unburned, and sat on a cot. She took a deep slug of the coffee. It was black, just the way she liked it. Opening the bag, she drew out a biscuit, which was heavier than any biscuit she'd ever held. She tried a bite of it and found it too hard. She had to dip it in her coffee to chew it at all.

Malcolm brazenly looked inside the tent. "Sorry about the hobnob," he said. "But it's all I've got."

"What's a hobnob?"

"Biscuit made out of oats. Took them from a horse bucket I found over yonder."

Elsie put down the hobnob but finished the coffee. When she looked up, Malcolm was still standing there. Fearful he might come inside the tent, she put down the cup and took Albert by his leash and walked him outside.

"Where you going?" Malcolm demanded.

"Is that any of your business?" Elsie demanded right back.

He reached out to touch her, then drew back when Albert hissed at him. His expression changed to one of bitterness. "You've got it all, don't you? A husband who is in the leadership of the party and a vicious alligator."

Elsie leveled her gaze at him. "And what do you have, Malcolm, besides a tendency toward lechery?"

Malcolm waved his hand around the field. "I have these men and soon I'll gather them and march on the mill."

"What good will that do?"

"We'll protest poor wages and unsafe working conditions."

Elsie shrugged. "It's a sock mill. You don't have to be educated to work there so no wonder the workers get poor wages. And unsafe? It's a mill. Lots of machines in tight quarters. How do you figure to change any of that by marching and waving signs?"

Malcolm raised his nose as if to get a whiff of Elsie's perfidy. "Karl Marx explained all that."

At that moment, it occurred to Elsie that it was men who caused most of the problems in the world and that included the Captain, Homer, Malcolm, Karl Marx, and even Buddy Ebsen. It made her angry, that women had not only to bear the children and raise them, but also put up with men who only saw the world through a man's eyes. These thoughts drove her to demand, "What about women, Malcolm? What can a woman do except be a housewife, a secretary, a nurse, a teacher, or work in sweatshops like that mill? At least a man can try to be a mill foreman. He might even be a doctor or a business owner or a banker if he's of a mind to get educated."

Malcolm studied her. "This isn't about women."

"What about Mother Jones? Isn't she a suffragette saint to you Communists?"

"I'm not a Communist. I'm a Democrat Progressive Socialist. And Mother Jones was a union organizer, not a suffragette. The unions are going to bring equality to everyone, even women."

Elsie looked over to the field where the men had gone. They were supposed to be making signs but most of them weren't doing much of anything. Some of them were even asleep and others were drinking. "That bunch isn't going to bring equality to themselves, much less everyone."

Malcolm smirked. "I suppose you could do a better job of firing them up. As if they would listen to a woman."

"They listened to their mothers, didn't they?" When Malcolm didn't reply but continued to smirk, Elsie marched over to the field. "Listen to me, you men! I'm Elsie Gardner Lavender. My married name is Hickam but I'm a Lavender through and through. My family came over here in 1712 after they were run out of England and escaped to Ireland and then got run out of there, too. They turned to America and came as indentured servants, which is another way of saying they were slaves. But that didn't matter. They worked until they could buy their freedom and then they headed west and fought the Indians and anybody else who got in their way. They took a dead land and plowed its rocky hills and, with their sweat and blood, made it grow fruit and vegetables and flow with honey. They raised their children in a place nobody else wanted. They were free!"

The men who were awake stared at Elsie, then nudged the ones who were asleep while the men who had bottles set them down. The pink, damp faces of the strikers seemed to shine in the sun as they turned in Elsie's direction.

Elsie glanced at Malcolm who was still smirking. She struck a defiant pose. "Then men came in silk hats came and stole the land from us and made us go underground and dig out the coal and breathe its nasty dust and hack up our lungs. They put us in camps where the only place little boys can play in the summer is in a creek filled with filth where they catch diseases that make their little bodies so hot it almost burns up until they die. They kill us and then don't understand why we say we're not going to take it anymore, that we're going to stand up for ourselves. That's what the people did up where I come from, up in Mother Jones territory. We fought for our rights! And now I'm telling you damn Tar Heels to get off your lazy tails and do the same. Stand up if you're any kind of man. Stand up beside me. Stand up and *let's march!*"

The men looked at her for a few silent moments and then, as if angels were lifting them up, rose in a body and, while Malcolm watched with mouth agape, held aloft their pathetic signs and roared their willingness to march into hell as long as Elsie Lavender Hickam led the way.

11

HOMER WAS SURPRISED TO SEE HOW SMALL THE MILL WAS. He had expected a big plant with belching smokestacks. Instead, it was just a little redbrick building with a thin pipe poking through the roof with no smoke at all. Two sagging power lines, a flock of sparrows sitting on them, were stretched between the building and a leaning pole. Big rectangular windows set along two floors were uniformly gray. A chain-link fence surrounded the mill. Atop its main gate was a sign that read STROOP SOCK MILL. A smaller hand-lettered sign on a gatepost read: WE ARE HIRING.

In front of the gate, three stocky men in suits and brimmed hats stood waiting. They drew back their coats to reveal pistols on their hips. Fearlessly, Homer and Steinbeck got out of the Buick and approached them. Steinbeck introduced himself and said, "I called Mr. Stroop and he gave us permission to go inside."

"We heard already," one of the guards said and nodded to another, who swung open the gate.

The door of the mill opened and a dapper man dressed in a suit and vest walked out. Behind him followed two men holding shotguns. "Mr. Steinbeck," the dapper man said.

"Mr. Stroop." Steinbeck nodded toward Homer. "My assistant. His name is Homer."

Stroop looked Homer over. "He's a workingman. I can tell by the way he carries himself."

"I'm a coal miner," Homer said. "But today, I'm working for Mr. Steinbeck."

"Well, come on in," Stroop said. "Got a half shift going today."

"Is that because of the strikers?" Steinbeck asked.

"No such thing as strikers. If a man doesn't come to work, he is permanently dismissed."

As they passed through the entry, Homer took a closer look at the mill owner. The coat he was wearing was worn, the elbows threadbare, and the pants shiny from too many pressings. His shoes, probably once elegant and fine, looked to have thin soles. Either he had dressed himself in his oldest clothes for the day or his mill wasn't very prosperous.

The first room they entered was noisy, the looms clattering away, and brown dust floated in the air. "They need to put safety guards on these machines," Homer said to Steinbeck. "Look how that woman reaches in there and plucks at the yarn. She could catch her hand real easy."

Stroop heard him. "She has to do that or the yarn gets kinked up. We train our people to be nimble."

"You get tired and things happen," Homer replied. "That loom could rip off a finger or an arm so fast you'd hardly know it happened."

"I don't design the machines," Stroop replied. "I just use them. My employees won't get hurt if they're diligent."

"There's no way you'll hire the strikers back?" Steinbeck asked.

"Hell, no! I got feelers out for other men and girls. It's the Depression. If you haven't noticed, people are desperate for jobs. It might take a while but I'll get them in here."

"It will take time to train them," Steinbeck said.

Stroop huffed. "Better than having to supervise a bunch of union louts."

Homer perused a stack of boxes filled with socks. "Who do you sell your socks to, Mr. Stroop?"

"Anybody who'll buy them."

"Looks like you have a big inventory."

"Things are a bit slow, I'll warrant," Stroop admitted.

Homer took Steinbeck aside. "This mill's about busted, strike or no strike."

"How do you know?" Steinbeck asked. "The economics of textile mills are quite complex."

"If you don't sell your socks, you go broke. That's not complex."

"You think the union's wasting their time with this mill?"

"I think Malcolm's trying to make a name for himself with the party, whoever they are, and figured this was going to be an easy nut to crack. It turned out to be tougher than he thought so now he's swinging for the fences."

"What does that mean?"

"It means I think he really means to blow this place up. Somehow, we've got to head that off."

"Agreed. But how?"

Homer considered. "He thinks I'm somebody important in the party. Maybe if I play along, I can get my hands on that dynamite and get rid of it."

"What if he catches you at it? Sounds dangerous."

"I'm a coal miner, Mr. Steinbeck. Dangerous is what I do."

Steinbeck squinted. "You know, Elsie's got quite the man in you. I'm not sure why she keeps going on about that Florida hoofer."

"It's hard to fight a dream," Homer answered. "And maybe harder to lose one."

"How about you, Homer? What's your dream?"

"I just want to live in Coalwood, mine coal, and have a family."

"Seems simple enough."

"With Elsie," Homer said, "nothing is simple."

12

ELSIE AND MALCOLM WERE IN THE FIRST LINE OF STRIK-
ers marching up to the gate of the Stroop Sock Mill. Most of the others
were holding back. Although they'd been excited when they'd left the
camp, their spirits had ebbed as they neared the mill. Their chants were
listless, their signs drooping. To revive their spirits, Elsie jabbed her
sign—which said STROOP IS A RATT!—at the sky and yelled, "Stay
with me, men. Stay with me and we can win!"

Beside her, Albert was in his washtub atop a toy wagon, liberated
from the host farmer's yard, pulled by one of the strikers. A sign attached
to the wagon read TAKE A BITE OUT OF UNFAIRNESS. Another man
carried a bucket of water to keep Albert cool. "How did you get them to
do that?" Malcolm asked Elsie out of the side of his mouth.

"I just asked."

"Elsie, do you have any idea the power you have over men?"

"And do you have any idea the power you men have over all of us
women? Let me tell you, the day will come when that will change."

Before Malcolm could reply, if he had a reply, the strikers stumbled to
a halt, their cries winding down to mumbled imprecations. Stroop had

appeared behind the fence with his big, rough-looking bodyguards. Homer and Steinbeck were also there.

The gate opened to let Homer and the writer out. "You shouldn't be here, Elsie," Homer said, then noticed her sign. "There's only one *t* in *rat*."

"I know that. I was going to write 'rattlesnake' and ran out of room."

Homer took her arm. "You're going with me."

She pulled away. "No, I'm not. The only reason these men came here was because of me."

"That's kind of true," Malcolm admitted.

"You keep out of it, Malcolm," Homer snapped. "This is between me and my wife." He leaned over and spoke into Elsie's ear. "Why are you doing this? Are you trying to put me in my place?"

"No, to put me in mine." She pushed past Homer to confront the owner. "You are a mean man, Mr. Stroop, and so are your scabs!"

"Woman, be careful!" Stroop snarled. "I respect women but when you pick up a sign and start waving it at me, you get on my wrong side!"

"All your sides are wrong!" Elsie yelled, then turned and addressed the strikers. "Listen to me! Here he is! Stroop! He's taken away your jobs and given them to scabs. You said you weren't going to take it."

A voice rang out. "No, we're not going to take it!"

"Don't tell me. *Tell him!*"

A quiet, almost apologetic chant began. "Not going to take it. Not going to take it."

"For crying out loud!" Elsie shouted. "Pick it up! *No more scabs!*"

The cries became a little louder. "No more scabs! *No more scabs!*"

"Elsie, you're playing into Stroop's hands," Homer said. "Look at him grinning. He's going to unleash his men."

Elsie ignored her husband, threw down her sign, and cupped her mouth with both hands. "Take the mill! Take the mill!"

"Stop it, Elsie," Homer said.

"Don't tell me what to do. Don't *ever* tell me what to do!"

"I'm your husband. That's my job."

Elsie glared at Homer and Homer glared at Elsie as the strikers and Stroop and Malcolm and even the mill turned into a gray, inconsequential mist that all but ceased existing around them. "Buddy wouldn't tell me what to do," she said.

Homer's eyes turned to blue ice. "Buddy isn't here. He's in New York dancing with other women. Lots of other women."

"You don't know that."

"Maybe not, but I think you do."

Suddenly, the mist dissolved and everything around them snapped back into focus. Stroop gave his order and his guards burst through the gate. They threw punches at the strikers and knocked them down and stomped on them. Rocks, hurled by both sides, started flying and one of them sailed in and struck Elsie on her head. "Oh," she said in a small, surprised voice and started to fall but Homer caught her, hooked his arm into hers, and grabbed the handle of Albert's wagon. Homer half-carried Elsie and pulled Albert through the battle until they were clear.

In a little woods nearby, Homer sat Elsie down against a tree. "Does it hurt?" he asked.

Confused, she stared at him. "Does what hurt?"

He took out a handkerchief and dabbed at the wound on her head. The handkerchief came away bloody. When he showed it to her, Elsie, undaunted, struggled to rise.

"Stay down," Homer said, pushing her back. "You got hit by a rock."

"I don't care," she protested. "My men are getting the worse of it."

Homer looked over his shoulder. The strikers had broken, their signs thrown down and trampled. The only ones left behind were either lying in the street or limping away. "They've been beaten," he said. "It's over."

"It's not right," Elsie said in disbelief. "Stroop should lose but instead he's won." She looked up at Homer. "And you won't help, will you? You're on his side. You're a . . . a capitalist."

Homer held her close but didn't say anything. Elsie looked over his shoulder and saw the men straggling away, some of them helping others but mostly by themselves. Stroop's strikebreakers were walking around, laughing and tossing the signs into a heap. "What's wrong with this world, Homer?" she whispered.

"Nothing you can fix, Elsie."

"Why not?"

"I don't know."

"You're supposed to know. You're my husband."

Homer didn't say anything. He just held her tighter.

13

WHEN THEY GOT BACK TO CAMP, HOMER TOOK ELSIE AND
Albert back to the tent, then helped her onto one of the cots. He washed
his bloody handkerchief out and used it to pat away the dried blood from
her wound. "How do you feel?"

"Terrible," she said. "Did you see how those men ran?"

"They were getting beat up, Elsie," Homer said. "They're mill workers, not professional ruffians."

"I need to think about this."

"Well, just relax for now. You can think later."

Steinbeck showed up, peeking into the tent. Homer came out to talk
to him. "Well, that didn't go well," Steinbeck said, drily.

Homer saw Malcolm arrive in his car. "John, would you look after
Elsie for a while?"

"Be my pleasure. What are you going to do?"

"Get hold of that dynamite and stop this before it goes any farther."

The camp was nearly empty except for a few weary stragglers wandering in. Malcolm was dourly contemplating them when Homer walked
over. "What's your plan to blow up the mill?"

"There's a locked gate in the back of the mill. Simple to cut the lock and sneak inside."

"What about Stroop's guards?"

"That's why I hung back, to see what they'd do. Every manjack one of them went off to get drunk. Far as they're concerned, they did their job. The strike's over."

"Where's the dynamite? I need to look at it again, make sure it'll blow."

"It'll blow. Anyway, it's already on its way. Slick and Huddie are trucking it over."

Homer had wondered why Slick and Huddie were involved with the strikers and now, recalling the bank teller's advice on how many sticks of dynamite it took to blow a steel safe, he thought he knew. "You really gave them your dynamite?"

"Sure I did. They not only have a truck, they volunteered."

Homer lowered his chin and shook his head. "You know, Malcolm, my boss back in West Virginia is a fellow named Captain Laird. He's a great man and knows a thing or two. He told me one time, 'Never be afraid to tell a man he's no good because how's he going to get good if he doesn't know he's bad?' Well, Malcolm, you're bad but I'm not sure telling you is enough. I guess I need to show you. Where's the nearest bank?"

"Over at Stroopsburg, I guess," Malcolm replied, his frown deepening. "Why? You need money?"

"No, but I reckon Slick and Huddie do."

Homer walked to the farmhouse and knocked on the door. A gray-haired woman in a flowery dress and a white apron answered it. "Ma'am, can I borrow your phone?" Homer asked.

The woman looked chagrined. "I'd say yes except it ain't workin'. Ain't been workin' all day."

When Homer came off the porch, he looked around the corner and saw why the phone wasn't working. It had been cut down at the last pole. He went back to Malcolm. "The phone line's been cut."

"I could've told you that. I cut it. I didn't want nobody warnin' Stroop about what we're up to out here."

Homer went back to see how Elsie was doing and discovered her resting in a camp chair reading a small, thin book. It was *The Red Pony* and Homer guessed Steinbeck had given it to her. Albert was at her feet, his head flat on the dirt. He looked unhappy. Homer supposed he was still missing the rooster. Homer missed him, too.

"Elsie, listen. I've got to take the Buick and do a few things. How's your head?"

Elsie raised her eyes, then touched the bump just inside her hairline. "I'm fine. Just a scrape." She looked away and bit her lip. "That thing I said about Buddy out there. I was just mad."

"I know. I was mad, too. But right now, I've got to know something. Do you still want to be a radical? Because if you do, I don't see how we can keep going to Florida."

She laid the book down on her lap. "Did you see how those men ran? I've done all I can for them. Let's just pack up and go."

"I have to do something first. Where's John? He was supposed to be looking after you."

"Said he was going to hitch a ride into town. Said he wanted to make some calls. I told him I'd be fine." Elsie studied him. "You look perplexed," she concluded.

"That's because I'm dealing with a perplexing situation."

Interrupting, Malcolm walked over. "You ready, coal miner? How you doing, Elsie?"

Elsie glared at him. "You ran away out there, Malcolm!"

"To fight another day."

Elsie looked doubtful. Malcolm took note of the book she was reading. "I thought you were going to read the copy of *Das Kapital* I gave you."

"Tried. It's the boringest book I ever read, bar none."

"That book has ignited the world!"

Elsie wrinkled her nose. "Then I guess the world must be some pretty dry tinder."

"Elsie's probably not going to make a good Communist," Homer advised Malcolm, "although she's no great shakes as a capitalist, either."

"I could be either one if I wanted to be," Elsie retorted. "In fact, I can be *anything* I want to be. I just need to figure out what that is. When I do . . ."

"You'll ignite the world," Homer finished for her, "and burn it down to the ground."

Elsie went back to her book. "Go on, do what you have to do," she said with a wave of her hand.

Homer nodded, feeling as usual a bit helpless in the face of Elsie's decisiveness, then climbed into the Buick, Malcolm settling in beside him. Homer was surprised when Elsie called out. "Don't blow yourself up," she said. "I need you."

Homer was so pleased by that, he grinned like a schoolboy. "You do?"

"Yes. I need you to take me and Albert to Florida."

Homer's grin faded.

Once on the road, Malcolm said, "She has no intention of staying with you, does she?"

"I don't know," Homer replied.

"Must be hard living with that every day."

"If she doesn't stay with me, I'll still be thankful for every day she did."

Malcolm laughed. "God, I wish I could love a dame that much!"

"No you don't. Now, listen, Malcolm, we're not going to the mill. We're going to Stroopsburg. Slick and Huddie mean to rob the bank there."

"I don't believe it," Malcolm scoffed.

"You'll see," Homer said.

At Stroopsburg, they found Steinbeck sitting on the stoop of the Western Union office. Beside him sat a homemade cage holding a forlorn fowl. "I bought this rooster," he said. "Is it yours?"

Homer looked closer, then laughed in delight. "It is! Where'd he come from?"

"I recognized some of the folks from the Hooverville where you found me. When I saw they were trying to sell a rooster, I took a guess it was yours and bought it."

Homer was glad to see the rooster. "That's the luckiest rooster I guess there ever was," he said. "I'll pay you whatever it cost."

"It only cost me a nickel," Steinbeck said.

Homer searched his pockets. There were the bills, nothing smaller than a five, counted out as change for the two fifties, and also the penny he'd robbed from the bank. Figuring he'd gotten all the luck he was likely to get out of it, he handed the penny over. "I owe you four cents. Do you recall seeing Slick and Huddie here?"

Steinbeck stood up, dusting off the seat of his pants. "Can't say that I have."

Homer peered up the street. "Where's the bank?"

"Closed, has been since the first year of the Depression. That's according to the telegram clerk. I was hoping to cash a check."

"Guess you were wrong about them," Malcolm said.

Homer looked at Malcolm. "Where do you think they are?"

"At the mill, of course."

Steinbeck asked, "Give me a lift back to camp?"

Homer shook his head. "Sorry, John. Malcolm and I have something to do. But Elsie's reading *The Red Pony*. Bet she'd like to talk to you about it."

Steinbeck beamed. "Is she, by God? Well, I'd like to hear what she has to say." He placed the caged rooster on the back seat of the Buick. "I saw a farmer come into town on his tractor. Maybe he'll give me a ride."

Homer wished the author luck and then drove the Buick onto the road that led to the mill. On the way, he said, "You do realize, don't you, that I'm not going to let you blow up the mill."

Malcolm stared at him. "Well, I guess that fries it. Are you a fed or state cop?"

"Neither one. I'm just a coal miner like I've tried to tell you I don't know how many times. Where did you tell Slick and Huddie to park the truck?"

"Why should I help you?"

"Because if you don't, I'm going to stop this car, drag you out into the road and beat you senseless, then run over you."

"I don't believe you'd do that," Malcolm replied. "Part of my training as a union organizer is to recognize a man's proclivities. You're not a beater or a runner overer."

Homer stopped the car and grabbed Malcolm's shirt at the collar. "You want to test my proclivities?"

"Keep following this road. I'll tell you where to turn!"

Homer followed his directions to a dirt road that wound through a pine forest until it ended at the rear of the mill. The truck was there but there was no sign of Slick and Huddie. Malcolm looked into the truck bed. "The dynamite's gone," he said. "I don't get it. They were supposed to wait for us."

"They're crooks, Malcolm. Whatever they're doing is for themselves."

"Well, we can't go in there until they come back out and tell us where they placed the dynamite."

"Yes, we can," Homer said, "and we are. And don't even think about running. If you do, I'll break your neck."

Malcolm reflexively put a hand to his neck, then gulped. Homer pushed him to the fence. The gate was ajar, and a snipped lock lay nearby. "I gave them bolt cutters," Malcolm explained.

Homer pushed the gate open. "Let's go."

The back door of the mill was unlocked and Homer and Malcolm went inside. On the second floor, they peeked through an open door and saw the mill equipment sitting idle. They climbed the steps to the third floor, which is where they found Stroop contemplating a box of dynamite. Without turning around, he said, "I told you to get out of here. Your job's done."

"What are you doing, Mr. Stroop?" Homer asked.

Stroop whirled about. "This is private property. Get out!"

Homer walked to the box of dynamite. A fuse was sticking from one of the charges. Then he noticed the factory owner was holding a box of matches. "I asked you what you were doing?"

Stroop eyed Malcolm. "A damn radical in my mill. Get out!"

Malcolm looked at the dynamite and the matches. "You're going to blow up your own mill?"

"It's mine. I can do anything with it I want."

"But blow it up?"

"I think I know why," Homer said. "He's broke. Your strike was the answer to his prayers. So was your dynamite. Blow up the mill, accuse you of it, collect whatever insurance might be on the place, and call it a day. About right, Mr. Stroop? How much did you pay Slick and Huddie to bring you the sticks?"

Stroop looked as if he meant to argue, but then shrugged. "There's no insurance. I haven't been able to afford any for a long time. But the mill is a family business, and I couldn't just close it and walk away. Everybody would think I was a poor businessman. I was going to blame its demise on this Communist."

"I'm not a Communist," Malcolm said. "I'm a Democrat Progressive Socialist."

Homer rolled his eyes, then took the matches away from the mill owner. "What you are doesn't matter right now, Malcolm. Look, Mr. Stroop, this looks like a nice mill. What would it take to make a profit? Rather than just giving up, have you ever thought about that?"

"Of course I have! My workers would have to take a big cut in pay for about a year. They'd never do that, of course, but if they did, we could probably get on our feet. Especially if we had a half-decent salesman. We actually make good socks."

Malcolm was astonished. "A cut in pay! My workers need more money, not less!"

"I answered the question honestly, Mr. Stalin," Stroop replied.

"Stalin? My name's Malcolm Lee. I'm related to Robert E. Lee. I'm as American as you, you damn fool moneymonger!"

Homer shushed Malcolm. "Have you asked your workers if they'd agree to a pay cut, Mr. Stroop? Maybe they would if you explained the situation."

Stroop looked doubtful. "Talk to mill hands? That's just not done around these parts."

Homer turned to Malcolm. "What do you think, Malcolm? You think your fellows might be willing to work for less with the chance they might keep their jobs and make more later?"

Malcolm raised a single eyebrow and cocked his head. "Are we nego-tiating, Mr. Stroop?"

Stroop studied Malcolm. "Let's say I am. You willing to talk turkey?"

"Let me see the books. If it's like you say, I might. But only for how-ever long it takes. The second you turn a profit, it goes to my people."

"You're holding some cards here and I might as well admit it. You get the fellows to take a temporary pay cut, I'll sign your damn union con-tract."

"Like I said, we'll sign after I have a look at your books. And I'll want safety lines painted around the machines."

"Paint is expensive."

"Arms and legs are expensive, too, Mr. Stroop. After you get up and running again, I want my people to get help from the company if they're injured."

Stroop looked askance, but then his expression softened. "I never wanted anybody to get hurt. Sure. I'll do what I can. Until you came along, my workers were like family to me."

"Then why didn't you think about helping them and keeping them safe on your own? Why does it take a radical like me to show you some sense?"

Stroop allowed a sigh, then put out his hand. "Radical? I don't think so. I think we're going to have an interesting relationship, Mr. Union Man. Do you think you could sell socks as well as you sell *The Communist Manifesto*?"

Malcolm put forth his hand but before the two men could shake, Slick and Huddie burst inside. Slick's eyes were wide and panicky. "What are you doing, Stroop?" he demanded. "Light the damn thing and let's go!"

Stroop smiled at the two bank robbers. "There's no need. I've decided to keep the mill going."

"You don't understand, you moron!" Slick yelped. "We lit the fuse to the other box on the floor below. *Run!*"

Slick and Huddie ran. With no hesitation, Stroop, Malcolm, and Homer were right behind them. Just as the last of them passed through the back gate, the mill erupted, turning into smoke and flying bricks. A secondary explosion completed the job. Homer threw himself behind a tree and covered his head with his arms until it stopped raining debris and dust. This took a considerable while.

14

INSIDE THE TENT, ELSIE WOKE TO HOMER STANDING over her. "Elsie, we're leaving!"

Elsie sat up and stared at her husband, who was covered in brick-colored dust. "Every time you leave me, you come back covered with dust," she said in mild wonder.

"No time to explain. Get your things and let's go."

She swung her legs around and put her shoes on. Albert was awake and nuzzled her legs. "You ready to go, little boy?"

"He is. Come on. You grab him up front. I've got his tail."

"What about John?" she asked as she picked her end of the alligator up.

"He'll go along with us to Winston-Salem to catch the train."

"We're going to Winston-Salem?"

"We are now."

"You still haven't told me why you're covered with dust."

"I'll tell you later."

"But it will make Albert sneeze."

"I'll clean up at the farmer's pump and change my clothes. Hurry!"

Elsie and Homer carried Albert to the Buick, which she noticed was also coated with dust. It also had a few new dents, a tear in its convertible top, and a rather familiar feathery creature peeking over the steering wheel. "Is that the rooster?"

"It is. John rescued him."

"How'd he do that?"

"Bought him for a nickel."

"It isn't worth it."

"Then you'll be pleased that I only gave him a penny. Now, hurry!"

Homer retrieved some fresh clothes from the Buick's trunk, then went off to wash up and also look for Steinbeck. He returned a few minutes later cleaned up and with the author in tow.

Homer stuffed Steinbeck in the front seat, Elsie and Albert in the back, waited until the rooster settled on his shoulder, then drove away from the union camp and turned in a direction the sun told him was south. He described the destruction of the mill to Elsie and Steinbeck, both of whom reacted in shocked silence, while wailing police cars passed them going the opposite direction. Everyone slid down in their seats.

"They might as well blow up Stroopsburg, too," Steinbeck said. "It will never recover from the loss of the mill."

"I don't know," Homer said. "This could work out if Mr. Stroop and Malcolm play the cops cagey. Maybe the two of them could join together and build a better mill where fine socks are made by happy workers."

"What are the chances of that, do you think?"

"Pretty much zero," Homer admitted.

The miles rolled on, the destroyed mill put far behind them. Elsie soon put what had happened behind her, too. If all radicals were going to be like Malcolm, she had decided she wanted no more to do with them! *On to Florida*, was her thought.

Before long, she and Steinbeck were engaged in a discussion of her literary aspirations. "I'll need a typewriter to get going, I suppose," Elsie said.

"I would recommend a Hermes Baby," Steinbeck replied. "It's portable and the ribbons are easy to change. For heavier duty, a Royal or Underwood will do."

"I recall Uncle Aubrey has a Remington," Elsie said, "but I can save up for one of my own."

"A pencil on a scrap of paper will do if the story's pouring out of you," Steinbeck advised. "That's the way I write, in spurts. All of a sudden, a chapter forms in my mind and I have to get it down before I lose it. I also like to write to music, especially Bach and maybe a little Stravinsky."

"Bach's nice," Elsie replied thoughtfully. "Not so sure about Stravinsky. Now that you've seen union organizing up close, what's going to be the title of your book?"

Steinbeck provided a gentle chuckle. "After seeing Malcolm at work, I've decided on *In Dubious Battle*. Of course, I'll have to spiff him up a bit, make him a *lot* smarter, and change the strikers from North Carolina mill workers to California fruit pickers. I know a lot more about California than North Carolina, you see."

"So you're saying you should always write about what you know?"

"Or think you know. The truth is that a lot of things we think we know we don't know at all. For instance, why are you on this journey?"

When Elsie didn't answer, Homer did. "We're carrying Albert home."

"Oh, I think it's a lot more than that," Steinbeck said.

Neither Homer nor Elsie objected to Steinbeck's comment, mainly because it was true. Instead, Homer changed the subject back to the literary. "What's next after *In Dubious Battle*, John?"

"You recall, of course, those nomadic people in the camp where you found me? I'm thinking about writing a novel about a poor family a lot like them except they'll be from Oklahoma and on the road to California to pick grapes."

"Got a name for it?"

"Not yet but the first title that comes to mind is *The Harvest Gypsies*."

"That's a terrible name," Elsie said. She took a moment to think before musing, "Grapes. Picking grapes. There was a Civil War song that had something dramatic about grapes in it. What was it? It's on the tip of my tongue."

"*Battle Hymn of the Republic*," Homer said. "They are trampling out the vintage where the grapes of wrath are stored."

"That's it!" Elsie cried. "*The Grapes of Wrath*! It's perfect!"

Steinbeck frowned thoughtfully, then shrugged. "Well, I'll give it some thought if I should ever write the blamed thing."

"Oh, you must," Elsie said, "and you will."

"Well, maybe just for you, Elsie," Steinbeck chuckled. "Maybe just for you."

I was sixteen and trying to figure out where I fit in the world. I was also about to get my driver's license, which, like all young men, I thought would help in that regard. To take the test, Dad let me get behind the wheel of his Buick and drive us to the state police outpost across the mountain from Coalwood. For some reason, Dad loved Buicks. It was the only kind he ever owned.

My father watched me critically as I carefully steered through the switchback curves of the mountain. "Watch the speed limit when the policeman takes you out," he advised. "He'll flunk you if you go one mile over it."

I was sweating, not because of the upcoming test but because my dad was paying attention to me. He was capable of being a severe critic when it came to his second son. "I will, sir," I promised.

"If you get your license, for God's sake, be careful. If you got killed, your mom would probably figure out some way to blame it on me."

In my defense, I pointed out a truism. "Mom drives too fast all the time."

"You're right," Dad grumped. "She learned how to do that when she was with those damn bootleggers."

Before I could respond, not that I had a response worthy of the name, he said, "I wasn't with her or I would've put a stop to it. But I was elsewhere writing poetry."

I thought Dad was making a rare joke but when I glanced at him, I saw by his expression he wasn't. "You wrote a poem?"

"My first and last."

"I don't get it."

He shook his head. "Gone this far, guess I ought to tell you the rest of it."

I steered through a curve, then another one, grateful that his critical eye was off me and on something else. "It was night," he began, "and we were in North Carolina. . . . You sure your mom never told you about this?"

"No, sir. Not a word." Actually, she had but I wanted him to keep talking.

"You know what a snub-nose is? No? Well, it's a little short-barreled pistol crooks like to use. Keep that image in your head." ✦

PART III

How Elsie Rode the
Thunder Road,
Homer Wrote a Poem,
and
Albert Transcended
Reality

15

HOMER EVENTUALLY FOUND WINSTON-SALEM BY DEAD reckoning and the occasional road sign. By then Elsie was asleep, as was Albert snuggled in his quilt, and the rooster atop the alligator's back.

At the train station, Steinbeck quietly removed himself from the Buick and came around to the driver's side for a last handshake. "It's been a pleasure," he said. "Take care of Elsie. She's pretty special."

"As long as she lets me stick around, I will," Homer said.

"You don't sound too hopeful."

"I don't know, John. She's a tough gal to figure."

"I'd give you some advice if I had some. The only women I understand are the ones I invent for my books, and half the time, I don't understand them, either."

Homer grimly nodded, then said, "Adios, John Steinbeck. I look forward to reading more of your books. And thank you kindly for the rooster."

Steinbeck walked away, then stopped and turned around. "There's something special about that rooster," he said, "although I can't quite put my finger on it. It's like he's, well, something bigger than himself. A lot bigger."

"He's just a rooster, John."

Steinbeck nodded. "Yes. Of course, you're right." He tipped his hat and walked away, Homer watching after him until he was safely inside the train station.

The rooster jumped up on his shoulder and nestled in. "Why are you here, rooster?" Homer asked but when the rooster didn't answer, only snuggled in closer, Homer steered the Buick through the city, then turned in what he thought was a more or less southerly direction.

Hours later, Albert's soft snores, the nestling rooster at his ear, and Elsie's sighs as she slept, were all that kept him company as Homer drove through the darkness along a road surrounded by deep woods. He'd always been reluctant to ask for directions but without so much as a glow of a distant kerosene lantern in the surrounding gloom, he began to wish he had somebody to ask. For all he knew, there was no end to this road and it might go on and on forever, even to the ends of the earth and over it. Such nonsensical thoughts were just his mind playing tricks on him but he couldn't help it. The forest, dark and mysterious, seemed to creep in closer with every passing mile.

To make matters worse, the Buick's engine was beginning to miss the occasional stroke. Homer kept his eye out for a clearing where he might pull off the road and wait for morning to do repairs when he saw a tiny but well-lit gas station in a clearing. Beside it was a garage and some junked cars. When the Buick's headlights caught a sign that read VAR-MINT'S GAS & REPAIRS, Homer felt he'd caught a bit of luck.

The lights in the garage revealed two men looking beneath the hood of a battered truck. The men, dressed in bib overalls, raised their heads and looked with some surprise as the Buick chugged in, choked, and died. One of them came over, wiping his hands on a dirty rag. "Sounds like you got a problem, mister," he said. When he peered into the Buick, he gave a low whistle. "Except in the woman department. That's one fine-lookin' female there. She your sister?"

"My wife," Homer replied. He didn't like the comment but he needed help and therefore kept his irritation restrained. "Engine started to miss. Guess I can fix it but I'll need to borrow a few tools if you'd allow."

The other man, his oil-slick hair shining in the harsh garage lights, came outside. "What we got here, Varmint?"

"Since Mildred never showed," Varmint replied, "maybe just what we need."

When another man came out, this one from the gas station, Homer began to feel a little surrounded. The third man was wearing canvas pants and a dirty T-shirt and was about the same age as the other two, which Homer guessed was mid-twenties. All three were caked with dirt and had missing teeth. He was about ready to start the Buick—if it *would* start— and leave when Varmint said, in a friendly tone, "I can tell it irritated you what I said about your wife. I apologize. Guess I'm worn-out, hardly know what I'm saying. Look, you need help, I'll help you. That's what we do around here. You okay with that?"

Varmint's expression was so sincere, Homer relaxed. "Sure. Thank you. I'd appreciate it."

Just then, Elsie came awake, yawned, stretched, then took in the lights and the garage and the gas station. She stuck her head out the window. "Got to pee. Go in the woods or is there an outhouse?"

The slick-haired man pointed to the gas station. "Outhouse in the rear, ma'am."

Elsie climbed out of the Buick, leaving the door open, and walked quickly into the shadowy passageway between the garage and the gas station. Homer lifted the Buick's hood and peered inside. "Spark plugs are likely shot," he said. "The ones they get at the company store are usually old before they get there."

"Not sure we got any plugs that'll fit your car," Varmint said. "But we can pull 'em out, see if we can clean 'em, and maybe figure out what else is wrong."

"How much for that?" Homer asked.

"Aw, hell," Varmint said, "it don't cost nothin' to clean up some spark plugs. Let's have a look."

When Elsie came back, she was gratified to see Homer and one of the young men at work on the engine. She coaxed Albert out of the Buick to stretch his legs. When she walked him past the two other men who were just leaning against the old truck, the one with the oil-slick hair said, "Well, hello, lady." The other one just stood watching with a slack jaw.

Elsie tried to always be at least polite so she said, "Hello," back.

"My name's Troy," the slick-haired man said.

"I'm Flap, ma'am," the slack-jawed man said.

"I'm Elsie," Elsie said, "and this is Albert."

"What the heck *is* that thing?" Flap asked. "A crocodile or sumphin'?"

"He's a Florida alligator. We're carrying him home."

"They got homes? What do they look like?"

"Well, I mean he's from Orlando."

Flap looked confused while Troy looked thoughtful. "Say, ma'am, unless I miss my guess, based on your alligator and other things I see about you, you're a woman what's a bit different than the average stripe. Am I too far off?"

Elsie considered the charge. "Well, I'm not sure what you mean by that."

Troy turned his head and spat a stream of tobacco juice, then wiped his mouth. "You been known to take a chance now and again, toss the dice, do something real different, am I right?"

"I still don't know what you mean."

"Well, I think you do."

Elsie didn't like the way either Troy or Flap was looking at her. It was like Malcolm had done, only worse. Homer walked by carrying spark plugs in his cupped hands toward the garage. "How much longer?" she asked.

"Working as fast as I can," he said and went inside the garage with Varmint.

Feeling his eyes exploring her, Elsie faced Troy. "Did you know Albert once bit off a man's leg?"

Troy grinned. "I think you're lying. He don't look big enough."

"It was a little man. Like you."

Troy's grin faded. "He comes at me, I'll kill him."

"Don't get any closer and he won't."

Before long, Homer came out of the garage and he and Varmint inserted the plugs, then started the Buick up. Homer climbed behind the steering wheel, Varmint getting in the passenger side. "Got to test these out," Homer said to Elsie.

"Come right back."

"No more than five minutes," he said, then steered the Buick onto the road and away.

In Elsie's estimation, Homer had just shown some very bad judgment and so had she by not insisting on going with him. She wrapped her arms around herself and shivered even though the night was warm.

16

FIVE MINUTES WENT PAST, THEN TEN. FOR PROTECTION, Elsie retreated with Albert inside the gas station, which was at least brightly lit. She knelt beside her alligator and patted his head, just to reassure herself. Flap and Troy came in, got themselves some pop out of a machine, and sat down in some chairs placed around an old black stove. "Never thought I'd see somethin' like that thang in these parts," Flap said, eyeing Albert. Troy kept his eyes on Elsie.

When a car stopped for gas, Elsie thought about going to ask for help but Flap said, "It's cousin Stuart," and then went off to fill up the tank. Troy, who'd moved over behind the counter, kept watching her. Elsie didn't like anything about Troy: the way he smelled, his dirty clothes, or his hair slicked back by surely a gallon of motor oil. She also didn't much care for the constant smirk on his face, like he knew something she didn't know.

Troy glanced at the clock on the wall and said, "Well, I think your husband and Varmint must have had some trouble. I think you and me, we'd best go see after them."

"You go see," Elsie said. "I'll keep Albert company."

"Naw, you got to go. You know the license plate number so if we don't find them, we can go to the police and tell them what to look for."

"I'll write the license plate number down for you."

"I was never good at reading numbers."

"Come to think of it, I don't know the license plate number, either," Elsie said. "I never looked to see what it was. It's from West Virginia, that's all I know. You can remember that, can't you?"

When Troy walked out from behind the counter, Elsie tensed, prepared to run, but as soon as he took a step toward her, Albert opened his jaws and hissed louder than she had ever heard him, a sound easily the equivalent of at least ten teakettles spewing steam at the same time. Troy stopped short, reached in his hip pocket, and brought out a little snub-nosed pistol. "I told you I'd kill that thing if it came after me."

"Walk back behind the counter, then," Elsie said.

Flap came inside, wiping his hands with a greasy rag. "Well, golly, Troy, put that gun away!"

Troy's smirk returned. "Just keepin' that critter off me."

"Something's wrong," Elsie said urgently to Flap. "I'm starting to think Varmint's done something to Homer. Please, Flap. You seem nice. Will you go after the police?"

Flap shook his head. "We don't need no police, ma'am. Heck, you got us all wrong, anyway. Ever'thing's on the up-and-up, no cause to fret. Ol' Varmint's a good ol' boy, wouldn't pull a tick off a dog and squash it."

"I told this pullet we needed to go hunt for 'em but she's got an attitude," Troy snarled.

Convinced that Troy was on the verge of attacking her, Elsie said, "I won't go with you, Troy, but I'll go with Flap."

Troy and Flap exchanged glances and then Troy shrugged. "Suit yourself. You heard the woman, Flap. Take her to look for her husband and Varmint."

"Albert will go, too," Elsie said.

"Naw, ma'am," Flap said. "Ain't no way I'm gonna let that critter next to me in the truck cab."

When Troy made another attempt to come from behind the counter, Albert hissed and snapped his jaws, causing Troy to jump back. "You leave him with me, he'll be dead when you get back," Troy threatened.

"We could lock him in the garage," Flap said. "He'll be okay there."

Elsie gave Albert a consoling stroke, then, because she had no choice if she was going to get away from Troy and find Homer, nodded agreement. "All right," she said. "Albert, you be good and I'll be right back."

After seeing Albert locked in the garage, Elsie climbed into the truck and settled onto its bench seat, which was nasty with grease. Flap put the truck in gear and drove onto the road. The headlights weren't very bright and all Elsie could see was a little of the road ahead and the deep forest on both sides of it. She only trusted Flap a little more than Troy but she didn't know what else to do. She said a silent prayer that Albert would be okay in the garage and that she'd soon be reunited with Homer. She was going to give him what-for for abandoning her, that much was certain.

After a few miles down the road, Flap turned off on a dirt road. "This is where Varmint lives," Flap explained. "I thought we'd look there first."

This made some sense to Elsie, although she still had her doubts that Flap was playing straight with her. She kept her hand on the door handle, ready to jump out and make a run for it if she had to. The dirt road was bumpy and curvy and after a few miles, Elsie said, "I think you should turn around," just as a cabin came into view, a light in its window. Several old cars were parked in front, one of them up on cinder blocks.

Flap parked by the cabin, got out, walked around the truck, and opened the door. "Go inside," he said.

"Who's in there?" she asked.

"A friend. He'll know where Varmint took your husband."

When she hesitated, Flap reached for her. Elsie pulled away and got out on her own. She started to run but Flap pinned her arms behind her. "Nothing's gonna happen to you," he promised. "Just go inside, have a talk with the man in there."

Flap pushed the door to the cabin open, its rusty hinges creaking, and forced Elsie inside where a man wearing a white shirt with red sleeve garters looked up from a small table. A stylish fedora adorned his head. Although he had a well-trimmed beard, he was young and Elsie thought, despite the situation, he was about as handsome a man as she'd ever seen. "Somebody for you to meet," Flap said, releasing her.

The handsome, bearded man was playing a card game, solitaire from what Elsie could see. Beside the cards and a half-full glass of clear liquid was a black revolver. "Who's the frail?" he asked, then leaned back and gave Elsie the once-over. Elsie noticed his eyes were blue, even bluer than Homer's, which were as blue as any she'd ever seen. But Homer's blue eyes were crisp. This man's blue eyes were warm. Very warm.

"She goes by Elsie," Flap said.

The man scooted his chair back, stood up, and walked around the table. He brazenly touched Elsie's hair. Startled, Elsie pulled her head back. "Easy, girl," the man said, then asked Flap, "How much did you pay her?"

"He didn't pay me anything," Elsie said. "Who are you and why am I here?"

The man frowned. "She ain't a hootchy-kootchy girl?"

"Couldn't find one," Flap said. "But maybe she's better. No makeup, sweet and innocent. Charlotte'll be fooled for certain."

"I want to leave now," Elsie said. "You've kidnapped me and that will get you in more trouble than you can shake a stick at."

The man took off his fedora. His hair was a nice shade of brown and parted in the middle. He smiled at her and Elsie saw that he had good teeth, not even a hint of tobacco stains like Troy and Flap and Varmint. "Well, my apologies, ma'am," he said. "I sent Troy and Flap after a pigeon but I don't need one that's been kidnapped. Flap, you're a fool. Get on out to the car and finish the loading. I'll deal with you later."

Flap shrugged and went out on the porch, closing the door behind him. Elsie looked at the closed door and then back at the man and his white shirt and red sleeve garters and, now that he'd stood, his freshly pressed gray pants. Yes, this man was of a much different stripe than the trio from the gas station. "Who are you?" she asked. "What do you want with me?"

"Denver's my given name," he said. "My mama, she went to Colorado once and never got over it."

"There's nothing wrong with Denver for a name," Elsie said.

"You thirsty?" Denver asked.

"Not for that rockgut I suspect you've got in that glass. But I guess I could use a glass of water."

Denver walked over to the kitchen sink, where there was a pump. He took a glass from a shelf, pumped water in it, rinsed, then pumped some more. He handed the glass over to Elsie, then pulled out a chair for her at the table. "You hungry?"

"No," Elsie said, even though she was. For all she knew, he was going to drug her, then drag her into the unmade bed in the corner and have his way with her. She sat in the offered chair and drank the water, which she guessed was safe since it had just been drawn. It tasted sweet and she discreetly wiped her lips with the back of her hand before asking, "Why am I here?"

Denver sat down at the table and studied her. Finally, he said, "I'm making a run tonight. All the way to Charlotte. If I have a woman with me, the police there will think I'm a regular Joe with a wife or out with my girl. I asked Troy to find me a hootchy-kootchy girl to play the part."

"I'm no hootchy-kootchy girl but I am a wife," Elsie said.

Denver smiled. "Then you should be perfect to go on a run with me. How would you like to make a hundred dollars? No, I take that back. Two hundred."

Elsie's eyes involuntarily widened but she answered, "I can't. I have a husband to find. He went off with Varmint in our car to test it after it got fixed at the gas station."

"If he went off with Varmint, he's going to be fine. Varmint's harmless. I see what's happened now. Kind of a misunderstanding. Where are you from?"

"West Virginia but I lived in Florida for a while."

Denver smiled. Elsie couldn't help but admire what a nice smile it was. "Tell you what," he said, "if you like, I'll leave you here and, after I make my run, I'll send word to Varmint to tell your husband where you are. But if you go with me tonight, I'll send Flap off to fetch your husband right away. They can meet us in Charlotte."

"I'd prefer you send Flap off to fetch my husband right now," Elsie said.

"Can't. I need him to finish loading my car. Besides, your husband might want to go to the police. No, the best thing is for them to meet us in Charlotte after the run."

"What about my alligator?" Elsie asked.

"You have an alligator?"

"He's the reason we're on the road. We're carrying him home to Florida, but because of all this mess, I had to leave him at the gas station. His name's Albert and if he or my husband's hurt in any way, I will track down every one of you and kill you." She tilted her chin up. "Don't think I won't, either. I have Cherokee blood in me."

Denver chuckled. "I'll have Flap fetch Albert, too," he promised. "All you have to do is go with me to Charlotte."

Elsie gave it all some thought, then looked at the cards on the table. "You're losing at solitaire," she said.

"I ain't much of a card player."

"What's this load that Flap's putting in your car?"

Denver raised his glass to her. "Liquor. Moonshine. White lightning. Corn squeezings. Clear death. Best stuff in North Carolina, bar none."

"So you're not only a kidnapper," Elsie said, "you're a bootlegger."

Denver smiled, then slowly shook his head. "No, ma'am, I'm a driver. The best one in this and several states. We move the 'shine at night from a couple of local distilleries."

"And you want me to join your gang?"

"It ain't no gang. There's just me."

"What about Troy, Flap, and Varmint?"

"Flap's my brother. Troy and Varmint are cousins. They just help out from time to time."

Elsie gave it all some thought. "You sure Flap will bring Homer and Albert to Charlotte?"

Denver put out his hand. "Yes, ma'am. I swear to you that's exactly what he will do."

Elsie looked into Denver's eyes, which seemed not only soft and warm but also sincere. She put her hand in his. "I want my two hundred dollars in advance."

Denver shook her hand, then stood up. "We have signed articles and that will be enough for now unless we could hug up a little and perhaps kiss to seal our bargain."

Denver was quite handsome and a hug and a kiss from him would not have been entirely unwelcome had they been in different circumstances but they weren't, so Elsie said, "I'm ready to go but let me tell you one thing, just so we're clear. You touch me and you're a dead man."

Denver threw back his head and laughed. "Well, ain't you the grittiest female I've been around in a coon's age!" Still chuckling, he stood up. "You're going to enjoy this. Trust me."

Unaccountably, Elsie realized she was excited by what lay ahead. "I've always wondered what it would be like to be gangster's moll," she admitted.

Denver shook his head. "Why, Elsie, I'm not a gangster and you surely ain't no moll."

"I could write poetry like Bonnie of Clyde. How did it go? *You've read the story of Jesse James, of how he lived and died. If you're still in need of something to read, here's the story of Bonnie and Clyde.* Of course, Denver and Elsie will be harder to rhyme but I can work on that. Can I drive part of the way?"

"No! This ain't no subject for poetry and it ain't no Sunday pleasure drive. This is my job. Your job is to just sit there beside me and be quiet like a good little pigeon."

Elsie frowned. Despite his warm blue eyes and dangerous air, Denver's insistence on controlling her was beginning to remind her of Homer and she didn't like it. In fact, even though she resisted feeling that way, she was kind of happy to be rid of Homer for a little while. He'd been getting at her with his being so kind when she'd compared him unfavorably to

Buddy at the plantation, and then when she'd led the mill workers and then been hit by a rock, he'd held her and told her it was okay when she knew very well he didn't think it was at all. In fact, since they'd been carrying Albert home, he hadn't tried to be very controlling at all. Her feelings toward Homer were so confusing, she decided to stop thinking about them. She concentrated, instead, on what was going to happen next with a man whose maleness was so strong, Elsie's legs were fairly made weak when he opened the door to his coupe and bade her to climb inside, to sit beside him, and, as he put it, "experience a little of life on the wild side."

17

HOMER DROVE THE BUICK DOWN THE ROAD. THE MOTOR wasn't knocking anymore although it was still a little rough. "With them cleaned-up spark plugs, all she needs now is prob'ly just the gunk run out of her," Varmint said. "Press down on the gas. Let the carburetor open up some."

Homer pressed down on the gas and the engine coughed, then caught and began to purr. After a mile or two, Homer slowed the Buick. "Best turn around and go back."

"Naw, go on for a few more miles. Let's make sure."

"I think I'll turn around," Homer said. "Elsie will be worried."

"You ain't gonna turn around," Varmint said with a menacing edge. "What you're gonna do is what I say you're gonna do. Keep driving."

Homer had halfway expected something like this. He braced his hands and arms against the steering wheel and slammed his foot on the brakes as hard as he could. Varmint was thrown against the dashboard, his head smacking into the windshield. Shocked, he subsided on the seat and looked at Homer. A trickle of blood rolled down his forehead. "What the hell did you do that for?"

Homer got out of the car, walked around it, pulled Varmint outside, and pushed him down on the road. "I guess you'll walk back," he said.

Varmint got to his knees. His nose was also bleeding and his hair was in his eyes, but he had the presence of mind to reach into his back pocket and pull out a snub-nose. "Don't get back in the car," he said. "Go down there." He waved the snub-nose toward the woods.

Homer stood his ground. "Why are you doing this? Are you after my money?"

"I don't want your money. I want your time." Varmint waved the snub-nose again. "Now, go on over there and sit on that stump and be quiet or I'll shoot you. You wouldn't be the first fellow I shot, neither."

Homer looked at the snub-nose, then looked at the stump. He went over and sat down. Varmint sat on a big rock across from the stump and wiped his nose with the back of his hand. He inspected the blood on the hand and then touched his forehead, which was also wet with blood. "Man, you did a number on me," he whined.

"How long are you going to make me sit here?" Homer asked after a few minutes.

"All night long," Varmint said. He waved the snub-nose around his head to chase away biting bugs.

"The mosquitoes will carry us away by then."

"If you move off that stump, they'll carry you away with a bullet hole."

There came the sound of a car and Homer looked in its direction. He thought about waving it down. As if reading his mind, Varmint said, "Don't even think about waving it down. I swear I'll shoot you if you so much as move or say a word."

The car, a long, low Packard, rolled to a stop, the driver rolling down his window. "Your car's gonna get hit, sitting in the road like that," he said.

"Mind your own business," Varmint replied, his snub-nose tucked out of sight.

The driver shrugged and the Packard went on. After that, there were no more cars and, sure enough, the mosquitoes began to seriously bite. Homer noticed with some gratitude toward the insect world that Varmint's blood was especially attractive to them.

When one of the insects bit Varmint hard on the cheek, he slapped at it with the hand that held the snub-nose and the pistol went off, the bullet taking with it a piece of his ear. Varmint threw down the gun and yelled and rolled and cursed and then sat up and put his hand on his ear and began to whimper. That was when he noticed Homer had come off the stump and was running toward him. He looked around and reached for the gun but Homer had already made his lunge. The two men grappled for it but Homer was much stronger. He pulled it away from Varmint and stood up. "Run," he said. "And don't stop running."

Varmint took one look at the snub-nose in Homer's steady hand and ran into the woods. Homer heard him cursing and crashing through the brush for some time until at last there was a scream followed by silence. Whatever had happened, Homer suspected it wasn't good. Maybe Varmint had fallen off a cliff or gotten eaten by a bear. Whatever had happened to him, it wasn't Homer's immediate problem. He climbed back into the Buick, put the pistol in the glove compartment, and turned around and headed back to the gas station, fearful of what he might find.

18

DENVER DROVE WITH ONE HAND, HIS RIGHT ARM UP ON the bench seat. Elsie pretended to ignore the fact that his hand rested very near her shoulder. It was past midnight. The gray road flew at them and passed behind in the dark.

At the end of a straightaway, Denver flashed through a sharp curve with scarcely a squeal of the tires. Elsie inadvertently slid toward him and Denver touched her shoulder. When he steered the low-slung coupe into another straight stretch, Elsie slid away. She brushed the hair from her forehead and tried not to act nervous because Denver was driving so fast and because he had touched her shoulder.

A collection of small houses came into view. The houses were all dark and there were no streetlights. Only the headlights of the car lit the houses briefly as they drove past. For just a moment, Elsie saw a cow standing behind a fence. "One," she said.

"What's that?" One of Denver's fingers was now tickling Elsie's shoulder.

Elsie drew her shoulder away. "I saw a cow back there on my side. If we were playing cow, I'd be ahead by one."

"What are you talking about?"

"It's a road game. You count cows on your side of the road, I count cows on my side. A white horse gets ten points. A graveyard on your side and you lose all your points."

Denver chuckled. "Do you like to play games, woman?"

"Yes, but probably not the ones you like to play."

"You see me too harsh."

Elsie reached up and pushed his hand completely off the back of the seat. "I see you for what you are, Denver. You think yourself a lady's man. Well, maybe you are but this lady's married."

"So I hear," he said, placing both hands on the steering wheel. "But I've known a few married women in my time. Like in the Bible kind of know."

"Now you're talking dirty."

Denver suddenly floored the gas pedal, slamming Elsie back into the seat. "Brace yourself and hang on," he said.

Shortly thereafter, Elsie heard a siren and a light swept through the back window. Denver's face was lit up by the reflection and Elsie saw that he was grinning like the devil.

No matter how fast Denver drove, the car behind kept up. "Looks like the sheriff's got hisself a new boy and he's pretty good," Denver said as he sped into one hairpin curve followed by another. The tires were shrieking but he maintained easy control.

Then Elsie saw ahead two cars parked sideways in the road and a half-dozen flashlights waving around. Terrified when Denver didn't slow down even a little bit, she braced herself by pushing against the floor with her feet and grabbing the seat between her legs with both hands. At the last moment, Denver slammed on the brakes. The coupe slid until it had turned completely around. When Denver next slammed on the gas,

Elsie thought his foot was surely going through the floorboard. Her screams were lost in the shriek of the tires, the stink of burning rubber boiling up inside the coupe.

They roared back at the car that had been following them. Its spotlight flooded the interior of the coupe but then flashed away. As they flew by it, Elsie saw in silent horror its undercarriage. When she turned to look out the rear window, she saw it had rolled into a ditch.

She hadn't realized it but Denver had been yelling the entire time. "Yee-haw!" he yelled again and again. He raced along for a while before turning onto a dirt road. When he finally stopped, he switched off the engine, its hot metal clicking like crickets as it cooled.

Elsie tried to catch her breath but before she could, Denver's arm went around her shoulders and pulled her close. He smelled sweaty but manly and Elsie struggled somewhat reluctantly from his arms. She admonished herself in her thoughts, although not too harshly, and said, "You can drive, Denver, I'll give you that. But you can't kiss me. Unless . . ."

He leaned back, a smirk on his face. "Unless what, Elsie?"

"Unless we get to Charlotte. You get us to the big city safe and sound and I'll kiss you. But that's only if you can get us to Charlotte."

His smirk dissolved. "What do you mean if I can?"

"How many more policemen are waiting to chase you?"

"Plenty, but they never caught me yet."

"Well, I'll say it again, Denver. You can kiss me in Charlotte but you've got to get us there safe and sound. Why don't you find another route where we won't get chased?"

"That would take too long."

"So what? Get there after the sun's up, we'll just be one more car. The coppers will never suspect a thing."

"Coppers? Where'd you hear that? In a Jimmy Cagney movie?" He laughed good-naturedly before turning thoughtful. "You know, you ain't even halfway stupid." He looked at Elsie. "You sure I can't have a down payment on that kiss?"

Elsie took a breath and tamped down the temptation that was urging her to do things she just couldn't—*mustn't*—do. "Charlotte, bub," she said, although her voice wavered just a little.

19

WHEN HOMER ARRIVED AT THE GAS STATION, HE FOUND
Troy there. Based on the astonished expression on Troy's face, it was
clear he was surprised to see Homer again, especially when Homer came
inside holding Varmint's snub-nose.

"Where's Elsie?" Homer demanded.

Troy's hand went for the snub-nose tucked in his belt. "Don't do
that," Homer warned. He reached over, took the pistol from Troy, and
tucked it in his own belt. "I'll ask again and don't lie to me. I swear I'll
shoot you if you do. Where's my wife?"

"She and Flap went looking for you."

"You're lying." Homer fired the pistol into the ceiling, dodging the
subsequent plaster powder that fell. When the smoke and dust cleared,
he demanded, "Where is she? Tell me or I swear the next bullet's going
into your face!"

Troy opened his mouth to tell a lie but then noticed Homer's trigger
finger tighten. "Easy with that, mister. She's been taken to a man who runs
the thunder road. He needs a woman to make him look like a family man
who just happens to be driving through the night at ninety miles an hour."

Homer absorbed Troy's confession but could make little sense of it. "What's the thunder road?"

"Any road you use to run 'shine to Charlotte. The man she's with is named Denver and he's the best driver out there."

"Tell me how to find him."

"In Charlotte, he usually hangs his hat at the Sunshine Motel."

Homer looked around. "Where's the alligator?"

"Locked in the garage."

"How about the rooster?"

"What is this? You gonna ask me next where the bears in the woods are? I don't know nothing about no rooster."

Homer looked past Troy to a closet where oil cans were stacked. "Get in the closet," he said.

"Hell, no."

Homer fired the pistol at the ceiling and dodged the plaster again and Troy ran into the closet and slammed the door. "You open it, I'll kill you," Homer said.

"I ain't opening it," Troy said in a muffled voice from within.

Homer walked to the garage and found its door padlocked. He looked around, found a rusty old wrench, and whacked the padlock until it fell apart. Inside, he found Albert asleep inside a big tractor tire. The rooster was with him. "Come on, boys. We got to go!"

Homer picked up Albert, his fear giving him strength, and carried him to the Buick and put him in his tub. The rooster hopped in and stood on Albert's back. Homer climbed behind the steering wheel. That was when Troy emerged from the gas station holding a sawed-off shotgun.

Homer pressed down on the gas, wheeled the Buick around, and headed back down the road. A mile or so later, after his heart had stopped pounding in his ears, Homer sent up a prayer. "Dear God, please don't let me be too late to save Elsie!"

As it turned out, God was apparently unconcerned whether Homer was too late or not. After an hour of driving in a direction he hoped was toward Charlotte, Homer realized he was completely, totally, and utterly lost. The Buick had also taken up spitting and coughing again. Homer desperately turned down one road and another but found nothing but the occasional fence marking a pasture containing cows, sheep, or goats.

Finally, the car provided a final and dramatic rattle and stopped altogether. Stranded, Homer had no choice but to set out on foot. Leading Albert on his rope leash, he walked for about half a mile before the alligator dug his paws into the dirt and provided his *no-no-no* sound. Homer picked him up and carried him like a baby. The rooster walked in front as if scouting the way for a while, then climbed up on Homer's shoulder for a ride.

It was with a great deal of relief when Homer spied a farmhouse up ahead. He knew it was a farmhouse because beside it sat a barn and a corral in which stood a white horse. "Ten," Homer said, recalling the car game that Elsie liked to play. This made him feel unhappy because Elsie was somewhere with a thunder road runner who was, for all he knew, probably a murderer on the side. He worked hard to keep his unhappiness from devolving into panic, which would do nobody any good. Like the Captain had told his foremen-in-training, "A man who loses his head is no good for anything. You got to train yourself to stop and think the situation through. Don't do anything until you're sure it's right."

All while he was walking, Homer had tried to think the situation through but couldn't come up with anything except to get the Buick fixed and get on to Charlotte and the Sunshine Motel, where he hoped Elsie would be. By the time he reached the farmhouse, he was very tired and the front porch had two rockers and a swing on it. He considered knocking on the door but the people inside were likely asleep and, anyway, probably wouldn't ask him in, especially when they saw Albert. There were also no wires of any kind leading to the house that Homer could see, so it was obvious they had neither electricity nor a telephone. The rockers beckoned and Homer sat down in one and removed his blister-producing shoes, careful not to make noise. He briefly sat there, wiggling his toes and lightly rocking and arguing with himself that maybe he should wake up the people in the farmhouse, anyway, or maybe keep going until he found a telephone. He did that for only a few minutes and then fell fast asleep.

When Homer awoke, it was to the sound of several roosters crowing. The sun was creeping up above the pasture across the road. When he heard a noise, he found himself staring into the pale gray eyes of a gaunt man dressed in coveralls sitting in the rocker beside him.

The man had a strange kind of face and Homer thought he'd never seen the like of it. He had skin that was white as plaster and his hair was also white, so white it looked like he'd stuck his head in a can of white-wash. He wasn't an albino, Homer didn't think, because he'd heard they had pink eyes and this man's eyes were gray, but, still, he had to be close to one.

Homer bent down and picked up his shoes. "I'm sorry," he said. "I was just resting."

"Oh, please stay," the man said. His tone was friendly. "Our porch was made for comfort and it appears you've availed yourself of it. That pleases me."

Homer put on his shoes, wincing as they pressed against his blisters. "My car broke down and I was walking," he explained, "and got tired. I have to get to Charlotte as fast as I can. Can you help me?"

The man ignored Homer's plea. "I also noticed that you have an alligator. And a rooster. It's a quiet rooster. When my roosters crowed, it didn't."

"It does seem to be a polite bird," Homer acknowledged. "The alligator is named Albert and is my wife's pet. We're carrying him home to Florida."

"I see," the man said. "And where is your wife?"

"That's why I need to get to Charlotte. She has been kidnapped by a man named Denver who runs the thunder road."

The man's mouth moved very slightly. It was almost a smile. "Yes, I know who you mean. Denver transports illegal liquor to Charlotte. He usually has a woman with him so he appears to be just an innocent family man. I suspect your wife is being used in that ruse, in which case you have little to fear from him. He is not by nature a rapist or a murderer. He merely likes to drive fast. I noticed you winced when you put on your shoes. Do you have blisters?"

Homer, relieved at the man's good report of Denver, looked unhappily at his shoes. "I do. These shoes are pretty new and not really meant for heavy duty. How can I find Denver?"

"When he goes to Charlotte, he usually stays for about a week. I have heard he prefers the Sunshine Motel. Most likely, he'll be there. My name is Carlos. What's yours?"

Homer felt more relief at the confirmation of the Sunshine Motel as Denver's destination. "My name's Homer," he answered.

Carlos clapped his hands. "Delightful! You are named after the original sage, scribe, writer, and poet! I, too, do a little writing. *Tempest toss'd the tide of woman, precious 'v' of life and love, yearns a man with bended knees, succor'd fast the nectar of gods.* I wrote that just last week."

"That's pretty good," Homer said even though he didn't really think it was.

"Do you write as well, Homer?"

"Well, I write in what's called a mine diary. Captain Laird wants all his foremen to do it and so I do even though I'm not quite yet a foreman."

"Can you give me an example of your prose?"

Homer thought about that, then said, " 'Loaded thirty-two tons on Three West. Water pump broke. Fixed with mine wire but liable to come loose.' "

Carlos looked skyward with an expression of rapture, even though the porch roof was in the way. Finally, he lowered his head and said, "Although it is difficult for me to follow, I sense great meaning there."

Through the screen door, Homer heard the sound of light footsteps and then a woman stepped outside on the porch. Homer thought she was perhaps the most beautiful woman he'd ever seen. Her olive-colored skin was without blemish, her nose was majestic, and her lips were full. On her hands were gold rings set with stones that looked like they could be rubies and garnets. She wore gold bracelets of various designs on her wrists, a white kerchief on her head, and a blue silk robe around her exquisite body.

Homer stood, not because she was beautiful and exotic (which she also was), but because he had been taught by his mother to always stand in the presence of a woman just met.

"Soufflé," Carlos said, "we have a guest. His name is Homer and he is a writer. He travels with an alligator whose name is Albert. That rust-colored rooster with the bright green tail over there has no name—for there are many gods or angels unnamed—but is also his companion. Homer, this is Soufflé. She is my mistress."

"I'm actually a coal miner," Homer said, noting that Carlos had called the lovely woman his "mistress," and not his wife. He had never known a man and a woman who lived together without being married except for an elderly brother and his sister over on Anawalt Mountain, near Gary.

The woman studied Albert, who responded by looking back at her with much the same expression he used with Elsie, that of adoration. Soufflé then turned her eyes toward Homer, who couldn't help but notice that her eyes were black as a bottomless well, a well in which Homer thought and even wished at that moment he might fall forever. He also had the unsettling sense that she knew exactly what he was thinking.

"You are most welcome to our house," Soufflé said. "Will you and Carlos write together?"

"Well . . . I am on my way to rescue my wife."

"He seeks Denver the driver who has kidnapped his wife, which worries him unnecessarily," Carlos said. "Yes, we shall write together. But first, our morning meal!"

Homer didn't intend to write with anyone but, in the hope he could convince them to help him, he followed Soufflé and Carlos through the parlor, which had ornate furniture, all red velvet and gilt and grander than any Homer had ever seen, and thence into the kitchen, where a table was already set. He sat in the chair Carlos pointed to and then Soufflé served pastry dishes and eggs and an odd-shaped fruit that tasted like a Fig Newton, only richer. She also served coffee that was darker and richer than any he had ever tasted.

After Homer's plate was full, Soufflé excused herself, saying she was going to feed Albert. She returned soon after. "He seems to like chicken," she said, "but yet I sense the rooster is his friend."

"Not sure what they are," Homer replied, chewing the figgish fruit with great satisfaction. "The rooster likes to sit on Albert's head and Albert doesn't seem to mind."

"You clearly are a remarkable man," she said, "to travel with such creatures. The rooster is much more than he seems, as is the alligator. But, of course, you know that."

Homer didn't know that but he nodded as if he did. He also noticed that Carlos did not suggest that Soufflé join them at the table and that she did not remove her head scarf even though the kitchen was warm from the wood-fired stove and the sun streaming through the window. When Soufflé left the kitchen again, Homer asked about the kerchief. "You will never see her without her *hijab*," Carlos said. "She must always wear it in the presence of men except for her husband. Since I am not her husband, she always wears it."

"Is that a North Carolina rule?" Homer asked.

Carlos sat back and laughed heartily. "No, Homer. It is because Soufflé is a Moslem woman, a follower of Mohammad of Arabia, although she is Persian. It is a stricture all good Moslem women follow."

Homer had heard of Moslems but the only thing he knew about them was mixed up in his head with stories he'd read as a boy about Ali Baba and the Forty Thieves and Aladdin and his flying carpet.

Carlos said, "Of course, she removes the *hijab* when we are performing relations but for that she requires complete darkness lest I see her hair."

Homer blushed. He imagined Soufflé's hair must be lustrous and ebony and thick and long, all the things he liked about a woman's hair. Still, he wondered what kind of den of iniquity had he fallen into where an unmarried man and an unmarried woman lived under the same roof and had relations. He glanced at Carlos and thought maybe the man was so pale because he was sick. And then Homer wondered how it was Carlos could perform properly with such a gorgeous and strong woman as Soufflé. But that was truthfully a sinful thought so Homer put it aside and focused on eating. He needed nourishment, after all, if he was to keep going after Elsie. When he finished, he said, "Thank you, Carlos, but I have to go."

"Where?"

"I have to walk back to my car and see if I can fix it."

"You didn't mention a car. I have a fully equipped machine shop where you can repair it. I also have a tractor. We can go after your vehicle and bring it here."

"Well, that would be fine," Homer said.

"Only one thing," Carlos said. "The tractor requires repair and I know nothing about machinery. Soufflé has been trying to fix it. Perhaps you can give her a hand?"

"Well . . ." Homer went through some sequential thinking. What use was it to hike back to the car if he couldn't move it? The tractor was the key to finding Elsie. "All right. Where's the tractor?"

Carlos smiled, Soufflé, coming back into the kitchen, smiled, and Homer decided to also smile. At Soufflé's invitation, he rose from the table and went with Soufflé to the barn where the tractor awaited.

After shooing out the chickens nesting in the engine box, Homer inspected the old tractor and discovered there really wasn't much wrong with it. The air filters and the carburetor needed cleaning, the oil needed to be changed, the belts tightened, and a leak in the radiator patched. This Homer did as quickly as he could although it took all morning.

After the tractor started right up, Soufflé gave Homer a kiss on his cheek. "You are the genius," she said. She was standing very close. Homer had never had any woman who wasn't his wife stand so close to him before. He felt a bead of sweat on his forehead.

Soufflé said, "Now we must eat again. I shall prepare a cold dish of nuts and dates. Stay here and I will return."

"I really need to get my car."

"Just a little while, my dear mechanic. You cannot go anywhere without nourishment."

Homer felt it would be impolite to turn Soufflé down and he supposed she was right about the nourishment, anyway. He went outside into the little pen where Albert had been placed, checked on him, then went back and waited in the barn. Before long, she returned with a plate of nuts and dates and also a jug of wine. "We make it with our own grapes," she explained.

Soufflé prepared a short-legged table and sat in a pile of fresh hay, patting a spot beside her. "Come. Let us eat and drink and celebrate the repair of our tractor."

Homer sat in the hay beside her. "Isn't Carlos going to join us?" he asked as she poured the wine.

"That dear man," she said. "He works so hard on his poetry in the morning, he must rest by noon. He has taken to his cot and will be asleep for hours. Try this. It is very good."

Homer sipped the wine. It was very good, indeed.

"And the dates. And the nuts. They go well with this wine, which you must drink after each morsel." A few strands of Soufflé's lustrous ebony hair slipped into view from beneath her *hijab*. Homer was surprised at how the sight of her hair affected him. He felt his temperature rising. She poured more wine, then offered the plate of nuts and dates. Homer took a handful.

"It is a fine thing we have done," Soufflé pronounced, putting the plate of nuts and dates on the table and then lolling back into the hay. "A farm without a tractor is no farm at all, just as a man without a woman is no man at all nor a woman without a man."

Homer tried to piece together what Soufflé had just said but the wine had seemed to dull his ability toward sequential thought. "A farm without a man is no woman at all?"

She smiled and languorously stretched. "A woman is no farm with-out a man." She touched his hand and ran her own up his arm. "But a woman with a man is a farm that needs a tractor."

Everything Soufflé was saying was starting to make an odd kind of sense to Homer and the wine was also very good. Upon her suggestion, as her hands went behind his neck, he thought he'd have some more of it, and also perhaps some dates and nuts. He might have done it, too, except his eyes were so heavy that he couldn't keep them open. When he next woke, he was lying on his stomach and there was straw in his mouth.

20

DENVER KEPT COMPLAINING THAT TAKING ELSIE'S ADVICE
had caused them to drive all night without any excitement at all. Elsie
didn't argue. She was just glad that they were no longer flying recklessly
across the roads with policemen chasing them. When Denver confessed
he was lost, he pulled behind an abandoned barn. While Elsie slept in
the back seat, Denver leaned back in the driver's seat and snoozed until
the morning sun woke them both up. When Elsie heard him get out, she
pretended to sleep until she heard him open the trunk. She sat up. "Are
you truly lost?" she asked.

"Pretty much," he confessed. "I thought I knew these roads but some
of them got washed out in the spring." He opened a thermos and poured
some coffee into its top. "You hungry?"

"I guess I am," she said. She swung open the door and came out and
stood in the grass in her bare feet. "Is there a bathroom in that barn?"

"I used the other side. You can, too, if you like. Just avoid the wet
spot."

Elsie squinted toward the barn, then took her leave. When she got
back, Denver had opened up a basket that had apples and oranges in it.

She chose an apple, then drank coffee from the thermos top. "More," she said, and Denver obligingly poured the last of it.

"We got to find the highway," he said after putting away the basket. "It's the only way we're going to get to Charlotte today. Might be some more thunder road out there. You up to it?"

"No," Elsie said. "I've decided I don't like being a gangster's moll. How about letting me out somewhere?"

"Your husband's going to be in Charlotte. If you want to see him, you need to stay with me."

"What if you get stopped and I get arrested?"

Denver shrugged. "That ain't the worst thing that can happen."

"No? What's the worst?"

"That!" he said as a car boiled up on the dirt road and, siren screaming, came racing toward them. Shots rang out. "State police! Get in the car!"

Elsie did not hesitate. She got in the car and Denver slammed down the gas pedal and drove across the pasture and through the line of bushes behind them. The bushes, it turned out, hid a fence, which was instantly turned into splinters. The wailing police car raced behind them, a uniformed man on the passenger side halfway out and squeezing off pistol shots.

Denver spun out, headed back, shattered the fence in another spot, and passed the police car, which slid to a stop, then turned around to give chase. Elsie realized she was grinning. Denver noticed it, too. "You enjoying this?"

"I guess I am," Elsie confessed.

"Maybe you *would* make a good gangster's moll!"

Bumping through a ditch, Denver drove the car up on the dirt road. "Okay, I know where I am now. The highway's that way. I missed this fork last night."

"They're back!" Elsie said as sirens wailed behind them again.

Denver took a look in the rearview mirror. "Hang on!"

Elsie hung on as they flew toward a covered bridge. A large sign at its entrance said: DANGER. DO NOT CROSS. The thrill of the chase died and was replaced by fear.

Denver plunged the car inside the bridge, which shook beneath the earthquake of the coupe's big engine. They passed through the bridge and bumped up on the highway. Elsie looked over her shoulder and saw the police car had stopped before crossing the bridge. "We got away!" she crowed.

Elsie's joy was curtailed when a bullet crashed into the rear window, filling her hair with glass. She screamed. Another car was behind them, its siren wailing.

"Watch this!" Denver shouted. He pulled a lever, then looked into his rearview mirror. "Aw, hell, it didn't work. Oil was supposed to come out of the back, make the road slippery."

"That would take a lot of oil," Elsie said. When she looked back, the chasing car was falling behind. This calmed her down enough that she could brush the glass out of her hair. "And oil doesn't flow very well. It's kind of thick."

Denver gave that some thought. "You know a lot for a West Virginia girl."

"And you don't much for any kind of man," she snapped. "You got a box of thumbtacks or something? I could throw them out the window and give them a flat tire."

Denver laughed. "I got something better. Climb into the back seat and pull it down. There's a box behind it. Bring it to me."

Elsie dutifully crawled into the back, pulled down the seat, and retrieved the cardboard box. Back in the front seat, she opened the box and beheld a half-dozen cylinders, each about the size of a big banana. "What is this? Dynamite?"

"Naw. Homemade firecrackers. There are matches in the glove compartment. Start tossin' them."

"Won't that make them mad?"

"They've already shot out our window," Denver pointed out. "If you don't, they're liable to catch us. You don't want that, do you? Now be careful. Toss 'em as soon as they're lit."

Elsie looked askance at such obvious advice, but when Denver deliberately slowed down to let the police car close in on them, she started lighting and tossing. The first two firecrackers bounced off the road but then she got the hang of it and put one on the hood of the chasing car. In response, it swerved into the roadside ditch, flipped, rolled over, and burst into flames.

"Oh, my stars!" Elsie cried. "We've got to go back!"

Denver chewed on his lip, then allowed a big sigh. He slowed the car and turned around and drove back to the upside-down police car. The flames had died down and it was only billowing smoke from the engine compartment. The driver, a uniformed state policeman and the only passenger, had dragged himself outside and was lying on his back in the grass.

Elsie saw the policeman was a young man. "Wake up, Officer," she pleaded. "Oh my gosh, Denver. Is he dead?"

Denver knelt beside him and slapped the policeman on the cheeks a couple of times. "Wake up, old son."

The policeman woke up, blearily regarded Denver, then sat up, although slowly. He rubbed his head. "You'll pay for this, Denver," he groaned.

Another police car stopped and a big man got out and walked over.

He had an old-fashioned handlebar mustache and was wearing a different uniform than the youth. "You couldn't just outrun him, Denver?"

"Thought to have a little fun," Denver said. "Elsie, meet Sheriff Sanders. That was one of his boys who rolled over last night. He okay, Sheriff?"

"He's fine but that's the second car from my department you caused to wreck this year. I've asked you to stop messing with them. My boys know to not catch you."

Elsie was confused but made a guess. "You two are in this together?"

"The sheriff is my first cousin," Denver said.

The sheriff smiled a crooked smile at Elsie. "What joint do you work at, sweet girl?"

"I'm no hootchy-kootchy girl. I was kidnapped."

"That's more or less true," Denver allowed.

Sanders shrugged. "Hidy, Bobby Hank," he said to the state policeman, who had climbed to his booted feet. He creaked with leather and rectitude.

State Trooper Bobby Hank hooked his thumbs in his belt. "If you think I'm gonna play along with your nefarious schemes, you've got another think coming. You're all under arrest."

"After you rolled over and caught on fire, we came back to see if you were all right," Elsie pointed out.

"I wouldn't have rolled over and caught fire if you hadn't thrown those firecrackers at me."

"It's still a lot your fault," Elsie insisted. "So you can't arrest us."

Trooper Bobby Hank considered Elsie's illogical logic, then said, "You know what? I'm gonna catch hell for wrecking my car, even if it wasn't my fault. My pay's probably gonna be docked, so you fellows owe me something."

"How much?" Denver asked.

"Quarter the profit on your load. No, make that half."

"Pay it, Denver," Sheriff Sanders said. "Ol' Bobby Hank's got us fair and square."

Denver shook his head, then held his hands palm up, a gesture of surrender. "You want to ride with us?" he asked Bobby Hank.

"No. I called in my location before the wreck. Troopers will be along soon. You'd better hurry. You know where to send my money?"

"I'll find you," Denver promised.

Denver and Elsie climbed back inside the coupe and drove on without incident to Charlotte and the Sunshine Motel. Denver escorted Elsie to the motel office. Elsie inquired about Homer but the clerk knew nothing of him. "You want a room, ma'am?"

Denver said, "She can stay in my room, Clyde."

"What about you?" the clerk asked.

"I'll be back a little later."

After squiring Elsie to the room, Denver stood at the door. "How about that kiss you promised?"

"You promised me my husband would be here."

"He will be. You want to pucker up?"

"Not until I lay eyes on my husband. You also owe me two hundred dollars."

"Damn, woman!" Denver declared. "You're tough as rawhide."

"That's the way they grow us in West Virginia."

"Then I'm glad I live in North Carolina."

"Give me my money and bring me my husband, Denver."

Clearly embarrassed, Denver rubbed the back of his neck. "I'll have to mail you the money. I don't keep that much on me and this load of 'shine got messed up. What's your address?"

"In the unlikely event you decide to be honest, you can mail my money to my mama, Minnie Lavender, Thorpe, West Virginia. That's all it needs to say. She'll get it."

Denver plucked a pen from a bedside table in the room, wrote the address down on a scrap of newspaper, and tucked it in his shirt pocket. "I swear you'll get your money."

"How about my husband?"

"Him, too. Trust me."

"I'd sooner trust a snake."

Denver grinned. "So a kiss really is out of the question?"

"See you around, Denver," Elsie said and pushed him outside.

Elsie watched Denver go down the steps and get behind the wheel of his car and drive off. The motel clerk came by, his arms laden with fresh sheets. "It ain't usual for Denver to leave behind one of his hootchy-kootchy girls," he advised Elsie. "How about a kiss?"

Elsie took the snub-nose, which she had filched from Denver, from her dress pocket. "I know how to use this."

The clerk handed over the sheets. "Sorry, ma'am."

"You'll be even sorrier if you come back," Elsie said, then took the sheets and closed the door behind her, contemplating a hot shower, a soft bed, and, she fervently hoped, a short wait until Homer showed up to carry her—*oh, please let it be so!*—and Albert home to Florida.

As Elsie showered, she realized she had learned something. She was attracted to the kind of man Denver was. He drove fast and was dangerous and handsome but, she reflected, he was also, in his own way, needy. If he wasn't showing off to a pretty girl, it was Elsie's guess he was fairly miserable. Elsie was happy she didn't have to put up with such a man all the way to Florida. Homer, despite all his many flaws—mostly, she had to concede, having to do with his good character—well, he would do just fine for that chore.

21

AFTER HOMER PLUCKED THE STRAW FROM HIS MOUTH AND sorted himself out from the numbing wine, he woke up Soufflé, who was dozing beside him, then hopped on the tractor and drove it out of the barn. Even though there was but one seat, Soufflé insisted on riding along to retrieve the Buick. She sat behind him, her arms around his waist, her hands holding a nearly empty bottle of wine, and hugged him close all the way there and then all the way back. "You have the best-smelling back in the world," she said above the clatter of the tractor.

Homer didn't know what to say. How backs smelled one way or the other was something he'd never thought about. He hoped he could get the Buick fixed in a hurry so he could go find Elsie.

At the Buick, Soufflé finished the wine and tossed the empty bottle into the back seat while Homer hooked up a cable to the car for retrieval. When they got back, Carlos was waiting for them at the entrance to the barn. The Buick was brought inside and the noisy tractor turned off and Carlos said to Soufflé, "I could not help but notice you and our esteemed guest had a lunch of nuts, dates, and wine while resting on a bed of hay." His eyes shifted to Homer. "I trust you enjoyed Soufflé's lunch, sir?"

Homer couldn't hide his blush. "It was very good," he said. "Then I took a nap."

"Did you?" Carlos removed a pitchfork from the wall. Its tines gleamed in the sunlight streaming through the open barn doors. Homer thought it best to stay in the tractor seat while Carlos came closer, holding the pitchfork in a stabbing position. "When I noticed your depressions in the hay and the remnants of your lunch," he said, "I was inspired. When I saw this pitchfork, I was also inspired. Would you like to hear what I wrote under these inspirations?"

"Very much, my darling," Soufflé said. "You know I am devoted to your work."

"How about you, Homer?" Carlos asked. "Are you devoted to my work?" When Homer didn't answer, mainly because he didn't know how to answer, Carlos said, "Of course you aren't. You haven't heard enough. But what poetry I'm certain you found with my Soufflé!"

"Alas, he found none, my love," she said. "The wine was too heavy for him, I fear."

"Is that true, Homer?"

"As far as I know," Homer said, cautiously.

Carlos turned and jammed the pitchfork into a sack of wheat, the grain pouring out like golden tears. Then he quoted himself:

> *Your body has the sharp tines of a pitchfork*
> *Plunging into my heart the release of my potent blood*
> *And my tempted zeal beyond the horizon of mirth*
> *There, my sweet soul, upon the litter of heat and oil and straw*
> *You showed me once more in my frenzied mind your nectar lips*
> *upon another and the joy of the other from which you*
> *know I must depend.*

There was more to the poem, none of which Homer comprehended. When Carlos finished his recitation he was breathing heavily as if he'd run for miles.

"You have done it again, my strength!" Soufflé applauded.

Carlos looked up at Homer. "Will you write with me now, Homer?"

"I need to fix my car," Homer said.

"A mundane requirement of life," Carlos said, sighing. "But I shall not detain you from that which you must do on your vehicle, although I insist that we write together before you go." He extended his hand to Soufflé. "We have an assignation, my dear, wouldn't you say?"

She smiled, her expression eager and salacious. "I would say so, my all."

The pair departed hand in hand, leaving Homer alone, relieved that they'd left him and also relieved that he hadn't been stuck with the pitchfork. He got to work, hoping to get the car going before Carlos and Soufflé returned. The carburetor was the focus of his attention because he suspected the gasoline in southern states was less than clean.

To his disappointment, Soufflé soon returned but all she did was sit in the straw and watch him with her big, soft, dark eyes, which made him feel uncomfortable. Still, he persevered, cleaning the carburetor and also affixing some tape on the convertible top to patch the hole put there by a fragment of the sock mill. When he was ready, he put everything back together and tested the Buick, which started up with an effective rumble that soon settled into a purr. That was when Soufflé rose and put out her hand. "Due to my tractor and tools, your vehicle is fixed. As my reward, you will walk with me."

"I need to look after Albert," Homer said because he didn't want to go anywhere with her. For all he knew, Carlos was waiting to stick him with that pitchfork if he did.

"I insist," she said. "You have nothing to fear from Carlos. Walk with me. It will be to your benefit."

She took Homer's hand and held it with a tight grip. Her hand was surprisingly strong and a bit calloused, the hand of a farmer. She led him from the barn to a small pond filled with reeds and cattail rushes and there he saw Albert, or more exactly, Albert's eyes protruding above the muddy water.

Soufflé took both of his hands and it seemed to Homer that there was a kind of electricity flowing through them. "You think you don't need anything," she said. "You think you know yourself completely. Yet, the paradox is that you are on this journey to discover who you really are."

"But I'm just carrying Albert home," Homer said.

"Dear one, we have only known one another a few hours, yet I know you are doing far more than that. What have you already learned on your journey?"

"That it takes a lot longer to get through Virginia and North Carolina than I expected."

She smiled. "That is a good thing to discover. Most things take more time than we believe they will. But, now, what about love? Will love take more time than you think?"

"I don't know anything about love."

"That is true," she agreed. "Yet, every mile you travel on this journey is for this thing you don't know anything about."

Homer blinked, the truth of his purpose flashing into his mind. "I need to find Elsie."

"Where is she?"

"Charlotte. The Sunshine Motel."

"How will you find her?"

"Get in my car and drive there and ask for directions."

"Yes, but how will you *find* her?"

Homer thought, then said, "I don't know."

"By carrying Albert home," Soufflé said, "but you already know that. You just don't know you know. Now, listen to me. We are going back now and you will sit with Carlos and you will write poetry together and you will fill the pages with all the things that are in your heart and have always been there."

"But that doesn't find Elsie."

"It is the only thing that will."

Which was the last thing Homer recalled of that moment on that endless green pasture with the pond he hadn't noticed before and Albert's eyes floating like scarlet fireflies in the darkness. In what seemed to be a very white room where even the air was white, he filled pages with all that he knew and hoped he knew and wanted to know. He kept writing until the sun came up and then he wrote some more until, at last, he wrote what he had to say. After that, the room turned back into the kitchen and he found himself sitting across the table from Carlos and Soufflé, who were reading what he had written. Soufflé looked up and smiled. "You're back," she said. She held up a sheet of paper on which he recognized his handwriting. "And look at what you've written. You have revealed a truth as important as the earth revolving about the sun."

"Quite astonishing," Carlos agreed.

Homer read his words and then felt like he couldn't breathe. He excused himself and went outside and walked around the barn until he came to a plot of patchy green grass that contained what appeared to be a rather fresh grave and several older ones. He stared at the graves, wondering whom they contained.

"They were not poets," Carlos said, walking up beside him. "They revealed no truths."

"What . . . *who* were they?" Homer asked.

"Though their souls were artless, Soufflé gave them a moment of poetic joy and then I made their deaths perfect."

Homer waited to see if Carlos was going to say something else, perhaps laugh and tell him he was only joking, but after an interval during which it became apparent that Carlos was going to do no such thing, Homer said, "I think I had better be going."

Carlos nodded. "Yes, I think you should."

When Homer turned to leave, Carlos called after him, "You were lucky wine does not suit you."

With Albert and the rooster snuggled down in the back seat, Homer drove away while looking in the mirror to see the poet and his mistress on their porch. Soufflé held up a single sheet of paper and pointed at it. He thought he knew which one it was, the one she had told him revealed a true truth. On it, he had written:

> *Let me find you.*
> *If you don't,*
> *I will still look.*
> *If you won't,*
> *I will still look.*
> *If you can't,*
> *I will still look.*
> *It is the looking that finds the love,*
> *Not the finding.*

Homer kept driving away, trying to sort out reality and dreams from other reality and dreams, and then, unable to do it, began to focus on finding Elsie. "The Sunshine Motel," he kept saying to himself as if the very words were a map, and, finally asking for directions from various people on the streets, eventually found himself there. When Elsie opened the door, he made to hold her but she pushed him away. "You abandoned me."

"You're right. I'm sorry."

"I want to see Albert."

Homer stood back, then watched as she rushed down the steps to the Buick and flung open the door and greeted her smiling reptile. He remembered what he had written at the farm no more than a few hours past.

Elsie was found.

But that wasn't what mattered.

What mattered was that he had looked.

It was only after he was back on the road that Homer realized Soufflé and Carlos had done more than give him an important insight. They had also stolen all of his money and both pistols he'd collected from the thunder road gang.

I was eighteen and it was summertime. Between my freshman and sophomore years at Virginia Tech, I was working for my father in the Coalwood mine. Mom was gone from Coalwood, for the summer. She'd finally convinced dad to go into debt to buy her a house near Murrell's Inlet, South Carolina.

To help celebrate the Fourth of July, a softball game was scheduled between a union team and a management team. Because I was young and not beat up like most of the older coal miners, I was tapped to join the union team. The management team consisted mostly of young foremen. To my surprise, my father took on the umpire's job. I had no idea he knew anything about softball or any kind of ball.

The game was played and our union team won. I even hit a home run. Afterward, Mr. Dubonnet, the United Mine Workers union boss, sought me out. He and my dad were forever arguing about how the mine was supposed to be run and, even though they had gone to high school together, they weren't friends. "Your mom called me yesterday," he said. "She heard you were going to play today and Homer was going to umpire. She thought you ought to hear a story about your dad. It's about her, too."

Mom always had an ulterior motive for anything she did so I naturally asked, "Did she say why?"

"She said you don't really know who your father is and it was about time you did." He scratched his head. "That story taught me a couple of things about him and your mother, too. She's an interesting woman."

"Yes, sir. I guess she is."

Mr. Dubonnet led me over the concession stand and bought himself a beer and me a Royal Crown cola. I drank my RC and heard my mom's tale through the voice of Coalwood's union boss, a man my father heartily disliked but thoroughly respected. Mr. Dubonnet, you see, was the captain of his high school football team. He was also the same football captain my mom had turned down so she could go to a dance with a certain blue-eyed, skinny young lad named Homer.

PART IV

How Homer Learned
the Lessons of Baseball
and
Elsie the Nurse

22

THE JOURNEY OF HOMER, ELSIE, ALBERT, AND THE ROOSTER changed abruptly with the sound of breaking glass. Splinters and shards pelted Homer's face, chest, and hands and he stared with incomprehension at the glittering mess in his lap. He picked a shard from his cheek, a trickle of blood seeping from the small hole left behind.

"What happened, Homer?" Elsie asked groggily from the back seat.

"Somebody busted our windshield," he answered.

"Who would do such a thing?"

Homer didn't answer because he wasn't sure. His first thought was that the gang that had kidnapped Elsie had somehow followed them and was now on the attack, but when he looked around, there was no gang. There was only the empty field where he'd pulled over for the night, which, he now understood, was actually the parking lot for a nearby stadium of some sort. Upon closer inspection, the sign heralding the entrance to the stadium clarified both the name and the kind of stadium that it was:

FELDMAN FIELD
HOME OF THE HIGH TOP FURNITURE MAKERS
COASTAL LEAGUE CHAMPS 1912

Homer got out and spotted the baseball that had busted his windshield and wounded his face. Angrily, he picked it up and threw it with all his might, watching it sail over the fence and bleachers. Although the angry pitch made him feel better, it didn't come close to solving his immediate problem: How was he going to get the windshield fixed, if it could be fixed at all? 1925 Buick convertible touring cars weren't mass-produced. Who in the backcountry of North Carolina might have a windshield to fit it? Even if there was somebody, he and Elsie didn't have any money. They also didn't have any food. There was even the possibility that they were being hunted by the police for being (a) witnesses to a bank robbery (during which he'd stolen a penny), (b) accomplices to the destruction of a sock mill, (c) knowledgeable of the possible murders of more than several unknown persons on a poet's farm, and (d) transporting illegal liquor along the thunder road. The end of his thoughtful sequence arrived at a singular conclusion: they were in a bad fix.

Elsie opened the back door and came out to contemplate the situation. "What did you do to bust the windshield?" she asked.

"I didn't do anything. It was a baseball." Homer gestured toward the stadium. "From there, I think." He looked around to see if he could figure out where they were. Past the parking lot and the stadium, there could be seen some low brick buildings that indicated a town of some sort. He supposed he could drive the Buick, even with its busted windshield, to the town, although what he'd find there in terms of car repair, or how he might pay for the work, he could not say.

That was when he saw a man hurry through the stadium gate beneath the sign, take obvious note of the Buick and its occupants, and turn steadfastly in their direction. The hurrying man wore a white shirt with suspenders, gray pants, and two-toned shoes, and had about him a determined look. He held up a baseball. "You throw this ball?" he demanded.

"If that's the baseball that broke my windshield, then, yes, I threw it," Homer said.

The man squinted at the windshield. "People who park here know they're liable to get hit by a ball now and again." He tossed Homer the ball. "Throw it again."

"Where?"

"Back inside the park."

Homer obligingly threw the ball. It easily cleared the stands and disappeared. Before long, a fellow in a baseball uniform, a catcher if his mask and pads were any indication, appeared. He was carrying the ball, which he held up, saying, "All the way to the other side of the field, Mr. Thompson."

"Give it back to this young man, Jared," the man in the suspenders said.

The catcher tossed Homer the ball and then ran a distance away and squatted down. "Right here," he called, smacking his glove with his fist.

"Pitch it to him," the man said.

"Homer played on the Coalwood Robins team, which won the league last year," Elsie interjected.

"You're a pro?" the man asked.

"I'm a coal miner," Homer said, then wound up and threw the ball to the catcher.

The ball flew with unerring velocity straight into the catcher's glove and the catcher yelped, then took his hand out of the glove and shook it. "Red hot!"

The suspendered man was looking thoughtful. "So this league you played in, it's not professional?"

"Coal companies sponsor teams," Homer said. "We don't get paid to play, if that's what you mean. We do it for the honor of our employers."

"You ever think about going pro? You got some arm on you."

"Most coal miners have good arms," Homer said. "It goes with the job. I don't think I'm anything special."

"He got a gold cup when he won the championship," Elsie said.

"We all got a gold cup, Elsie. The Captain got them made for us."

"You were still the best player on the team."

"I bet he was, ma'am." The man with the suspenders put out his hand. "Jake Thompson. I'm the manager of the High Top Furniture Makers. Coastal League. I also scout a little. Want to try out?"

Homer frowned. "What I'd like is for you to pay for my windshield. We're on our way to Florida, you see. Anybody in this town could fix it?"

"I think I could find somebody," Thompson replied. "I'll call around. Take a little while to get it in, though. Likely would have to be a special order and come all the way from Detroit. In the meantime, why don't you come on inside the park, let us feed you and your wife, and let you use the bathroom if you're of a need. Then, maybe you could take a few swings of the bat. Like to see what you can do."

"Homer knocked a home run almost every game," Elsie said. "They started calling them Homers."

"They called everybody's home run a homer, Elsie," Homer said, then allowed a bashful smile. "I did hit a bunch of them."

"Well, I imagine the pitching wasn't up to the level of our league," Thompson said, "so let's see how you do today."

Elsie nodded toward Albert. "Our alligator is also hungry."

Thompson peered at Albert, who had come awake and was hanging his head out of the window. "Quite a fine-looking animal," he said.

"He is beautiful, isn't he?" Elsie gushed.

Thompson shrugged. "Sure, bring him on. We got hot dogs aplenty inside. And popcorn for that rooster I see sitting atop the front seat."

Elsie put Albert in the washtub and Homer and the catcher carried him into the stadium and over to the hot dog stand, where a cook was cleaning up. "These folks are hungry, Bob," Thompson said. "Cook them up some dogs, will you?"

The cook took a look at the odd assembly. "I got eggs and toast I could fix, too."

"Fix 'em, then. In the meantime, Homer, come on over here to home plate." Thompson put his fingers in his mouth and whistled. "Franco! Get your lame butt out to the pitcher's mound. Got a batter for you."

There were bats lying around and Homer picked up the first one he came to. He stepped into the box while the catcher settled in behind him. "Watch this fellow," the catcher said. "He'll try to dust you."

Homer wasn't sure what that meant until the baseball came straight at his head. He dodged just in time. The ball slammed into the catcher's mitt with a resounding *whack*!

"Quit that, Franco!" Thompson yelled out to the pitcher's mound. "Give him one right down the middle."

Franco, a skinny youth with a uniform that was at least a size too big for him, spit on the ball, then shrugged. "Sure, boss," he said and wound up.

The ball flew from the pitcher's hand and seemed to wobble midflight. Homer recognized the trick: spitballs were used in the Coalfield League, too. It was a pitch perfect for a sequential thinker with a very fast mind. All Homer had to do was follow the ball's wobble, calculate the spin, and apply the bat appropriately and this is what he did, blasting into it with the heaviest part of the bat and sending it screaming into the air and over the farthest fence.

Thompson, who'd inserted his thumbs in his suspenders, let them go with a slap. "I'll be blamed," he said.

"He can hit one, can't he, Mr. Thompson?" Elsie asked with a proud grin.

"I reckon he can, ma'am. Franco, give him a curve, then a slider. Best you got."

Franco, looking decidedly peeved, performed the pitches. Homer easily swatted them out of the park.

"You know how to hit a single, son?" Thompson asked. "Give him a change-up, Franco."

Franco served one up, hard, fast, and high. Homer knocked it down past third base, just inside the line.

Thompson smiled. "Come on over here, son. Got somebody I want you to meet."

Homer followed the manager, as did Elsie. A man in a wheelchair, pushed by a young woman, was rolling into the park. Thompson went up to the pair. The woman was a young blonde dressed in a tailored, navy blue suit with white pinstripes. "Mrs. Feldman," Thompson said, tipping his hat to the woman. "Mr. Feldman, I want to sign this boy for twenty dollars a game, pending we see how he works out."

"Twenty dollars!" Elsie could not hide her astonishment. "How many games?"

Thompson waved at her to stay silent. "How about it, Mr. Feldman? I think we got a good one here."

The man's voice was shaky and barely intelligible. "Argh arghproof," he said.

"Now, honey, let me be the judge of that," the blonde said.

"What did he say?" Elsie asked.

"He said he approved," Thompson replied.

"My mister is on his way to Hot Springs, Georgia, for the cure," the woman informed the manager. "That's why we're here, for him to say goodbye. I will be running the club in his absence."

"Nah," Feldman said. "Nah go'n ha spring."

"You have to go, honey," his wife replied with an irritable edge. "There are no nurses to care for you here."

"I always wanted to be a nurse," Elsie said.

"Did you say you're a nurse?" Thompson asked.

"Professionally qualified?" the young wife demanded, and rather archly.

"I have a diploma," Elsie answered.

Homer noticed that Elsie had neglected to say that her diploma was from secretary school. "Elsie, you're not . . ."

Elsie's smile was frozen as she said, through clenched teeth, "We need the money, Homer."

"There you go, Mr. Feldman," Thompson said, although Mrs. Feldman continued to look dubious. "In this young couple, we got ourselves a new pitcher and long ball hitter and also a nurse. What could be finer?"

"Thaghh alahater."

"What did you say, sir?"

Feldman raised his palsied hand and pointed a trembling finger at Albert. "Thaghh alahater!"

The manager looked after the point and saw Albert looking back with a curious expression and a hot dog protruding from his lips. "That alligator did you say?"

"Yeh. Thaghh alahater. Noo makot."

"New mascot," Mrs. Feldman said, rolling her big blues.

"Albert a mascot?" Elsie questioned.

"Albert a mascot?" Homer questioned.

"A new mascot," Thompson mused. "Makes sense. Alligators are tough and mean. But we're the furniture makers, not the alligators."

"Hoo giff a chit?" Mr. Feldman demanded, which settled the question.

23

ELSIE HAD ALWAYS FELT HER LIFE WAS LIKE A JIGSAW puzzle with no picture on the box to show her how the puzzle pieces should fit together. To her delight and complete surprise, as soon as Homer started playing baseball for the High Top Furniture Makers (soon renamed the Chompers in honor of its new mascot), it seemed as if the pieces suddenly fitted themselves together in a way that made complete and utter sense. Homer seemed to have become a changed man. When they saw each other, baseball was all he talked about. The two weeks the Captain had given him for the journey came and went but he never mentioned that or anything about Coalwood. Elsie didn't know what her husband was thinking, especially about going back to the coal-fields, and she didn't care to find out. As her daddy often said, it was best to let sleeping coal miners sleep.

Homer had taken lodging in a broom closet at the stadium while Elsie lived in the Feldman mansion. To her way of thinking, their lives were now completely perfect. She could do what she wanted to do and Homer could do what he wanted to do and their lives, still officially joined together, were separate. If this seemed selfish of her, she supposed it didn't matter. It was a fact, one she had not planned but had just happened.

Each morning, Elsie eagerly dressed in the nurse's white starched skirt and blouse and low-heeled white shoes that Feldman provided her. He was a delightful patient. He appreciated everything she did and there were many things she did that nobody seemed to have ever thought of doing. She was there when he woke with a breakfast she cooked herself—eggs, bacon, toast, coffee—sweeping away the gruel the cook had said the patient was usually served, and then she saw to his bath, lifting him out of his chair into the tub by herself—she was a strong West Virginia girl, after all—and then wheeling him into his library, where she sought out the books he asked for, and gave him his pills, which were not washed down with tap water but sweet, fresh water from the well in the yard she hand-pumped because he liked the taste and she thought it better for him. While he read his books, she massaged his legs to turn them pink and no longer the gray of death, and combed his thin hair, and rubbed his bony shoulders, and sat nearby should he need anything.

More than anything, she loved the conversations she had with Mr. Feldman, his garbled words gradually becoming completely understandable to her. Their talks were more stimulating than any she'd ever had with Homer or anyone in the coalfields, all about life and past loves (she waxed on about Buddy, and Feldman of his first wife, who had died of tuberculosis), and the philosophies of the ancient and modern world, and politics (he hated the New Deal but she thought it might work, given time), and Hitler and Stalin, who were both despicable, and Mussolini, who Feldman thought was more comedic than evil, and religion, of which Feldman was a Jew and Elsie a Methodist, which they found weren't at all alike except those parts that were, and so forth. Within a week, he could not live without her and said so, not only to her but also to Young Mrs. Feldman (as she was universally known) and anyone else who came within the range of his voice, including his doctor.

The town of High Top was a small town, its main street but a hundred yards long, and every house, whether it was old, new, mansion, or shack, was less than a mile from its Courthouse Square. The Feldman house, built on a hillock, was a neo-Georgian mansion with big porches and lots of bedrooms, one of which had been turned over to Elsie. She loved the spacious room and the huge canopied bed and the antique chairs and tables and bookcases filled with gilt-inscribed classics. Although Feldman's library was extensive, Elsie still walked to the library beside the courthouse and applied for a library card, whereupon she proceeded to check out every book she could find on the science and procedures inherent to the profession of nursing. So top-heavy was her selection toward nursing, it came to the attention of Dr. Martin Clowers, the only physician in High Top and therefore the general practitioner in charge of Mr. Feldman's health. With stealth and guile, the doctor arranged to place himself so that he might meet Elsie in the stacks.

She was at the time wearing her nurse's uniform. "Nurse Hickam," Dr. Clowers said, "I am Dr. Clowers. You may recognize my name as the attending physician for your Mr. Feldman. It is good to meet an angel of mercy such as yourself."

Clowers was a man Elsie judged to be in his sixties, distinguished, with silver hair and a mustache and a bowler hat, the latter of which he held primly while addressing her.

"Mr. Feldman told me about you," she said. And he had, too. *Damn quack,* he'd said more than once. It was the first time Elsie had heard the phrase but it didn't take long before she understood what it meant. It had taken her a bit longer to understand that Mr. Feldman was using it in an affectionate way. He and the doctor were old, old friends.

"Feldman also told me about you," Clowers went on. "He seems pleased with the care you are giving him. But, tell me, all these books about nursing . . . what school did you say you graduated from?"

The doctor's question placed Elsie in something of a corner, one from which she recognized there was no escape, and so she fell back on the truth. "I matriculated at the Orlando Secretary School," she said.

Dr. Clowers smiled. "So, young woman, it appears you are something of a fraud."

Elsie looked the doctor squarely in the eye. "I never said I was a nurse who'd gone to school for it. It just sort of happened that Mr. Feldman thought that was so."

With an amused expression, Dr. Clowers studied her. "If you had to do it, do you think you could give Feldman a shot?"

Elsie reddened. "Well . . . I've never tried anything like that."

Clowers put his bowler hat on the floor and opened his black bag, producing from it an orange along with a wicked-looking needle. "Practice on this." He demonstrated the proper technique and handed the orange and the needle to her. "Now, if you please."

Elsie gave it a try. "Like this?"

"You're a natural." He dug farther into his bag and gave her two needles and several vials. "Should Feldman begin to shake uncontrollably, or his eyes roll back into his head, or if he begins to gasp while unable to speak, inject this medicine, preferably in the hip. I will depend on you to be my eyes and ears and sometimes hands." He tapped the books. "And these will be our little secret."

Elsie took the syringes and medicines and tucked them into her purse, thanked the doctor, then got back to her studies. Mr. Feldman's needs, she now understood, were far more serious and immediate than she had supposed.

During one of her excursions to the library, Elsie read a book that included a description of fever, the very thing that had taken her little brother Victor, and what to do about it. Her eyes softened and then became damp when she read: *It is imperative to lower the body temperature as soon as possible. A very effective means of accomplishing this is wrapping the patient in ice packs.*

Elsie took a short breath, then a longer one. "Ice packs. I could have saved Victor!"

But Elsie had also read a biography of Florence Nightingale, the first nurse who'd set the standard for all nurses to come. She forced back her tears, since Nightingale believed they were unworthy of a nurse. Still, she couldn't help that her tears fell inside her just the same. Again and again, the thought came to her: *I could have saved Victor!*

Elsie often took Mr. Feldman to the field to watch his team practice or, if it was playing a home game, to watch the game itself. It was a disappointment to her that Homer sat on the bench during all the games. Why this was, she could not understand, seeing as how in practice Homer threw the ball as fast as Mercury's lightning, and hit the ball with great regularity across the fence or into the stands. Once, when the manager came up to say hello to Feldman, Elsie got in a private word. "Mr. Thompson, why isn't my husband playing?"

Thompson clearly did not like explaining the management of his team to the wife of one of his players but he unbent enough to say, "He will play, ma'am. I will know when is the proper time. You are not to worry about that."

"But I *am* worried," Elsie replied. "What if Homer hates sitting on the bench so much he decides he'd rather mine coal?"

"All in good time," Thompson advised. "Be patient."

Elsie considered the manager's advice, then said, "I wonder what Mr. Feldman would think of this."

Thompson's eyebrows went up. "You would complain to our boss about my managerial decisions?"

"Not complain. Merely wonder out loud why Homer doesn't play."

Thompson considered her response, then said, "Let me explain something to you, Nurse Hickam. The Coastal League has a peculiarity in that it has two championship series, one halfway through the season and one at the last. The owners believe they get more people to attend if their teams are in contention for a championship more often. It is a headache for managers but a boon to the owners and so it is done. Next week will begin a round-robin to determine the final two teams for the initial portion of our season. I am saving your husband for that series as something of a surprise."

"You mean Homer is a ringer?"

Thompson cleared his throat and nodded.

"Do you bet on these games?" Elsie asked.

Thompson cleared his throat again, tipped his hat, said, "Good day to you, madam," and left. Elsie squinted after him, her mind alive with nefarious plans to force him to let Homer play. One by one, she dismissed them until she reached the most probable, the same one she'd threatened, to convince Mr. Feldman to make the manager bend to her will.

Next to visit Elsie was the lumpy bat boy, Humphrey, who also looked after Albert. "Ma'am," Humphrey said, "I forgot how often you said I should feed Albert. He seems hungry all the time."

Humphrey was small enough that most spectators thought he was a boy rather than his factual age of thirty-two. Elsie liked Humphrey, mostly because he was eager to please her. "Once a day is plenty. Is he happy?"

"He seems happy although he has bitten me twice," Humphrey replied, rolling up his sleeve to present tooth marks.

Elsie made a nursely inspection of Humphrey's wounds and was unimpressed. "Did he bring the blood? No. These are clearly warnings that perhaps you were doing something wrong. Do you recall what you were doing at the time?"

"I don't recollect doing anything wrong, ma'am, although I'm not entirely sure what is right around an alligator. You might find it of interest that both times Albert bit me, those two men over there were nearby. Their presence seemed to make him nervous."

Elsie peered toward the two men Humphrey referred to. One of them was a big, tall, black fellow, the other shorter than even Humphrey. They appeared to be the same fellows she'd met at the union camp, the ones Homer claimed were bank robbers but this, of course, was impossible. Still, Elsie studied the lopsided pair with an intention of calling Homer's attention to them for further identification. But then they spotted her, the little one tipping his cap as they slinked back into the shadows, a location in which they seemed to correctly inhabit.

Elsie dismissed the two as inconsequential. "I am depending on you to look after Albert," she told Humphrey. "Does he still have his rooster?"

"Yes, ma'am. I've been feeding him crumbs from the leftover hot dog buns."

"That's fine. Is there anything else? No? Toddle off then. I have nurse duties."

Humphrey saluted Elsie, then toddled off. Watching him go, Elsie allowed a short sigh. It wasn't easy for her to keep everything going at the ball field and at Mr. Feldman's house, although she was doing her best.

She was also burdened with an awful knowledge. She saw Homer walking by with the other ballplayers on their way to the field. "I could have saved Victor," she called out.

Homer stopped in his cleated tracks. "What?"

"I could have saved Victor."

He came near. "How?"

"Ice packs. It said so in a book."

Homer looked doubtful. "Where would you have gotten ice in Gary hollow?"

It was just then that Young Mrs. Feldman presented herself to Elsie. "You brought my husband here without letting me know," she said accusingly, and accurately. "I'm his wife. I should know where he is at all times."

"I told the chauffeur," Elsie said. "I thought he'd tell you." She could have added, *During the times during the day while you are in the chauffeur's room*, but she didn't.

"Well, he didn't tell me," Mrs. Feldman said with her nose in the air. "From this moment on, Mr. Feldman is not to go anywhere without you letting me know, nor are you to give him his meals without my confirming the menu, nor shall you give him any medicines without my express permission, nor may you do anything having to do with his care without my granting you leave. Do you understand?"

"Does that include when I take him to the bathroom?" Elsie asked in her sweetest voice. "I could use your help then. He's a little unsteady on his feet."

Mrs. Feldman's face clouded over. "You had best remember who signs your checks. It isn't Mr. Feldman."

This observation from Mrs. Feldman struck home. Elsie said, all fake sweetness aside, "Yes, ma'am."

"You know, Elsie, I used to be poor," the wife said.

Yes, I bet you didn't know where your next husband was coming from.

"I'm a working girl, too," she added.

I bet you are, and as long as there are sidewalks and corners to stand on, I guess you'll have a job that suits you.

Elsie said none of those things, of course, but she thought them. "As soon as he's finished looking at his silly ballplayers, bring him home," Mrs. Feldman commanded, then walked away with her high heels clicking on the concrete. Despite her annoyance, Elsie had to admire how Young Mrs. Feldman could go anywhere she liked in those stiletto heels.

She also thought about what Homer had said about Victor. *Where would you have gotten ice in Gary hollow?* It was true there was no ice to be had there, not even in the company store, nor did her parents own a car, nor did anyone else except maybe the owner of the mine, but there were horses on which a determined girl could ride to the county seat of Welch and there find ice and figure a way to get enough of it back before it melted.

In fact, the more she thought about it, the more Homer's question about getting ice rankled her. Did he think she was not resourceful? She was certain she knew what Buddy Ebsen would have said to her. She could almost hear his voice. "Well, Elsie, if anybody could have done it, you could have. But you should not blame yourself. Blame the coal company that did not have an ice house on its property."

Yes, she thought to herself, that is what her erstwhile husband should have said to her, not the all-too-Homerish and therefore overtly logical, *Where would you have gotten ice in Gary hollow?*

"I would of got it, bub," she muttered to herself. "If I'd have known Victor needed it, *I would of got it.*"

Back at the house, Feldman, who had apparently overheard the exchange between Elsie and Young Mrs. Feldman, said to her, *Sarmywifesezmeentingsoo*, which Elsie correctly interpreted as "I am sorry about the mean things my wife says to you."

"It's okay, Mr. Feldman. Have you ever heard of Florence Nightingale?"

Firsnurrs.

"That's right. First nurse. She's tougher on me than your wife."

He smiled. *Likoonurzickem.*

Elsie provided him with a fetching smile. "And I like you, too, Mr. Feldman. Would you like your bath now? By the way, Homer still hasn't played in a single game."

24

HOMER WAS IN A STRANGE PLACE. THE QUICK JOURNEY he'd planned to carry his wife's alligator to Florida had come completely undone. The Captain would have probably called it kismet, but if that's what it was, it didn't much matter. It seemed the whole world outside the coalfields was crazy. Homer was embarrassed that he hadn't been up to its challenges and now found himself stranded. He'd considered wiring the Captain with a plea for enough money to get home but his pride wouldn't allow it. After the two-week deadline had passed for when he was supposed to return to Coalwood, he thought about wiring the Captain about that, too, but he couldn't bring himself to do that, either. The Captain had a calendar and would surely notice the number of days Homer had been gone and would take appropriate action. He required no sniveling telegram from his former assistant foreman to do what had to be done. He'd probably even consider it an insult. No, when Homer returned to Coalwood, he'd come with the one hundred dollars he owed and be prepared to take his medicine. In the meantime, all he could do was try his best to get back on track. Considering that the baseball team had promised to fix his Buick, and that the team had also given him and

Elsie jobs, he saw nothing else to do but to stay until the car was ready and they had enough money to leave. With that philosophy fixed in his mind, Homer relaxed into the strange place he found himself, making the best of it and even occasionally allowing a little of an emotion he usually thought of as frivolous. It was that odd, peculiar, and somewhat un—West Virginian sensation called fun.

One of the things Homer thought was fun was leaning on a post in the dugout and looking across the baseball field. He loved the bright green grass of the outfield and the garish colors of the advertisements on the surrounding fence and the brownish-red baselines and the bright white bags spaced just so and the yellowish home plate backed by a gray net to catch errant fouls. He loved the pitcher's mound, a place of business where a man might find greatness, and he loved the surrounding bleachers that always seemed to stir with excitement even when they were empty.

He also loved the way the field smelled. Its grass smelled green and alive and the dirt had a rich, wormy perfume. The wooden stands smelled of paint and tar in the midday heat and the fragrance of hot popcorn seemed never far away. He loved the crisp smell of his freshly laundered cotton uniform and the tart aroma of the shoe polish on his cleated shoes. He even liked the smell of his ball cap, that of well-earned sweat and Wildroot Creme Oil, and he especially liked the fresh, rawhide smell of the baseballs.

Most of all, he liked that he was learning something new every day at the field. He did not mind at all that he had yet to play in a game. He knew he needed more instruction before he was fully prepared. No matter how talented his teammates might have been back in Coalwood, Homer recognized that they were still coal miners. In the Coalfield League, it was all about strength and intimidation and pitchers threw as hard as they could without many tricks past a spitball now and again. Nine times out of ten, the ball was going to come fast and hard, either high, low, somewhere in the strike zone, or at your head. Coal miner batters had been killed by coal miner pitchers. The game they played was almost entirely physical. Base runners were contested by blocking or hooking their arms and spinning them to the ground. Sometimes they were even punched in the nose. Umpires were lax about all the rough play. The more bloody noses and broken bones in the coalfields, the better the miner crowd liked it and the umps knew it.

Such play was not tolerated in the Coastal League. Finesse was required. This became evident during a practice game when Homer had three men on base and Mr. Thompson had walked out to the pitcher's mound. "Don't know what I'm doing wrong, Mr. Thompson," Homer had said while scratching up under his cap.

"What you're doing wrong, Homer, is throwing as hard as you can every time. They've got your number. All they have to do is to get some wood on it and it's going to get knocked out of the park. Let me ask you something: what kind of pitcher do you want to be?"

"Well, I guess a good one."

Thompson spat tobacco juice. He wasn't a good spitter, usually hitting his own shoes or pants, but he knew something about pitching. "I've seen lots of good pitchers who couldn't win a game to save themselves. You want to be a pitcher who wins games, forget about being good. Just beat each batter that stands before you. Do you understand?"

Homer understood very well. In fact, it made eminent sense. That was why he'd replied, "That makes eminent sense, sir."

"Fine. I've been watching you and I think you're a natural forkball pitcher."

"Forkball, sir?"

"You've got big hands, perfect for a forkball, which some folks call splitters. Look at the way I'm gripping the ball. What you do is choke the ball deep, grip it moderately tight, put your index and middle finger on the upper side of the horseshoe seam, and throw it just like a fastball but with your palm aiming straight at where you want the ball to go. Keep your wrist stiff." Thompson nodded toward home plate. "Now, look at Burnoski there, see him staring at you, swinging his bat? He knows what you're gonna do, and he's ready for your fastball. Only you're gonna throw something completely different that looks exactly the same until it's too late for him to do anything about it. You got it?"

Homer got it. He worked his fingers over the seam, feeling the threads like they were roads on a map.

"Pitching's like building a house," the manager went on. "You've got to first lay in a good foundation. You've got the talent and the skill, Homer, but not the mechanical technique. But I think you're going to learn and you know why I think you're going to learn where a thousand others as good or better haven't?"

"No, sir."

"Because you're not only strong, you're smart. You intellectualize this game. You see all the moving parts, the sequences, how it all fits together."

Thompson embarrassed Homer. He blushed and muttered, "I'm not so sure about that."

"Sure you do! You've got muscles like steel." Thompson gripped Homer's right arm. "But your real strength is here!" He pointed at Homer's head. "After a couple of pitches with change-ups, a batter's gonna look at you and give up. He can't help it. He'll give up and not even know he's giving up. You're smarter than he is and deep down at some kind of molecular level, he'll know that. And something else," Thompson went on. "You've got heart. Pluck. Grit. Whatever you want to call it. Saw that first thing about you in that parking lot. You and me, Homer, we're going to go all the way. You ever think about the majors? Well, I have. A manager, he gets the right player, he can go along with him to the top. You're my ticket out of here, boy!"

Homer wasn't sure about the idea of the majors but he held the ball the way he'd been shown and threw it. It was a fastball to everybody who watched it leave his hand but it dropped at the last moment to the batter's knees. Burnoski swung hard and the ball pounded into the catcher's mitt.

Burnoski cursed. "I didn't see that coming," he said to the catcher.

The catcher stared at the ball in his mitt. "A forkball," he muttered. "A goddamn forkball. Who the hell can throw a forkball that fast?"

It didn't take long for Homer to learn several other kinds of pitches besides the forkball. He learned the curve, the modified light curve, and the slider, but, most of all, he kept improving on his specialty, the fork-ball. He also studied the opposing pitchers and made mental notes about their change-ups and strategies. He was applying to baseball a lesson he'd learned in coal mining, that it was the man who studied success who succeeded. After a while, Homer started to believe Thompson was right. If he worked at it hard enough, and if he wanted to, he could go all the way to the pros.

Homer kept believing it until the day Ty Kerns arrived. Kerns had played in the majors on several teams, and had even been in a World Series game. He was an angry man, a big-bellied, beefy-armed, red-faced kind of angry man who was certain he'd entered a kind of hell when he'd been sent down not to a triple-A or double-A or even an A ball team but to a club in North Carolina that surely didn't even rate a B. When he first entered the clubhouse, he talked to a couple of players he knew, got the word on who was who, and, determined to show these amateurs how it was done, tossed a stuffed cloth bag with a pair of baseball shoes tied to it at Homer's feet. "Clean up my gear, rookie," he demanded.

Homer had never had a man ask him to see to his laundry and his shoes and therefore hesitated. Kerns's eyes narrowed and he stuck out his whiskery jaw. "I said, clean up my gear, boy."

Homer knew about hazing. Fresh new coal miners got hazed all the time. He'd been sent after a rail straightener, had his lunch bucket emptied out, and had grease put in his boots. Those were things to be expected. But this fellow, this big ballplayer, was different. The manner in which he was hazing was without any of the humor and good-naturedness Homer was used to in the mines. Therefore, Homer said, "Clean it yourself."

Kerns was surprised by the response. "I'm a professional baseball player, been wrote up in the papers. What are you? I heard a coal miner."

"I'm a pitcher now."

Kerns's laugh was more a snarl. "Pitching from the bench, I heard. If you ever want off it, clean up my gear. I'll put in a good word."

Homer, irritated, said, "You look pretty old. I figure you'll be the one sitting on the bench."

Kerns growled like a bear startled out of hibernation. "You think you can get a ball by me, boy?"

"One? I could get them all by you."

Astonished, Kerns pawed inside his jacket and brought out a pouch of Red Man tobacco. He stuck in a chaw, accomplished a test chew, grinned a nasty, tobacco-stained grin, and shifted his gaze to the bat boy. "You! Yes, you! I gave you my bat to be oiled. Get it ready."

Humphrey tried to pull in his head like a turtle. "I'm supposed to feed the alligator right now, Mr. Kerns," he said from between his shoulders.

Kerns's mouth, leaking tobacco juice, dropped open. "Feed the alligator? You making fun of me, boy?"

When the ball boy hesitated, Homer said, "The alligator's name is Albert. He belongs to my wife."

"He's our mascot," a second baseman named Ziff said.

"Have I got myself into a friggin' loony bin?" Kerns demanded, wiping away tobacco drool. "Get my damn bat and forget the damn alligator!" He leveled a quivering finger at Homer. "And you! Meet me on the field."

The other ballplayers began to exchange money in a quick series of bets, then followed Kerns and Homer onto the field. Homer picked up a ball and walked to the pitcher's mound while Kerns waited impatiently near home plate. Humphrey appeared with Kerns's bat, Albert following on his leash. "You drop that bat, you damn midget, I'll kill ya," Kerns growled.

Kearns's threat had the precise opposite effect. Humphrey dropped the bat. Albert, not paying attention, straddled it. Kerns stopped short when he was met with a full mouth of alligator teeth.

Homer walked over and, wordlessly, took Albert by the tail and dragged him off the bat. He then strode back to the pitcher's mound, bent over, and put a baseball into the small of his back, fingering it hungrily.

Kerns gave Humphrey an angry look, picked up the bat, and lovingly ran his hands over it to remove the dust. After a couple of practice cuts, he stepped into the batter's box and nodded to Homer. "Let's see what you've got, rookie!"

Homer instantly let fly with a forkball. Kerns grunted massively as his bat cut through nothing but air and the ball slapped into the catcher's glove.

By then, Manager Thompson had arrived on the scene. He stepped up to play umpire. "Strike one!" he called with some glee, then called out to the pitcher's mound. "Homer, throw this bum a curveball, break to the left." He grinned at Kerns. "You can get a hit off a rookie when you know what's coming, can't you, Tyrone?"

Homer threw the curve. It came flying in, then jerked to the inside. Kerns did not swing, just dumbly watched it go by. "Strike two," Thompson called. "Just caught the inside corner. Homer, give old Tyrone here a fastball, straight down the middle. He ought to be able to hit that, at least."

Homer threw as instructed and Kerns swung. He would have hit it had the bat made it around in time but it was late and the catcher was shaking his hand from the impact while Kerns was still swinging. Incredulous, the old ballplayer stared at the ball the catcher held up.

Homer had gone from being proud of taking down this arrogant man to feeling sorry for him. He saw the power in the man's swing, much more power than any he'd seen from the other players. He looked at Kerns and saw a pathetic fellow whose eyes were filled with a sad desperation and the haunted look of an old man who still wanted to play a young man's game.

"Give me one more!" Kerns yelled. "I got your number now, kid!"

Thompson shook his head. "Three strikes and you're out, Kerns. You don't get another chance."

"This don't concern you, Thompson," Kerns spat. "That boy said I couldn't hit anything he throwed. Well, I'm warmed up now. Bring it on, rookie. I'm going to show you how a pro can hit a ball!"

"Don't do it, Homer!" Thompson yelled but then subsided to see what his pitcher would do. "Your call, Jared," he said to the catcher.

Homer looked over the sign from the catcher. Jared called for a forkball. Homer's fingers moved deftly to the seams, but then he looked down the barrel between the pitcher's mound to home plate, moved his fingers off the seams, and placed them instead on the smooth rawhide. He wound up and threw and was not the least bit surprised when Kerns nailed the ball so hard it was still accelerating when it cleared the fence at center field.

For just a moment the old player's eyes met Homer's eyes. Homer knew that Kerns knew the truth of what had just happened. Still, the old pro laughed aloud and turned to Thompson. "What do you think now, Mr. Manager?"

"You can still hit a ball over the fence, Ty. That's what I think. Welcome to the club."

Thompson met Homer coming off the field. "You lost me some money," he said.

Homer shrugged. "Officially, I struck him out."

"The bet was he couldn't hit you. You should have stopped at three."

"I guess my forkball still needs work."

"No it doesn't. You let Kerns hit the ball. Question is why?"

"I wanted to let him keep his dignity."

Thompson squinted at Homer. "I guess I was wrong about you, which is a shame. You're a good player, Homer, could be great, but I see now you're missing something inside. You letting Kerns down easy means you think this is a game for the players. Those of us who love the game will tell you it ain't for the players at all. It's for the game. A fellow who believes in the game will never let up on another man just because he can't play to the level he wants."

Thompson walked off, leaving Homer to think things over. He looked at the dugout, where the other players were applauding Kerns and slapping him on his back. Try as he might, Homer just couldn't feel bad about what he'd just done.

25

THE GAMES TO DETERMINE THE WINNER OF THE COASTAL League midsummer series were best three out of five. The Chompers backed into the series after the league-leading Alexander City Clam Stompers lost ten straight games after half of their players were sent up to the double A's. High Top and the Marion Swamp Foxes ended up being the teams in contention, with the first two games to be played in Marion. The Swamp Foxes were a talented club filled with young rising professionals and nobody gave the Chompers much of a chance.

Elsie accompanied Mr. Feldman to Marion in his chauffeured Cadillac. For a man who had trouble with his speech, Elsie thought he had a lot to say. On the road, they talked their usual philosophy, religion, and politics. She also got up enough nerve to tell him at least one truth.

"You know, Mr. Feldman, I'm not a registered nurse or any kind of schooled nurse."

"Knowit," Feldman responded. "Doctolme."

"The doctor told you? That rascal! Well, I'm sorry I lied to get my job."

Feldman's hand shook as he reached out to touch her arm. "Elzee . . . pay . . . yurskool."

"You'll pay to send me to nursing school?" She kissed him on the cheek. "Thank you, Mr. Feldman!"

" 'appy," he said and touched his chest. " 'appy."

"I'll come back and work for you. I promise I will!"

Feldman smiled at her. " 'appy," he said again.

Ball games in Marion were well attended. The bleachers were packed full, enough so that overflow spectators were allowed to bring their own chairs. They were a pleasant people, Marion folks, and they watched with enthusiastic contentment as their boys destroyed their opponents, the hapless Furniture Makers or Chompers or whatever the fellows from High Top chose to call themselves for the series. The Marion folks also thoroughly admired the new mascot of the opposition.

Elsie was proud of how well Albert fulfilled his mascot role. Homer had affixed a handle and wheels to his washtub and Humphrey rolled him around, coaxing him out with hot dogs for the edification of the spectators. After being given a tiny bat to hold between his teeth, Albert even took swings at tennis balls Humphrey tossed to him, hitting them nearly every time. Albert seemed fascinated by nearly everything: the smells of the food, the excitement of the crowd, the sudden cheers, the running players, the *thok* of the bat on the ball, and the frenzy of the play. When Elsie came down from the stands to say hello, he swished his tail in delight and provided her his toothiest grin. "He surely loves you, Mrs. Hickam," Humphrey said.

"He was a gift from Buddy Ebsen, the dancer and actor," Elsie said. "He and I had some good times."

"I've never heard of Buddy Ebsen," Humphrey confessed.

"That's okay. You will. He's going to be famous someday."

"Does Mr. Hickam know about him?"

Astonished at the bat boy's impertinence, Elsie rubbed Albert's head, hard enough that the alligator flinched. "Of course he does."

"Well, doesn't he . . ." Humphrey stopped.

Frowning, Elsie looked up. "Doesn't he what?"

Humphrey plunged on. "Well, doesn't Mr. Hickam get jealous about Mr. Ebsen? I mean because I think I would get so jealous I couldn't stand it."

Elsie stood up and narrowed her eyes. "Just take care of Albert, Humphrey."

The bat boy ducked his head. "Yes, ma'am."

Elsie gave Humphrey a final look of warning and started up into the stands to be with Mr. Feldman but, for a reason she couldn't quite discern, deviated toward the dugout. She found Homer sitting on the bench. He was startled by her appearance and startled anew when she asked, "How are you?" in a tone that was more of a demand.

"F-fine," he stuttered. "Never better. What's the matter?"

"Nothing's the matter."

"Yes, there is. I always know when there's something the matter."

"Nothing, I tell you." She turned to leave, then looked over her shoulder. "I hope you get to play today."

Homer shrugged and Elsie turned back around. "You know what, Homer? Your trouble is you have no ambition."

"So that's what the matter is," Homer replied. "You know that isn't so. I was studying to be a foreman when we left Coalwood."

"That was then and this is now. Anyone who would sit on a bench and not say something about it can't be ambitious. That's what I think."

Homer looked around to see if anybody was listening. Every player in the dugout was, of course, but was pretending he wasn't. Homer got up and went over to Elsie, leaning in. "I'm doing my best," he declared.

"Do better," she said, and walked away. As she walked, she expected to feel vindicated, that she'd done the best she could do for her husband, but it was shame that she felt, instead. That stupid bat boy had come entirely too close to the truth. Buddy Ebsen was still in her heart where Homer ought to be and, as far as she could tell, that's where he was going to stay.

→ ←

The Chompers lost that day eight–zip while going through five out of six pitchers on the payroll, the sixth being Homer, who toiled away in the bullpen but did not play. He didn't play the next day, either, and, once more, the Chompers lost. If they lost one more, it was all over.

As Homer walked back from the bullpen at the end of the game, he was met by two men, one very short and the other big and tall. They were wearing suits and ties and expensive fedoras.

Homer stopped and stared at them. "Go away, Slick. You, too, Huddie. Go away before I call the manager and have you turned over to the police."

"You can't do that," Slick said. "We're season ticket holders."

"How is that possible?" Homer demanded.

"How's your arm?" Slick asked.

"My arm's fine."

Slick cut his eyes toward Huddie. "What do you think, Hud?"

"I ain't paid to think," Huddie growled, scratching up under his armpit.

"Truer words have never been spoken, son," Slick said, then put two fingers to his hat brim in a salute to Homer and moved off, Huddie in his wake.

Homer watched them go, and felt unsettled. Those two were up to something. But what?

26

ELSIE ROSE THE DAY OF THE THIRD GAME IN THE SERIES and sensed something different. When she went on the balcony to greet the morning sun, a falcon appeared and performed a series of small acrobatics, apparently for no other reason than her delight, and then when she looked up, the clouds had formed what appeared to be an alligator just like Albert, its jaws wide and smiling. A window opened in the basement and she heard the chauffeur's phonograph playing a Cole Porter song she really liked titled "What Is This Thing Called Love?"

Elsie sang along with the song for a while, feeling a little deliciously sorry for herself because she'd been with Buddy the last time she'd heard the song. Afterward, she got dressed and went to Mr. Feldman's bedroom. After helping him to the bathroom and checking all his vitals, she went down to the kitchen and brought up his breakfast. "Wih-we win, Elzee?" Feldman asked.

"If Homer plays, Mr. Feldman," Elsie answered, "we will."

→ ←

The game began. By the fifth inning, Marion had scored three runs and High Top none. Thompson visited Homer in the bullpen. "Get in there, Homer. Let's see what you can do."

"Why now?"

"Because it is now. Now is when it is. Now is when you're ready."

"There were two fellows who came to the bullpen the other day. A small one and a big one. I know them. I think they're up to something."

Thompson stared at Homer. "This is baseball, Homer. Everything that happens in baseball happens in the game. If those fellows are in the stands, they can't change the game. Now, get in there and win one for us."

Homer got in there. The Marion batter swung at his first pitch and missed. Encouraged, Homer threw twice more. The batter missed those pitches, too. No Marion batter came close to a hit for the rest of the game. When the game was over, the score was 5–3 in favor of High Top. Homer had scored one of those five with a mighty home run over the left-field fence.

As Homer came around third, heading toward home, he looked up in the stands and saw Elsie standing beside Mr. Feldman. She was wearing her nurse costume and also a proud smile. After placing his foot on home plate, he doffed his cap in her direction. She waved and even sent him an air kiss. His chest swelled.

In the second game, Homer started at pitcher, hit two home runs, and the Chompers coasted to an easy win, 5–0.

All was tied with one more game to play.

Thompson rested Homer the first five innings of the deciding game, until the score was tied 6–6. Then the manager beckoned to him and Homer walked out to the mound. Atop the mound, he leaned over, the ball behind his back, then wound up and threw, the ball a blur to the batter and everyone in the stands. It was an unswung strike, as were the next two pitches, the ball pounding into the catcher's mitt with a mighty *thwak*!

But the score remained tied. As it did for the next two innings.

At the bottom of the ninth, the Chompers' last try at bat, Homer rose from the bench to take his turn. Before he emerged from the dugout and made his way across the grass, Thompson put his hand on his shoulder. "You recall that time you let up on Tyrone?" he asked. "I think you've played enough now that you know you were wrong to do that. Play for the game, son. Play for the game."

"Play for the game," Homer repeated to himself as he walked the thirty feet from the dugout to the line of bats Humphrey had set out. As he approached Albert in his wagon, Humphrey suddenly started to jump up and down and clap, urging the High Top fans in the stands to join in. As they did, the bat boy also began to make disparaging gestures toward the Marion fans, pointing at Albert and making chomping-jaw movements with his hands. Homer thought he heard shouts that sounded like "Kill the alligator!", which was very strange, considering how normally polite the Marion fans were.

Before Homer reached the line of bats, a man in a pair of dirty coveralls leapt from the stands and snatched up one of them, raised it, and ran toward Albert. Instinctively, Homer raced to stay the blow, reaching out his right hand just as the man slammed the bat down. As Homer fell, the man flung away the bat and ran through the gate.

Homer made certain Albert was okay. The reptile looked back at him with a puzzled expression. Homer next looked into the stands, seeking out Elsie. She was there, looking back at him in shock. He next looked at his ruined hand and his knees felt weak. The docs from both clubs came running, but it was Thompson the manager who reached Homer first. When he saw Homer's smashed hand and bent wrist, he looked like he might vomit.

Dr. Clowers arrived next. "Sit down and lie back, Homer," he said. Homer did as he was told. His hand and wrist didn't hurt, not yet, but he knew they would. He'd seen hands crushed between coal cars and wrists broken by drills that caught a rock in the mine. At first, the afflicted miner would joke about it but before he was out of the mine, he'd be whimpering like a baby. Pain did that. It was like an ambushing animal, quiet at first, then all teeth and claws.

Doc took Homer's hand and felt all about. "Bones busted inside for sure," he said, "and your wrist's broke. We've got to get you to my office. I'll need to get a cast on."

Homer pulled away. "I'm going to take my turn at bat," he said to both the doctor and manager.

"What are you talking about?" Thompson demanded. "You can't hold a bat with a broken hand and wrist."

"I'll bat left-handed. Put a bandage around it, Doc. Do it or I'll go into your bag and do it myself. Put it on tight as you can."

Doc looked at Thompson, who lowered his eyes and looked away. Doc went into his bag, got out a bandage, and wrapped it tight around Homer's hand. "You pick up a bat, you'll destroy your hand for baseball," he warned.

"It's destroyed already," Homer answered. "Anyway, Mr. Thompson, you're wrong. I don't have greatness inside me, not the kind you want me to have. I don't believe in the game. It's people I believe in and it's people I'm going to win this game for. Or person. Namely, Mr. Feldman, who has been so good to me and Elsie."

Thompson frowned. "Homer, I'm a baseball manager. Don't you know we're all full of shit? I didn't mean half what I say."

"Well, I mean all that I say," Homer said and picked up a bat and walked to the left-handed batter's box. He nodded to the umpire and the catcher and raised the bat. The Marion pitcher looked at Homer in disbelief. "Throw the damn thing!" Homer shouted, wincing from the pain of the broken bones as he stood in the batter's box and gripped the bat. "Give me your best."

The pitcher did. Three times he threw, the ball slapping into the catcher's mitt, the result two strikes, one ball.

The fourth pitch the pitcher threw as hard as he could, the ball hissing through the air as if it were puffing steam. Homer, his teeth clenched, his eyes mere slits, swung at it. The bat cracked like a bullwhip and the ball screamed. Or perhaps it was Homer screaming. Homer couldn't tell. All he knew was the ball was sailing, sailing, and sailing until it was all the way over the right-field wall.

"He did it," Elsie said in more of a breath than a voice. "Homer did it, Mr. Feldman!"

But Feldman, despite the smile on his face, was quite dead. Elsie didn't have to be a certified nurse to figure that out as she knelt beside him and took his hand. "I told you if he played, we would win, and we did," she whispered, putting Feldman's cooling hand to her hot, flushed cheek.

27

MR. FELDMAN'S ATTORNEY WAS A DIGNIFIED GENTLEMAN
by the name of Lewis Carter who had moved to High Top to get away
from his two wives in New York City, both of whom he had neglected to
divorce and who, upon learning of one another, jointly filed charges of
bigamy in the hope of getting his money. What they didn't know was
Lewis Carter had already spent all his money on a string of showgirls.

Fortunately, Carter did not need New York; he also had a license to
practice in North Carolina, mainly because he had gone to Duke University.
He therefore had a place to abscond from wives, showgirls, and their
pursuing lawyers. To date, his Duke frat buddies, which included the Tar
Heel State's governor, were just fine with having him in their fair state
and had no intention of sending him back to the Yankees for prosecution,
if not persecution. Carter had established himself a fine little practice
in High Top, which counted among its clients the very wealthy Mr.
Feldman.

Two days after Mr. Feldman died, and well before he could be buried,
Lewis Carter sat at the head of a mahogany table and watched with benign
interest, and not a little bubbling joy, as Mr. Feldman's family filed

inside. The bereaved widow, Young Mrs. Feldman, was still dabbing at her eyes (although her mascara remained remarkably intact). She was followed by Feldman's two children, a great lout named Amos and a fat grouch named Ethel, both looking with more than a little disdain at the theatrical grief of their stepmother, who was at least a decade younger than they. "Can it, Louise," Ethel finally said when Young Mrs. Feldman raised her eyes from her hanky and glanced her way.

"Yes, by all means can it," Amos declared. "It's too late for him to change his will so you can wail and gnash your teeth all you like but it will do you no good."

"Nor us," Ethel said, whereupon Young Mrs. Feldman stopped crying and, with a faint smile, put her hanky away with a click of her silk purse.

Carter made a steeple with his fingers. "Actually, he changed his will just two weeks ago."

The shocked looks on all three potential recipients of the Feldman fortune were compounded when the door opened and Elsie Hickam, Feldman's nurse, walked in. "I'm sorry I'm late," she said.

"Why is *she* here?" Young Mrs. Feldman demanded. Her stepchildren were having difficulty closing their hanging jaws.

"Because she's in the will," Carter said. "Please, Mrs. Hickam. Have a seat. No, here, please, beside me." After Elsie sat, Carter patted her hand. "I know you were distressed by your patient's death." He shoved a box of tissues toward her. "If you need them."

Elsie looked at the tissues but didn't reach for them.

"Read the damned will, Carter," Amos growled.

Carter nodded toward a young woman in glasses sitting primly, notepad and pencil poised, in one of the chairs that lined the room. "This is my able assistant, Mrs. Jo Ann Nelson. She will keep notes on the proceedings unless anyone has any objection."

When no one did, Carter opened the leather cover of the document and spread out its papers. He pretended to study them for a moment although he could quote them by rote. A good lawyer is also a good actor and a dramatic pause seemed in order. When he looked up, he found the three Feldman family members were having a contest on who could glare the hardest at the nurse. It was, he decided, Young Mrs. Feldman by several yards.

Carter cleared his throat and got going. After reading some legalese, a requirement of state law, he divulged the particulars of the will. Young Mrs. Feldman was to receive the three houses and the horse farm plus one hundred thousand dollars. Ethel and Amos would also receive one hundred thousand apiece. "The remainder of my estate," Carter read on, "will go to my nurse and friend Elsie Hickam."

"The remainder of the estate?" Ethel blanched. "How much is that?"

"About three million dollars, not including the value of the ball club. There are further instructions in a codicil to Mrs. Hickam requiring her not to sell the club."

Young Mrs. Feldman was astonishingly calm, which instantly put Carter on alert. "This will not stand," she said.

"On that, we agree," Ethel said. Amos nodded vigorously.

"It is all legal," Carter replied. "There's really very little you can do." He turned to Elsie. "Do you have anything to say, Mrs. Hickam?"

"He was a good man," she said.

"He was, indeed," Young Mrs. Feldman said, hotly. "And easily manipulated."

"Of course he could be! He was sick!" Ethel cried. "She manipulated him! Turned his head!" Ethel suddenly came across the table, reaching for Elsie's throat.

Young Mrs. Feldman pulled Ethel back and raised her hand to Amos, who was halfway out of his chair. "I believe our business is finished here," she said and calmly nodded to the attorney. "I trust you have already been paid by the late Mr. Feldman? You are therefore discharged from all duties in terms of Feldman family business."

"Except the will makes me the executor of the Feldman estate," the attorney reminded her. Still, he felt a bead of sweat on his brow. Young Mrs. Feldman was truly a force to be reckoned with. He hadn't completely realized that until that very moment. It was the way she held herself together, the steel of her gaze, the tightness of her lips. He silently bet to himself she probably also had her buttocks clinched so tight a dime wouldn't fit between them.

"We will be in touch," the new widow said. She rose with dignity from the table, smoothed her skirt, and nodded to her stepchildren, who also rose and followed her out the door.

"Mrs. Nelson, could you give us a moment?" Carter asked.

"Of course, sir," the assistant said and quickly exited.

When they were alone, Carter said, "Well, Mrs. Hickam, congratulations."

Since the reading of the will, Elsie had been expressionless. Now, with only Carter in the room, she exhaled and allowed a smile. "Three million dollars! And the ball club. All I can say is . . ." She looked up at the ceiling. ". . . thank you, Mr. Feldman."

Carter chuckled. "Just so you understand, Mrs. Hickam, this wasn't done entirely to reward you. It was also meant to be a punishment for the others. He knew very well Young Mrs. Feldman was only in the marriage for his money and he knew his children are selfish creeps. Regardless, you'll need to be patient. There's a lot of paperwork to be done before anything can be transferred. And if any of those three approach you, don't say anything. There's no use arguing with them or rubbing their noses in it."

"Can I spend the money any way I want?"

"I don't see why not."

"Even buy a coal mine?"

"A couple of them, I would imagine."

Her smile faded. "What would Homer think of that, I wonder."

"Your husband? I was at the game. Will he play ball again?"

"No, sir. I doubt that he will."

Carter rose and shook Elsie's hand. He looked at the tissue box. "You didn't cry. I thought you might."

Elsie shrugged. "Mr. Feldman knew he was going to die. He told me not to cry when he did. He told me to be happy. I just didn't know he was planning on helping me feel that way."

"Be careful, Mrs. Hickam," Carter said as he walked her to the door. "I have a feeling Young Mrs. Feldman doesn't care if you're happy or not."

*Elsie walked to the baseball stadium, the reading of the will and its after-*math running over and over in her mind like a stuck record. She could scarcely believe it but yet she did. After all, why shouldn't she have received a reward for the work she'd done? She grinned to imagine what would happen if she bought the Coalwood coal mine. She'd have the Captain in her office first thing and he might learn a little about kismet, the old faker!

Since the game and Homer's injury, she and Homer had moved into a little room at the stadium that Mr. Feldman had sometimes used to relax. She went there but found it empty of her husband. She found him sitting in the stands looking at the ball field. He seemed to be thinking about something so she sat beside him and asked, "What are you thinking about?"

"I was just thinking that I like this place. It's nice."

"It's good you think somewhere besides Coalwood is nice."

Homer held up his bandaged hand. "Coalwood is where I make my living. Coal mining is what I do. It's what I'm supposed to do. This hand confirms that."

Elsie smiled, the secret of her visit to the Feldman attorney quite delicious in her mind. When she told Homer about it, she was going to love the look on his face. But when to tell it? She wanted to hold on to the secret for a little longer. She so rarely had such a grand secret to hold.

"The Buick is fixed and we have some money," Homer was saying. "Let's head on to Florida, let Albert go, and then go home."

"I'd like to wait a few days," Elsie replied, laughing inside. *Oh, what a hoot it was going to be when she told him she could buy Coalwood!*

Someone took seats behind them. When Elsie looked, she saw it was Slick and Huddie.

"Go away," Homer said.

"That's not nice," Slick said.

Homer shook his head. "Well, as long as you're here, tell me something. Was Humphrey in on it?"

"Of course," Slick answered. "And the fellow who bashed you, too. Only that wasn't the plan. The plan was for the bat boy to act the fool to make the Marion crowd mad, which would give that fellow an excuse to race out and brain the alligator, which was supposed to demoralize you. Of course, breaking your hand was even better." He shrugged and looked sad. "Not that it did any good."

Elsie was confused. "You paid for that man to come out on the field?"

Slick made a hapless gesture. "I don't know why I do bad things. Maybe it was because I was raised in the orphanage. True, they tried to teach me right from wrong but their message never stuck. Maybe if they'd had more time before I burned the place down . . ."

Elsie was still confused. "I still don't understand what happened."

"The reason the man came out to hit Albert, Elsie," Homer said, tiredly, "was because Slick paid him to do it. Slick, you see, bet on Marion to take the series."

Slick chimed in. "With Homer playing, most folks thought High Top was going to win so we stood to make a pile of money by betting on the other team. Of course, I didn't intend that he'd be hurt, just the alligator. I thought that might upset Homer enough he wouldn't be able to get a hit."

"*You paid for somebody to hit Albert?*" Elsie jumped up and punched Slick hard in the face.

Slick fell backward. "You busted my nose," he groaned.

"Well, you hurt my hand," Elsie said, wringing it. "And Homer's, too!"

Homer put a restraining hand on Elsie's arm. "Take it easy, honey," he said.

Huddie had scrambled away. "You better not hit Slick again," he called from a place safely out of Elsie's reach.

Slick wiped the blood from his nose. Even with a freshly broken nose, he managed to look devious. "Do you know where your alligator is? I heard he's been kidnapped."

Elsie wrenched her arm away from Homer and made a fist. "What have you done with him? Tell me or I'll hit you again!"

Slick dug into a pocket and brought out a handkerchief and then dug into another pocket and held out a scrap of paper. Elsie snatched it.

"That will tell you where to find him," Slick said. "Better hurry. Otherwise, you might never see him again."

"What do you want, Slick?" Homer asked.

Slick stood up and pressed the handkerchief to his nose. "Me? Not a thing. I'm just a paid messenger. It's the young Feldman wife who thinks she can extort you."

Homer wrinkled his forehead in confusion. "Why would she want to extort us?"

"Ask your wife," Slick replied before stalking off, beckoning Huddie after him.

Elsie was studying Slick's paper. "I know where this is! Madison Park! It's just south of town. I used to go over there with Mr. Feldman and push him along the river. We've got to hurry!"

"All right, Elsie, we'll hurry, but why would Feldman's wife want to extort us?"

"It's complicated. I'll tell you on the way. Come on!"

Homer came on. "Okay, tell me," he said after they'd climbed into the Buick.

"Mr. Feldman left me three million dollars and the ball club."

Homer stared at her. "If I'd have known you were going to tell me a lie, I wouldn't have asked."

Elsie rolled her eyes. "Please just drive," she said.

Madison Park was thirty minutes away and it only took a couple of minutes more before they found Albert down by the river in his tub on wheels. Humphrey was with him. When the bat boy saw Homer and Elsie, he took off running. He didn't get far; Homer chased him down and walked him back.

"Humphrey," Elsie said, "who brought you and Albert here?"

"Nobody. I drove myself."

"But you don't have a car, do you?"

"No, ma'am, but Young Mrs. Feldman does. She said I should bring Albert down here for a nice day by the river and I could use her Cadillac. She said not to come back until it was dark. She also said that you might be coming to pick him up."

"Why did you run from us?"

"Well, you both looked kind of mad."

Elsie gave his answers some thought. "She sent Albert here so we'd have to drive out of town," she concluded. "Homer, we've got to go back to High Top, straight to Attorney Carter's office. I'll direct you. Come on, fast as we can!"

"What are you talking about?" Homer demanded.

Elsie didn't answer. She just snatched up the handle to Albert's tub wagon and started pulling it. Homer followed, then helped load Albert and the tub into the Buick. "When are you going to tell me what this is about?" he demanded again.

"I didn't lie about the money. Mr. Feldman really gave it to me, a fact Young Mrs. Feldman didn't like one bit. I think she's up to something."

To Elsie, Homer's response was so very much Homer. "He shouldn't have given you that much money," he said. It was an admonishment.

"Oh, here we go," she declared. "Your grand pride. Well, it isn't your money. It's mine. Now, shut up, and drive."

Homer shut up and drove. He didn't get far. At the city limits, he had to stop at a roadblock set up by the sheriff, a man named Posner. Elsie had met him at the games.

"What's this about, Sheriff?" Homer asked.

"Hang on a second," the sheriff said. He went to his car and returned, carrying the rooster, and tossed him into the back seat with Albert. "Thought you might want this thing."

Confused, Homer asked, "Why do you have our rooster?"

"Because you're not going back to town and I thought you'd want him. You see, this roadblock is just for you. Turn around and get going. Don't come back."

"But I have business in town," Elsie said. "Important business. Law business with Mr. Carter the attorney."

The sheriff scratched up under his cap. "Sorry, Mizz Elsie. Story I got was Mr. Carter just went on vacation. Yep, pretty sure that's right. I was told to patrol around his house, keep watch till he got back."

"The sheriff is lying," Elsie said to Homer. "Mr. Carter would never go anywhere until I got my money."

Elsie got out of the car, hooked the sheriff's elbow, and marched him off into the grass alongside the road. "Now, listen, Sheriff—"

"No, you listen, Mizz Hickam," the sheriff interrupted. "I don't like this any better'n you but I know who runs High Top and it ain't me. Mr. Carter was reminded of this, too. It's purely amazin' but he discovered Mr. Feldman's will he read to you and the others was plumb wrong. The new one doesn't have you in it, that's all you need to know. Now, you can skirt around me, come into town a different way, yell at folks, and generally be a pain in the keester to all concerned but it won't change a thing. Best you just keep on movin'. I'm sorry you got caught up in somethin' bigger'n yourself and sorry your husband got hurt."

"This isn't right," Elsie said.

"No, ma'am, it ain't," the sheriff agreed. He looked back toward town and shook his head. "There's lots of things that ain't right just about everywhere you go. I thought when I got into the sheriffin' business, I could fix some of those things but so far . . . well, it's been disappointin', that's all I got to say. You got to know there was never no way you were ever gonna get any Feldman money. Likely Mr. Feldman knew it, too. He just wanted to make Young Mrs. Feldman and his two kids work for it, sweat a little, you might say. He told them what he thought of them and what he thought of you. Guess that's your gift from him, if you can stand it."

Homer walked up. He had obviously overheard. "Let's go, Elsie. It's over."

Elsie was outraged. *This was her money!* "I'm not giving up! I never give up!"

"Mr. Hickam? You need to talk some sense into your wife."

Homer put his arms around her. She struggled against him until he tightened his arms around her so hard she could scarcely breathe. "Come on, Elsie. It's over. Let's go while we still have our pride."

"I don't have any pride," she said in a muffled voice against his shoulder.

"One thing, Sheriff," Homer said. "There are a couple of fellows, one real short, the other real big and tall. I last saw them hanging around the ball field. They're bank robbers and general scofflaws."

"Slick and Huddie? I arrested them about an hour ago. They were caught trying to steal the mortuary's hearse. Can't figger out what they were gonna do with it."

"I recommend you beat them both senseless," Elsie said, coming up for air from Homer's bear hug. She pushed at Homer to try to get away from him but his grip only got tighter. "I wish you hadn't had that pouch of Brown Mule," she said with her mouth pushed into his chest. "I wish I hadn't married you. I wish you would just go away forever!"

"I know," Homer said, quietly.

"Now, Mizz Elsie," the sheriff said, "you and your baseball player coal miner boy, you be on your way."

Elsie's outrage left her like air out of a balloon. Of course she wasn't going to get the money. Since when had she ever gotten what she wanted?

Homer must have felt her wilt because he released her. She pulled away from him and stalked to the car. When he settled behind the steering wheel, she noticed him grimacing. "Your hand or your wrist?" she asked, not sympathetically.

"Both are killing me."

"I'll drive," she volunteered and got out while he slid across the bench seat and leaned back. The rooster took up station by his head, fluttering sympathetically and cuddling at his ear.

Elsie turned the Buick around, reached back and petted Albert on the snout, then headed back toward Madison Park, which she knew was in a southerly direction. She drove past the park, then drove all day, watching the sun slide across her view until it was on her right. Her anger at Homer went up and down and twisted around like a mountain road. *How dare he tell her she didn't deserve her money? How dare he have that pouch of Brown Mule?*

She hadn't gone far before a sudden thought occurred to her. She'd left her wages from Feldman in the room at the stadium. She pulled over and shook Homer awake. "Homer, do you have any money?"

Homer blinked awake. "Money?"

"Mine is back at the stadium. Do you have any money with you?"

He pointed at the glove compartment. "In there."

Elsie opened the glove compartment. The snub-nosed pistol she'd stolen from Denver was there and she was surprised the mechanics who'd worked on the Buick hadn't stolen it. She supposed there were at least a few North Carolinians who were honest! There was also some money and she pulled out the bills and counted them. "Eighty dollars? That's all?"

"I sent the rest home to Daddy to keep for us."

"Your daddy? Your daddy plays poker *and loses!*"

Disgusted, she tossed the money back into the glove compartment and slammed the lid shut. She considered turning around and heading back to High Top to get her money but it was miles back and, most likely, the little room had been stripped bare. "The devil! What next!" she wailed.

She drove on, stopped for gasoline once, took Homer to the toilet, bought some aspirin from the attendant, gave it to Homer, and then inspected his cast. Above it, his arm was hot and red. When she asked him about it, he merely shrugged and tried unsuccessfully not to moan. She was tempted to squeeze his afflicted hand and hurt him like he'd hurt her. But, no, she'd take care of her husband even though he clearly did not deserve it.

Elsie drove on into the night, taking roads that looked like they might be the best ones, rolling through little towns and past cotton mills and through fields of crops—she couldn't tell what kind—until she began to smell something she thought was maybe the ocean. Big trees hung over the road, her headlights illuminating Spanish moss dripping from them. "I am lost," she confessed. "Lost," she repeated, eliciting only a groan from Homer.

At last she arrived at a place where she had to stop. There was no more road in front of her. The headlights of the Buick lit up an old house and beyond it Elsie thought there was water, although she could not see for certain because the lights didn't reach that far. The smell of the sea filled her nostrils as Albert stirred, perhaps also smelling it. Homer moaned anew. The rooster was silent.

Elsie said, "Lost" again, and switched off the motor and leaned back to wait for the sun. When it came up, everything was different from anything she had ever known.

I was fifteen and we were vacationing in Myrtle Beach, South Carolina. It was the third summer we'd stayed at a place called Lazy Hill, a collection of clapboard cabins behind a small ocean inlet. Mr. and Mrs. Glasgow ran the place. He'd been a Hollywood writer, and she an extra in a few of his movies, and they had a lot of stories to tell about that.

During our time at Lazy Hill, Dad rarely left the grounds and Mom only occasionally walked the few short blocks to the beach, where she would briefly sit in the sand and watch the sea before walking back. She and Dad seemed to be satisfied doing nothing and going nowhere.

One morning after breakfast, the Glasgows came by our cabin. Mr. Glasgow was building another cabin and needed Dad's advice on pouring concrete. After they'd left, Mrs. Glasgow said, "Elsie, how about we take my Jeep and drive down to Murrell's Inlet? Sometimes conch shells wash up there. It's a special place. I think you'd like it."

I was surprised at my mother's reply. "Oh, I know that beach," she said. "Almost every inch of it."

Mrs. Glasgow was also surprised. "How is that?"

Came the answer, "Spent some time there. It was a long time ago. Before Jimmy and Sonny."

Jim had already gone to the beach but I was hanging back to read a new Hardy Boys book. At Mom's comment, I asked, "Was it when you carried Albert home?"

Mrs. Glasgow turned to me. "Who's Albert?"

I couldn't help myself. It was too good not to tell. "An alligator!" I blurted. "Mom raised him in the bathtub! Dad was afraid of him! Buddy Ebsen the actor gave it to her!"

Mom's look told me I had overstepped my bounds but the damage was done. Mrs. Glasgow sat herself down in the nearest chair. "I'm not leaving until I hear this one!"

Mom gave me another unhappy look, then poured a couple of mugs of coffee, handing one of them to our vacation landlady. I laid myself down on the floor with my hands behind my head, just staring up at the ceiling and imagining everything while Mom told her tale. She gave a quick synopsis of who Albert was and why he was being carried home and then said, "So after we got out of North Carolina, I wasn't sure where I was but Homer and Albert were with me. And the rooster, although I didn't know then and don't know now why he was there...."

PART V

How Elsie Came to
Love the Beach and
Homer and Albert
Joined the Coast Guard

28

CAPTAIN OSCAR'S BOARDING HOUSE, WHICH SAT BESIDE an ocean sound, was surrounded by pin oaks dripping with Spanish moss. It was a lovely old manse built of cedar planks weathered gray, with a roof covered with slate shingles, and a front porch boasting a swing and a dozen rocking chairs. The front yard consisted of sand, saw grass, and sea oats and abutted a well-maintained wooden dock with iron cleats for the one boat that was most often moored there, a fishing trawler named the *Dorothy Howard*. The *Dorothy*, as she was affectionately known, was a working boat and fair sailer although not one you'd want to broach up too far in a steep sea and stiff wind. Captain Bob, her skipper, knew all her idiosyncrasies and tricks and treated her like he would treat a generous great-aunt, which is to say with deference and respect.

The boardinghouse required help, and a sign to that effect greeted Elsie on the morning of her arrival. She straightened her shoulders, fluffed up her hair, smoothed her skirt, and knocked on the door. A man dressed in the formal clothing of a sea captain, that is to say a navy blue coat, matching pants, and a white-brimmed cap, came to the door.

Elsie pointed at the sign. "Whatever you might need," she said, "I can provide if the pay is suitable."

The man leaned on his cane and stumped out on the porch, there to observe the Buick. Homer was resting, his eyes closed, on the passenger side, and Albert was looking with eager interest through the open window on the same side. The rooster stood on the alligator's head. "Quite a menagerie you got there."

"It is, sir, and I'm responsible for the lot. My husband's hand is crushed and his wrist is broken but he's not applying for this job. I am."

"Why do you have an alligator?"

"We hail from the West Virginia coalfields, an unsuitable place for an alligator, or anyone for that matter. I am therefore carrying him home to Florida. He was a gift to me from Buddy Ebsen of Orlando, the movie actor and dancer."

"I saw a movie once in Chicago," the man said, wistfully. "It was silent although there was a piano player on the stage." He approached the Buick and inspected Homer. "He is sweating and his face is pale. I think he is very sick."

"His hand is infected," Elsie explained. "I know that because I was once a nurse."

The man yelled, "Hey, Bob, get up here!" and a bearded young man, dressed in working khakis and a seaman's cap, walked up from the dock. "Fetch us the sawbones, Bob. And *toot sweet*, you hear? This young man may be dying."

"Who do we have here, pops?"

"Never mind that now. Take Wilma and be off with you!"

"Bob" tipped his hat to Elsie, went into a shed, and came back out riding a brown mare. He proceeded to clip-clop up the road Elsie had blundered down the night before. "That's Captain Bob, my son," the man said. "I shall introduce you to him at length but first things first. I am Captain Oscar, the owner of this establishment. Now, let's see to your husband."

Elsie and Captain Oscar helped Homer inside and laid him on a couch in the parlor. "Tell me how you feel, Homer," Elsie said in a cold voice. She felt no sympathy toward him, only responsibility.

Homer didn't reply. He didn't even moan. He only looked at her with glassy, uncomprehending eyes.

"How did he hurt himself?" Captain Oscar asked.

"He was struck with a baseball bat," Elsie answered, "and life. They don't always go together but this time they did."

An hour later, the doctor arrived in a chuggy old Ford and went inside to see his patient. After his examination, he asked, "Who speaks for this man?"

"I do, sir," Elsie said. "He is my husband."

"His hand and wrist are terribly infected and the infection has reached into his arm. If there is no improvement by tomorrow, I will have to take it off." The doctor handed her a bottle. "These are aspirin. Every three hours, give him two. They will lower his temperature. The infection he'll have to fight off on his own."

"He is a coal miner," Elsie said, her pride overcoming for the moment her anger, "and therefore strong."

"Bacteria has a way of taking down the strongest of men," the doctor said as he strapped his black bag shut. "But on the morrow, we shall see what we shall see."

Homer was moved to a downstairs bedroom, the second on the left, and then Captain Oscar, who was one of those men of indeterminate age who might be anywhere between seventy and ninety, bade Elsie sit with him in the parlor for a while. "You wish for a job," he said. "I have an opening. It is a maid's job."

"I can be a maid," Elsie said. "I have always wanted to be a maid."

"And it is a cook's job."

"I can be a cook," Elsie said. "I have always wanted to be a cook."

"And it is a manager's job." He waved his hand to indicate the dusty parlor and its somewhat mildewed furniture. "My wife ran this place until she died and then my daughter Grace took over until she came down with the tuberculosis. Now it has fallen into the general state of disrepair you presently observe. Would you be willing to be the maid, the cook, *and* the manager of my boardinghouse? I cannot pay you other than room and board until we become more prosperous but then I will give you a percentage of the net, to be negotiated later. What do you say?"

"I have always wanted to be the manager of a boardinghouse," Elsie swore and stuck out her hand. Captain Oscar shook her hand and Elsie became the maid, cook, and manager of Captain Oscar's Boarding House, an establishment dedicated to clean rooms and fine food, especially if it was fish.

The next day, the doctor returned as promised and examined Homer's arm. Homer continued to be generally unresponsive, although when the doctor ran his hand up and down his arm, he flinched. "The arm has not improved," the doctor announced. "I shall need to cut it off."

"You shall do no such thing," Elsie declared, then transitioned into a nursely description of what she had observed the night before while, out of a sense of responsibility, she had tended to her husband even though she could scarcely stand the sight of him. "Although his arm has not improved much, it has improved some. I can tell by a subtle color change that may not be apparent to you. I didn't rest at all last night. I gave my husband his aspirin but also kept him cool by dipping a towel in ice water and placing it across his brow, a procedure I'm surprised you didn't prescribe."

"It did not occur to me that you had ice," the doctor said.

"I found some in the icebox where the fish is kept fresh. Now, I think what should be done is that you remove the cast, which has become nasty and is too tight, and put on a clean one a bit looser."

The doctor was affronted. "Madam, I am a graduate of a state-approved medical school and have years of experience. I assure you that if I don't amputate your husband's arm, he will be dead within a couple of days."

"He will keep his arm," Elsie said, resolutely, "and if he is dead as a result, I will admit that you were right."

The doctor regarded Elsie, his frown changing to an expression of consternation. "You are a pigheaded child," he said, "who is gambling with this man's life."

"He is my husband," Elsie replied, "and if a wife can't gamble with her husband's life, then what's a marriage for?"

"You have an interesting take on marriage," the doctor replied, but then opened his black bag and removed a saw and a little sack of plaster. "I shall give him a new cast, as you wish."

"And I will help you," Elsie said. "You see, I have training as a nurse."

Afterward, as the doctor put his saw and the empty plaster sack back into his black bag, he said, "Pray that he is stronger than I perceive. I will not return unless sent for."

"I doubt that will be necessary," Elsie replied.

The doctor's face was pinched. "Then good day to you, Madam."

Over the next few days, Elsie plied Homer with the occasional aspirin and kept him cool by wiping him down with ice water every hour. After the fish ice ran out, she drove the Buick five miles up the road to the icehouse and bought more on Captain Oscar's credit.

Captain Oscar was impressed by her constant attention. "You must love your husband very much," he said while holding a kerosene lantern aloft in the middle of the night to assist her in her ministrations.

"I could have saved my brother Victor if I'd brought ice to him," Elsie said while wiping Homer down. "A fever will not catch me unawares again. If this man was the worst villain in the world, Captain, I would do no less."

It took two days but finally came a break in Homer's fever. The swelling in his arm and wrist and hand receded and the angry red streaks dissolved. While Elsie was tending to him, he blinked once, then stared at her. "Hello, Elsie," he said. "I'm pretty cold."

"Hello, Homer," Elsie replied. "You had a fever but I've saved you with the application of ice." She dipped a towel in the pan of ice water and raised it up so Homer could see.

"You still couldn't have saved Victor," he said.

"So you say," she answered and turned his face to the window and its view of the sandy road lined by pin oaks. "Look how lovely this place is. I brought you here."

"Where are we?"

"In South Carolina along the coast."

"We are off course."

"I am now plotting our course. You have abrogated that responsibility."

Homer raised his ruined hand and wiggled his fingers. "It works," he said, "but not well."

"It will get better," Elsie said, "and that's all you have to do for now, let yourself get better. In the meantime, I will provide."

He gazed at her. "You seem angry."

"I am angry. I will forever be angry. You said I did not deserve the money I earned. You did not back me up when I needed you."

Homer frowned as if trying to recall, then said, "But that's the way I felt."

Elsie dumped the pan of ice water on Homer's lap. "And this is how I feel."

Elsie left Homer with his mouth open to object or ask more questions—she didn't care which—and got busy cleaning the boarding-house from top to bottom. When she arrived with her mop, bucket, and broom at the second upstairs room on the right, she was surprised to find within it a young woman seated in a wingback chair, facing the window that overlooked the sound, which Elsie had learned the low-country folk called a swash.

"Oh, sorry," Elsie said. "I didn't know we had a guest."

The woman, who wore a high-necked white blouse, a brocaded skirt, and laced black boots, turned her face from the swash. "I am not a guest. I am Grace, Captain Oscar's daughter. And you are Elsie, our new maid, cook, and manager."

Elsie had forgotten that Captain Oscar had mentioned his sick daughter. She had presumed the daughter was off in a sanitarium. "If you would like me to come back later . . ." she began.

"No, please come in," Grace said, a faint smile forming on her sunken-cheeked face as she nodded toward the implements that Elsie was holding. "That mop, bucket, and broom were mine before I caught the consumption."

"The consumption?" Elsie asked.

"Tuberculosis. I laughingly refer to it as my Victorian novel's disease."

"You laugh about it? Isn't it bad?"

Grace shrugged, her thin shoulders barely moving beneath her blouse. "I laugh to keep from crying. It is bad enough to send me to this room, here to contemplate all that might have been. I'm certain my future would have included a handsome husband, intelligent and lively children, and a long, romantic life beside the sea."

"I am sure all those things will yet be yours," Elsie said.

The woman coughed a phlegmy cough and shook her head. "My fate was preordained. I can see that now. And perhaps," she said after a moment's reflection, "it was so that your fate might be fulfilled. Who are we mere mortals to know the plans of the angels who control our lives?"

"No one," Elsie answered. "My husband is also very ill."

"Yes, I know," Grace answered. "I slipped downstairs to observe him. He appears strong and I believe he will return to health." She turned businesslike. "So tell me, Elsie, what experience do you bring me and my father?"

"None whatsoever," Elsie confessed. "But I am eager to learn."

Grace smiled. "Why do you think he hired you?"

"He said I was the only one who applied for the job."

"There is truth to that observation," Grave observed. "But I suppose it was also because a turn of your pretty ankle caught his ancient but still appreciative eye. But never mind. I think he made a good choice. The first thing you should do is delve into the top right drawer of the rolltop desk in the kitchen. There you will find the daily log I kept during the years of my managership. It will tell you how I did things. Read it and then come back to me and I shall answer any and all questions."

"I'm sure I will have many," Elsie said. "I hope I won't be a bother."

"Never. In fact, I take great comfort in you. You are the answer to my father's prayers—and mine."

"You will find no more ardent worker than me," Elsie swore.

"You must make certain every occupied room has fresh sheets each day."

"I have already found your scrub board, washtub, and clothesline and I will make it just so."

"Fresh flowers in every room every day."

"I shall range far and wide to find them."

"The kitchen is in dire need of a good scrub and our icebox is empty."

"I shall scrub the kitchen and, given money, will fill the icebox with ice and fresh vegetables and as good and clean meat as I can find."

"Splendid. Along the road, you will find farmers offering their produce and meats, both fresh and salted. My brother Captain Bob will provide plenty of fish. Can you cook?"

"Unfortunately, I am only fair in that department."

"There are recipes aplenty in the cupboard over the kitchen sink. Use them diligently."

"They shall be my guide."

"There is something else," Grace said. "There is a child. Her name is Rose. She lives a mile northward on the sound. I would have you hire her. Tell her you will pay her in food. She is very smart and knows where everything in the inlet is and who you might need to see for this and that."

"As soon as possible, I will go to her," Elsie vowed.

After a few more days of cleaning, and once everything had been put away in its proper place, Elsie felt she could take the time to find and hire the girl named Rose. She walked along the muddy edges of the sound northward until she came upon a weathered, windblown old house made of driftwood and scrap. It was there she found a girl, not more than ten years old, sitting on the porch as if waiting for her to arrive.

"Good day, missus," the girl said, swinging her bare legs. "My name is Rose."

"I know what your name is, Rose. Would you like to work for me at Captain Oscar's? I would pay you in food."

Rose cocked her head. "I heard you have an alligator. Is it true?"

"Yes, it is."

"Might I touch him?"

"Of course. You may even feed him if you like."

"Then I will work for you." Rose gathered up her things, her very few things, and walked with Elsie to Captain Oscar's. Without being told, she made her bed in an outbuilding that had once been a shed for goats. Then, also without being told, she washed all the windows, and scrubbed all the copper pots and pans in the kitchen until they gleamed like new pennies. After that, she went to Elsie, who was on her hands and knees scrubbing the parlor floor. "Might I touch Albert now?"

Elsie put her fist in her back and stretched, then wordlessly took the girl to see Albert, who was in his washtub on the screened back porch. The rooster was asleep on his head but woke up and jumped off when Elsie and Rose walked in.

Albert grinned and grunted a hello as Elsie knelt beside him and petted his head. "Albert, I would like you to meet someone. Her name is Rose. She is a hardworking child. You should allow her to touch you."

At Elsie's nod, Rose went down on her knees and, with a trembling hand, reached out to touch the alligator's knobby head. At her touch, Albert's eyes rolled back. "I think he likes me," Rose breathed.

"Albert is a very sensible boy," Elsie said, "who knows a friend when he meets one."

"I *will* be your friend, Albert," Rose said. "Forever and ever."

"That is a long time," Elsie mused.

"Time is the best gift, missus," Rose replied. "Time is really the only gift we receive from God that we can give to others."

The mention of God took Elsie aback. She had been raised attending the company churches of the coal camps where her father had worked, but the thought that God gave out gifts like time was a novel one, never covered by dogma or the preachers she had listened to. "I was told you were very smart, Rose, and it seems you are."

"Thank you, Miss Elsie. It pleases me that you might think so."

Rose, besides being a hard worker, proved to be good company. She taught Elsie things such as how to catch blue crabs with nothing more than an old fish head, a string, and a long-handled net, and then how to cook and clean them. She was also fearless, and in that respect, reminded Elsie of herself.

Rose had been working for Elsie less than a week when a huge dog presented itself in the yard. When Elsie came out on the porch and saw that it had foam dripping from its mouth and its eyes were busy with hate, she called for the girl. "It is surely rabid," Elsie said when Rose arrived. "It will not leave before it has bitten someone."

Rose studied the creature. "I know that dog," she said. "It's old Sandy, belongs to the Buford family. They never fed it much so it had to go into the woods to feed itself. Must've been bit by a sick raccoon."

"If we move, it will attack us," Elsie said. "I shouldn't have called you and put you in the same pickle."

"Oh, yes, ma'am, you should have!" Rose declared. "But now we must work together. Do you see that spade leaning against the fence? I used it to work in the garden this morning. I must get to it and then I can do what must be done. You must distract old Sandy without getting bit."

Elsie considered where she was in relation to the dog. "I will do my best," she said. "But do you mean to hit the dog with the spade?"

"This isn't Sandy," Rose explained. "Sandy has already died."

"I know you're right but it's still hard."

"Hard or not, it must be done."

Elsie exhaled. "All right, I accept your premise. Ready?"

Rose nodded and Elsie stamped on the porch. "Sandy! Sandy! Here, here! Come get me!"

The dog shook its head, wisps of foamy drool slung from its mouth, and then came running toward Elsie in a strange, half-crippled gait. It stumbled at the steps but kept coming after regaining its footing. Elsie jumped up on the porch banister and balanced there as Rose leapt over the banister, plucked up the shovel, sprinted back to the porch, and brained the dog with one sure swing, the blade of the shovel making a sickening sound as it crushed the dog's skull.

Rose tossed the shovel away and knelt beside the dog. "Poor Sandy," she said, her hand hovering over its bloody head.

"Don't touch it," Elsie said as she stepped down from her perch. "It can still give you its disease even when dead."

"It led a poor life," Rose said. "But it lived until it died and, until this moment, never tried to hurt a soul." Rose looked up at the sky. "Bless this old dog, Lord, and let him finally get a good meal in heaven today."

"Do you think dogs go to heaven?" Elsie asked.

"If they don't," Rose said, "God is a poor excuse for a god."

Elsie looked at Rose. "You saved me."

"One might say I saved us," Rose responded. "Or, more appropriately, we saved each other. It's what friends do."

Elsie reached across the dead dog and touched Rose's cheek and her hair. "Thank you," she said.

Rose also took Elsie to the seashore, where she'd never been before. They walked around the sound, then through a shallow inlet to reach the Atlantic Coast. In every direction, the sea appeared endless. Elsie was enthralled by the wind, the waves, the thunderous noise, and the way the sand felt between her toes. "They call this the Grand Strand," Rose reported.

"It is aptly named," Elsie replied. "I have never imagined a beach so grand."

Rose pointed at the flat round shells that littered the beach. "Those are sand dollars, missus," she said. She picked one up and broke it open to reveal what looked like tiny sculptured birds of fine white china.

"Why are they in there where no one can see them?" Elsie asked.

"Nobody knows," Rose said, "except as a hidden glory of God. It makes you wonder what other glories He keeps hidden."

"You have spoken of God before," Elsie said. "What do you know about Him?"

"I have never set foot in a church," Rose answered, "but somebody must have made all this."

"A sensible answer," Elsie said, her admiration for the child growing.

Rose pointed out the gray driftwood, twisted like gargoyles and shoved back along the dunes. "The sailors say those are formed by mermaids. Maybe they sculpt the sand dollars, too."

Elsie picked up what she thought was a black arrowhead. Her brothers were always bringing arrowheads home from their hikes into the surrounding mountains but this one was a bit strange. "What is this, Rose?" she asked.

"Why, it's a shark's tooth, missus," Rose replied.

Elsie studied the tooth, noting now the fine serrations along the edge like those on a butcher's bone knife. She worried it between her fingers, its smooth surface soothing to the touch. "But why is it black?" she asked.

"I'm sure I don't know," Rose answered. "I've seen the fishing boats bring in a shark now and again and their teeth are always white as ivory."

"Maybe black teeth are very old," Elsie proposed. "Like dinosaurs."

"Things usually bust up in the sea when they're old," Rose scoffed, then bent down and picked up something blue and sparkling in the surf. "Like this piece of beach glass."

Elsie took the glass. It was smooth and rounded on its edges and glittered in the sun like a jewel. "It's beautiful," she said.

"It's just a piece from an old bottle," Rose replied, "tumbled in the sand by the sea for a long time. You can keep it."

Elsie put the beach glass and the tooth in her pocket. "Thank you, Rose."

Rose shrugged, then pointed at a large shell just at the ocean's edge. "Look there. It is a queen conch, a true beauty!"

Elsie followed Rose to the big shell, all turned into itself, pink and white and smooth. Elsie picked it up and held it to her ear. "I thought I could hear the ocean in this kind of shell but I don't hear anything."

"That's because its animal still lives in it," Rose said, taking the shell and showing Elsie the hard gray foot of the sea creature within. "It will soon die here in the air and the sun."

"Then let's return it to the sea," Elsie proposed. She took the shell and waded into the water, past the first row of waves, where she dropped the shell. "There," she said, walking out.

Rose said, "Oh, missus, you are very bold. There are sharks in the surf this time of the year."

"Fortune favors the bold, Rose," Elsie replied, although she was shaken by the belated warning. There was so much about the sea she didn't know, including its dangers. Still, for a reason she couldn't discern, Elsie wanted to tempt the sea just to see what it would do.

Rose led Elsie farther down the beach. With every step there seemed to be another wonder: an egg of a manta ray looking for all the world like a lady's purse, a shell that was the shape and color of an exotic butterfly wing, little birds that scampered along the surf but never got their feet wet—"Sandpipers, missus!" Rose explained.

Elsie also gasped at the strange creatures just beneath the shallows with bulbous heads that flew more than swam—"Horseshoe crabs!" came Rose's explanation—and the air itself, which was clean and fresh yet smelled of a vast underwater kingdom.

"I have never been happier," Elsie said, as much to herself as to Rose. It was the sea, the glorious sea. Here beside it, near it, in it was where she felt she belonged. "I should like to stay here forever and ever and learn everything there is to learn."

"There is no reason why you can't," Rose replied.

"Oh, there is," Elsie said. "It seems anytime I am close to happiness, it is snatched away from me. How about you, Rose? Are you happy?"

"Moderately so, although I am an orphan," Rose replied. "Happiness will not be fully mine until I find a family."

They walked on for a while, Elsie mulling over Rose's declaration. Finally, she said, "If I knew my own fate, I would be pleased to make you part of my family. Although I have a husband now, I'm not certain I will always have one. You see . . ."

"Oh, missus, don't say it!" Rose cried. "He is getting better. I go into his room to look at him now and again and I'm certain his health is returning."

"It is not his health that will see us apart," Elsie replied. "It is who he is and who I am."

Rose looked away to the line of sea and sky. "Look there," she said, suddenly. "Porpoises! See their bottle-shaped noses and the smiles on their faces? They are good and wonderful creatures that have saved many drowning sailors. They're also supposed to be good luck."

Elsie watched the cavorting animals but she took no joy from them. Instead, a great sadness washed over her. The world was indeed beautiful, but she still had many decisions to make.

29

WITH ELSIE IN CHARGE, IT DIDN'T TAKE LONG BEFORE
Captain Oscar's Boarding House rose sufficiently in reputation that its
weekly rooms were filled with sailors. Dozens of weekend visitors also
came by for good meals and the view of the swash and to meet the
friendly alligator who always seemed to be smiling. To help this trade
along, Captain Oscar put up a road sign on a tree:

FREE! COME SEE ALBERT THE ALLIGATOR!
ALL DAY SATURDAY AND SUNDAY AFTERNOONS!
FINE FOOD AND DRINK
CAPTAIN OSCAR'S BOARDING HOUSE

Albert was at first presented in the front yard on a leash, but after
some boys tried to pull his tail, Homer built a pen for him, placing it in
the shade of a willow tree. He also provided a water-filled bathtub (discovered in an abandoned shed) for the alligator to loll in as he wished.
When there were too many visitors crowding about, Homer sat protec-
tively in a chair beside the pen and read a selection from Captain Oscar's
library titled *Moby-Dick*, a novel Homer found tedious but brilliant.

At times, the rooster shared the pen and pecked along Albert's back, keeping it free of parasites, but, at other times, chose to sit on Homer's shoulder, tucked next to his ear. Parents would sometimes tell their children Homer was Long John Silver and the rooster was a parrot. Homer was patient with the visitors and willing to answer all the questions they had about Albert, and whether he and the rooster were a pirate and a parrot.

These were confusing times for Homer. Though on the mend, he still got easily tired. He also liked the boardinghouse but didn't like that Elsie only treated him with polite disdain. He knew partially why she was angry, having to do with what he'd said to her about Mr. Feldman's will, but he still didn't think it was right that she receive so much money from a man she wasn't related to. What he might to do return to her favor, or if he ever would, he had no idea.

Although he was aware that Captain Oscar was sharing a portion of the boardinghouse's net proceeds with Elsie, he knew it wasn't that much. Since he supposed that she still wished to continue to Florida, he thought he'd better find a job. One afternoon, after his cast was removed and fair movement had returned to his hand and he felt his strength returning, he asked Captain Bob if he might be of some use. "In what way?" the surprised captain asked.

"Well, I could help you fish," Homer said. "I have noticed that you take the *Dorothy* out to sea every day."

Marley, the first and only mate, looked up from the deck he was mopping. "I wish *somebody* would help us fish," he said. "These days, we can't seem to catch much of anything."

Captain Bob thought a bit, then said, "A dollar a day, take it or leave it. But you won't do any fishing. You'll cut up bait, bait the hooks, scrub the decks, polish the brightwork, and do whatever else I or Marley might require. Workdays will last until everything is done to my satisfaction. If that's agreed, see you at sunup."

Homer agreed and showed up at the dock with the rising sun. Thus began his fishing career. For three days it consisted of hanging over the rail and feeding the fish with the contents of his stomach, and Captain Bob chose not to pay him on those days. But on the fourth day Homer found his sea legs and got to work chopping up bait and baiting hooks and scrubbing and mopping and polishing. Because of his obvious love of learning new things, coupled with a willingness to work hard, it wasn't long before he'd gained the grudging admiration of the captain and mate. He was even allowed to fish, although he didn't have much luck.

On the tenth day of Homer being a fisherman, Elsie pleased him very much by voluntarily walking with him to the dock. She was wearing a bonnet, which gave her a winsome look, like a little girl playing grown-up. Homer, enamored all over again with his wife, asked, "What are you doing today?"

"Baking bread," she said. "Using one of Grace's recipes. I have always wanted to be a baker."

"I have yet to meet Grace," he confessed. "She stays holed up in that room of hers."

"She is much too ill for casual guests," Elsie replied.

Homer was wounded to be considered only a casual guest but he let Elsie's comment slide. She put her hand on his arm, the first time she'd touched him since he'd recovered from his busted hand and broken wrist, and said, "I want to thank you for taking this job and also for looking after Albert on weekends."

"You're welcome," he said and leaned over to kiss her lips, catching instead her quickly turned cheek. He raised his head and said, "Marley says I'm turning into a fair sailor now that the seasickness is gone away."

To his joy, Elsie smiled up at him and put her hand on her bonnet as a freshening breeze swept across the swash. She gave Homer a quick peck on his cheek. "Away with you, sailor man."

Homer looked fondly at his wife, then crossed the board that served as the *Dorothy*'s gangplank. "Get back on the dock, you scurrilous knave," Marley mocked. "Untie our lines, then come aboard and pull the plank. Have you no sense in how a boat leaves her harbor?"

Homer went back and properly untied the lines, then climbed on board and pulled the plank. Captain Bob called Homer up to the wheelhouse. "Take the wheel," he ordered, stepping aside.

Homer was astonished. "You want me to steer the boat?"

"You've earned the right. Just keep her along the channel between those piers and all will be fine."

Homer took the wheel. He could feel the power of the *Dorothy* as he guided her through the piers and toward the opening in the sand that led across the bar and into the open sea. "Give her a little more power," Captain Bob said as they approached the bar. "The sea will slap you back if you don't."

Sure enough, as Homer pushed the throttle lever forward, he felt the energetic pushback of the Atlantic. Beads of perspiration broke out on his forehead. "Maybe you better take it," he said.

"*Dorothy* is a she, not an it," Captain Bob replied as he struck a match and fired up his corncob pipe. "And you're doing fine." He clenched the pipe between his teeth and took a puff.

Homer didn't feel like he was doing fine. He felt as if the fishing boat was slipping out from under his bare feet and that the sea was more in control of her than he. But then the waves gave a final, hard slap and he and the vessel were through the pass. Homer's delight manifested itself in a grin and, for the briefest of moments, he was nearly content.

"I'll take her now," Captain Bob said. "Go cut up bait."

Homer walked astern and opened the chest holding squid and octopus. He took a fish knife and began to cut them into small squares for the multiple hooks that would go down once they found a spot to drop anchor. When Captain Bob found his spot, Marley threw out a line to see if it was any good. He got a bite, reeled in a small snapper, and Homer tossed out a buoy to mark it, then began to put out all the rods and reels and lines.

At the end of the day, the catch was one grouper, one wahoo, and three snappers. "Scarcely worth the gasoline," Captain Bob griped as he aimed the bow toward shore.

On the way in, Homer took a moment to admire the richness of the sky as the sun set in a wash of blazing pinks and blues and purples and yellows unlike any he had ever seen. Marley handed him an iced bottle of beer. Homer didn't much like beer but he knew the gesture was meant in friendship so he took it and drank with feigned pleasure.

"What are you thinking about, Homer?" the first mate asked.

"Refraction," Homer said. "That's what causes the colors in the sky."

Marley shoved his gnarled hand up under his cap and gave his head a good scratch. "Then you ain't thinking about nothing," he concluded, "at least nothing that makes any kind of sense to be thinking about."

Homer sipped his beer. "What do you think about?"

The first mate grinned. "Women, booze, a warm bed, a roof that don't leak, and fish."

"I envy you," Homer said, and meant it.

After the *Dorothy* was tied up and the fish unloaded and Homer was finished mopping the deck and cleaning the brightwork, Captain Bob said, "Something's wrong with us. The other boats are catching fish but we aren't."

"I think it's bad ju-ju, Captain," Marley said. "We got to change it."

"Ju-ju?" Homer asked.

"Luck, providence, what have you," Captain Bob answered.

Homer was intrigued. "How do sailors change their luck?"

"Well, let me see," Marley said. "There are quite a few ways, I suppose. Whistling aboard a boat causes bad luck but touching your collar, if you have one, is supposed to change it back. Pigs and hens on boats are supposed to be good luck, too. Say, maybe we should take your rooster aboard! He seems to be a lucky fowl."

Captain Bob said, "The alligator seems the luckiest of all."

"Albert *is* lucky," Homer acknowledged. "He came all the way to Coalwood in a shoe box and was taken in by a woman who treats him better than most mothers treat their children."

"Well, then, let's take him with us," Captain Bob proposed. "Maybe he'll change our ju-ju. It would be worth a try."

Homer shook his head. "I can't allow that. What if he got seasick?"

Captain Bob studied him. "You really love that alligator, don't you?"

Homer laughed. "I am only Albert's chauffeur. And Elsie's."

→ ←

Later that evening, Captain Bob found Elsie frying potato pancakes, using a recipe Grace had given her, and alternately minding a big, bubbling pot of shrimp. "I need to change our luck," he said. "I would like to take Albert fishing."

Elsie pushed back strands of hair from her sweaty face. "No," she said. "It's too dangerous."

"You husband goes fishing with me. Is it too dangerous for him?"

"That's his responsibility. Mine is Albert."

Captain Bob smiled. "I believe you to be the prettiest girl I have ever seen, bar none. What do you say about that?"

"I say I'm married."

"That is but an excuse. You do not care for your husband. I've noticed the way you ignore him most of the time."

"That is none of your business."

"Ah," Captain Bob said with a nod, "the confirmation. Well, then, Elsie, here we are, the handsome young sea captain and the lovely young woman who finds herself unhappy on the beach and needing more, much more, of that which this seafarer is more than pleased to provide." He put his hand on her waist. "*Give me women, wine, and snuff until I cry out, 'Hold, enough!' You may do so sans objection until the day of resurrection. For, bless my beard, they aye shall be my Trinity!*"

"Really, Captain!" Elsie pried his hand from her waist. "Do you think my head is turned so easily? I mean, Keats! Who quotes Keats to a woman? That ancient reprobate, of all the bards!"

Captain Bob took off his captain's cap and said, "I was just testing the waters. I know other poems that might cause you to beg me to kiss you but I recognize now is not the time or place. Such will come. In the meantime, I respectfully request that you please let Albert go aboard the *Dorothy*."

Elsie shook her head. "It will never happen. It is much too dangerous for my little boy. Now, please remove yourself from my sight."

Captain Bob laughed softly, then walked out of the kitchen while Elsie furiously stirred the shrimp, muttering, "*Keats!*"

➤ ◄

That night, in their tiny room, which was not much more than a closet with a door and a narrow bed, Homer asked, "Where are we going, Elsie?"

"Going? What do you mean?"

"Are we going to Florida or have you decided to stop here?"

Elsie took her time to reply. "I don't know anymore," she answered in a near whisper. She turned her face to her husband. "If I stayed, what would you do?"

"I'm not a fisherman."

"Then you would leave?"

"I didn't say that. I don't know what I'd do."

"I love the beach, I love the sea, I love everything about this place."

"Do you love—?" But Homer couldn't bring himself to finish the question he really wanted to ask. Instead, he asked, "Do you love Albert? You said he'd never be happy in Coalwood. Do you think he'd be any happier living behind a fence in the sand?"

"I don't know. I will think on it."

Homer pressed. "Have you forgiven me, at least a little, for challenging you on Mr. Feldman's money?"

"I've nearly forgotten it. I've nearly forgotten everything. The here and now, those are my concerns."

Elsie turned over and went to sleep. Homer stared at the ceiling for a long time. What did Elsie really want to do? The only thing that kept him from shaking her awake and demanding an answer was that he, too, fell asleep.

The next morning, Homer went aboard the *Dorothy*. Captain Bob and Marley seemed to be looking at him oddly but Homer couldn't imagine why after he checked his fly and found it buttoned.

Once they were through the pass, he discovered the reason. "We shanghaied Elsie's alligator," the first mate confided. "Don't look at me that way. Captain Bob and me, we are desperate for some good ju-ju. Albert is below. The captain and I had the devil of the time getting him there."

Homer threw open the hatch, clambered down it, and was relieved to find Albert in his washtub and looking around the boat with interest. After making certain he was unhurt, Homer stormed to the wheelhouse. "I can't believe you stole Elsie's alligator!"

"We are only borrowing him," Captain Bob said, mildly. "And we'll have him back onshore in good order. What's the problem?"

"Other than the fact you kidnapped Albert, the problem is Elsie will be sure I helped you."

"You really have to take that woman under more control," Captain Bob advised. "And now, with the authority vested in me as the captain of this tub, I order you to help Marley carry Albert to the bow where the gods of the sea can have a better look at him."

Recognizing the futility of further objection, and giving in to the ancient authority of boat captains at sea, Homer went below and helped the first mate carry Albert to the bow. Once he was there, Albert's grin broadened and he began to make his *yeah-yeah-yeah* sound. "He likes it!" Marley crowed. When Homer glared at him, he added, "It was Captain Bob's idea, every bit of it."

"But you agreed to it. I thought you were my friend."

"I'm a fisherman who needs to feed his family first."

"Do you really think having Albert on board will make the slightest bit of difference?"

Marley shrugged and then, after Captain Bob chose a spot, baited and tossed in a hook. At first nothing happened but then there was a tug and Marley reeled in the biggest grouper the *Dorothy* had caught all year. Homer baited more hooks and tossed them in. To the astonishment of everyone aboard the fishing boat, with the possible exception of Albert, the sea frothed with fish of every size and shape, almost as if they were desperate to be hauled aboard.

Captain Bob howled with delight as the fish piled up on deck. "Albert, you old creature. You are the best luck any fisherman ever hoped to have!"

How Albert slipped off the boat was never clear to Homer. He only knew that he was on the stern pulling in fish left and right when Captain Bob came up to him. "Homer," he asked, pointing out to sea, "is salt water bad for alligators?"

Homer wasn't certain. All he knew was that when he looked along Captain Bob's point, he saw Albert swimming away from the boat in the direction of a flock of bobbing seagulls. "Go after him!" Homer cried.

Captain Bob was astonished. "Leave this spot? With all these fish on our hooks? That would be crazy!"

"But Albert's fixed your ju-ju!"

"That he did." Captain Bob saluted the departing alligator. "Thanks, Albert!"

Homer had no choice. His duty to Elsie, Albert, and maybe the entire universe was clear. He dived overboard into the foamy sea.

30

THE SEA WAS INVIGORATING AND TERRIFYING ALL AT
once and its wetness reminded Homer of something pertinent. He didn't
really know how to swim.

He dog-paddled as hard as he could, too fearful to stop and look over
his shoulder to see if the *Dorothy* was coming after him. He didn't catch
up with Albert so much as the alligator turned around and met him
coming back the other way. When they were nose-to-snout with one another, Homer desperately wrapped his arms around the alligator. "Help
me, Albert!" he cried.

Albert swam a little way with Homer hanging on while Homer looked
all around for the *Dorothy*. She was nowhere to be seen. He felt a tug and
realized he and Albert were caught in a powerful current that was sweeping them rapidly in a direction Homer suspected they didn't want to go.

How much time passed, Homer didn't know, but it was surely hours
because the sun was dipping toward the westward horizon. He just hung
on to Albert, who kept swimming. "Take us back to the beach, Albert,"
Homer begged, and the alligator might have, too, except for the boat that
heaved up next to them. Homer was shivering, the heat sucked from

him by the cold Atlantic, but he managed to raise his head to see two men in bib overalls and straw hats looking back at him. Both, based on their expressions, were not thrilled to see either Homer or Albert.

"Well, this is a fine howdy-do," one of the men said, a man whose arms and face were burned brown.

The other man had red hair and a cigarette at the corner of his mouth. "We got to save him," he said.

"No, we don't got to save him, nor nobody else," the brown-faced man replied.

"Is that a crocodile holding him up?"

"He's an alligator," Homer said, his teeth chattering. Then, not wishing to be impertinent, he added, "But I can see how you might make such a mistake."

Eventually, the redheaded man lowered his hand and Homer grasped it while holding Albert with all his remaining strength, to be pulled aboard. "Thank you," Homer said, rolling over on his back and gasping for air. "You are the answer to my prayers. Who has saved me?"

"Roy-Boy's his name," the redheaded man said. "We ain't never been the answer to nobody's prayers,"

"Merganser's his," the brown-faced man said, "and he's right, we ain't. So who you be, boy?"

"My name's Homer," Homer said, "and this is Albert."

"What the hell you doin' out here with this reptile?" Roy-Boy asked. "You ain't with the Coast Guard, are ya?"

"Fell off a fishing boat. Well, I didn't exactly fall. Albert somehow got into the water and—"

"If this ain't a queer mess," Merganser interrupted. "Who'da thunk we'd end up with stowaways!"

"Technically, we're rescues," Homer advised.

Roy-Boy made a dismissive gesture. "Look, get in our way, it's back into the drink with the both of you."

"Just think of us as not here," Homer said.

Merganser wasn't convinced. "What if he tells on us?" he demanded. "Maybe we shouldn't have told him our names."

"You told him mine," Roy-Boy accused. "That's why I told him yours." Roy-Boy swept his eyes across the empty ocean. "But who's he gonna tell, anyways?"

"I don't mean now. Later."

"I swear I won't tell anybody anything," Homer swore. "Albert and I don't care what you do as long as you give us a ride back to the beach. I'm staying—well, my wife and I are—at Captain Oscar's in Murrell's Inlet. You heard of it?"

"Yeah, I heard of it," Roy-Boy said. "So you fell off the *Dorothy*, did you?"

"Yes, sir. The *Dorothy* she was."

Merganser shook his head. "Captain Bob gets wind of this, he'll turn us in, sure. I say we throw this fellow and his crocodile back into the ocean."

"Albert's an alligator," Homer reminded Merganser and then reflected it probably wasn't good to correct a fellow who could throw you in the ocean to drown.

Roy-Boy was thinking it over. "Naw, we can't do that," he said at last.

"Thank you," Homer said, relieved. "Albert thanks you, too," he added.

Homer crawled down with Albert onto a pile of woolen blankets. They were wet but Homer didn't complain. After a while, Merganser asked, "You want some water? Got some in this bottle if you do."

Homer gratefully took the offered bottle, which was an old whiskey bottle, and gulped its contents down. The water was warm and a little slimy but it wet his dry mouth. He shared the remnant left with Albert, who, refreshed, slithered out of Homer's grasp and made a run for Roy-Boy's feet. Roy-Boy raised an oar. "Another step closer, I'll bash ye, ye damned croc!"

Albert stopped and cocked his head, considered the raised heavy oar, then retreated back to the wet blankets. Homer wrapped a protective arm around Albert and together the two remained quiet until it got dark.

The stars came out, millions of them, all bright and sparkly, and then Merganser turned off the motor and they began to drift. Summoning up his courage, Homer asked, "Are we anywhere near Murrell's Inlet?"

"Shut up!" Merganser hissed. "No, we ain't. You say another word, one single little word, it don't matter what it is, I'll pitch you and your croc into the sea. We clear?"

"Clear," Homer said before realizing he wasn't supposed to say another word, one single little word, but Merganser apparently wasn't the literal type and Homer and Albert were left alone, although damp, in the bottom of the boat.

Above, Homer could see a crescent moon with purple clouds scudding past. The sea slapped gently against the hull. Then a lantern popped into view and something huge began to draw next to them. It appeared to be a wooden wall topped by three giant trees.

"Hello, the *Theodosia*," Merganser quietly called out.

A face appeared next to a lantern. "You ready?"

"You might want to send somebody down to help us," Merganser answered. "Make it go quicker."

"Right." In a trice, a cargo net fell down the side followed by a black man in dungarees and a canvas jacket. When Albert hissed and the fellow caught sight of him, he screamed, "Crocodile!" and clambered back up, fast as his bare feet could carry him.

"He's an alligator," Homer said, then wished he'd remained quiet because Roy-Boy gave him a kick in his ribs.

"It's just a little croc," Merganser said. "Come on back. It won't hurt you."

The man crept back down the side of the wooden wall, his eyes as round and bright as bone china saucers. "Keep that thing away from me," he said before being distracted by a creaking noise from above. Homer saw a sling being lowered from a steel boom.

"Hold the burlocks steady," the black man ordered Roy-Boy as he grasped the netting of the sling. Together, they eased it down into the boat, where it fell away to reveal a number of wrapped burlap bundles.

"Hurry!" someone called from above. "Scuttlebutt is there's a cutter out here somewhere."

The black man was counting. "Shit!" he moaned.

"What's wrong?" Roy-Boy asked, nervously.

"You got thirteen burlocks."

"Fletcher!" the voice from above called out. "If you got them unloaded, get back up here!"

"They's got thirteen burlocks, Mr. Marsh," the black man replied. "That's bad ju-ju."

"Get your tail back up here, Fletcher."

The black man reluctantly complied and climbed the netting onto the ship. When the man at the lantern looked down, Homer saw he had a square face and a large mouth, creased at the corners with laugh lines. "That completes our business for this evening, gents. Take those burlocks—don't look to see what's in them, you hear?—and carry them directly to Crab Pinch Inlet. There'll be a truck there waiting for you. Get going. We've got our steam up already and I've given orders to rig the sails to push us along even faster."

The wall of wood pulled away. Merganser started the lighter's small motor and steered them about.

"We did it!" Roy-Boy exulted.

"Not yet. You heard that smuggler. There's a patrol boat out here somewhere. We'll get by her, though. If they see us, they'll just think we're a couple of drunk locals."

"Yuh, and a half-drowned fisherman and his crocodile."

"Alligator," Homer said and then, because he was so tired, allowed curiosity to overcome his good sense. "What's in those thirteen bundles?"

"Never say thirteen on a boat!" Merganser admonished. "It's bad luck."

Homer refrained from pointing out that he hadn't been the first one to say thirteen on the boat. The black man named Fletcher had that honor.

"And don't ask what's in them because we don't know. We're just hired to bring in the goods."

The boat puttered along but they hadn't gone more than a half a mile before a spotlight struck the boat. "Heave to!" a harsh voice commanded, apparently amplified through a megaphone. "We are prepared to shoot if you don't."

At first, Merganser and Roy-Boy threw up their hands to shield themselves from the blinding glare but then Merganser yelled, "Hang on!" and threw the boat over in a hard turn.

"We ain't kiddin'!" the voice yelled.

"Ho ho!" Merganser laughed. "You got to catch us first!"

Merganser's challenge was apparently accepted because, within seconds, a storm of crashes battered the boat and boards splintered, their remnants falling on Homer, who quickly shielded Albert with his body.

The pounding continued—by bullets, Homer realized—until Homer heard the sound of two large splashes. When he looked up, he saw that Roy-Boy and Merganser were gone. The gun or guns had stopped, the reason for that soon evident when water rushed inside the boat and it sank. Homer found himself once again in the sea, this time without Albert, who had slipped from his grasp. *Elsie will kill me if I lose her alligator,* he thought.

But then he realized she wouldn't have to kill him. For one thing, he was drowning. For another, he was about to be run over. A luminescent wave rushed at him, parting from the sharp bow of a big steel ship aimed precisely in his direction.

31

WHEN THE *DOROTHY* RETURNED TO PORT THAT EVENING, its hold was filled with fish but its deck contained a sheepish captain and mate who had to confess to Elsie that they had, while making their fine catch, lost both her husband and her alligator. Hearing this, Elsie's first reaction was abject misery and she swayed toward hysteria. But upon reflection, and the fierce stoicism of the coalfields still embedded in her soul, she drew back from the cusp of wails and tears and gnashing of teeth that she teetered about. She reminded herself that Captain Bob hadn't told her that her husband and alligator were drowned, only that they were last seen swimming in the ocean. Alligators, according to what Elsie knew about them, were supposed to be pretty good swimmers. She wasn't certain about Homer but most Gary hollow boys knew how to at least dog-paddle. So there was hope for both.

There was also a load of customers inside the boardinghouse, sailors off a big trawler down from the Outer Banks, and they needed tending to. Elsie made her decision. She owed it to Captain Oscar to do her job.

She'd see to her customers, then decide what next to do. She warned Captain Bob, "We are not done here."

"I did all I could, Elsie. The sea is unforgiving."

"So am I."

Holding herself together with iron will, Elsie went back inside and worked with Rose to get out the big supper to the starving men of the sea.

After the sailors were sated and all had left the table, she carried a tray of food to Grace, noting, "You never eat what I bring but I thought I'd try one more time."

"I eat all I need," Grace said. "And you need not bring more. You see, I steal down to the kitchen at night and take what I wish for sustenance. Now, what is this about your husband lost at sea?"

Elsie burst into tears, the dam in her heart breached by Grace's words. "And my alligator," she said. "Oh, Grace, what shall I do?"

Grace leaned forward. "Well, Elsie, what do you think you should do?"

Elsie wiped her eyes. "I don't know."

"Think, Elsie. Your husband is lost at sea. . . ."

"And my alligator."

"Yes, your alligator. What should you do?"

Elsie thought it over. "I should find them," she said at length.

"At sea? How would you do that?"

There was only one way and Elsie knew it. "Thank you, Grace," she said and stepped downstairs and outside onto the porch, where Captain Bob and Marley were holding court with the trawler sailors, all of them relaxing and smoking and digesting their large meal. "I need your boat," Elsie told Captain Bob.

"Whatever are you talking about, Elsie?" Captain Bob asked, taking his corncob pipe from his mouth.

"I need your boat. To look for Homer and Albert."

Captain Bob pondered Elsie's demand, then said, most condescendingly, "There are two things wrong with this idea. Firstly, you don't know anything about boats. Secondly, it's become night and the sea is a dangerous place after dark."

"I don't care," Elsie said. "Just get me started, aim me in the right direction, and I'll take it from there. I have always wanted to be a sailor."

Captain Bob leaned back and smiled, then rose from the rocking chair, nodded to the trawler boys, and led Elsie over to Albert's empty pen beneath the willow tree, where they might not be clearly heard. "Now, see here, Elsie," he said, pointing the stem of his pipe at her, "they're lost, your husband and alligator, and there's nothing to be done about it. You must accept that you're a widow, the sea being the harsh mistress that she is, and commence with your grieving and then get on with your life. Give it a few days, even a week, and then I'll come a-courting. You can stay here forever, which I know is what you want. It's kismet. Do you know what kismet means?"

"I certainly do," Elsie answered. "Wait here." She marched across the front yard, up the porch steps, across the porch, and through the screen door, which slapped loudly behind her, startling the somnolent sailors. She kept going until she reached her room, where she opened a small trunk, provided by Captain Oscar to hold her things, and removed the snub-nosed pistol she'd stolen from Denver the thunder road driver, which seemed months, perhaps years ago. She made certain it was loaded, descended the staircase, and marched out onto the porch, the screen door slapping shut anew behind her, which startled the dozing sailors once again, and continued down the steps and into the sand and across to Albert's pen, where she soon had the barrel of the pistol tucked up under Captain Bob's chin. "You will take me to sea and you will find my husband and my alligator *toot sweet*, Captain Bob, or I swear I will blow off your head."

Captain Bob spat out his pipe. "Well," he said in an aggrieved tone, "since you put it that way, I suppose I will."

32

A LIGHT FLASHED INTO HOMER'S FACE, NEARLY BLINDING him, and then, as the sharp bow turned aside, a giant hand seemed to claw up out of the deep and pull him under until he felt something slip beneath him, then lift him to the surface. Once his head popped above the water, Homer could see that Albert had saved him once again. He hung on to the alligator and started yelling for help.

The boat that had nearly run him down circled about, then edged in alongside. Muscled arms reached for Homer from above and grasped his shirt, then his belt, and pulled him from the sea. Somehow, he hung on to Albert.

Dumped on the deck, Homer rolled over and gulped air while seawater ran off him. When he opened his eyes, it was to see the face of a rough-looking man wearing a seafarer's cap. Other faces also appeared. They were all rough-looking men. "Thank you," Homer managed to say in a strangled voice.

Albert looked around with interest and hissed when one of the men tried to grab him by his tail. "Don't do that," Homer said as he sat up.

A boy with a tub hat shoved on the back of his head pushed through the other men and stared at Homer and Albert. "You're lucky to be alive," the boy said.

"Where am I?" Homer asked him.

"Why, the cutter *Helene*," the boy said. "Of the United States Coast Guard."

"Coast Guard! You were looking for me?"

"Why, no, sir. We're on smuggling patrol. Just happened acrost you."

"What kind of smuggling?"

"Gold, silver, jewels, just about anything they ship up here from old Mexico. Uh-oh. Here comes Chief Vintner."

Chief Vintner was the rough-looking man Homer had first seen. He shoved into Homer's view, then kicked the boy in the buttocks. "Move it, Doogie! Help throw that crocodile or whatever the hell it is overboard!"

"He's an alligator," Homer said, "and please leave him alone. He belongs to my wife. His name is Albert."

Vintner turned on Homer. "Who are you, smuggler man?"

"I'm no smuggler. My name is Homer Hickam. I'm a coal miner except I've been working on the fishing boat *Dorothy Howard*. My alligator jumped off and I jumped with him. Then I was picked up by that boat you sank."

Vintner's face darkened and he raised his hand as if to strike Homer. Then, apparently having a second thought, he lowered it. "It's not often I hear so many lies told at the same time. For not much, I'd flog you to an inch of your life. However, you're saved from the cat for the moment because the captain wants to see you. Come with me."

The other men were grabbing at Albert, trying to get a grip on him, but Albert was holding his own. He turned to present his teeth to each man who came near. Homer crawled over to shield him. "If you're going to throw my alligator overboard, you'll have to toss me in with him."

"Leave the creature alone, you boys!" Vintner growled. "We'll let the captain decide what to do."

"Do you have a rope I could use to make a leash?" Homer asked. "Albert will walk on a leash."

"There's no *rope* on this tub, you gnarly landsman," Vintner snarled, "but there is *line*. You'll not use the foul word *rope* again as long as you're a crewman on this boat. Understood?"

"But I'm not a crewman," Homer said.

Vintner laughed, and harshly.

Homer was handed a length of what appeared to be a rope by the boy in the tub hat, who said, "Here's your line."

"Why do they call this a line and not a rope?" Homer asked in a whisper.

"No idea, sir. And if you know what's good for you, you won't ask any more questions about it. Chief Vintner will take a loop of rope, I mean *line*, and give you a bash for it, don't think he won't."

Homer shrugged, then used what still appeared to be a rope to fashion a leash for Albert. When he was done, Chief Vintner took Homer by the arm. "Come now, we'll meet the captain!"

Vintner, holding a sack filled with the burlap bags, also recovered from the sea, dragged Homer along while Albert waddled behind. Now that nobody was trying to grab him, he began to inspect the boat with interest. Soon he was grinning.

On the bridge, Chief Vintner knocked on the hatch and a booming voice yelled, "Enter!"

Vintner dragged Homer and Albert inside. "Captain Wolf, these are the two fellows we pulled out of the drink!"

The man who turned toward Homer was gaunt as a scarecrow, his face cadaverous and horribly scarred. His cheeks were bewhiskered and one eye seemed to enjoy wandering off on its own. "Well," he growled, "what do you have to say for yourself? Be careful. It will all go into the record."

Homer didn't understand what the record was but he nevertheless said, "It started when I jumped off my fishing boat. . . ."

"Deserted!"

"No, sir. You see, my alligator—well, actually, he's my wife's alligator—he jumped off and I had to go in after him since—"

"So far, all you've heard are lies, Captain," Vintner said. "This man and his crocodile were on that smuggler's boat. We hauled them out of the drink."

"Deserters *and* smugglers! Chief, what in blue blazes are you doing with criminals on my bridge? This will not abide! Is this all of them?"

"Two more, sir, but they drowned. We're hauling in the bodies now."

"What were their names, boy?" the captain growled at Homer.

"Roy-Boy and Merganser, sir."

The captain huffed. "Those two! Don't bother. Let the sharks have them. What else you got for me, Chief?"

"Bags of doubtlessly illicit goods, sir." Vintner held up the bag he was carrying. "I believe they are called *burlocks* in the arcane terminology of smugglers."

"Open one of them, man!" the captain demanded.

Vintner reached in the bag, drew out a bag, and opened it, spreading its contents on the captain's gray metal desk. The dim light inside the wheelhouse did not diminish the sparkling jewels that were displayed. The captain plucked up one of them and held it next to the porthole. "Emerald. Finest quality." He carefully replaced the gem and picked up another one. "Opal. Perfect and full of fire." A necklace caught his eye. "Topaz and silver, very nice workmanship. Colonial period, no doubt. How many packages?"

"Thirteen, sir."

"Toss one of them back into the drink."

Vintner raised his eyebrows. "Which one, Captain?"

"How the hell should I know? Choose one and do what I say! I'll not have thirteen of anything on my cutter!" The captain turned to Homer and Albert. "Where did these packages come from?"

Homer searched his memory. "The name of the boat that delivered them was the *Theodosia*, sir."

"The *Theodosia*! Those lowlifes. I've been chasing them for years." He pondered Homer. "Hold up your hand!"

"My hand, sir?"

"This one, recruit," the chief said, taking Homer's right hand, twisting it palm out, and jerking it and his arm upward.

"The crocodile, too, Chief," Captain Wolf said. "Raise its right paw up to take the pledge."

"He'll bite me if I do, Captain," Chief Vintner said.

"Then call Doogie."

Vintner opened the hatch and yelled for Doogie and, very soon, the boy with the tub hat ran in, breathing hard. "Yes, sir!"

"Kneel by that crocodile, Doogie, and raise its right paw."

"But it will bite me, sir!"

"I gave you an order."

Doogie knelt and, cringing, picked up Albert's right paw. Albert looked at Doogie with interest and curiosity, and then smiled. Doogie smiled crookedly back.

Captain Wolf squared his shoulders. "Repeat after me. I swear to be in the Coast Guard and do exactly what I'm told when I'm told to do it by just about everybody but mainly my captain and chief petty officer." When Homer didn't immediately respond, mainly because he was too shocked at the turn of events, the captain added, "Say it or I'll have you flogged and flung back into the ocean. That includes the crocodile."

"He's an alligator," Homer grumbled, but did his best to say what he'd been told to say. He mangled most of it but thought he got through it okay, considering. When he was finished, or at least stopped, everyone turned to Albert, who responded with a grunt, which seemed to satisfy all concerned.

"Welcome to the United States Coast Guard," Chief Vintner said. "In case you wondered, our unofficial motto is 'You have to go out but you don't have to come back.'"

Homer, whose wits were returning, considered the unofficial motto. "That's sort of like coal mining," he concluded.

The captain put the gems back into the burlap bag. "You may leave the burlocks with me, Chief, except the one you are to toss overboard. And get these two out of my sight. The next time I see them, they will be proper sailors."

The chief replied with a hearty "Aye, aye, sir!" and chose a burlock before escorting Homer and Albert down from the flying bridge and put to work mopping the deck. At least, Homer was put to work. Albert instantly became a favorite of the crew and given a little white tub hat to wear (a drawstring kept it on his head) and treated with a mixture of deference, amusement, and awe. The chief, having disposed of the thirteenth burlock in his quarters (since, after all, it was no longer thirteen but just one), considered Albert. "You know," he said to no one in particular, "I think that crocodile must be a very lucky creature whose luck will surely now be ours."

→ ←

Sure enough, before too many hours passed, the Helene *luckily came across* the ship she had looked for so diligently over the months, the *Theodosia.*

Chief Vintner barged into the captain's office, catching Captain Wolf studying the illegal gems, several of them already in his pocket for safe-keeping.

"What the hell do you want?" the captain demanded.

"Sir, enemy in sight!"

"I presume you refer to the *Theodosia.*"

"Aye, sir, the *Theodosia* she is and showing us her heels."

"Then get after her, Chief! We'll teach her captain and crew to break the sovereign antismuggling laws of these United States! Blood will flow, Chief! Do you hear me? *Blood will flow!*"

33

ALL THROUGH THE NIGHT, THE *DOROTHY* WANDERED ACROSS the sea. If there was anything to see, it was not seen, but that did not deter Elsie, who peered into the gloom for any sign of life, any splash that might indicate a struggling husband or beloved alligator. The rooster, who had rushed across the plank at the last second, stood on the bow, looking fiercely into the darkness. Nothing was seen.

When the sun peeped above the horizon, and the gulls rose from the sea to greet the newborn day, though she looked until her eyes were raw, Elsie could still see nothing except the everlasting sea. Until Marley called out, "There's what looks like a body over there!"

A lump rose in Elsie's throat as Captain Bob steered his boat alongside. Marley, his face screwed up in fear—dead men afloat were surely bad ju-ju—turned it over to find its face chewed off by sharks.

"It is not Homer," Elsie declared after willing herself to look.

"Well, I don't need to see his face to know him," Captain Bob said. "See that tattoo of a duck on the back of his hand? It's Merganser Finney from up Myrtle Beach way. He comes from a long line of beach trash."

"Don't go talking about the dead that way, Captain Bob!" Marley cried, making secret signs with his hands to ward off the spirit of the man still bobbing in the sea.

"Set Merganser back adrift," Captain Bob directed. "His kin won't care and there won't be nobody wantin' to bury him. It'd be left to us and I'm in no mood to dig a grave nor find a preacher to stand over it."

"Don't you dare push him away," Elsie said. "He is still a man and deserves respect."

Captain Bob looked grim but nodded reluctant agreement. Marley, after gulping several times, caught the body with a boat hook and, with Elsie's help, hauled it in to sprawl on the deck. An eel of some type crawled out of the cadaver's ear and wriggled across the deck and through the scupper into the sea.

"It don't take long before the creatures of the ocean make anything their home and hearth," Marley marveled, making more secret signs.

Elsie went below, fetched a tarp, and covered the body. The rooster came over and looked up at Elsie with an inquiring expression on its beaked face. "What is it, rooster?" she demanded and then noticed the boat was aimed toward shore and making headway. She turned to Captain Bob. "What do you think you're doing?"

"Why, taking Merganser to the beach, Elsie. That's what you wanted when you had him brought aboard, is it not true?"

"It is not true. Turn us around and keep looking. I have a hunch this man had something to do with what's happened to Homer. Besides that, you're responsible for my husband going overboard, him and Albert, and I won't have you give up the search so easily."

When Captain Bob resolutely kept churning toward shore, Elsie marched up beside him and pulled back the throttle. The engine groaned, then died.

"You are a crazy female," Captain Bob said. He tried to start the engine but it only sputtered. "Now you've done it. We're adrift with a dead body."

"It will begin to stink, Miss Elsie," Marley explained, nodding toward the covered body. "Stink unto high heaven such that you will never take a breath without thinking of that stink."

"I am willing to chance that, Marley," Elsie answered, resolutely. "Now, Captain Bob, stop playing games with me. You are deliberately pretending not to be able to start the engine just to scare me. Well, I'm not scared. Do I have to go after my pistol?"

"Hark!" Marley called, a hand cupped to an ear. "Did you hear that?"

Elsie and Captain Bob both cocked their ears toward the open sea. "Gunfire," Captain Bob said.

"And a volume of it, too," Marley said. "Who declared war, I wonder?"

"Has to be that crazy bastard Captain Wolf."

Elsie faced the gunfire. "They're there," she said. "I know they are. We have to go see!"

"We're not going anywhere," Captain Bob said. "Captain Wolf is as crazy a gent who ever donned Coast Guard blue. He starts his boys shootin', there's no way we dare run up on him. Bullets will be flying everywhere."

Elsie squinted toward the noise of the battle, and then pulled Captain Bob aside. "You've admired me, Captain Bob, and made no secret of that. I presume if I'm a widow, you'll take that as an advantage, but how are we to know if we don't have a look?"

Captain Bob narrowed his eyes. "Are you saying that there might be room for me in your heart if in fact your husband is gone?"

"It is well known," Elsie replied, "that a woman uncertain of her widowhood can go years spurning all other men for no other reason than she must be sure of her status. I call to your attention Penelope, who waited twenty years for Ulysses."

"Twenty years, madam?"

"Such is the lot of the uncertain spouse." Elsie batted her eyes.

Captain Bob quivered with outrage. "I shan't wait so long!"

Elsie pointed toward the ever-increasing barrage of gunfire. "There might be the answer to your prayers . . . and mine."

Captain Bob cranked the engine, which started up immediately. He steered the *Dorothy* away from shore and toward the noise of battle, the rooster once more taking up a position on the bow.

"Oh, Captain, my captain!" Marley wailed. "We're in for it now!"

34

"THERE, LADS, IS THE QUARRY," CAPTAIN WOLF SHOUTED
to his assembled coastguardsmen. "And the glory I know you've always
wanted!"

His crew stared at him with uncertainty. Most of them were just boys
who'd left their mother's arms for the promise of being paid on a regular
basis or had been jerked awake after being found asleep on the beach
and pressed into the service of an armed force of the American federal
government. Their training consisted entirely of service aboard the
Helene. They knew nothing of glory or even much about the rifles and
cartridge bags that Chief Vintner had given a few of them. Cutlasses,
knives, and brass knuckles had also been handed out. They looked at
their implements of war with more curiosity than eagerness.

Captain Wolf was not unaware of the situation. "Now, boys, most of
you have never been in combat but that don't change the fact that you're
American fighting men. Once in battle, you'll get the hang of it. Chief,
make sure our lads know how to load and fire their rifles. The rest of you,
swipe the blade or bash 'em in the teeth! Nothing to it!"

Chief Vintner showed those who'd been issued a rifle how to load it. "Aim carefully, fellows, and pull your triggers only when you have the enemy in your sights."

Homer, observing all this, was wondering if he was expected to fight. All he had in his hands was a mop. He scanned the deck, noting several hatches that led below. Accordingly, he set his sights on the nearest of them but was caught up short by Chief Vintner. "Here now, recruit," the chief said, taking Homer by the neck of his shirt. "Where do you think you're going?" He broke off the working end of Homer's mop and handed the handle back to him. "There, a staff good as Little John ever used to knock down Robin Hood. You'll join the assault, boy, even though it will be against your friends in the trade."

"They're not my friends," Homer said. He looked at the mop handle and wondered what he was supposed to do with it.

"What about the crocodile?" one of the men asked.

Chief Vintner seized on the remark. "Aye, lads, our lucky charm, the croc of the sea! Give praise and thanks we have this fierce creature with us for no one can deny us victory with, um . . ." He leaned in close to Homer and asked, out of the corner of his mouth, "What's his name?"

Homer allowed himself a quick sigh. "Albert and he's an alligator, not a crocodile."

"Albert!" Vintner cried. "Albert the crocodile will lead us to victory! Who shall carry him across?" He pointed at the boy. "You, Doogie, you and the former smuggler will carry Albert across to the *Theodosia* and thus we shall all follow and smite them, yea to victory!"

"Huzzah for Albert!" a crewman yelled out. "Huzzah!" came back the answering cry from the rest of the coastguardsmen. "Three cheers for our crocodile! *Rah! Rah! Rah!*"

"You men!" Captain Wolf shouted from aft the bridge. "Prepare yourself. We shall be on the enemy in a nonce!"

Although none of the Coast Guard crew had the slightest idea what a nonce was, apparently the smugglers did as the *Theodosia* suddenly came about. From her bow came a puff of smoke followed by a sharp *crack* and a whistle and a thrum of the air as something heavy and very fast flew over the *Helene*. Chief Vintner raced forward as the rest of the crew dropped to the deck. "I see a smoke ring! They have a cannon on board, Captain! Get up, you swine! Get up, I say!" He turned to the bridge. "Faster, Captain Wolf, faster so we may close with these thugs and destroy their terrible machine!"

→ ←

Captain Wolf raised an eyebrow at the chief's theatrics, then went back inside the wheelhouse to take the wheel himself. "Horatio Nelson said it best, my lad," he advised the crewman just relieved of the wheel. "No fancy maneuvers. Just go straight at 'em!"

"Horatio who, sir?" asked the crewman.

"The greatest admiral in history even though he was a goddam Limey!" Captain Wolf yelled just as a cannonball smashed into the bridge, punching a hole fore and aft. Captain Wolf turned to look at the holes and then noticed the crewman lying on the deck. "You all right, lad? Your eyes are as wide as a hooked swordfish."

"I'm okay, sir," the crewman said as he slowly picked himself up.

"Then arm yourself! We're about to collide with the smuggler!"

"Collide, sir?" the crewman asked just as the collision occurred, knocking him back to the deck. The bridge tilted crazily and Captain Wolf, staggered for a moment, threw open a locker and pulled out a cutlass before stomping out on the flying bridge. "At 'em, men!" he yelled, waving the cutlass. "Show 'em the spirit of the United States Coast Guard!"

What came next was complete confusion. Shots were fired and the coastguardsmen ran to and fro, uncertain what they were supposed to do. "At 'em, lads!" Captain Wolf kept yelling from the bridge but his men hung back, not exactly certain what "At 'em!" entailed.

Chief Vintner, seeing his hapless crew so confused, took Albert away from Doogie and tossed him across to the *Theodosia.* When Albert landed, he snapped his jaws at the smugglers, who took one look and ran. "Follow our crocodile!" Vintner screamed.

The coastguardsmen still hesitated until Homer, worried for Albert, jumped across the space between the two boats. A smuggler tried to cut him down with a machete and he used the mop handle like a baseball bat, knocking the machete from the man's hands and then whacking him hard on his head. The man dropped like a sack of beans. The other smugglers shrank back from the formidable pair suddenly in their midst.

"Follow the recruit and the crocodile!" Chief Vintner demanded. This time, seeing the good example of both Homer and Albert, the coastguardsmen rose up and leapt onto the smuggler's deck like a flying wave of humanity. The battle was quick and bloody although not particularly deadly because most of the smugglers instantly dropped their weapons and gave up the ship. This was fortunate, seeing as how the *Theodosia* was hopelessly holed by the *Helene's* bow and was already settling in the water.

Two of the smugglers, however, did not give up. They advanced on Homer, their machetes raised. One of the men was very big and one was very small. To his amazement, Homer recognized them both. "Slick? Huddie? Is it really you?"

The two men stopped and peered at Homer and then Albert. "It is not us," Slick said.

"Stop lying, Slick. I recognize you. What are you doing on this boat?"

Slick and Huddie looked at one another and then Slick answered, "We can't make an honest living robbing banks or blowing up sock mills or betting on baseball games so we decided to go to the sea and seek our fortune."

"I thought you got money from Young Mrs. Feldman," Homer said.

"We did but it was took by the sheriff after he arrested us for stealing that hearse. We can't catch a break."

Despite all their criminality, Homer felt a little sad for Slick and Huddie. They obviously had poor ju-ju. "You must live beneath an unlucky star," he said.

"Quite honestly, I believe our bad luck is knowing you and that alligator. You both therefore have to die. Huddie, let us take care of business."

Huddie nodded and both men raised their machetes and came forward. Homer blocked the first swipe of Huddie's blade with his mop handle but then the giant raised his machete for a killing blow. Homer, his back to the sea, had no choice but to dive into the water. After he plunged in, he heard another splash and saw Albert had joined him. Slick and Huddie were left behind on the *Theodosia* to helplessly wave their machetes and curse, both of which they accomplished with exceeding zeal.

Albert swam over and Homer grabbed hold of him, and then both watched until the two boats, smuggler and federal cutter, drifted out of sight. The sun began to set amid a burst of flamboyant pinks and purples and blues and Homer drew Albert closer, fearful of spending another night on a dark, cold, and dangerous ocean. But then a distant hull drew near, nearer, and found them.

It was the *Dorothy*, whose captain, first mate, and supercargo named Elsie and a rooster with no name had come after their orphans and miraculously found them, coal miner and reptile, which was followed by great rejoicing by some but not all.

35

ELSIE SOUGHT OUT GRACE IN THE MORNING, FINDING her as always in her room. The sun had penetrated the parted curtains behind her and she seemed but a shining wisp in the streaming light. "You are leaving," she said before Elsie could open her mouth.

"Yes," Elsie said. "I am here to say goodbye, Grace, and to thank you for showing me how to properly run a boardinghouse." Elsie looked past the woman toward the swash, which was a-shimmer with sunlight. "My God, how I love this place!"

"Yet, you are going."

Elsie rushed to explain. "It is clear I have broken Captain Bob's heart. I don't want to continue to cause him pain. That and he has put Homer ashore and won't allow him to work as a fisherman anymore."

Grace cocked her head and said, "Homer could work on other boats and my brother could be contained. He is a good man—although lonely—but another woman will come along for him by and by. No, Elsie, I believe you are leaving because you know it is time for you to go. Your journey is not yet complete. There is much for you to see and do before you can return."

Elsie's eyes were wet and her voice choked with emotion. She hated to leave but knew she must for the very reasons Grace had said. "Do you think I will ever come back?" she asked her friend.

"Of course. But before you go, I think you should walk the beach, the big beach, not the one on the sound, and contemplate what will come and what it is that will bring you back to this place when the time is right."

"Oh, I will!" Elsie cried. She moved forward to give Grace a farewell hug.

Grace held up her hands and backed away. "Please understand. It is not proper to embrace me for my condition makes me untouchable. But it is time for you to turn about and go. Know that I shall be watching you as time goes by and waiting for you to return. Someday, Elsie, you and I will walk the big beach together, the one that goes all the way to the tip of the peninsula. Do you understand? Now, give us a smile and be off."

Elsie gave Grace the requested smile and went off, thence to climb into the Buick, which was, at Captain Oscar's insistence, loaded up with food and drink in the trunk. In the back seat, Albert slept in the washtub lined by Homer's mother's quilt and the rooster sat on the alligator's head. On Homer's side of the car stood Captain Oscar, who wore a sad smile. On Elsie's side was Rose, who was crying softly, her tears dripping into the sand.

"Well, goodbye, goodbye," Captain Oscar said.

Rose leaned in the window and wrapped her thin arms around Elsie. "I shall miss you forever," she said.

Elsie hugged her tight. "I hope you'll be here when I come back."

"She will if I have anything to say about it," Captain Oscar said. "This place couldn't operate without Rose."

Rose ducked her head and smiled. "Thank you, Captain. I will stay and work for you for as long as you like."

Homer shook Captain Oscar's hand and turned to his wife. "Well, Elsie," he said, "let's get going if we're going."

Elsie and Rose shared another hug, and then Rose stepped back and looked away while trying unsuccessfully to hide the awful sadness on her face and her unabated tears. "Look after Grace, honey," Elsie said to her. "She acts like she doesn't need anything but she enjoys conversation, I think."

"Wait just a minute," Captain Oscar said. He stared at Elsie with an expression of dismay. "What did you just say about Grace?"

Elsie was confused by the anxious manner in which the captain asked the question. "Just that Rose should look after her," she answered.

"You've been talking to Grace?"

"Nearly every day since I've been here."

Captain Oscar took off his cap and worried it between his hands. "Elsie, my daughter has been dead for three years."

Elsie looked into the captain's eyes and saw that he was not joking. She looked through the Buick's back window and saw the faint outline of a human figure in Grace's bedroom. "I'm sorry, Captain," she said in an attempt to comfort him. "I have always been told I have an overactive imagination. Of course I couldn't have possibly talked to her."

Captain Oscar looked back at the house. Whether he saw the figure in the window, Elsie didn't know. He reached across Homer and grasped Elsie's hand, then let it go. "I wish you'd stay," he said.

"I just can't," Elsie replied evenly. "Grace said . . ." She took a breath. "I have come to understand I'm on a journey that is more than a journey. It has to have an end but this isn't it. Not yet, anyway."

Homer, not understanding anything of this, pressed the gas pedal and drove to the highway. "I need to go to the beach," Elsie said before he could make the turn.

Homer looked as if he wanted to argue but then turned in the direction of the sea. "Whatever you want," he said, quietly.

At the beach, Elsie got out of the Buick and took off her shoes. "Wait here," she said, dropping the shoes onto the floorboard. Without looking back at Homer, she threaded a path through the sea oats to the ocean's waves and the vast strand of sand that went for miles until it ended at the tip of a peninsula.

Elsie breathed in the tangy sea air. She walked to the water's edge, picking up shark's teeth and sea glass. When she felt someone beside her, she thought it was Homer, but when she looked up, it was Grace.

Startled, Elsie dropped the teeth and the glass. "Why are you here?"

"I love the beach."

"No," Elsie said. "I mean why are you *here*?"

"You mean why am I not in heaven?"

"Yes."

"I am, Elsie. And when the time comes, this will be your heaven, too."

Elsie took a deep breath and watched the seagulls wheeling overhead and sandpipers running across the sand. On the horizon of the otherwise crystal blue sky, puffy white clouds lay like strewn cotton balls. *God, she thought, it's so beautiful I want to be here forever!* She turned to tell Grace how she felt but discovered she was alone again. When she turned around, she saw only one set of footsteps, her own.

Pushing any thoughts out of her head except the beauty of all that surrounded her, she stood for a while, looking out to sea, then followed her footprints until she reached the Buick. She pulled open the door, waking Homer up.

"Did you see anyone else on the beach?" he asked as Elsie sat down on the front seat and pulled the door closed. She shook her head.

"Are you ready to go to Florida?"

Elsie nodded.

"Are you all right?"

"No."

"What can I do?"

"You can drive."

The rooster jumped up and nestled on Homer's shoulder, and Albert, coming awake, provided his *yeah-yeah-yeah* happy sound. Homer, still without a map, drove to the nearest highway, put the sun on his left, and headed tenaciously south.

I was nineteen, a student at Virginia Tech. A friend of mine who had his pilot's license took me flying in a small one-engine plane. It was a windy day. After flying over the beautiful spring countryside around Blacksburg, he made his approach at the airfield. As we landed, a powerful crosswind pushed up a wing. The other clipped the ground and we nearly cartwheeled. We were lucky to survive and knew it. "Hope nobody saw that," my buddy said.

My heart was stuck in my throat. "Me, too," I croaked.

The next time I saw my mom was when she was passing through Blacksburg, on her way to the house she and Dad had bought on the peninsula of Garden City Beach, just a little north of Murrell's Inlet. She sent word she was in the dormitory and I came down to see her.

Mom wasn't much for hugging. She waved me to a chair in the dayroom. "What's this about you being in a plane crash?" she demanded as I sat down in the chair across from her.

"Who told you that?"

"You think I don't have my spies down here? I know everything you do. Tell me what happened."

"Crosswind on landing," I said. "It wasn't the pilot's fault."

"How would you know? Did he apply downwind rudder and opposite aileron?"

I studied her. "How do you know anything about flying?"

She tilted her chin. "Oh, I could tell you a few stories about things I know that you don't know that I know."

"You've already told me more than a few," I pointed out.

"Don't get snippy," she warned, then relaxed into the chair. "I've missed our talks, Sonny. Since you've been in college, about the only people at the house I can talk to are the cats. Your dad ..." She shook her head. "Well, you know. He's always busy at the mine."

For the first time in the entire history of my life, I thought my mom looked a little pathetic. Maybe it was because she was getting older. She was all of fifty, after all. "So tell me how you learned about airplanes," I urged.

She instantly warmed to the task. "It was in Georgia," she said, "and we were still carrying Albert home...." ✦

PART VI

How Albert Flew

36

ELSIE THOUGHT THE SIGN ON THE GEORGIA BORDER WAS
the biggest, gaudiest sign she had yet seen announcing a state. It had a
gigantic peach-colored peach on it, a smiling blond woman holding a
basket filled with what appeared to be more peach-colored peaches, and
curving atop the sign the words:

WELCOME TO GEORGIA
OUR MOTTO: WISDOM, JUSTICE, AND MODERATION

Elsie read the motto, tried to make sense of it, failed, then closed her
eyes and tried to sleep. But sleep didn't come. Instead, she thought about
what was going to happen next and concluded she just didn't know.
She'd threatened to kill a man and risked her own life on the sea to save
Homer (and also Albert, of course) but she still didn't know how she felt
about her husband. She kept hunting through her heart to find a shim-
mer of love, but it just wasn't there. But maybe, she thought, that was
because she didn't know what love was. Homer was a good man, despite
his overly logical inclinations and tendency to criticize her, and other
women would probably be grateful to have him as a spouse. So why

didn't she? Maybe, she thought sadly, it was all because of Buddy. Buddy had spoiled her for Homer, perhaps for all other men. Buddy was so handsome and fun and, every time she'd been with him, he'd made her feel good about herself. But Buddy was gone, gone to New York and maybe Hollywood, gone to fame and fortune, and gone to women with big blue eyes and platinum hair. She allowed a long sigh. *So sad, so sad. What is to come of me?*

→ ←

On the other side of the bench seat, Homer occasionally sneaked looks at his wife and smiled inwardly. She loved him, he knew that now for certain, because why else would she have forced Captain Bob to look for him and then got aboard the *Dorothy* herself to make certain the job was done right? This thought caused his heart to soar and made him want to drive through Georgia as fast as the Buick would go, across the border into Florida, thence to Orlando. He had some money in his pocket—pay from Captain Bob—and there was food and drink from the boarding-house in the trunk. If he could just keep going, he figured they'd be across the Florida line in a day and a night, maybe less, and then only another day to Orlando to drop Albert off in a suitable swamp. After that he'd make as straight a shot as he possibly could to Coalwood, where he would beg the Captain for his job back. Because, after all, when a husband and wife were in love, what did it matter where they lived?

As the hours passed, the countryside became flatter and Homer saw cotton bushes in fields, row upon row. Wood frame houses, their tin roofs glittering in the hot sun, could be seen set far back from the road. No towns, big or small, appeared, nor did many traffic signs except occasional ones that identified the number of the road. Without a map, the numbers didn't mean anything, so Homer kept driving by instinct, choosing the best road that appeared to be heading south.

When he got hungry, he turned off the paved road and took a narrow dirt road that led beneath some shade trees. On the other side of the trees, he was pleased to find a lovely expanse of green grass and, upon it, a fine-looking, well-proportioned horse grazing on the grass. He drove up under a tree and touched Elsie's shoulder to wake her. "I've found us a fine spot for a picnic."

Elsie looked around. "Where are we?"

"Still in Georgia."

"Oh, yes, the state that intends to provide us with wisdom, justice, and moderation."

"A fine purpose," Homer said, "and so far, it appears to be a lovely state. I think you also know that Georgia shares a border with Florida, so we only have to get across it and then, before you know it, we'll be in Orlando, where we can let Albert go and drive back to Coalwood!"

Elsie reached over the seat and patted Albert's snout, then presented a forced smile. "Well, isn't that wonderful," she said.

By her forced smile, Homer suspected his wife didn't think his comment was wonderful at all. "What's wrong?" he asked, instantly regretting the question.

"Nothing," she replied.

"Are you sure?" Homer asked, also regretting that question.

"Well, actually, there's something we need to talk about."

At this declaration, Homer recalled some instruction from Captain Laird. "When a woman tells a man there's something they need to talk about," the great man had advised, "my advice is to avail yourself of the nearest door."

The nearest door in this case was the car door and Homer fingered the handle, then let it drop. He would hear her out. "What would those things be?" he asked.

"When we get to Orlando, I'd like to stay awhile," she said.

Homer relaxed and breathed out. "Well, sure. You'll want to visit your Uncle Aubrey."

"More than that," she said, "I'd like to stay for . . . as I said, a while. A good while."

"What do you mean a good while?" Homer asked, then felt something nudge his elbow. Startled, he looked up to see the horse had come over and was nuzzling his arm with its big nose. "Shoo, horse," he said.

Elsie opened the door and got out. "It's got a saddle and a bridle. It must have escaped from somewhere."

"It's not our responsibility, Elsie," Homer said. "What do you mean a good while?"

"I've always wanted to be a cowgirl," Elsie said, and before Homer could say anything else, she swung up in the horse's saddle with practiced ease, although, as far as Homer knew, she'd never been in a saddle before. She clicked her tongue, and the horse walked ahead and then broke into a trot with Elsie looking like she knew exactly what she was doing.

She must have learned in Orlando, Homer said to himself and then allowed his imagination to go into overdrive as his wife urged the horse into a gallop and he imagined the glamorous bachelorette Elsie Lavender and the oh-so-smooth Buddy Ebsen as they rode together along some romantic and tropical path in deep and decadent Florida. He found himself clenching his fists and was on the verge of chasing after Elsie, pulling her out of the saddle, and demanding how she knew how to ride, and whether "a good while" meant she had no intention of ever returning to

Coalwood. Angry and sad at the same time, he told himself that now was the time to finally get the truth out of his wife on why they were really on this journey.

But he didn't get the truth because there came from the sunlit sky a gigantic bird swooping low over the Buick, the rush of air from its wings knocking Homer to the ground, and then continuing on to dive at Elsie and the horse. The horse responded to this unexpected attack by bucking.

Homer, looking up from the grass, realized it wasn't a bird at all but an airplane and actually a vintage biplane. He climbed to his feet and watched the double-winged aircraft as it pulled up in preparation for another run. Then he saw that Elsie had been bucked off and, afraid that she was hurt, ran to her. "Are you all right?" he anxiously asked, going down on one knee and taking up her hand.

Elsie pushed herself up on one elbow. "Of course I am," she said, although she looked a bit dazed, her eyes slightly unfocused.

Homer ran his hands along her arms and down her legs.

"What are you doing?" she demanded.

"Feeling for broken bones."

"I don't have any broken bones," she said, and climbed to her feet to prove it just as the aircraft came whooshing over again, this time inclining its path and slowing enough to land in the field.

The plane's engine sputtered, coughed, and died. Then a man wearing a brown leather cap, black goggles, brown leather jacket, forest green jodhpurs, and brown boots climbed out of the aircraft and walked over to Homer and Elsie. He put his hands on his hips. "Were you stealing my horse?"

"No, sir, I was just riding her," Elsie answered, taking the occasion to brush off her skirt. "We supposed she'd gotten loose from somewhere and I thought if I rode her, she might take me to where that was."

The man pushed up his goggles and, though his face was dusty and spattered with oil spots, Homer saw it was a brown face, about the same color as the man's boots. He gave that a quick ponder, a Negro man flying an aircraft, and then inwardly shrugged for he believed the same thing Captain Laird believed, that a man should be judged by his skills and productivity, not by the color of his skin or who his parents were, either.

"Well, I believe you," the man said. "I call the mare Trixie. She's full of tricks and one of them is untying her rope." He stuck out his hand to Elsie and then Homer. "My name's Robinson R. Robinson but most folks call me Robby."

"Homer Hickam," Homer said. "This is my wife, Elsie, who apparently is also something of a trickster because, until today, I didn't know she knew how to ride a horse like an expert."

"I learned in Florida," Elsie said.

"This does not surprise me," Homer answered with a jealous frown.

Elsie changed the subject. "How did you become a pilot?"

"The late great war, Miss Elsie," Robby answered. "I was but a mechanic at an aerodrome in France but we ran short of pilots one day and since I'd practiced a bit with one of the instructors, they gave me a plane just like this one and a couple of bombs and off I went. When I hit my targets, they kept sending me up until the war ended. When I got back, I bought old Betsy here and we barnstormed all over the country. When I settled down, I started a crop-dusting company. Been bombing bugs for about ten years."

At this revelation, Elsie looked thoughtful. "You're wondering what the locals think about a black fellow in an airplane?" Robby asked. "These old boys around here are cotton farmers and if I take care of their crops, I could be sky blue pink for all they care."

Elsie walked to the airplane and ran her hands across the fabric of the fuselage and along the wing. Robby and Homer walked up just as she said, "I've always wanted to be a pilot."

"Elsie, no!" Homer blurted. "You can't keep wanting to be everything there is!"

"Well, I guess I can want to be anything I want to be," she answered, then asked, "How much for a lesson, Robby?"

Robby grinned. "For you, Miss Elsie? Well, I guess I'd do it for a smile and a quarter."

Elsie smiled. "I have a quarter, too," she said.

Homer said it again, although this time with a lower and quite defeated tone. "Elsie, no."

Elsie walked past Homer and he hurried to catch up with her. "I want to be more than you want me to be," she said, taking big strides toward the Buick.

"That's not true, "Homer replied when he caught up with her. "I just don't believe you have any idea what you want. Are you going to tell me what 'a good while' means?"

➤ ◄

Elsie did not answer. After going to the Buick and retrieving a quarter and handing it over to Robby, she began to receive instruction from the pilot on how to climb up and into the aircraft and what the various instruments were for and all about the rudder pedals and the throttle and the stick. With every word, Elsie's heart beat a little more strongly. She really had thought about being a pilot, or at least a stewardess for an airline. She had often stretched out on the grass in the backyard in Coalwood and looked up into that narrow strip of dusty air that passed for a sky and imagined herself flying in some manner from cloud to cloud. If, she had proposed to herself, she kept flying from cloud to cloud, just as if they might be islands, she might fly herself completely out of Coalwood and into a different place, even to a different reality. But her reveries never lasted long because the locomotive pulling the coal cars would rumble through town and the clouds and the sky would be obscured by dirty gouts of smoke, and then the coal dust, whipping off the coal cars as they gathered speed, would spread across the little town like a gray cloak, settling down on roofs and seeping into rooms, and cloaking dreams as if they had never existed.

Elsie settled into the hard wooden seat of the biplane and stared at the dials and gauges, and put her hands on the stick that came up through the floor. "Don't touch the stick until I tell you," Robby cautioned. "I'll get us in the air. When you get comfortable, I'll let you take over."

Robby turned the necessary switches on in his cockpit, then got out, grasped the propeller, and gave it a pull. The engine sprang into life and he climbed back in. "Are you ready?"

"Forever ready!" Elsie cried, her grin so wide it hurt her face.

Robby pulled his leather helmet down around his ears, then pushed the throttle forward and the old plane lumbered across the grassy meadow. When it got near a fence, Robby turned it around, then pushed the throttle to the firewall. With a puff of smoke, the aircraft rolled forward and gathered speed. Faster and faster it went until it hit a bump in the meadow that bounced it into the air. Elsie yelped in delight. When Robby put the biplane into a bank, its right wing pointed nearly straight down, she gasped at the glory of the sight of the meadow and the forest beyond and the red clay cotton fields and the Buick and Homer and Albert looking up. Robby leveled the plane and began to circle to gain altitude.

"*Wonderful, wonderful, wonderful!*" Elsie yelled and it really was. Every circle caused the biplane to go higher and with altitude came more wonders. Now she could see a river she had no idea was anywhere near and a big house that looked to be perhaps an old plantation house with gardens and a brick-paved driveway.

"Are you having fun?" Robby yelled.

"Oh, yes!" Elsie trilled.

"Mind if I do some acrobatics?"

"What?" Elsie asked

Robby proceeded to dive the biplane and pull up into a stall, which put the aircraft into another dive, this one ending up inverted and in a partial inside loop. The unhappy result of this was that Elsie, who did not have her seat belt on, started to drop out of the cockpit. She managed to jam her knees into the lip of the cockpit and she cried out, this time not in joy but fright.

Robby took note of his error and flipped the plane over and Elsie fell back into the seat. "Sorry!" he yelled. "I should have told you to put your seat belt on. You must be sitting on it."

Elsie discovered a leather belt she was indeed sitting on and latched it around her waist as tight as she could. She gave Robby a thumbs-up.

"Okay, let's do a touch-and-go," Robby said. He lined up on the meadow and descended until the biplane's wheels kissed the grass and then gunned the engine to take off again. The maneuver produced a throbbing wave of energy from the engine that caused Elsie to gasp in pleasure.

"You ready to fly her?" Robby asked.

"Oh, yes!" Elsie shouted over her shoulder.

"Take the stick and wobble it to the right. Feel that? When you start to turn, make it smooth and use the pedals, which control the rudder.

Okay. Turn right, press gently on the right pedal—that's it! Give it a little throttle, your nose is dropping. Perfect!"

Elsie made slow turns and gained and lost altitude and then learned how to land, her first touch-and-go perfect. "You're a natural-born pilot!" Robby called out. "Now, take us in. Land us."

And that's what Elsie did and she did so, perfectly. When the biplane stopped close to the Buick, Robby looked over at Homer. "How about you, young man? Would you like to fly among the clouds?"

"No, thank you," Homer politely answered.

"I flew, Homer!" Elsie yelled over the engine noise.

"I saw that you did," Homer replied in a voice that was diminished and sad.

The look on Homer's face caused Elsie to lose her joy and her smile faded. Could this man not ever be pleased with her accomplishments? "You need to go up, Homer," she said, climbing out.

"I'm not interested," Homer said, but then something clicked in his head. "But I think Albert would like it."

Elsie frowned. "That's crazy! Albert can't fly!"

"I think he can. And I'll go with him to make sure he's okay."

Elsie crossed her arms and stamped her foot. "Albert is my alligator and I forbid it!"

Homer slapped a ten-dollar bill in Robby's hand. "Let's go, Robby. You've got some new customers." Cradling Albert in his arms, he climbed in the aircraft, buckled up, and then looked out at Robby. "You either get in this airplane or I'm going to fly it myself," he growled.

Robby, after an apologetic glance at a clearly fuming Elsie, climbed into the biplane and soon had it in the air. Over the cotton fields and summer rivers of Georgia, Albert flew and flew and flew, grunting in pleasure at every new thing he saw while Homer, his mouth a hard line, saw virtually nothing at all, since he was thinking too hard. Elsie didn't need to tell him what "a good while" meant. As he flew through the wispy clouds with an alligator on his lap, he began to accept the truth. She was never going back to Coalwood. She didn't love him. Their marriage was over.

After landing, Homer handed Albert down to an anxious Elsie. "My little boy," she crooned. "I was so worried about you. Dammit, Homer! What were you thinking?"

Homer's anger made him brash. "Thinking? Who needs to think? I just thought I'd let Albert fly for *a good while*."

"Listen, Homer . . ."

Homer held up his hand. "Forget it," he said, then turned to Robby and shook his hand. "You have done a fine thing, Mr. Robinson," he said. "You gave Albert the sky."

"Elsie, too," Robby said.

"Yes, well, she always gets what she wants."

Robby briefly took Homer aside. "You've got a fine woman there, Homer," he said. "Full of adventure and sass. A woman like that is delicate in her feelings. I think you need to give in to her, if only a little."

"Giving in to her is what I do best, sir," Homer said, bitterly.

"You took that alligator up to irritate her, didn't you?"

"At first that was why. But then I remembered he saved my life not too long ago. I thought I'd show him my appreciation."

"Don't give up on her yet," Robby said and clapped him on the shoulder.

Homer shrugged. He wasn't the kind of fellow who gave up on much of anything but he was also a realist. Wherever Elsie was heading, he wasn't invited.

I was fifty-five. I had sold my memoir *Rocket Boys* to Universal Studios and they were making a movie based on it. Mom was invited to the set, where she met Chris Cooper, the actor who was playing her husband. I didn't tell her they were calling him "John" in the movie because the screenplay writer wanted to call me "Homer," instead of "Sonny," and there couldn't be two "Homers" in the film. I'd fought against the change and lost. "That's what you get for selling your baby to the slave traders," Joe Johnston, the director, quipped. He was right.

Mom hadn't been told about the name change. All she knew was she was standing in front of a man dressed in the same kind of work khakis my father wore, and the same hard-toe work boots, and the same white foreman's helmet. Chris had asked me for a few personal things of my father's and Mom saw her husband's Masonic ring and Bulova wristwatch right away. "I hope I do him justice," Chris said.

Mom looked Chris in the eye. "Are you a good actor?" she asked.

Chris was a bit startled by the question. "Well, some say so, Elsie," he said.

She eyed him up and down. "You'd better be," she said, and then walked away.

I caught up with her. "Mom, what's gotten into you?"

She was eighty-six then, and easily fatigued. We were in the tiny Tennessee town of Petros, which was busily pretending to be Coalwood. A scene was being set up in the yard of the house, which was supposed to be the Hickam house. Without asking for permission, Mom sat down in the assistant director's chair. I pulled up a chair beside her. "Are you okay?" I asked.

"That house doesn't look much like ours."

"It's just a movie, Mom."

"Well, you'd think they'd try to get a few things right. What's this about them calling Homer John?"

I winced. "I didn't know you knew that."

"You think I can't read a script? I've read the whole thing. I don't much like the way I'm in it, either. I wonder if Buddy knows about this movie."

"Buddy Ebsen? I could let him know if you want me to."

She considered my answer, and then shook her head. "No. After all this time, it wouldn't be right." She looked

CARRYING ALBERT HOME

out at the movie people. "That fellow is a gaffer," she said. "And that one's a best boy. Those good-looking girls, they're script assistants." She sighed. "They were always the prettiest things when your father and I made that movie. He told you about that, right?"

"About you making a movie?" I couldn't help but laugh. It was ridiculous.

She cocked an eyebrow. "You don't believe me? Albert was in it, too."

The assistant director came over. The scene they were setting up was ready but when he looked at his chair, he saw it was full of my mother. "You want me to move?" she demanded.

I could tell he did. I could also tell he didn't have the nerve to say it. "No, ma'am," he said. "I'll get another chair."

Mom saw Natalie Canerday, the actor playing her, standing on the front porch of the "Hickam" house for the scene. She shook her head. "If I'd known you were going to make me famous, Sonny, I'd have stayed younger and thinner."

And then she told me about the movie she and Dad and Albert made. ❧

291

PART VII

How Homer and Elsie
Saved a Movie
and Albert Played
a Crocodile

37

THERE IT WAS.

At last! *At long last!*

Homer could scarcely believe it and, in fact, wouldn't have believed it except there was the proof staring him in the face. The welcoming sign declared:

WELCOME TO FLORIDA, THE SUNSHINE STATE

There was a great big golden sun in the center of the sign and oranges all around the edge and a buxom woman in a swimsuit looking as if she was inviting the world to sample her pleasures.

Homer peered past the sign and decided the place didn't look that much different from Georgia. Green, flat, and hot. "Well, we made it," he said anyway. He thought something needed to be said to mark the occasion. He also wanted to break the silence that had been in the car for many miles.

Elsie's contribution was, "We need a map."

"Why? Right there's a sign that points to different places including Orlando."

"We don't know that's the best way. Maybe there's a shortcut."

"If there is, I'll figure it out," Homer replied stubbornly.

When darkness overtook them, and no signs had been seen for many miles, Elsie said, "We're lost."

"We're not lost," Homer replied. "We're just not sure where we are."

Elsie looked incredulously at Homer, then shook her head. "Truer words have never been spoken," she said.

Morosely and hopelessly, Homer kept driving until they at last came upon a big red and white sign that said:

ENTRANCE
FLORIDA'S SILVER SPRINGS
RELAX AND REFRESH AT THE
SHRINE OF THE WATER GODS

The promissory note that the sign provided was inviting enough that Homer turned off in the direction shown by the arrow on the sign. Before long he came upon a pleasant parking spot among a stand of pine trees. Homer parked and Elsie took a deep breath. "I've always loved the smell of pine," she said. "We never got that smell in Coalwood, only the stink of the train smoke and the coal dust."

"That stink, as you call it," Homer replied, "is the price of progress, that which paid for our food and the roof over our heads."

"It still stinks."

Homer tapped his fingers on the steering wheel, willing calm and dragging back his anger. He wanted to argue with Elsie, wanted to shout at her, but he just didn't think it would do any good. "Let's eat," was what he finally said.

After a dinner made from the fixings in the trunk, Elsie, Albert, and the rooster bedded down in the car while Homer unrolled a blanket on the ground, pulled another one over him, and slept with the hope that it wouldn't rain.

It didn't, and the morning was also very nice, cool and misty. Homer, after climbing from beneath the blanket, decided a change of shirt was in order. After stripping to the waist, he was looking in the trunk for another shirt when he heard the putt-putt of a motorcycle, which soon drew alongside. Astride it was a slim woman in jodhpurs, boots, canvas shirt, and a beret. Her brown hair was cut short in the modern style. "Oh, thank goodness, you've come, after all!" she exclaimed.

"Ma'am?" Homer responded, his eyebrows raised.

"You *are* Omar, right?"

"No, ma'am. My name is Homer."

"Oh, marvelous! We thought you weren't coming. This is going to please Eric so much!"

Elsie climbed out of the Buick, rubbing the sleep from her eyes. "Homer? Who are you talking to?"

"Who's this?" the woman on the motorcycle asked. "Oh, I see. Your agent sent an actress hoping for a gig." She squinted at Elsie. "And I can see why. There decidedly is a resemblance. Well, come along the both of you. Eric's waiting." When neither Homer nor Elsie moved, she added, "Why are you just standing there? I said come along. Chop-chop!"

Elsie opened the back door and coaxed out Albert. Scrabbling down, he waved his head and stuck his snout into the air, sniffing, after which he rolled onto his back. Elsie knelt and rubbed his belly while he made his *yeah-yeah-yeah* happy sound and waved his paws around.

"Good Lord!" the woman cried. "Your agent is a wonder! How did he know we needed a crocodile?"

"He's an alligator," Homer said.

The woman stared at Homer for a short second, then said, "Close enough. I'm Miss Mildred Trumball, assistant to the director, and that includes location casting. You, girl, get in my sidecar. Omar, you behind me. Can you carry the crocodile?"

"Albert needs to do his business before we go anywhere," Elsie said.

Miss Trumball considered Elsie's comment, then asked, "What's your name, girl?"

"Elsie. This is Albert."

"Eloise," she mispronounced. "What a beautiful name! Okay, here's what we're going to do. You take your crocodile to do his business, then walk down that road around the curve to the first cottage on the right. That's where Eric is. I'll take Omar—excuse me, young man, don't put your shirt on!—along to meet him first. Don't be long, Eloise. Come along, Omar. Eric's going to love you. I'm sure of it!"

Elsie walked over to Homer and, while Miss Trumball watched with her eyebrows raised, whispered into his ear, "Who *is* this?"

"I don't know," Homer whispered back. "Maybe we're in a park or something and need to pay our fee to this Eric person. Guess I'd best go along."

"But why no shirt?"

"Maybe he's weird and we'll get a discount."

"Okay, but don't take off your pants."

Homer, thinking he had just been given very good advice, climbed into the sidecar. As he motored away, he glanced back at Elsie and Albert, both of whom were headed for some nearby bushes.

Homer enjoyed riding in the sidecar but he didn't get to enjoy it long. Just around the curve of the dirt road was a line of cottages built of concrete blocks set back in the saw grass amid a grove of palmettos. On the porch of the first cottage sat a man in a metal chair. Two other men sat on the porch rail and a woman was on the steps. She was holding a notebook and was apparently reading aloud from it to the three men. When Miss Trumball shut down the motorcycle, Homer heard the woman on the steps say, ". . . and then Tarzan cries out and we see a montage of elephants and lions and buffalo. They come crashing down on the pygmy village and . . ."

To Homer's astonishment, the man in the chair swore vehemently. "That's the same gawdam ending there is in every other gawdam Tarzan movie! When are you buncha hacks ever gonna give me something original? Not a gawdam original thought in your gawdam heads. Get out of here! All of you, gawdammit! Who you got there, Miss Trumball?"

"Buster's stand-in, sir," she answered as Homer got out of the sidecar.

"Is this where I pay my fee?" Homer asked.

"Lemme have a look at him. Didn't I tell you gawdammed writers to get out of here? *Get!* And don't come back until you bring me something original."

As the two men and the woman scattered, the man rose from his chair and walked down the steps into the grass. A bandy-legged fellow in sunglasses, a baggy shirt, and khaki pants stuffed into high-top brown boots, he imperiously inspected Homer with the intensity and arrogance of a Roman senator choosing a slave. "Damned if he ain't close enough, Mildred," he said, reaching out and plucking a hair from Homer's chest. Homer winced. "We'll need to shave him, though."

"I just want to pay our fee, and then we need to go," Homer said, putting up his hands to protect his chest from further hair plucking.

"What's he talking about? Is he worrying about his fee? Well, you'll get fifty a week, young fellow, and not a penny more. And your food and lodging will come out of that. Why haven't you explained this to . . . what's his name?"

"His name is Omar, Eric. Omar, what's your last name?"

"Hickam," Homer said. "But I think there's been a misunderstanding here. My name isn't Omar, it's—"

"Now, listen to me, Omar," the man interrupted. "Clearly, you don't know who I am. Perhaps you think I'm a grip or a gaffer or the best boy on this flick but in fact I'm Eric Bakersfield. Yes, *that* Eric Bakersfield."

When Homer looked blank, Miss Trumball said, helpfully, "The famous director of many great movies."

Bakersfield, after a brief frown in her direction, continued, "But from here on, I am God almighty to you. What should you call me? You'll call me Mr. Bakersfield but mostly you'll call me 'Yes, sir, right away, sir,' and that's about all I want to hear out of your mouth. And who the gawdam hell is *that*?"

The director's gaze had shifted to Elsie, who had just come around the curve in the road with Albert.

Miss Trumball jumped in. "That's Eloise, Miss O'Leary's stand-in. The agency sent a crocodile along, too. They should get a gold star for that, don't you think?"

"Her name isn't Eloise," Homer pointed out, "and that isn't a croc—"

"What did I just tell you, Omar?" Bakersfield snarled. "Yes, sir, Mr. Bakersfield. Right away, Mr. Bakersfield. Mildred, this fella better learn the rules or I don't care how much he looks like Buster."

Homer wrinkled his forehead in consternation. So far, he had not understood much of anything these odd people had said. But before he could try once again to correct their various errors, a woman wearing a silk kimono and a man also wearing a silk kimono plus a beret ran up to Elsie like they were going to attack her. Instead, to Homer's relief, they only touched her hair and crooned over her figure. "She is gonna look so good in Maude's clothes," the woman said.

The man said, "She's gonna look *better* than Maude. Do we have to dye her hair, Mr. Bakersfield?"

Bakersfield walked over and ran his fingers through Elsie's hair, giving it a careful perusal. "Her color is fine but I'd like to see a little less curl in it."

A rugged-looking man in khakis and a pith helmet walked over from the cottage next door and knelt down beside Albert. "What a fine animal!" he enthused as he ran his hand over the alligator's bumps and ridges. "Very healthy, too. I can tell by his well-formed osteoderms. Obviously well trained and docile as well, not like our wild fellows here in the Springs. A little small for the wrestle scene, though."

"Camera angle and quick cuts can handle that, Chuck," Bakersfield said, loftily. "I'll make that creature look big as a house."

The man in the pith helmet looked up at Elsie. "I'm Chuck Noble, known around here as the reptile wrangler." He patted Albert on his head. Albert responded with a toothy grin. "Who trained him?"

"I guess I did," Elsie said, flustered and pleased while the man and the woman in silk kimonos continued to fuss with her hair and coo over her clear skin.

Bakersfield clapped his hands. "All right, Trish and Tommy, let's give the little lady some room, let her breathe."

"Did you pay the fee?" Elsie asked Homer.

"Fee? Is that all you care about, your fee?" Bakersfield demanded. "You're supposed to be artists!" He produced a hefty sigh of exasperation. "All right, fifty dollars a week for each of you and ten for the crocodile.

Fair enough? Right. Mildred, take Omar to meet Buster. Trish and Tommy, you take Eloise to meet Maude. Chuck, go forth and train the crocodile. Go on now! I've got to flesh out this gawdammed script with these gawdammed writers who couldn't write their way out of a gawdam mudhole. Go on, now. Chop-chop!"

In short order, the makeup artists dispersed with Elsie in tow. Chuck the reptile wrangler headed off with Albert on his leash and, Homer, his head spinning, found himself back in the sidecar bumping down the dirt road. When Miss Trumball next stopped, six cottages away, Homer decided to demand some answers. "I'm not getting out of this sidecar until I find out what's going on."

"What do you mean?" Miss Trumball asked.

"Elsie and I didn't mean to cause any trouble," Homer explained. "We parked overnight and meant to be on our way this morning. To tell you the truth, I don't understand anything about any of this."

Miss Trumball frowned until her eyes registered a glimmer of understanding. "You mean you're not from the agency?"

"Actually, we're from West Virginia."

"With a crocodile?"

"Albert's not a crocodile. He's an alligator. And he came from my wife's former boyfriend as a wedding gift. Her name is Elsie, not Eloise, and my name is actually Homer, not Omar, although I'll confess that's close. We're carrying Albert home, you see. We've been on the road for . . . well, I don't know how long. A long, long time."

"Well, ain't this a crush?" Miss Trumball erupted. "Eric's gonna be so disappointed! You and your wife are perfect and so is Albert! Couldn't you see your way to work for us, anyway? We're talking about one hundred and ten dollars a week! That's not chicken feed, you know!"

It was decidedly not chicken feed and Homer gave the offer some thought. He was, after all, uncertain of the finances he would need once they reached Orlando. He also didn't know exactly what was needed to get back to Coalwood, considering how long and difficult the journey had been so far. With those thoughts fixed in his mind, he shrugged and nodded. "Where do I sign up?"

"Oh, Omar! You're the best."

"Did I mention my name is really Homer?"

"Yes, you did, but you have to be Omar now. It'll confuse Eric too much to change. He doesn't do well with change."

"What if the real Omar shows up?"

"I don't believe he will. We heard last night he's in jail, which was why I was so surprised to see you here. Something to do with being drunk and disorderly and maybe murdering his girlfriend." She sighed. "Actors."

"Does Elsie have to be Eloise?"

"I'm afraid so." She brightened. "But Albert can be Albert!" She stuck out her hand. "So, do we have a deal?"

It was a deal and they shook on it. Then Miss Trumball led "Omar" to the cottage. "Buster!" she called. "It's Mildred. May I have a moment? I've got somebody I'd like for you to meet."

There came from within the cottage scurrying sounds, a crash as if something heavy and glass had fallen and broken, and then a male voice calling out, "Just a minute!"

The requested minute passed, then another, and then Homer saw a pretty much nude blond young woman, holding her clothes, run from the back of the cottage into the bushes. Miss Trumball lit up a cigarette. "Pretend you didn't see that. Well, hello, Buster!"

Her greeting was to a young man who'd stepped outside on the
porch. He was wearing a white terry-cloth robe and a grin on his cheerful, handsome face. "Who you got here, Mildred?" he asked.

"Buster, meet Omar. He's your new stand-in. Omar, this is Carl
"Buster" Spurlock, otherwise known as Tarzan the ape man!"

"Hiya," Spurlock said, giving Homer a wave. He turned to Trumball.
"I've been studying my lines."

"Yeah, I noticed. I must've missed the page where Tarzan takes off
his loincloth and lays the script girl."

"Aw, Mildred, it ain't like that."

"Buster, I'm not your mother or your wife. You want to play around,
that's your business. Just show up and know your lines when you're on
set, that's all I ask."

"Sure, sure," Spurlock said. He nodded again to Homer. "Good to
meetcha. See ya around the set." The screen door slapped shut behind
him.

Homer turned to Miss Trumball. "Was that really Buster Spurlock?"
he asked in astonishment.

"In the flesh. Don't get the wrong idea. Buster's not a bad fella. Neither smokes or drinks, can you imagine? But he's got an eye for the
dames. How about you, Omar? You got an eye for the dames?"

"Just one."

"Eloise?"

"Whatever you want to call her, she's the only one for me."

Miss Trumball laughed. "Well, you'd best be careful around here.
These young girls—and Eric doesn't hire one unless she's a beauty, save
yours truly—get kinda crazy on a movie set. It's like if they're making a
fantasy, they want to live one. You get me?"

Homer was starting to get Miss Trumball. He even liked her. He only hoped Elsie was doing all right, wherever she was. And he also hoped they weren't straightening her hair. He liked it curly.

→ ←

Elsie was led by the makeup artists to another cottage along the road. After Trish and Tommy explained to her that she was going to be part of a movie titled *Tarzan Meets His Mate,* Elsie discovered she was thrilled. "I have always wanted to be an actress," she said.

"You're a stand-in, not an actress," Trish said.

"I've always wanted to be one of those, too," Elsie replied.

The cottage in which the famous actress Maude O'Leary was staying had been painted pink just for her. Its interior was also done up in pink, including the little heart-shaped pillows on the couch and chairs. When Elsie came in, she glanced in at the bedroom, which had also been painted pink, although the bedspread was blue, which made, in Elsie's opinion, a nice contrast. The famous actress, dressed in an incongruously green silk robe, was sitting on the couch, a script on her lap, a cigarette dangling from her pink lips. Despite the color clash, Elsie thought O'Leary was just about the most beautiful woman she'd seen in the entire history of her life. When she looked up and blinked her gorgeous big blues, eyes Elsie would have gladly traded her own hazels for in a heartbeat, Elsie was completely, utterly, and totally ready to fall down and worship this mortal goddess.

"Who the fuck is this?" the goddess demanded. She removed the cigarette from her mouth and ground it into an ashtray.

"Her name is Eloise," Miss Trumball said, coming in through the screen door. "She's your new stand-in."

"What happened to the old one? Oh, don't tell me. Buster screwed her until she can't stand up long enough to piss in a pot. Am I right?"

"Nearly so," Tommy acknowledged, "except I think Eric added to the young lady's distress by offering her a side of his bed, too. She got so confused, she stole a thousand dollars out of petty cash and took off."

"I don't blame the bitch!" O'Leary declared. "Those bastards are the worst lays in Hollywood. Or so I've been told." She stretched out her legs and made a scissoring motion. "You'll never catch either of them between these lovely gams! You want a drink, honey?"

"Well . . . I am kind of thirsty," Elsie replied, still awed at being in the presence of the famous actress.

"Water's not what she has in mind, Eloise," Miss Trumball said as she entered the cottage without knocking. "And I'm sorry, Maude, Eric says the liquor cabinet stays locked until he declares the sun's over the yardarm."

"Fuck you, Mildred, and fuck Eric," O'Leary growled, then laughed and patted the cushion beside her. "Sit down, dear, let me have a look at you. Oh, you are a pretty one. I would murder someone—especially my husband, who's probably banging our maid even as I speak—to have your hair. And your skin. It's translucent! What are you? German?"

"English, Irish, and Cherokee," Elsie said.

Mildred smiled. "Like I said, German."

"Yes, ma'am," Elsie replied.

"Yes, ma'am! By gawd, we got here a true southern lady, too. You know where I'm from, Eloise? Ellis Island by way of Poland, that's me! My real name is Oshinski. Can you believe it? My agent said it sounded like 'oh shitski,' said I was henceforth Maude O'Leary and here I sit, a Polack pretending to be a lass of the Emerald Isle. Now, that takes some true acting chops, girl! Stand up. Twirl around for me, won't you? Oh, gawdammit! Your ass makes mine look like a pair of fat pillows. Shit! You see that, Mildred?"

"Sure, Maude," Miss Trumball said while Elsie blushed furiously. "Well, come on, Eloise. Let's let Miss O'Leary study her lines. She's got a scene this afternoon."

"I'm gonna chew up the scenery with it, too," O'Leary said, then grinned broadly. "Bet you a hundred bucks I give both Buster and Eric a hard-on."

"I would never bet against you giving any man a hard-on, Maude," Miss Trumball said, winking at Tommy before ushering a thoroughly flustered Elsie outside.

"Mercy, I never knew a woman could cuss like that," Elsie said.

"Honey, she was just getting started. But she's got some acting talent, I'll give her that much. All Buster has to do is mostly grunt while the writers give her soliloquies to make up the difference. Don't know how she does it but she pulls it off."

"Do you think she'd teach me how to act?" Elsie asked.

"Just watch her, honey, that's the best way to learn."

"Oh, I will watch her," Elsie declared. "I will watch her every second I can." She shyly looked behind her. "Is my, um, bottom really all that . . . nice?"

"Oh, honey." Miss Trumball laughed. "I suspect it's a good thing you have no idea how beautiful you are. You'd be some trouble, I'm thinking."

"I used to have a boyfriend who said I was beautiful but I didn't much believe him. He's an actor, too. Buddy Ebsen."

Miss Trumball frowned. "I've heard of him. He's a dancer, too, right? And he was your boyfriend? Where did Omar come from?"

"West Virginia."

"Really? What does he do there?"

"He's a coal miner."

"That explains his muscles. What an Adonis you have there, young lady!"

To Elsie's astonishment, her lower lip trembled and a tear escaped and dribbled down her cheek. She wiped it away quickly.

"Here now. What's this?" Miss Trumball touched Elsie on her shoulder. "What could put a cloud across that pretty face?"

"Until this moment, I was certain I was going to leave Homer. I mean, Omar."

"Really? Well, when you're ready to cast him off, let me know. I'll get in line. Likely it'll be a long one."

Startled by her admission, Elsie looked up and sniffed. "You think so?"

"I know so, honey. That man of yours is a keen Joe."

Elsie studied Miss Trumball's expressive face and realized she wasn't lying. Then she recalled when she'd first seen Homer at the basketball game and how she thought he was so handsome. Well, he was still handsome and he was smart, too. Captain Laird sure thought he was, and who was smarter than Captain Laird? Now, with this unsought adulation of her husband, Elsie considered that maybe she was being a little rash about wanting to be shed of him. Maybe she needed to give him another chance. Maybe.

38

TO HOMER'S ASTONISHMENT, THAT NIGHT ELSIE CLIMBED in bed with him, just as any married woman would with her husband. She was obviously in the mood for romance and Homer cautiously complied although he feared her favors were only temporary. The next day, they read over the movie script and, because Elsie insisted on it, practiced some of the scenes. Homer felt ridiculous doing the scenes. His part mostly called for grunting.

Elsie clasped the script to her chest and said, "You were raised by apes, it is true, but you are not an ape. You are a man! A man, Tarzan! *A human man.* Do you understand me?"

"I don't know, Elsie," Homer said, lowering his script. "It seems to me Tarzan would have kind of noticed he wasn't an ape. I mean, why else would he have fashioned a loincloth? Apes don't wear them, far as I know."

Elsie glared at him. "Do you always have to be so literal?"

Homer gave her question some thought, then said, "Maybe it's a coal mining thing. If you don't look at the roof literally, it might fall literally on top of your head."

Elsie opened her mouth as if to argue, then shook her head and flipped the pages of the script. "All right, let's do this one. Jane sees Tarzan up in a tree and tries to coax him down."

Homer flipped to the scene. "I don't have any lines."

"Perfect," Elsie said, then launched into hers. Homer went to the refrigerator for orange juice.

Later that afternoon, Miss Trumball arranged for Homer and Elsie and Albert to go aboard a glass-bottomed boat. The water of Silver Springs was so clear that when Homer looked through the glass, it appeared that the boat was floating on air.

Albert started making his *yeah-yeah-yeah* happy sound and then over the side of the boat he went. Elsie was astonished to see him through the glass bottom. He was effortlessly keeping up with the boat while making corkscrew spirals through the water. "My little boy," she swooned. "He's such a good swimmer."

"I guess he is, Elsie," Homer allowed. "He is, after all, an alligator."

"I bet he can outswim any alligator there ever was."

Homer didn't argue; Albert had twice saved him in the ocean. But then a big, dark shape swept past the glass. Homer realized it was another alligator and it was a lot bigger than Albert.

"Oh, my stars!" Elsie screamed. "He's after Albert!" She turned to the boat operator. "Do something!"

"I'm sorry, ma'am," he said, "but there's nothing to be done. That's a bull alligator and he don't much like another gator come sniffin' around his harem. Reckon you just lost your pet."

Homer confidently predicted to himself the next three words out of Elsie's mouth and was not surprised. "Homer, *do something*!"

Homer rose from his seat and picked up a boat hook that was leaning in the corner of the boat. "Follow those alligators!" he demanded.

The boat operator could tell Homer was serious, mainly because he was holding the boat hook like he might use it on him, so he turned after the two alligators. When they came alongside the big bull, Homer climbed up on the bow and jabbed him in the head. The alligator abruptly turned away.

A minute later the boat caught up with Albert. Seeing no recourse, Homer leapt into the water, grabbed him by his tail, turned him around, and then put his arm across him for support. "Come on, Albert," he said, "you're worrying your mother." Albert waved his head back and forth, perhaps looking for the big bull, and then pulled Homer back to the boat.

Homer, kicking hard, handed Albert up to Elsie, who grabbed him beneath his front legs, the boat operator helping. Elsie fell back into the boat with her arms around her alligator. "Oh, Albert, I was sure you were going to be eaten!"

Homer, climbing aboard, started to remind her that, had the big bull alligator decided to turn around, he, Homer, could have been eaten, too, but recognized the futility of it.

"She surely loves that gator," the boat operator said.

"More than anything," Homer said, "or anybody."

That night, Miss Trumball came by their cottage. "Tomorrow's an important day," she said. "We're doing the tree house scene and you'll stand in for Buster and Maude. You saw that warehouse down by the boat dock? That's where the set is. You'll need to be there precisely at six A.M. Here's an alarm clock. Don't be late!"

Homer was not the type to be late for anything. He set the alarm clock for 4 A.M. and got up and made coffee, then woke Elsie up and fixed her buttered toast. "I could have made breakfast," she said, stretching prettily in the silk pajamas that Miss Trumball had loaned her. She was a beautiful sight and it fairly took Homer's breath away but he kept his focus on the day's work. "This should be fun," he said.

"Do you have your costume?"

"It's not much to have. A loincloth. They said I could wear my underwear if it was black. I said I'd never heard of black underwear and for some reason they thought that was funny."

"I get to wear a safari outfit," Elsie said. "Even a pith helmet!" She tried it on. "What do you think?"

Homer thought she looked fetching in the pith helmet but said, just for fun, "You look ridiculous," and got a frowny face for his trouble. It wasn't a serious frowny face, though, and Homer thought maybe, just maybe, Elsie was ready for a kiss. He took a step toward her but she turned toward Albert and gave him a kiss atop his head.

"Chuck the reptile wrangler is coming for you today, Albert," she said. "He's going to train you to wrestle with Buster Spurlock. Won't that be fun?"

Albert made his *yeah-yeah-yeah* sound.

Homer watched Elsie hug the alligator and, at that moment, wished his blood were cold. "Come on, Elsie," he said. "Let's not be late the first day."

At the warehouse, the gaffers and grips and director and assistant director were working furiously to set up the scene while the script girls and the writers looked on with feigned interest and nursed their hangovers.

"I'll show those bastards who think they can cheat John Bakersfield!" Bakersfield yelled just as Homer and Elsie walked in. "I don't need their soundstages. I can do it right here for nothing!"

Miss Trumball came over to greet the couple. "Eric's a little upset. He got a wire that the studio wants to charge us an exorbitant fee to use their soundstages for the interiors so John's decided to shoot everything right here."

Elsie noticed the grass hut set. "It's beautiful," Elsie said, enthralled.

"Glad you like it," Miss Trumball replied. "You're going to see a lot of it today." She waved at one of the assistant directors, a trim young man in tight khakis and brown boots. "Donald? Come over here and escort our stand-ins to makeup."

Donald hustled over. "Go with this young man," Miss Trumball ordered Homer and Elsie.

Donald escorted Homer and Elsie to their makeup rooms, which were actually nothing more than curtained-off areas in the warehouse. In Homer's room, a young woman holding a shaving mug and a razor, asked, "Would you mind if I shave your chest?"

Homer blushed. "All right," he said, giving in to the demands of the job.

Elsie's dressing area adjoined Homer's. "Your skin is just perfect," Homer overheard Trish say to her.

"If it's so perfect, why do you have to put all this stuff on my face?" Elsie responded.

"The lights are harsh and the camera doesn't always tell the truth," Tommy explained. "Trust us. We know what we're doing."

After Homer's chest was shaved, and he and Elsie were properly powdered and lipsticked, they emerged from behind the curtains and were told by the second assistant director, a nice young man named Claus, to stand in front of the tree house. After that, they were directed to kneel, then hold each other. After that, Elsie was supposed to crawl into the hut and Homer was to follow. These things they accomplished while Bakersfield fiddled with the lights before ordering the setup for another shot.

"That's it?" Homer asked Miss Trumball.

"What did you want to do? Load a few tons of coal? Movie acting is mostly waiting around."

Homer pondered Miss Trumball's revelation. "I'm not very good at being still," he confessed. "Maybe I could help sweep up or haul garbage."

Miss Trumball stood on her tiptoes and gave Homer a kiss on his cheek. "You are truly a piece of work! Are all coal miners like you?"

"Pretty much."

"Then, as soon as this movie is over, I'm going to rent a bus and ship as many coal miners as possible to Hollywood. It could use some men like you!"

Elsie didn't mind waiting around for the director and the lighting people and the gaffers and grips and cameramen to get the next shot ready. There were just so many interesting things to see! She could not recall ever having quite so much fun. She finally understood why Buddy had gone off to work in pictures.

"Omar is so handsome, Eloise," Trish gushed as she powdered Elsie's nose.

"You think so?"

"Oh, we all do," Tommy said. Elsie raised her eyebrows at him. He raised his eyebrows back. "Don't look so surprised, honey," he said. "You're not the only pretty thing who likes boys with muscles."

Then Elsie overheard Bakersfield say, "I'd like to make a complete run-through of the seduction scene but we just don't have time to teach these two amateurs their moves."

Elsie broke away from the makeup people and walked up to him. "Mr. Bakersfield," she said, "I know all of Jane's lines and Homer—um, I mean Omar—knows all of Tarzan's. We've been practicing."

"Who gave you the right to practice anything?" Bakersfield growled. "Do you know the blocking, too?"

"If it's like it says in the script, we do."

Bakersfield shrugged. "All right. I'm desperate. Let's give it a go."

And a go they gave. Elsie pretended to wake on the tree limb that held Tarzan's hut and then when she saw Homer in his loincloth standing a few feet away, she screamed. In response, Homer walked along the limb and knelt in front of her and stared. In spunky fashion, Elsie demanded, "Who are you? *What* are you?" When Homer looked suitably confused, she said, "Why did you bring me here? What are you going to do to me? Are you going to kiss me?"

"There's no line about kissing," a script girl said to the director.

"Keep rolling," Bakersfield snapped. "I like it!"

"Do you want to kiss me?" Elsie demanded.

"She's acting her little heart out!" Miss Trumball said.

"It ain't her heart the men in the audience will notice," Bakersfield replied. "Who unbuttoned her blouse?"

"Well, I think she must have."

Homer had stopped acting. He was truly confused. Did Elsie really want him to kiss her or was it Jane asking Tarzan or Eloise asking Omar? Taking a gamble, Homer kissed Elsie. "Cut!" Bakersfield shouted. "Omar, act like you want to take her clothes off!"

"Mr. Bakersfield?" Homer asked, turning and shielding his eyes against the glare of the lights. "What was that?"

"Pull her clothes off, boy! Oh, I see. You want motivation. Well, your blood is up. Jane, you scream, resist, then give in. You got it?"

"Yes, sir!" Elsie cried.

"All right." Bakersfield looked at the cameraman, who, despite the beret slung off-center on his head, looked more midwestern farmer than French. "Clarence, you ready?"

Clarence hitched up the belt beneath his ample gut. "Just give me the word," he replied in a laconic voice.

"Word, gawdammit!"

"Speed."

"Action!"

Homer touched Elsie's blouse but she grabbed his hand and pressed it to her chest. "Grab hold, buddy!" she hissed, and though he was initially shocked at her audacity, he played along because it was, after all, apparently his job. She pulled back, popping her blouse open, the buttons flying. Bakersfield rose from his chair. He began to cheer as Homer continued to tug at the blouse (with Elsie's hand clasped over his, holding it in place). Stumbling, Elsie fell back into the tree house. Homer, after a moment of indecision, crawled in after her. Within seconds, Bakersfield came in on his hands and knees to join them. "Bravo, *bravo*! Now, if I can only get Buster and Maude to do it that way!"

When Homer and Elsie and the director emerged from the tree house to the applause of the assembly, Buster Spurlock and Maude O'Leary had joined the set. Spurlock was conspicuously not applauding. When Bakersfield saw him, he demanded, "Did you see that performance, Buster? If I can get just half of that pure animal lust out of you, we'll pack them in."

The actor pushed his chest out. "Are you saying my performance hasn't been good enough?"

"You said it, Buster. Not me."

Spurlock turned and stalked out of the warehouse and slammed the door behind him. Maude O'Leary laughed and said, "Shit, I'll do that scene better. Just give me *that man*!"

Bakersfield gave the proposal some thought. "If Omar will turn his head just so . . . yes, I think it can be done. Get up there, Maude. Make it extemporaneous. You there, Eloise. Get down. Maude, there you go."

Homer watched Elsie reluctantly leave the set. "Do you want to kiss me, big boy?" O'Leary demanded before laughing raucously. "Yeah. You do. They all do!"

"Speed," Clarence the cameraman sighed.

"Action!" Bakersfield bleated.

"Why did you drag me up here, you big ape?" O'Leary demanded. "Oh, you think you're so big and strong . . . well, you *are* big and strong . . . now listen, you, don't even think about kissing me."

Homer, remembering how it was done with Elsie and presuming the director wanted him to do it again, put his hand on the actress's blouse and gave it a tug. O'Leary quickly turned so the blouse tore, buttons flying. Satisfied, she shrieked and fell backward, her boots scrabbling against the leaves and sticks as she pushed herself on her back inside the tree house opening. Homer fell on his knees and scrambled in behind her.

"Cut!" Bakersfield cried. "Oh, perfect, perfect. Oscar-winning performance, Maude. What an actress!"

Inside the tree house, O'Leary grabbed Homer and dragged him down on top of her. "You know," she said, "I never lock my cottage."

"We don't, either," Homer said. "Miss Trumball never gave us a key."

O'Leary laughed, then put her hand on the back of Homer's head and pulled him in for a long kiss. "No underwear!" She laughed. "I like that in a man." Shocked, he pulled away and rolled off of her. "Didn't you like it?" she asked.

He considered her question and told the truth. "I surely did," he said. "But I knew it wasn't right."

O'Leary laughed again. "Boy, if you were a box of chocolates in my house, all you'd be in ten minutes is empty little paper cups."

→ ←

Outside, Bakersfield was still excited about what had just happened. "Mildred, that scene's going to sell our movie."

Elsie, who was standing beside Tommy, sniffed. "I don't see what all the fuss is about."

Tommy grinned. "Girl," he said, "that man looked like he truly was going in after Maude to make some hot love."

"Well, he can't do that."

"Why not?"

"Because he's . . ." Elsie stopped and considered her next words, then said, "Because I'm his wife."

"Really? I've always wanted to be a wife."

"Me, too," Elsie said in a wistful tone. "Me, too."

39

WHAT HAPPENED NEXT COULD ONLY HAPPEN IN THE movies or, in this case, in the making of a movie. Spurlock was so mortified by the director's praise for Homer that when Homer climbed up on a limb and swung from one vine to another vine for a long shot of Tarzan, Spurlock insisted on repeating the shot.

"You can't do that, Buster," Bakersfield replied. "If you get hurt, we have to shut down."

"If I'm your star, why didn't you let me do that scene at the tree house with Maude?"

"Because the way Omar did it was perfect. Don't worry. He had his face turned so people will still think it's you."

"But it wasn't, and it won't take too long before everybody knows that. I'll be a laughingstock."

"Just stay off that rope, Buster, and that's an order!"

Spurlock waited until the director's back was turned, then climbed up the ladder to the limb where the vine was hung. "Watch this," he said and jumped, yelling the Tarzan yell all the way down until he hit the ground, whereupon he broke his arm.

Then Maude O'Leary received an offer from John Ford to star in one of his westerns. "Sorry, darling, I've already been here longer than what the contract requires," she said to Bakersfield, kissing him on his bald head. "And fame calls only once, you know."

"Ford will make you the drunk prostitute in the bar, you'll be on-screen less than thirty seconds, and it'll be the last anyone ever sees of you," the director predicted. But he gave her a kiss on her cheek and sent her on her way. She left for California on the next train.

Bakersfield slumped in his director's chair while the gaffers and grips and assistant directors and writers slipped away and hid. The only person with courage was Miss Trumball, who pulled up an empty chair with MAUDE O'LEARY printed on the back and leaned forward with her elbows on her thighs and her chin cupped in her hands. "Speak to me," she said. "Tell me all your troubles."

"I'm doomed, Mildred. Doomed. I'm out of money and out of time and I have five exterior scenes yet to film." Bakersfield tossed the script in the air. It landed with a thud.

"There is a way," Miss Trumball said. "Omar and Eloise."

Bakersfield chuckled mirthlessly. "They're beautiful young people but despite that one scene they did, they're still amateurs."

"Listen, Eric. Before I became your Miss Do Everything for the Director, I was one of the best drama coaches on Broadway. I can train them to move just like Buster and Maude."

"But even if you accomplish that," the director said, "one look at their faces and the audience will know they aren't Buster and Maude."

"You're the best director in Hollywood. You're a camera master. You can have a head turned here, a distance shot there. When you get to the editing room, you'll have miles of close-up footage of your stars to cut in."

Bakersfield raised his head. "Do you really think it can be done?"

"I think *you* can do it." She took his hand. "I know it."

"Get them," Bakersfield declared, giving her hand a squeeze. "Get those two wonderful, marvelous young people and *let's make a movie!*"

➜ ⬅

"Here's the setup, Omar," Bakersfield said to Homer. "Eloise over there, aka Jane, has been captured by vicious pygmies and—"

"Vicious pygmies?" Homer asked. "I thought pygmies were nice."

"Where did you hear that?"

"*National Geographic* magazine."

"A scurrilous rag filled with falsehoods. You must get it into your head that there are no more vicious people in the world than pygmies. These particular pygmies are especially evil and they're cannibals to boot. They've got Jane tied up, you see?"

Homer saw that Elsie was indeed tied up, her arms stretched between twin poles driven into the ground inside a fake pygmy village. Apparently, the pygmies didn't like her clothes, either, as they had been partially torn off, leaving Jane in nothing but two strips of cloth artfully and necessarily placed for the edification of the censors. Homer was embarrassed to have his wife so displayed but Elsie seemed to be enjoying it.

"Shall we rehearse the scene, Mr. Bakersfield?" Elsie asked.

"We are rehearsing, my dear," the director replied.

"Oh, help me," wailed Elsie as the brown-painted midgets who'd been hired as pygmies gathered around. "I am so very much in trouble! These vicious pygmies are so mean and one of them—*ouch!*—pinched me!"

"You have no lines, dear," Bakersfield pointed out. "Harry, stop that. I've warned you about pinching girls, haven't I? So, anyway, Omar, put this knife in your mouth—no, the other way—and run in, knock the pygmies aside, and cut Jane loose. She will then faint and you will carry her—"

"Excuse me, Mr. Bakersfield," Elsie interrupted. "Jane wouldn't faint. She lives in the jungle. She's very brave. Why would she faint?"

"Because it's in the script," Bakersfield replied.

When Elsie opened her mouth to argue, Miss Trumball interjected, "Because the pygmies haven't fed her or given her anything to drink for days. She is about to pass out from the heat of their pressing bodies, too, so it's coincidental that she faints just as Tarzan arrives."

Elsie gave that explanation some thought, then said, "I can live with that."

"Well, gooooood," Bakersfield said, stretching out the *o*'s. "Now, Omar, are you ready?"

Homer was ready. He was even starting to believe he was good at the acting business. Maybe coal mining wasn't all he could do, after all. "Yes, sir, I am," he said with steely resolve.

"All right. Ready, Clarence?"

The cameraman shrugged and said, "Speed."

"Action!"

When Bakersfield yelled "Cut!" after the scene, everybody cheered the grand new actors. The pygmies broke out the smokes.

→ ←

"Now, dear," Bakersfield said to Elsie as Chuck the reptile wrangler walked on set carrying a huge snake draped over his shoulders. "Take the snake and pretend it's strangling you."

Elsie's eyes widened. "It's awfully big."

"Just relax," Chuck said. "Her name is Gertrude. She recently ate so she's sleepy. Don't worry if she coils around you. That's just her way of using you for support while she takes her nap."

Homer was proud of Elsie when she allowed the giant snake to be draped on her shoulders. It was clearly heavy because her knees buckled beneath it. She looked at him and said, "Save me, honey." He looked at his script but didn't see that line. She was apparently improvising again. He smiled at her while she looked back with what he took to be mock horror.

"All right, Omar," Bakersfield said. "In this scene, Jane has been taking a little walk, sampling the delights of the jungle. But an evil snake has dropped from a tree and is determined to choke and eat her."

The snake's head had moved to circle around Elsie's throat. "Um, excuse me, but—"

"You have no lines, dear," the director interrupted her, then turned to the reptile wrangler, who was busily chatting up a script girl. "Chuck, kindly stop chatting up Martha there and tell Omar how best to peel Gertrude off Eloise."

The wrangler stepped in, put his arm under the snake, ran his hand up to its head, and pulled it back. "There you go. Nothing to it."

Elsie took a deep breath while Chuck held the snake but when he let it go, she bleated, "I can't breathe!"

"If you had a line, that would be a good one," Bakersfield said. "Okay, Omar. You're up when I say action. Do you feel motivated?"

"I don't know, Mr. Bakersfield," Homer answered. He frowned at Elsie, who was staggering around, making choking sounds when the cameras weren't even rolling and clearly overacting. "How does Tarzan know Jane is being attacked?"

"Hmmm, good question. Gawdammed writers didn't make that clear."

"Maybe she could yodel for help?"

"Yes, of course! Damn, Omar. You're a better writer than the writers.

Yes, she would yodel a kind of feminine version of the Tarzan yodel and then you—or Tarzan in real life or not real life or, oh, forget it—*you* would yodel back with your manly yodel and fly through the trees to save . . . Chuck, why has Eloise fallen down?"

When Elsie made a strangled and somewhat desperate yodel, the director rolled his eyes. "We'll dub that in later. Clarence? Are you ready?"

"Speed," came the laconic response.

"Action!" Bakersfield said.

Homer rushed in and pulled the snake off Elsie. Then he fell to the floor and pretended to wrestle with it while Elsie flopped around and sucked in air.

"Cut!" Bakersfield said at length. The snake had gone limp and was all but snoring. "Omar, that was perfect!"

The reptile wrangler took the snake away and Homer got up and walked over to Elsie, who was sitting up. "Are you all right?" he asked.

She looked at him in a way he'd never seen her look at him before. "You saved me," she said.

"It was in the script," he replied.

She stood and threw herself into his arms. "*You saved me!*"

Bakersfield looked at Miss Trumball and shrugged. "It was in the script," he said.

Miss Trumball smiled benevolently at the embracing couple. "This part wasn't in there, Eric," she said, "but it should have been."

➜ ⬅

It was the final scene. The cameras were in position by a lagoon where great cypresses hung over the water draped with Spanish moss and fake vines.

"Eloise," Bakersfield said, "you go into the water. Albert will follow. The underwater camera, configured on that platform, will capture everything as he swims up to you. The next shot will be you yodeling on the surface for help."

"Yes, sir, we can do that," Elsie said. She reached down and patted Albert's head. Albert responded with his *yeah-yeah-yeah* sound. "But Mr. Bakersfield?"

"Yeah?"

"I'm wearing a swimsuit."

"And a fetching one at that, my dear."

"Where would Jane get a swimsuit?"

When the director faltered, Miss Trumball said, "Jane found it in a trunk that fell off a passing safari."

"I don't recall that in the script."

"It's, um, implied."

Bakersfield intruded. "Clarence?"

"Yeah, okay. Speed."

"Action!"

Elsie dived into the cold water. "Come on in, Albert! Come to mama!"

The reptile wrangler let Albert loose and he slid on his belly into the water and swam over to Elsie, who flailed her arms and sank. Albert sank with her. When Elsie came up, she was laughing. In fact, everyone was laughing. "I love you so much, little boy," Elsie said, hugging Albert in close and being rewarded with a big grin.

"Cut," Bakersfield said. "We'll fix it in editing. Okay, Omar, you're up."

Homer went into the water, dog-paddled beside Elsie, and waited for the director to say, "Action." When he did, Homer grabbed Albert while Elsie swam away. Seeing her go, Albert tried to wiggle loose but Homer held on to him and let him struggle. Albert opened his mouth and brought his jaws down on Homer's arm, although he stopped before he brought blood. "No, Albert, no!" Homer said and kept pretend-wrestling. Pretty soon, Albert understood the game and joined in.

"Cut, cut, cut, and that's a wrap!" crowed Bakersfield. "Children, you have made my movie for me. We shall sell a million tickets!"

→ ←

For Elsie, the wrap party was great fun. Everyone kept saying how wonder-ful she was and that maybe she and Omar might have a future in show business. Afterward, Miss Trumball sought the couple out. "What are your plans?" she asked.

Homer and Elsie looked at each other. "Maybe we can be actors," Elsie proposed.

"I don't think you're cut out for show business," Miss Trumball replied firmly. "It's a tough business. It destroys most of the people who get into it, one way or the other. Trust me. Take this experience and savor it but let it end here."

Homer nodded. "After we carry Albert home, I guess I'll go back to coal mining," he said.

He looked at Elsie, who shook her head. "I still don't want to go back," she said.

"Why is it necessary for either one of you to go back there?" Miss Trumball asked.

"Well, I'm a coal miner," Homer explained. "And you just said I shouldn't be an actor."

"What if there was another kind of work you could do? Something a lot like coal mining that would let you stay in Florida?"

"There's nothing like that here."

Miss Trumball handed Homer a flyer. Elsie looked over his shoulder and read what the flyer said. "Could you?" Elsie asked Homer. "Would you?"

Homer looked at Elsie and his eyes softened. When she looked closer, she saw with a thrill that he had, at last, given in. "Yes," she heard him say, resolutely. "I could. I would. And, if I can get this job, I will."

The next morning, after packing up and carrying Albert in his washtub and placing him on the back seat, Homer and Elsie hugged the delegation of Hollywood folks, then waved their goodbyes. As Homer aimed the Buick out of Silver Springs, there was a flutter of feathers and the rooster landed inside the Buick. "Hey, rooster," Homer said. "Where the heck have you been?" The rooster hopped over and stood on Homer's shoulder, then settled by his ear.

Homer laughed and then, still with no map, turned at the entrance sign and steered south, ever south to their new life.

I was twenty-three and an army lieutenant assigned to the Fourth Infantry Division. We were headed to Vietnam. Just before we were to queue up and climb into our airplane for the long flight across the Pacific, I managed to find a telephone inside the terminal to call home. Mom wasn't there but Dad was. Since I'd been in the army, Dad had never written to me or said anything about my service. He left all that to Mom. Not sure what to say, I settled on the obvious. "Well, I'm off pretty soon," I told him.

"I'll tell your mom you called," came Dad's reply.

"Thanks."

With our conversation, such as it was, apparently exhausted, I started to say goodbye but then Dad suddenly said, "Before there's trouble, there's always signs. Get ahead of it by always paying attention to everything going on, even things that seem ordinary. Figure out what's the worst thing that could happen and be prepared."

I realized he was giving me advice about being in a dangerous place. "Like in the coal mine," I said.

"Yes, but it was the hurricane where I really learned about paying attention to the signs."

I could hear the NCOs calling out the names of the men in their platoons. "Dad, I'm going to have to go. Tell Mom I probably won't be able to call but I'll write."

"Let me tell you about the hurricane."

I glanced across the tarmac. The men were forming up. I waved at the first sergeant and pointed at the phone. He gave me a curt nod. I turned away and gripped the phone next to my ear. "Okay, Dad," I said, "I'm listening."

"Back then, I was full of myself," he said. "Filled with piss and vinegar. Bulletproof. Indestructible. That's because I was young—like you—and nothing bad was ever going to happen to me. But that's when you can get into the most trouble...."

PART VIII

How Homer, Elsie,
and Albert Endured
a Hurricane, a Real One
as Well as the
One in Their Hearts

40

THE ROAD OUT OF MIAMI FOLLOWED THE COASTLINE
past Homestead and kept going straight as an arrow across the vast
soggy grasslands of the Everglades until it reached Key Largo, after
which it followed a chain of coral islands, crossing a series of bridges and
ferries, until it reached the last island of the American southern archipel-
ago, called Key West.

The recently appointed chief rail inspector for the Florida East Coast
Railway was a former coal miner named Homer Hickam, who was on an
inspection trip to a new section of track on Key West. To journey there,
he had received special permission to drive rather than take the train.
This was so he might stop along the way, whenever he pleased, and inspect the track at his leisure. He was also given permission to take along
his wife, one Elsie Lavender Hickam, who chose to carry with them her
pet alligator, named Albert, as well as a rooster, unnamed.

➜ ⬅

Homer was enjoying the scenery provided by the narrow gray road that led
across the keys. Key Largo was the first. It was a long, narrow island

(thus its Spanish name) lined by mangroves and rocky beaches. Before they got to the first bridge, Elsie exclaimed, "Put the top down, Homer. Please! Put the top down!"

"I don't know, Elsie. The sun's pretty hot," Homer replied. "Wouldn't want you and Albert to get burned."

"We're tougher than that, boy," Elsie declared.

Homer pulled over and put the top down, strapping it tight against the buffeting wind coming off the Atlantic. Above, seagulls wheeled in the sunlit sky, calling out to their companions. He took a deep breath and slowly released it. He'd never been so happy, which gave him tremendous concern. If past experience was any guide, something was going to happen to take his happiness away. "Your hair's going to be a mess," he advised his wife as he started out again but Elsie didn't seem to care anything about her hair. In fact, she stood up and let the air blast into her face, her hair whipping back and forth like a flag.

"Please sit down, Elsie," Homer urged.

"Homer, you've got to loosen up," Elsie said. "We're Floridians now. That means we can be a little crazy when we want to be. Look, we're both young. We're never going to be young again. Come on. Why don't you take your shirt off, just fling it away? I'll hold the wheel."

Elsie sat down and held the wheel and Homer, after a moment of resistance, gave in and unbuttoned his shirt and took it off. He held it over the back seat to drop it beside Albert.

"Uh uh, boy," Elsie said. "That won't do. You got to fling it." She grabbed his shirt and threw it in the air. It fluttered for a moment before flying off the bridge into the Atlantic below.

"Elsie, I loved that shirt!" Homer complained, but seeing the cheerful expression on his wife's face, he smiled benevolently at her. "But it was just a shirt, after all. You're not going to get naked, are you?"

"Don't fret, Homer. I know that would embarrass you all over Florida. But I'm tempted!"

After crossing the bridge, they found themselves on Matecumbe Key. Homer stopped the car and put on a spare shirt, then drove on, soon encountering men who seemed to be moving in slow motion while working on the road. When the Buick rumbled by, they stopped even that motion and leaned on their shovels and watched with morose interest. Most of them had sad, gaunt faces, the pinkness about their eyes and noses indicating too much alcohol drunk too often.

"I read about these men," Homer told Elsie. "They've been sent down here by the New Deal. Most of them are veterans of the Great War and desperate for jobs."

To his astonishment, Homer recognized two of the men. "Slick and Huddie," he said in disbelief.

The pair took note of the Buick and its passengers. "Help us!" Slick cried. Huddie grunted a desperate bleat. They were dressed in ragged clothes.

Homer was so moved by their sad appearance, he stopped. The two threw down their shovels and came running. Slick whipped a cloth cap off his head and held it pleadingly. "Might you help us, kind sir? Ma'am? Albert?"

"What are you doing here?" Homer demanded. "I thought you were surely lost at sea."

"Them what washes ashore oft stays ashore," Slick answered mysteriously. "Anyway, we have ended up here in this chickenshit outfit, pardon the language, ma'am, and we really need to get away. The mosquitoes here are so big, t'other day one lifted me clear off my feet. I ain't got an inch on my body what ain't been bit. Huddie's in the same shape. They don't feed us too well here, neither. How about a lift?"

"I can't," Homer said. "I'm on official business and, anyway, there's no room."

"We'll ride on the bumper, on the hood, anywhere. Please, I'm begging you. If we don't get out, we're going to die here!"

"I hope you do," Elsie said. "You can rot for all I care."

"Oh, ma'am, we've changed!" Slick cried. "We've been brought so low we've even found the Lord. Huddie and I are always saying God's name out loud."

Elsie turned away from the ragged pair. "Homer, you're a kind man," she said. "You'd feel sorry for killing a hornet after it's stung you, but please don't help these creatures."

"But they look like they mean what they say," Homer said.

Elsie looked at him with an incredulous expression as Homer laid down his conditions to the nefarious pair. "We're headed to Key West but will be coming back in a couple of days. If I can, I'll pick you up and carry you to Miami. But you have to ride the entire way in the trunk. It's the best I can offer. After that, you have to promise me we'll never meet again."

"Oh, bless you, sir, bless you," Slick simpered. "The trunk is fine. Give us a lift and I swear you'll have seen the last of us. If we ain't here on the road, see those shacks down yonder on the beach? That's where we stay when we ain't working."

"You don't seem to be working at all," Elsie pointed out. "You seem to be standing around."

"Yes, ma'am, a crime, ain't it? I mean we make an entire dollar a day for doing not much of anything. But lots of these fellows, even though they are otherwise heroes of the Great War, are actually psychos, drunks, and bums. This is just a Roosevelt make-work project, if you get my drift. There's a couple guys, you see them there actually turning a shovel, they do all the work that gets done. The rest ain't worth the powder to blow 'em to hell, beg pardon, ma'am."

"Maybe you should help the ones who are working," Elsie said.

Slick put his cap back on and tipped it to her. "Yes, ma'am, you're right. We will, too, won't we, Huddie?"

Huddie's eyes were unfocused. At the sound of his name, he grunted. Slick waved his hand in front of Huddie's face. "You see? Huddie's done checked out of his brain."

"All right," Homer said. "See you in a couple of days."

Slick put his hands together in a prayerful pose. "Please don't forget us," he begged.

As Homer drove off, Elsie said, "Forget them, Homer."

"Now, Elsie . . ."

"They're bad men," Elsie said. "Why you want to help them is beyond me."

Homer shrugged. "I guess I feel sorry for them."

Elsie shook her head. "You'd feel sorry for a wolf that was chewing off your leg because it wasn't a prime cut of meat."

The Buick didn't travel far before a man in khakis and sunglasses waved it down. "Mornin', ma'am. Sir. Those two you were talkin' to, you mind tellin' me who they are?"

"I don't mind," Homer answered, "if you'll tell me why you're interested."

"I'm Delbert Voss, boss man of this work crew. I was forced by the higher-ups to put your friends to work but they seem shady to me."

"They seem shady to everybody," Elsie said. "And they're not our friends. I'd keep an eye on them if I were you."

The boss man patted a pistol at his waist. "Yeah, figured them for criminals of some type."

"Who're you with?" Homer asked.

"Federal Emergency Relief Agency," the boss man answered. "How about you?"

"Railroad," Homer answered. "Track inspector. Heading to Key West to check out some new track."

The boss man took off his hat and wiped his forehead with a red bandanna plucked from his back pocket. "How long you gonna be down south?"

"Just a couple of days."

"Word is there's a storm coming. Locals been boarding up their shacks and sinking their boats in the shallows. Most of them are idiots but they must know somethin' to survive this shithole they got down here."

Homer looked out the window and saw only blue sky and a few puffy clouds. "Looks okay to me," he said, "but I'll start paying attention."

→ ←

Afterward, standing beside the Buick on the ferry to the next key, Elsie asked Homer, "Are you worried about the weather?"

Homer studied the horizon. "Well, the railroad didn't say anything about a storm and it looks peaceful enough. But if the local people are worried, maybe we should be, too. When we get to Key West, we can ask the folks there what they think."

Elsie took Homer's arm and put it over her shoulder. "Well, I trust you to get us through no matter what happens."

"You can be sure of that," Homer answered, although he truthfully wasn't sure of anything. Now that he'd been alerted, he sensed something threatening about the fluffy clouds in the sky, something he couldn't quite put his finger on. He hugged Elsie closer and she leaned her head on his shoulder. Since he'd begun working for the railroad, he felt they had finally become true lovers, their intentions at last the same. He had sent the Captain the hundred dollars he'd borrowed along with a note explaining that he wouldn't be coming back to Coalwood. He'd put a lot more in the letter, telling the great man how much he appreciated all that the Captain had taught him, and that he guessed kismet had meant all along for him and Elsie to live in Florida with Albert. Disappointingly, the Captain had not written back but Homer knew how busy the great man was.

For the rest of the day, while Elsie admired the scenery and Albert slept and the rooster dozed atop the reptile's head, Homer drove across lonely spits of land connected by bridges and ferries until they finally reached Key West, a pastel village of houses with peaked metal roofs and wide overhangs, gingerbread trim, large balconies, long porches, and louvered shutters. "What an enchanting town," Elsie declared. "What do you think, Albert?"

Albert had come awake during the last ferry ride and had his head hanging out of the window. He made his *yeah-yeah-yeah* happy sound.

The main part of Key West was quiet and sleepy, the only person on the street a man dressed in a white shirt, shorts, and sandals who stared at them as they drove by. He had a square, intelligent face bearing an inquisitive expression and a dark mustache. He waved them down. "Is that a 1925 Buick convertible touring car?" he asked politely. "If so, you made a wise purchase."

"Yes, sir, it is, and I did," Homer answered. Elsie gave the man a demure smile. He smiled back at her.

"You're a railroad man, aren't you?" the man asked.

"How did you know?" Homer asked.

"My agent in Miami told me you were coming. I like to keep up with who's coming to my island, especially government and railroad men. Typically, I don't like either one but considering your girl here and your car and the fact that you have an alligator with a rooster on his back, I would guess you might be at least interesting. Name's Ernest. Some people call me Hem." After a brief pause he added, "As in Hemingway."

Homer answered, "I know who you are, sir. My boss told me we might be lucky enough to meet you. I'm Homer Hickam and this is my wife, Elsie, and the alligator is Albert. The rooster doesn't have a name. Do you live here all the time?"

"Mostly. Big limestone house over on Duval Street. You're welcome to swing by. Do you like cats, Elsie?"

"Oh yes, sir, I do!"

"I have some that have six toes."

"How can that be?" Elsie asked, skeptically.

"Something called genetics, I'm told. Homer, let's confirm between us that you will dine with me tonight. Come toward dusk. I want to hear all about your Buick, your alligator, your rooster, and your lovely lady, who has such a winning smile. If you have trouble finding the place, just drop by Sloppy Joe's and ask anybody for Papa Hem's house. One of those splendid lowlifes will walk you over for a quarter."

"Mr. Hemingway is delightful," Elsie commented after they'd driven on. "I wonder what John Steinbeck would think if he knew we were going to sup with him?"

"John's a kind man so he would probably wish us well," Homer said, silently kicking himself for not asking Hemingway about the weather. The author looked like a man who probably kept up with everything.

"I read one of his books," Elsie went on. "*To Have and Have Not*. I forget what it was about except there was some killing and a little romance."

Homer was half-listening. He couldn't drag his mind too far from the weather. Or his job. "The new section of track is over by the old fort," he said. "I want to go ahead and take a look."

"Aren't we going to check in at the railroad hotel first?"

"No, I want to see the new track."

Elsie gave him a look of despair. "Are you never going to learn to enjoy yourself? Look at this beautiful place. Let's check into the hotel, then walk around town. You can look at the new track tomorrow."

"I'd better look at it now," Homer said, stubbornly. "If there's a storm coming, we might have to leave before I can inspect it."

"You are such a worrywart," Elsie said. "Look at the sky! It's blue as your eyes." She reached over the seat and gave Albert a few love pats. The rooster got up and moved away from her hand. "Albert, your father is a sourpuss who can't have any fun. A shame, really."

"Leave Albert out of this," Homer said, smiling. "But you're right, Elsie. I should have more fun and I promise I will."

"Right after you inspect the new track."

"Yes, right after I inspect the new track."

"Worrywart," Elsie sang to Albert. "Sourpuss!"

The new section wasn't hard to find. Not only was it near the old fort but it was also a spur that had been added near the Key West depot. After rousting out the foreman, Homer walked the track with the measuring stick he had placed in the trunk, checked the distance between the tracks, and studied the spikes and the rails. "A barely tolerable job," he concluded. "There are at least three sections I'll want pulled up and put down again."

"If I had better-quality men, I would have laid a better track," the foreman whined.

"It's your job to make them better," Homer said. "To be a leader, you have to know how to motivate your men."

The foreman turned sullen. "They get paid. Ain't that motivation enough?"

"Not for most men," Homer said. "They want to know what they're doing is important. Captain Laird said to make a man his best, he's got to believe his best is truly necessary."

"Who's Captain Laird?"

"A great man who taught me pretty much all I know. Pull up these last three sections and put them down again. I'll be back to make sure it's done right."

"Sure, okay," the foreman said, shrugging. "But it'll be a few days before I can get started. Most of my guys are staying home to wait out this storm."

"We heard something about that," Homer said. "Is it supposed to be a big one?"

"Maybe even a hurricane. I tell you what, Mr. Hickam. If I was you, I'd take your missus and get out of the Keys real quick."

Homer politely thanked the foreman, told him again he expected him to pull up the sections of the track that were inferior and lay them down right, then drove Elsie to the railroad company hotel. It was a pleasant place, though simple, and Homer and Elsie and Albert found the accommodations suitable. The rooster had disappeared somewhere. Based on the ragged, hungry-looking characters Homer had observed on the streets of Key West, he wondered if this time his feathery friend might find more trouble than he could handle.

Toward evening, Homer and Elsie heard a knock at their door. When Homer opened it, the hotel clerk handed him a telegram. Homer was surprised at its content. "The railroad wants me to drive back to Miami as soon as possible."

Elsie was lounging on the feather bed. "Does it say why?"

"The storm. They're afraid it might turn into a hurricane."

"I remember Uncle Aubrey saying hurricanes are like tornados," Elsie said, "only a lot bigger. They go around like a whirlpool and in its center, which is called an eye, he said the wind doesn't blow at all. But once the eye has passed the wind starts blowing again, only in the opposite direction. Are we going to stay long enough to go over to Mr. Hemingway's?"

"We are since we can't leave until morning. The ferries are closed at night."

"Oh, fun," Elsie said. "Let me find Albert's leash."

After applying the wheels and the pull handle to Albert's washtub, Homer and Elsie set out. Just as Hemingway had said, the first person Homer asked, a man leaning against the wall outside the bar called Sloppy Joe's, not only knew where the house was but led them to the uneven brick wall that surrounded it. "Can I pet your alligator?" the man asked and, after receiving permission from Elsie, gingerly stroked Albert's tail. "That'll make some story back at Joe's," he said, then held his hand out. Homer filled it with a quarter and he wandered off in the general direction of the bar where he'd been found.

A knock on the door brought Hemingway himself. Dressed in slacks and a linen shirt and sandals, he greeted them effusively and walked them inside, insisting that Albert be wheeled inside as well. A maid scurried out of sight as a woman in a white dress with a green-and-white polka-dot tie, a loosely fitted belt of the same material, and white linen sandals came into the foyer. "So this is the couple you met, Papa," she said, holding out a gloved hand. "I am Pauline. The wife."

Homer shook the lovely woman's hand and Elsie curtsied. "I love your dress!" Elsie said. "What is it made of?"

"Shantung silk," Pauline answered. "Very practical and serviceable in the tropics."

Homer felt underdressed, although he had worn his best work khakis. Elsie, however, looked marvelous in the sundress with a floral pattern she had purchased from a shop near the railroad hotel.

Elsie introduced Albert and Pauline knelt beside him. "Oh, jolly," she said. "Does he bite?"

"Scarcely ever but he likes his ears scratched," Elsie said, showing Pauline where Albert's ears were. When Pauline scratched him there with her long, manicured nails, Albert preened and stretched and sighed with pleasure.

"You know," Hemingway said, thoughtfully, "I might have to get me one of those."

"None else are like Albert, sir," Elsie said. "He is a very special boy."

"I believe you," Hemingway said. "What would he like to eat?"

"He favors chicken, sir," Elsie answered. "But he doesn't have to eat."

"Nonsense. If we eat, so does he. Jim!" At the call, a servant dressed in all white appeared. "Wheel the alligator into the kitchen, Jim," Hemingway said, "and cook him up some chicken."

After Hemingway conducted a brief tour of the foyer, parlor, and dining room, dinner was served. They ate heartily of the succulent fish called a dolphin along with spiced beans, rice, and a delicious, robust cornbread. Wine was liberally served and, before long, Elsie became quite loose with her tales of growing up in the coalfields.

"You make the place sound inviting," Hemingway said, "although you must have seen your share of tragedy."

"Oh, yes, sir," Elsie answered. "Men were forever getting killed in the coal mine and my little brother Victor died of not much of anything except the lack of care. One day he was in the creek playing, the next day he had a fever that took him from us. If I had only thought to get ice to cool him, he might yet be alive."

"Ice was not available in our little town," Homer pointed out.

Hemingway reached over and took Elsie's hand. "Do you know Dylan Thomas? I have always admired his take on death. Like he, I intend to go raging against the dying of the light."

"Dear," Pauline said, "please don't tax yourself with such thoughts. And I fear you might be distressing our guests."

"Nonsense, woman!" Hemingway growled. "These two were not born with silver spoons in their mouths. They're working class! I'm certain they can handle talk about the sharp stones of death."

When a moment of quiet prevailed, Homer, who didn't care to be reminded of his abandoned coalfields, said, "Elsie is interested in writing, Mr. Hemingway."

"Is she, by God! Well, what have you written, young woman?"

"I wrote a short story about Albert. Well, it was actually a letter to my mother but another writer, a Mr. Steinbeck, who we met in North Carolina, admired its description."

"Not John Steinbeck!"

"Yes, sir."

Hemingway's dark eyebrows plunged. "He has a simple style that has proved popular, although I know not why. What kind of man is he?"

"He seemed kind."

"He was brave, too," Homer added, providing a condensed version of what had transpired at the sock mill.

"I don't think of Steinbeck as a man of action," Hemingway mused, "but perhaps I am wrong." He called for the maid to clear the table. "How is the alligator doing in the kitchen, Myrtle?" he asked upon her appearance.

"He ain't no worse than t'others you've fed in there, Hem," Myrtle answered, pertly.

Hemingway laughed heartily and beckoned his guests into a drawing room where there was a fireplace, not lit, and some comfortable leather chairs. Three of the long-haired, six-toed cats he had promised Elsie lounged nearby. After presenting them by name, then scratching each behind the ears with long stretches and purrs from the felines in response, Hemingway ordered port for himself and Homer. "Paulster, why don't you give Elsie a complete tour of the house and also visit the other cats?"

Pauline smiled. "I believe Papa wants to have a word with your husband," she said, then took Elsie by her hand and led her from the room.

→ ←

"So, you met Steinbeck," mused Hemingway over his port after the women had left. "It is a fateful peculiarity that you might meet him and me at virtually the same time. To what do you attribute that, Homer?"

"I don't know, sir," Homer answered. "Just the way it worked out, I guess."

"Don't you believe it. There are no coincidences in life. Although the big God of the Hebrews might be the greatest of them, I believe there are small gods who watch out and sometimes determine our fate. I believe they also like to have a little fun with us from time to time. Kismet. You heard of it?"

"I may have, sir."

Hemingway nodded. "There is a reason you met me and Steinbeck but what that might be, I will probably never know. Maybe Elsie will indeed become a writer. To be successful, perhaps she needed to meet writer bookends, the alpha and omega of American literature, so to speak."

"Yes, sir," Homer said, uncertain which of the two writers was the beginning of American lit and which one was the end of it. He hastened to change the subject. "I've been ordered by the railroad to head north first thing in the morning due to a storm coming," he said. "Do you know anything about it?"

"I do, indeed. The navy told me all about it this morning so I got out my charts and figured its path. From my calculations, it will be here on Monday, three days from now. The Conchs—that's the locals around here—say it's going to be a bad'un. The railroad company is right. You'd best get out of here."

"How about you, sir?"

Hemingway made a dismissive gesture. "We'll be safe enough. This house is a limestone fortress. You're welcome to stay here if you can't get out. But if you're going to go, go at first light and don't stop until you reach Miami. Even there, seek out the strongest possible structure to withstand this storm."

"You give sound advice, Mr. Hemingway. Thank you. Elsie and I will leave in the morning."

"Cigar?" Hemingway asked, proffering a box of Cubans.

Homer took one. Hemingway showed him how to cut the ends off with a little cutter and then how to light the tight roll of tobacco. When Homer took a puff, it was so strong it made him cough, which caused Hemingway to chuckle. "It has to be savored in the mouth, not inhaled," he advised. "No matter how long you live, Homer, you'll never have anything finer in your mouth than an expensive Cuban cigar after sipping fine port. That is, of course, other than the voluptuous parts of the female body."

Homer didn't know how to reply so he instead concentrated on learning how to smoke the cigar. Before long, he thought he'd mastered the process. He listened while Hemingway told fish stories and the wonders he'd seen at sea. Although Homer could have told how he and Albert joined the Coast Guard and fought a sea battle, he decided it would be impolite to interrupt the famous writer with a tale that might be even more outlandish. He listened quietly as Hemingway went on and on with how he'd caught marlins and sailfish. Afterward, he launched into several tales of France during the Great War.

After a while, Homer was feeling warm and sated and was looking forward to a nice sleep in the plush feather bed in the railroad hotel. When the women returned, Homer and Elsie collected up Albert—the kitchen staff was most reluctant to let him go—gave their thanks, and said their goodbyes.

On the stroll back to the hotel, Elsie said, "You reek of tobacco and alcohol. I think I like it."

"What did you learn during your tour?" Homer asked.

"That it is not easy being married to a famous writer. His mind is never in the present reality. It is more inside his stories. It made me decide that maybe I don't want to be a writer after all." She leaned in closer. "Yes, I like the way you smell."

The nice sleep Homer was looking forward to was put off after the feather bed was reached, Elsie still liking the way he smelled, but the rest of the night was pleasant and he slept as if he'd been drugged. He was awakened just before the sun was up by a patter on the metal roof.

"It's raining," Homer said, rousing Elsie. "We need to get going. Fast as we can."

When Homer and Elsie and Albert got to the Buick, they discovered the rooster waiting for them in the back seat. Homer thought the rooster looked worried, which made Homer even more worried. "Get in the car, Elsie," he said. "We've got to go."

Elsie sat and pulled the door closed. "I swan, Homer. Look about you. This is just a little rain cloud that's already passed. Over there's a glorious sunrise and you don't even see it. There's no poetry in your soul at all, is there?"

"Roses are red, violets are blue, if we don't hurry, we'll be in a stew. Okay?"

Shaking her head, Elsie leaned back in the seat. Homer grimly set his jaw, his eyes, and the Buick north and prayed nothing would keep them from reaching Miami before the storm hit.

On Matecumbe Key, they saw nothing of Slick and Huddie or any of the work crews. Homer drove to the shacks along the shore and found a camp cook, his occupation apparent from the dirty apron he was wearing. He was sitting on a stoop, smoking a hand-rolled cigarette.

"Looking for two men, one very short and one very big," Homer said.

"Slick and Huddie? Foreman took all the fellows down to Lower Matecumbe and some of the other keys to pile sand up in case there's a storm."

Homer thanked the man and, after a moment's hesitation, continued driving north. "It's not your fault," Elsie told him. "You can't take the time to look for them. Anyway, they'd not turn over a leaf to help you."

"I know, Elsie, but—"

"No buts, Homer. Keep driving."

Homer kept driving. Clouds were scudding in and more than a few of them were gray. Once in Miami, he, Elsie, Albert, and the rooster settled in their room at the railroad hotel located there.

All day Sunday, Homer kept checking the sky, which kept filling up with more clouds. That night, the hotel clerk knocked on his door with a message. He was to go to the North Miami Depot, there to await further orders.

"What is it, Homer?" Elsie asked.

"I don't know," Homer answered. He handed her the message. "But something to do with the storm, I'll bet."

Elsie read the note. "I'm worried," she said.

"Don't be. I'll probably just need to help shore up the track around here in case it floods."

"I'm still worried," Elsie answered, then impulsively took his hand. "Don't do anything dangerous."

"I won't."

"Yes, you will," she said. "If you think it's your job. Well, your job is right here, me and Albert."

Homer smiled. "And the rooster?"

"I don't know about him," Elsie said. "I can't figure him out."

"Maybe there's nothing to figure. Not everything has to have a meaning, does it?"

"How about love?" she suddenly asked. "Does it have a meaning?"

"I don't know about love," Homer admitted, "but your kisses surely do."

"That doesn't make a lick of sense," Elsie declared, but she kissed Homer anyway.

41

MR. JARED CUNNINGHAM, SUPERVISOR OF TRACK FOR the Florida East Coast Railway, met Homer and several other railroad men at the station in North Miami. "Boys," he said, "according to the ships at sea, this storm is a big and bad'un and it's liable to hit pretty soon, which means we got ourselves a bit of an emergency. The government's got a bunch of vets on the Keys working on the road and they've got no way to escape because the ferries have left to keep from being sunk. The feds should've figured this was going to happen but they didn't so we've been asked to go get their workers. I'm looking for volunteers." He turned to Homer. "Homer, if you're willing to go along, I need you to assess the track and the bridges. You've got the best eye for structures of anybody I've got. How about it?"

Certain of his duty, Homer instantly nodded his agreement.

The locomotive engineer, a man named J. J. Haycraft, said, "I'll go, too, Mr. Cunningham. Old number 447's way too heavy to get blown off a track by any storm. We'll do just fine. What say you, Jack?"

Jack was the fireman. "Sure, I'll go," he said.

Cunningham solemnly shook their hands. "Get going, then, and hurry."

Elsie and Albert were waiting inside the depot. "I'm going on the train to pick up the vets," Homer said after the meeting.

"We're going, too," Elsie said.

"No, Elsie. I can't let you do that. Take the Buick and you and Albert hole up at the hotel. I'll be okay. We should be back by midnight. I'll hitch a ride with Jack. He's also staying at the hotel."

It was as if Homer hadn't spoken. "Albert and I are going to ride in one of the passenger cars," Elsie said, "and there's nothing you can do to stop us."

"That's true, beyond common sense," Homer replied. "But if you stow away I'll have to be worried about you and Albert the entire time and I won't be able to do my job. Elsie, for just this once, do what I ask. Go to our room, take Albert with you and the rooster, too, please, and wait for me. I'll be along safe and sound. That's my promise to you."

Tears streamed down Elsie's cheeks and she fell into his arms. To his utter shock, she was violently trembling. "Don't go," she said. "I'm so afraid."

Homer had never seen her so vulnerable. It was almost as if she were a different woman. The journey *had* changed her, probably had changed him, too. He would have to think about that if he ever got the chance. "The engineer and the fireman are going. How can I not go?"

Elsie took a step back, wiped her cheeks, and held her head up. "All right, Homer Hadley Hickam, and if I never see you again, I will say that I love you and I guess I will still love you to the end of my days. But go. *Go!* And be done with it and your precious job and your precious duty."

Homer grinned. Having heard with his own ears Elsie Gardner Lavender Hickam tell him that she loved him, he could die happy now. He admired her as she marched away with Albert scrambling behind her. He was the luckiest man in the world to have married this beautiful, wonderful woman.

Albert, after a glance back at Homer, grunted his *no-no-no* unhappy sound. Homer nodded at him and silently bade him to take care of Elsie.

Haycraft, the engineer, came over. "Homer, don't know if you counted but we've got six passenger cars, two baggage cars, and three boxcars. That's more than I like, considering our job, but it would take too long to change them out so that's the way it is. You stay up here in the cab with me and Jack. If I see something on the track I don't like, I'll slow enough for you to get off. You run ahead, check it for me. Understood?"

Homer understood very well, said so, and climbed into the cab with the engineer and fireman. The steam was already at the necessary pressure and old 447 was soon pumping its way down the track toward the Homestead yard.

When they reached the rail turntable, Haycraft said, "I'm going to turn us around and push the cars down the track backwards. That way we can head north at top speed after we pick up the boys on Matecumbe. It'll probably be dark by then but we can use the headlamp to watch the track. Homer, you go down to the last car and keep watch. Take this lamp. Wave it if you see something and I'll stop. When it's clear, wave it again. You up to that?"

"I am," Homer said. He climbed out of the cab and walked down to the last car, which was fortunately a passenger car that afforded him a view. He climbed inside and set the lamp down, then walked out onto the back platform. To the south were dense gray clouds and the occasional flash of distant lightning. The wind was picking up and he could feel a slight change of pressure in his ears.

After the train was turned around, it continued down the single track while Homer watched for debris on the track. The wind was howling and a driven rain slapped the windows of the passenger car. The sky turned a sickly yellowish green, the sand and brush along the track disappearing into the nasty, vaporous soup. There was a low-pitched hum, which Homer realized was coming from power and telephone lines being vibrated by the high wind. When a telephone pole fell, the broken wires hanging on it whipped around like deranged snakes. A grove of myrtle bushes suddenly flew into the sky and whirled away.

When the train reached Key Largo, the sea had risen so high, it was lapping along both sides of the track bed. Homer saw that a lot of gravel had eroded, threatening to remove support of the rails. Homer considered waving the lamp but decided Haycraft could see the embankment, too. He would stop if he thought it was unsafe.

The train rolled on. Sheets of rain began to fall, making it nearly impossible to see the track ahead. Even if he saw something on it, or saw that its rails had separated or washed away, Homer estimated the train was traveling around fifteen to twenty miles per hour, too fast for him to signal Haycraft in time to stop. If his car turned over, it would be crushed like flimsy cardboard by all the other cars piling on. Still, he remained at his post.

Using a map of the railroad he found in the train car, Homer tried to figure out where they were, guessing that they were approaching Windley Key. When the rain briefly subsided, he saw a mountain of black clouds lit by flashes of blue-yellow lightning. When a lightning strike revealed people alongside the track, he leaned out and waved his light and the train slowed and stopped.

Homer braved the pelting rain and stepped down from the car. The first people he came to were a man and a woman who had collapsed beneath the onslaught of wind and water. Homer helped them to their feet. They looked at him with dazed expressions. "Get on the train," he said and pointed at the last car. "I'll get the rest."

Fighting his way along the slippery embankment against the howling wind and rain, Homer found more people huddled along the track. "Go that way," he said, pointing up the track into a wall of rain. "Trust me. There's a train there. Go!"

When he had helped aboard everyone he could find, he made a head count. There were five women, one holding a baby, three children, and three men. They were locals, none of them the veterans the train had been sent to rescue. They were all soaked, shivering, and appeared to be in a state of shock. Homer went up and down the aisle to reassure them. "You're safe now," he said, smiling at the mother with the baby. She stared back at him, speechless and eyes wild. Homer went outside and waved the lantern and the locomotive pushed the cars into the gloom. The baby started to cry and then the children and the women started sobbing, too. One of the men shouted, "We're going the wrong way!"

"We have more people to pick up," Homer replied.

"You fool! We'll never make it!"

Homer suspected the man was right. The train was descending ever farther into the storm. Shrieking demons shook the car and waves slammed against it, sounding more like cascades of rocks than water. "We're going to die," the man said. "We're all just going to die."

In an attempt to see better, Homer stepped out on the car platform but was immediately driven back by the wind, the rain blown so hard it felt like it was shredding his skin. When lightning briefly lit up the tracks, he saw the ribbons of steel were nearly underwater. He anxiously peered ahead, hoping to see a sign of the veterans. When the train slowed to a crawl, Homer caught sight of a building of some sort and then a

passing sign identified it as the Islamorada Station of Upper Matecumbe. Dark forms rose from the platform. People!

Homer waved the lamp but the train kept rolling until Homer could
make out not only the station but also a warehouse and some other out-
buildings. A roof spun off one, then disappeared into the steel-gray sky.
More shadowy people rose up but the train kept going. As Homer
watched, someone—he couldn't tell if it was a man or a woman—was
picked up by an unseen hand and flung away into the darkness. Debris
slammed into the struggling people and, one by one, they disappeared.
One man got close enough that Homer could see his desperate eyes and
his open mouth. He was yelling something but then a strip of roofing
sliced through his neck like a guillotine. The head blew away instantly
and the body cartwheeled into the water.

Finally, the train stopped. Homer put his hands over his eyes to keep
them from being pierced by the needles of rain and, through the gaps of
his fingers, looked south. Everything was underwater. As far as he could
tell, the train was resting on the only strip of track still above the ocean.

Suddenly, dozens of men, women, and children began to climb
aboard the passenger cars. Homer jumped outside and did his best to
help them aboard. There were at least a hundred of them. Drenched,
gasping in fear, they crammed inside.

The water suddenly rose to his waist and Homer lunged for a car handle and pulled himself aboard. Inside, the people yelled curses and pleas
to God for deliverance but Homer found himself preternaturally calm. It
was the coal miner in him, he supposed, or maybe it was just stupidity.
He didn't have time to figure it out.

A steel pole, ripped up from somewhere, hit a man in the back just as
he climbed aboard. He was impaled, blood spurting around the spike
that poked from his stomach. His head fell back and, with a final crim-

son jet from his mouth, collapsed on the steps. Homer, with the help of one of the other men, pushed the man and the pole back outside. "How many more are out there?" Homer screamed over the whistling wind. The man who'd helped him just shook his head. When Homer looked closer, he realized it was Huddie. "Where's Slick? Where are the rest of the veterans?"

"Don't know," Huddie gasped. "Blown away and drowned, I reckon."

"Get in a seat," Homer commanded and Huddie staggered away.

Homer leaned outside to look for more survivors. The wind kept scouring his eyeballs and he had to rub them over and over to see anything. When no one else came, he retrieved the lantern and waved it. In response, the train lurched northward but only went a few feet before grinding to a halt. When Homer again stuck his head outside, he saw a boxcar had blown off the track. The train was hopelessly stalled.

The women began to keen and the men picked up the chorus. Babies shrieked and children wailed. "Stop that!" Homer shouted, instantly regretting his harsh command.

The rescued people were looking eastward in horror. Homer pressed his face against a window. What he saw was beyond his comprehension: A wall of water at least sixty feet high was coming straight at the train.

There was nothing to be done. Homer, giving in to almighty God or fate or kismet or whatever determined the fate of all the people of the world, sat down and waited for the wave to hit. When it did, it struck the train broadside. The car was swept off the track and began to roll. Black water rushed inside and pinned Homer beneath the seats torn off their attachments. He clawed through the broken seats until he saw a flash of light and realized the car had broken apart.

The body of a woman drifted past, her dead eyes accusing him. A dead baby trailed behind her. He wanted to tell them how sorry he was, that he'd done his best to save them, but they kept moving along and, to his shame, he felt relief when both disappeared into the swirling water.

Homer swam in the direction he hoped was up and pushed through the surface, only to find the wind and water sweeping by so fast, it was impossible to breathe. A gigantic force began to turn the water all around him into a mighty, irresistible swirl and he felt himself being lifted up. For a brief moment, he was provided an aerial view of the destruction. Every car had been swept away. Only the old No. 447 locomotive remained, sitting on the only piece of track left as far as Homer could see.

The wind shot Homer away until it dropped him back into the water. He struggled for a time, but at last, completely exhausted, let the waters take him. He sank almost gratefully beneath the waves.

It was then that Albert swam past and circled back around. Why Albert was there, Homer didn't know, but he enjoyed watching him swimming around while bodies and pieces of bodies swept by. After a while, Homer began to wonder if maybe it wasn't Albert but something else, something that did not exist, yet had always existed and would forever exist.

Albert, or whatever looked like Albert, seemed to sense Homer's thoughts and beckoned with a jerk of his head, then swam off, turning around from time to time to make sure he was being followed. Homer obediently kicked after him until, finally, he discovered he'd reached the surface. Gasping, spitting out seawater, Homer grabbed hold of Albert.

But it wasn't Albert.

It was a log, a big floating log, a log with a broken branch that he could wrap his arms around. Homer did so, listening to the howl of the wind, and the roar of the sea, and the screams of the people.

42

HOURS LATER, AFTER THE HURRICANE FINALLY BLEW IT-
self out, Homer lifted his head and discovered he was lying on his back
in a bed of oozing, stinking mud and putrid-smelling grass. When he
struggled to his elbows and looked around, he saw what appeared to be
a battlefield. Splintered and shredded, the remnants of the Matecumbe
depot were strewn everywhere.

Homer got to his knees and looked for the train but there was no sign
of it. When he managed to stagger to his feet he sank into a foot of mud.
His shirt had been torn away and he had no shoes and only one sock.
The sucking mud dragged at him as he slogged through it until he
reached what he realized was the track bed. It was completely covered in
muck, and absent any rails or ties. "How am I still alive?" he asked aloud
but no one answered. He briefly thought of Elsie, and hoped the storm
had not struck Miami. After that, he set about rescuing himself.

When he found a pair of boots sitting on the track bed, he tried them
on. They fit perfectly. Why there was a pair of boots that fit him perfectly
sitting there side by side while an entire railroad had been swept away, he
could not imagine. He put them on anyway, then looked at the sky. Dark

clouds were busily scudding away. *I must find someone,* he said to himself and, careful of tens of thousands of broken planks with nails sticking out of them and coils of twisted wire with ragged ends, he followed the remnant of the track bed. Before long, he saw the first car. It was lying on its side, mud spilling out of its broken windows. Then, he saw the first body, but only the first of many.

Looking for signs of life, Homer wandered among the bodies for a long time. He climbed inside the train cars and searched them, too. Only corpses were found. He tried not to look at their faces, especially those of the children, but some of them were turned in such a way he couldn't help it. One girl, he reckoned she was about six years old, lay atop one of the cars and he supposed someone, her mother or father, perhaps, had pushed her up there. She was still dead, her eyes on the sky, where clouds were rapidly scudding away, revealing a sky the innocent blue color of a robin's egg.

At the locomotive, he pulled himself into the cab where he found Mr. Haycraft sitting on the floor, his eyes closed. Jack the fireman was also there, his head down. "Are you alive?" Homer asked.

Haycraft's eyes flew open and Jack raised his head. "You made it!" Haycraft erupted. "I was sure you drowned." He looked thoughtful. "Why didn't you?"

"I don't know," Homer said. He lifted one of his boots. "And I found these boots that just fit. I don't know why, either. How is it you're sitting here and all the rest of the train got blown off the track?"

"Old number 447 is about ten times heavier than the cars," Haycraft explained. He passed Homer a jug of grayish water, then allowed a sigh. "But I fear she will never cross another track."

"Why not?" Homer took a long swig of the warm and slightly brackish water, and realized the hurricane had even forced seawater inside the tightly capped jug. "Won't they build everything back?"

Haycraft shook his head. "No, it was foolish to build this railroad in the first place. Man who built it was named Henry Morrison Flagler, partner of John D. Rockefeller himself. He had more money than sense, you might say. Mr. Flagler's gone now and everybody like him. Nobody has the guts for great enterprises anymore. We're all out of a job, I reckon."

"What should we do now?" Homer asked.

Haycraft shrugged. "Nothing to be done. All we can do is wait until the railroad sends somebody after us. It'll be a few days, I would imagine."

"I think I'll keep looking for survivors," Homer said.

"Be my guest," the engineer said, and shrugged. "If you find somebody, give a shout and we'll come out to help."

Homer climbed down from the cab and picked through the debris around the cars. When the smell of the decaying bodies soon drove him to the water's edge, he was surprised to find a small boat bobbing at anchor. He was even more surprised to discover one of the three men aboard it was Ernest Hemingway.

Hemingway waved at him. Homer waved back. "Hello, Mr. Hemingway!" he called. "It's me, Homer. Elsie and I had dinner with you the other night."

"Yes, I recognize you," Hemingway called out. "What are you doing here?"

Homer gestured behind him. "Came on the train to rescue the road crews but the storm hit us first."

"That's because you came too late," Hemingway scolded. "Why didn't you come earlier?"

"We came as soon as we could, sir," Homer replied.

"It's always too damn late when it comes to looking after our veterans!" Hemingway railed. "Homer, I wish the feds could see this, see the bodies hung up in the mangroves, smell the stink just like in the Great War. I hoped I would never have to smell death again. Those damn rich bastards who start wars! They're cranking up the war machines in Europe even as we speak and we'll get involved, you can count on that. Those Washington, D.C., bastards will send poor men into battle, then forget them like they always do. Who left them to drown, Homer? And what's the punishment for manslaughter now?"

Taken aback, Homer could only reply, "I don't know, sir. The engineer said the railroad died here, too."

Hemingway put his hands on his hips and looked around. "So it has. So it has."

"Are you going north, sir?" Homer asked. "I could use a ride."

"We're going north for a little while," Hemingway said. "But I'm not sure where we'll turn around. Wouldn't want to strand you. Somebody'll be along to get you. Just be patient."

"Yes, sir," Homer said.

"I'm a Republican, you know," Hemingway said, for no apparent reason Homer could figure.

Homer heard footsteps in the sand and was both surprised and yet not surprised to see Slick and Huddie coming his way. The clothes of both men were rags and their faces were sandblasted. "How did you two survive?" Homer asked.

"Only the good die young," Slick said. He cupped his hands and yelled to the boat, "Hem, it's me, Slick! We shared a drink at Sloppy Joe's a few weekends back. Huddie's here, too. You got room for a couple old vets?"

"We're going north for a while, then back to Key West," Hemingway replied.

"That would suit us both just fine," Slick said. He jumped into the water and began to swim out to the boat. Huddie followed and both were hauled aboard. To Homer's astonishment, Hemingway handed them bottles of beer from an ice chest, then pulled the anchor, turned the boat around, and headed north.

Homer briefly thought about waving his arms and shouting and insisting on being carried away but his awful pride and the stoicism of generations of coal miners overcame that urge. Instead, he watched until the boat was a little white dot, then walked back to old No. 447 to wait for whatever was going to happen next. When he found a ragged shirt, he sniffed it to make certain it didn't stink too bad, then wrapped it around his face to smother as much as possible the terrible odor of the rotting bodies bloating beneath the savage sun.

*It was three days before a chartered boat sent by the railroad company ar-*rived to take away the crew of the rescue train. By then, their clothes, their hair, and even their skin were saturated with the horrific smell of death. Aboard the boat, Homer, Haycraft, and Jack cast off modesty, stripped off every inch of their clothes and dumped them into the sea. Then they jumped in, too, with a bar of soap apiece. After thoroughly scrubbing, they were welcomed aboard the boat and given some old coveralls to wear.

It would be another two days before Homer, barefoot and thumbing rides up the road, reached the railroad hotel in North Miami, there to fall into the arms of Elsie and, after holding her for a while, to pet Albert's head and thank him for coming to save him, even if it was only in a dream. Homer was not surprised that Elsie did not sob and cry with relief. Instead, she reacted with a certain detachment, like coal miner wives so often did when a feared disaster had not materialized. What was important, what *mattered*, was he had not been killed.

Later that day, Homer and Elsie sat on chairs opposite one another and just looked at each other. Finally, Homer stretched out his hands and Elsie took them. "Will you go back to work with the railroad?" she asked.

"There is no more railroad, Elsie. It's gone."

She looked into his eyes. "Tell me what happened. Everything."

He told her. At the end of the tale, he said, "I really felt like it was Albert who came to me during that hurricane."

"He's a strong boy in both body and spirit," Elsie said, gripping her husband's hands a little tighter. "So maybe it was."

"You know, when I asked Captain Laird to let me take Albert home, he said maybe this journey was so I would find out the meaning of life. But, instead, it's only created mysteries I can't even begin to understand."

"Maybe that's what life is," Elsie said. "Mysteries atop mysteries. We think we know everything but we don't know anything, not really."

"Wouldn't it be strange if Albert knew? Or maybe the rooster? They know what life means and what it is for but can't tell us except to show us."

"And we don't even realize they're doing it and don't pay any attention," Elsie said.

"God's little joke," Homer said.

"No," Elsie replied, "God's *big* joke."

As philosophizing has a tendency to do to people who engage in it, Homer and Elsie became very tired and fell silent. They slept soundly that night, then loaded up the Buick and headed in the only direction left for them to head: north.

As Homer drove, he sensed a nothingness in the air, as if everything that meant anything had been blown away, dispersed, expelled, destroyed. Outside the Buick, there was only darkness even though the sun was out. What Homer and Elsie wanted to see, they could not see and they knew it. What they wanted to see was the life they thought they were going to have before the storm. They wanted to unwind the clock, set back the calendar, cause the billions of permutations and perambulations of life to be altered just ever so slightly so that the hurricane that had so utterly destroyed the Upper Keys of Florida would have instead wobbled off to destroy some other place or destroy nothing at all but just push around a lot of wind and water.

But it was not to be. The storm had been the storm it had wanted to be and no human could change that. They could only take what the storm had wanted to give them and what it had given them was the end of a dream.

"Kismet," Elsie whispered.

Homer heard her, said nothing, but knew she was right. The storm had been given no name but Kismet would have been a good one. Kismet, the destroyer. Kismet, the torturer. Kismet, the murderer. Kismet, the assassin, thief, and demolisher of all that was right and holy if anything ever was.

→ ←

On a whim, Homer turned onto the Silver Springs road to see if the Tarzan movie folks were still there but their cottages were empty and the sets struck. Summer was over and the park itself was mostly closed, although Chuck the reptile wrangler was there. He heard their story and then looked in on Albert. "What's to happen to him?" he asked.

Homer and Elsie looked at each other and confessed they didn't know. "Before long," Chuck said, "he'll be a lot bigger and he'll be interested in the girls, too. He needs a nice swamp if he's to be happy."

"Could we leave him with you?" Elsie asked.

The wrangler shook his head. "He wouldn't fit in with some of the big old bulls that are here. They'd likely kill him. What you need to do is find a place where he could be the new fellow on the block, like someplace where there's a new lake. Some of the towns popping up for retired folks are putting in dams to make their acreage waterfront. You might look for one of those."

Chuck went back to work, leaving Elsie and Homer looking at each other. Elsie finally broke the staring match. "You think we should go back to Coalwood?"

Homer nodded. "I could wire the Captain and see if he'll take me on again. I could ask him if we still have a house, too."

Elsie put her face into her hands and shook her head. When she looked up, she had a compliant expression. "I hate the thought of it, Homer, but I will go back with you. Whatever controls us wants us to go back to Coalwood. I make no sense of it but I'm tired of fighting. Send your wire."

Homer sent the wire from the next little town. They bedded down in the car in an alley until the answer from the Captain came: YOUR JOB AND HOUSE SECURE.

"Are you ready to head north?" Homer asked Elsie.

"Just let's go," Elsie said, hanging her head.

Homer felt terrible that Elsie was still so unhappy but he figured she was right. The journey was forcing them back to West Virginia. Even when he had tried something else, a hurricane had come along and blown it all away.

It was Homer's intention to go as far north as they could go until they just couldn't go anymore. At midnight, the sign for the Georgia border loomed. "Please stop," Elsie said, then wiped furiously at her tears she could no longer hide.

Homer stopped and waited until Elsie got control of herself. He was afraid to hear what she was going to say.

"Turn around," she said at length. "We can't take Albert back to Coalwood. You heard what the reptile wrangler said. We have to find him a place to live."

"Where should we look?" Homer asked.

Elsie looked over her shoulder at Albert, then reached out and touched his nose. In response, he stretched and made his *yeah-yeah-yeah* happy sound and then went back to sleep. She turned back toward Homer. "Where we've always been going," she whispered. "Orlando."

I was sixty. Mom was ninety-one. I'd just had a book published titled *The Keeper's Son*, which was about a lonely Coast Guard captain on a windswept island. It was also about loss. The captain's father, a lighthouse keeper, had lost his wife and his son, which meant the captain had lost his mother and his brother. A woman, freshly arrived on the island, had lost all hope of ever finding love. And off the coast, ships plying through the tumultuous seas were being lost to a marauding German submarine commanded by a captain lost in nearly every way possible.

"What do you know of these things, Sonny?" Mom asked as she placed her hand on the cover of the book, which rested beside her on the couch in her South Carolina home.

"What things, Mom?"

"All that death and dying in your book. You're still too young to know about that."

In my defense, I pointed out, "My dad's gone and most of my uncles and aunts. I lost some friends in Vietnam. And accidents have taken away a few more."

She shrugged. "But not everybody. That's what happens when you get as old as I am, when loss wakes you up in the morning and puts you to sleep at night." Her hazel eyes turned a bit misty. "You never get used to it."

I had the sudden feeling that if I didn't ask, I might never hear the end of the story she and sometimes Dad had told over the years. "Mom, you never told me what happened to Albert."

She looked a bit startled. "Well, maybe that's because it's kind of hard to tell."

"Was it that bad?"

Her expression hardened. "You think I can't tell it?"

"I don't know. Maybe you shouldn't. It's up to you."

"That's right. It's up to me." She took a breath. "It always was."

PART IX

How Albert Was Finally
Carried Home

43

THEY DIDN'T MAKE IT TO ORLANDO THAT NIGHT. WHEN his eyes couldn't stay open a minute longer, Homer pulled over beside what turned out to be, at first light, an orange grove. The oranges had been picked during the summer, but the trees were still fragrant and the sweet, citrus smell slightly lifted their spirits.

After taking Albert for a walk between the trees and feeding him some chicken and then feeding themselves some ham sandwiches and miner's coffee (boil water, add coffee grounds, wait for the grounds to settle, drink), they set out again, the rooster on Homer's shoulder and Elsie doing her best not to cry at the impending loss of her alligator, and Albert poking his head out and enjoying the scenery as he had done so often on the journey. Soon, the city limits of Orlando slid by.

After he got a look at the place, Homer thought maybe he understood a little why Elsie liked Orlando so much. It was a pretty town with its Spanish architecture and waving palms and peaceful atmosphere, and the people, based on their dress and the smiles on their faces, seemed friendly and prosperous. After meandering through the quiet downtown area, Elsie recalled various buildings and streets and was able to direct Homer to a place where there was a small trailer parked beside a little lake. Behind the trailer were several palm trees. This was the new home of her rich Uncle Aubrey.

"Rich Uncle Aubrey lives in a trailer?" Homer asked.

"It's a very nice trailer, Homer. When I first came to Orlando, he lived in a big house. Now he lives here."

Uncle Aubrey soon presented himself, a dapper man wearing a straw hat, a pin-striped shirt, baggy plaid golf shorts, and spats over brown and white oxfords. Homer thought he looked more than a little bit like the comedian W. C. Fields.

Aubrey greeted Elsie effusively, hugged her close, was introduced to Homer, Albert, and the rooster, and then waved them all to a picnic table to wait for refreshments. He climbed inside the trailer, returning with a tray containing a pitcher of lemonade and three glasses. "Now, my favorite niece, what brings you back? And how did you come about this strapping man for a husband, and this grinning alligator, curious rooster, and the rare Buick, hmmm?"

Elsie's lips trembled and her eyes welled with tears. "What's this?" Aubrey asked.

Elsie had another swallow of lemonade and said, "I've come to bring Albert home, Uncle Aubrey. Do you recall the fellow I once brought to meet you, the boy whose parents owned the dance studio?"

"Why, yes," Aubrey replied, "the Ebsens. I know them fairly well. He went by the nickname Buddy, as I recall. A fine family and he seemed a decent chap. Did a few dance steps for me when I asked him about the latest craze among the young people."

Elsie nodded. "Yes, sir, that was him. Well, he gave me Albert for a wedding gift."

Aubrey arched an eyebrow. "He gave *you*? Isn't it customary that a gift goes to the couple? Did he say the alligator was just for you?"

"I assumed it was," Elsie said. "Anyway, you can see him now, a fine little boy and, well, I'm afraid he would not be happy in Coalwood where, for now, anyways, we . . ." She stopped long enough to sigh. ". . . will make our home." She looked out at the lake. "Do you think he could live here with you?"

Aubrey shook his head. "I'm sorry, sweetheart. That lake is nothing but a mud flat flooded by the land developers. It isn't suitable for alligators. You will have to look elsewhere."

Homer said, "Elsie, I have an idea. What if we drove around and looked for a new lake like the Silver Springs reptile wrangler said?"

Elsie hesitated, not certain all of a sudden she really wanted to find a place for him. *Maybe he could live in Coalwood. Maybe . . .*

"Go on, Elsie," Aubrey said. "I'll look after Albert and the rooster."

→ ←

Homer sipped his lemonade and allowed Elsie to sort things out for herself. After a few minutes, she said, "I guess it wouldn't hurt to have a look."

"I suppose it wouldn't," Homer said and got up and opened the passenger door on the Buick for her.

Elsie got in and Homer drove her back into town. Along a road with large homes and big trees, Elsie's eyes widened in disbelief. "Homer, stop the car!"

Homer stopped the car. Elsie got out and ran to a man who was walking down the street. He was a young man, and tall, and had very long legs and was dressed in a suit and vest. He was also handsome, with a square jaw and bright blue eyes. Adding him all up, Homer knew who Elsie was hugging: his nemesis. Mr. Buddy Ebsen himself.

Taking a deep, resigned breath, Homer got out of the car and approached the couple, for couple they were, Buddy's long arms wrapped around Elsie's trim waist while she pressed her lips to his, then snuggled in close.

Buddy looked up querulously when Homer approached. He released Elsie, who, clearly flustered, took a moment to catch her breath, then said, "Buddy, this is Homer. Homer, this is Buddy."

The two men shook hands. "Her husband," Homer added.

Buddy was all grins. "Well, ain't this a fine howdy-do! How are you both doing? Elsie, why are you back in town?"

"Elsie wanted to bring your wedding gift home," Homer said in a voice cold as ice.

Buddy seemed confused but then his face brightened. "The alligator! Did it truly get to you? I figured it might die along the way. Well, I just wanted you to have a little bit of Florida. I'm sorry if it caused you any trouble."

Homer discovered he was angry. "Oh, no trouble at all. Your marvelous gift merely made us abandon our house, get caught up in a bank robbery, run illegal moonshine through North Carolina, get cast adrift in the Atlantic Ocean, act in a jungle movie, and get all but blown away in the Keys! No, sir. No trouble at all."

Buddy blinked thoughtfully, then said, "Elsie, would you mind if I have a word with Homer?"

Elsie clearly did mind but she acquiesced with a tilt of her head. Buddy, taking Homer's arm, walked with him a little farther up the street. "What did she tell you about us?" Buddy asked.

"Oh, she didn't have to tell me much," Homer said. "It's all in her eyes and her voice when it comes to the great Buddy Ebsen."

"That's what I thought you thought. Listen, Homer, nothing ever happened between Elsie and me. Oh, it could have, I suppose, but I had my eye on New York and Hollywood and when I asked her to go along with me, you know what she said? She said neither of those places was for her, that they weren't real places, and then she mentioned a boy back in West Virginia. She said before she went anywhere with me, she had to know what you wanted to do and if that included her."

Homer was astonished. "Well, it did," he said. "I married her and then you sent her Albert. That's what she calls the alligator."

"Albert. Good name." Buddy chuckled. "But I didn't send him just to Elsie. I sent him to the both of you. Yes, I wanted Elsie to be reminded of Florida but I also thought an alligator might give you both a good laugh. Most people flush them down the commode after keeping them around for a week or two but Elsie . . ." He shook his head. "So she loves this critter?"

"Yes. And so do I. But we can't keep him in Coalwood. It's no place for an alligator. That's why we're here. This is his home."

"Actually, I got him at an alligator farm near Okefenokee," Buddy confessed, "but I see your dilemma." He looked over his shoulder and saw Elsie watching them. "Since I caused your problem, the least I can do is provide a solution. Let me think about it."

Homer had little confidence that the actor-dancer was really going to do anything. Still, he thanked him, then looked past him to his wife, who cocked her head as if asking, *What in the world are you two talking about?*

That was, of course, the first thing she asked as Homer drove her back to Aubrey's trailer. "Just man talk," Homer said.

"What is man talk?"

"The price of tea in China. Not much."

"I wish we'd taken Albert with us. I miss him even after a few hours."

Homer knew what she meant. The car felt lonely without Albert and the rooster. He wished he could go back to the trailer and gather them up and drive with Elsie by his side forever.

But that was impossible. Every journey has an end and this one was no exception. The only question was how.

44

TWO DAYS PASSED. EXCEPT AT NIGHT, WHEN SHE TOSSED fitfully beside Homer on the mattress laid down on the floor of the trailer's tiny kitchen, all Elsie did was sit in a cane chair in the grass with Albert beside her while she sighed and dabbed at her eyes with an old dish towel and drank strong coffee. She didn't want to go anywhere or do anything and refused to make much in the way of conversation with either Aubrey or Homer. Although she knew it was crazy, she was afraid if she said anything, it would be the excuse the two men would need to take Albert away from her. Even when she slept, she ferociously gripped his leash.

On the third day, toward evening, Aubrey pulled up the other cane chair and sat down beside her. Homer had taken Albert for a walk to let him cool down in the shallow water of the mud flat. "Now, Elsie . . ." Aubrey began.

Elsie shook her head. "I know I'm acting silly but I don't know any other way to act." She looked at Homer standing on the grass watching Albert in the water. "Albert can't live in Coalwood and we can't live anywhere else."

"You know," Aubrey tried again, "you should have children. If you care this much about an alligator, think what a great mother you'll be! Maybe, in fact, this entire business with Albert is nature's way of telling you it's about time to start a family."

Elsie glared at her uncle. "If this is nature's way, I don't want anything to do with it."

"Well, some might say it's God's way then," Uncle Aubrey replied. "Though I don't know much about God beyond the preachers I've listened to and reading the Bible some. He seems too big to me, never could get a handle on him with his making the Israelites wander around in the desert and burning bushes and flooding out the earth and sending his only son down to get crucified. The mind boggles at the whole enterprise." Aubrey waved his hands expansively. "Consider all this. The grass, the sky, the air, the water, even the metal my trailer is made of. Where did it all come from and how does it all fit together and how *has* it all fit together?" He shook his head. "It's really impossible when you think about it, everything that had to happen to bring us to this moment. Or maybe it's predestination, instructions writ down in a book somehow that our lives have to follow." He sat back, dug a flask out of his coat pocket, took a swig, and said, "Anyway, have some kids, Elsie. That'll fix you."

Elsie shook her head. "Nothing's ever going to fix me, Uncle Aubrey. Nothing."

Aubrey smiled. "Maybe you're right, honey," he said, "but maybe you're wrong, too. There's a lot of love just drifting around this old world that could fix you. Could fix all of us."

Elsie leaned forward and took her uncle's hand. "I'm sorry. I'm a hopeless case. I'm going to take a nap."

"You can't sleep your way through your problems, Elsie."

"Maybe not, but at least I won't have to think about this one for a little while."

→ ←

When Homer returned with Albert, he sat down with Aubrey. Albert stretched out at his feet. "Aubrey, I have a question for you. Did Elsie ever talk about me when she lived here?"

"All the time, although she never said your name. She described you as this very smart boy with vivid blue eyes she'd met in high school who was now a coal miner, an occupation she hated."

"What about Buddy Ebsen?"

"Far as I could tell, they were only friends. Oh, likely, they necked some but she had to know she had no future with him."

"That confirms what Ebsen told me. I wonder why she thought it was more."

Aubrey gave the question some thought, then said, "The kind of man Buddy is—all bright and cheerful and dancing around—is the kind of man she wanted and then there he was. But there was always you."

While Homer was absorbing Aubrey's words, a pickup truck came trundling down the road and stopped in front of the trailer. The driver, a farmer from the looks of him, held out a scrap of paper and said, "Hidy, Aubrey. Fellow called on my phone, asked me to give you a message."

As it turned out, the scrap of paper with the message was really for Homer.

→ ←

The next morning, after breakfast, Homer said, "Elsie, how about we take a drive?"

Elsie was suspicious. "And go where?"

"Just for a ride. It'll be like old times."

"You're not trying to fool me, are you?"

"Fool you? In what way?"

"Like carrying me off to Coalwood."

Homer smiled benevolently. "I promise we'll come right back." He bent down and stroked Albert's back. "Would you like to take a ride with us, too, Albert? It'll be fun."

Albert grinned and made his *yeah-yeah-yeah* sound and, before long, he was loaded up in his washtub and Homer was behind the Buick's steering wheel with the rooster on his shoulder and Elsie was seated beside him. It was indeed like old times.

After driving through downtown Orlando, Homer steered the Buick to a well-to-do part of town where every house seemed like a mansion. At the gate of what appeared to be a park, he pulled over to the curb. Elsie was surprised to see none other than Buddy Ebsen leaning against the ochre stucco wall that guarded the park. He was dressed in an all-white suit and a spiffy straw hat. "Buddy?" She looked at Homer. "Did you know he'd be here?"

Homer made no reply, just kept looking straight ahead. Buddy walked over to the car and opened the door for Elsie. "Welcome. This"—he made a grand gesture—"is the Country Club of Orlando, of which I am a member. I would love to take you for a tour. What do you say?"

Elsie turned to Homer. "Did you plan this?"

"Of course not," Homer said, looking at her at last. "Buddy did. He wanted to talk to you."

"Bring Albert along, too," Buddy said. "I would love to get to know him."

"It's all right, Elsie," Homer said. "Talk to Buddy. You still have something to say to him, don't you?"

"I . . . I suppose I do."

Homer got out and connected Albert's washtub to its wheels, attached the handle, and handed it to Buddy. He turned to Elsie. "I'll be here if you need me." He put his hand on Albert's head and patted it. "Have fun, little friend."

"You never called Albert your friend before," Elsie said.

"I regret that," Homer replied.

Elsie could tell by his expression he meant it. She smiled at him but something still didn't feel right.

Buddy swept his hand toward the gate. "This way, Elsie." He tugged on the washtub handle. "Come along, Albert."

The brick sidewalk led past a magnificent white building with a portico and along manicured grounds. "It's beautiful here," Elsie said, breathing in the sweet perfume of the tropical flora. As they walked farther along, she marveled at the colorful gardens and the other features of the park. "I like all these little sandy beaches. What are they for?"

"What do you think they're for?" Buddy asked.

"Places to lie in the sun?"

"Yep. Bet Albert would like that. Did you notice all the little ponds, too? They're deep and full of fish and turtles."

"Really? I bet Albert would like those, too." Elsie stopped in her tracks. "No, Buddy."

"He would love it here, Elsie."

"Those little sandy beaches, these little lakes . . . I'm not stupid. This is a golf course."

"Yes, with a groundskeeper who is one of my father's best friends. I have pledged him some considerable funding if he would watch out for a friend of some friends of mine."

Elsie shook her head. "This is a golf course," she said again.

"Of course, it is," Buddy answered. "Come with me."

They walked on until, at last, Buddy stopped and nodded toward a lake that was larger than the others. "This is the seventh fairway," he said. "Here is Albert's home."

Elsie looked at the lake. It was a beautiful lake, blue and sparkly and surrounded on one side by a shady grove of pin oaks. Perfectly spaced palm trees circled the rest of the lake except for a wide opening that met the green grass of the fairway. Nearby was a large sand trap. She looked down at Albert and then up into Buddy's face. Her stomach was churning. She thought she might be sick.

"I'll think about it," she told Buddy.

"No, Elsie," Buddy said. "You can't think about it. You just have to do it." He dropped the handle of the washtub, walked around it, and picked up Albert's tail. Albert looked back at him with an expression of curiosity. "Help me. Help me carry Albert home."

Elsie knelt at Albert's head and wrapped her arms around his snout. "I can't do it."

"Yes, you can," Buddy said.

"I love you, Albert," she said, simply, and it was all she could say because of the gorge in her throat.

Albert grinned and made his *yeah-yeah-yeah* happy sound. Elsie picked him up beneath his front legs and, together, she and Buddy waddled down the slight slope to the water's edge, where they set Albert down.

Albert turned and looked up at Elsie. He was still smiling, eager for whatever new adventure she had in mind for him. Elsie knelt beside him while Buddy walked back to the washtub and pulled it along, back up toward the building with the portico, which Elsie now realized was the golf course clubhouse.

Elsie pointed toward the lake. "Go home, Albert," she said, her voice cracking. "Please go home."

Albert's smile faded. He stared at her, then nuzzled her with a questioning grunt. She pushed him away. "No! You have to go home. This is home! Don't you understand? Get in that water, Albert!" She pointed at the lake. "Go on! You can't be with me anymore. Go!"

Albert cocked his head and seemed to be thinking. He turned around and made a tentative step toward the water, then looked back. Elsie waved him on. "That's it. Go take a swim. It will be all right, Albert. I'll be right here. I'll never leave you."

Albert put a foot in the water, then two, then pushed off. He waved his tail and slipped through the water.

Elsie ran past Buddy, past the clubhouse and through the gate. Homer was leaning against the Buick, holding the rooster. She threw herself at her husband and he opened his arms to her, the rooster fluttering away. "Carry me home," she cried. "Homer, *carry me home*!"

EPILOGUE

AND SO HOMER CARRIED ELSIE HOME TO COALWOOD. The rooster did not go with them. Where he went, no one ever knew.

As for Albert, well . . . here is what little I can tell you.

Once in Coalwood during my growing-up years, my father read in the paper that a huge alligator in Florida had scared a woman golfer by abruptly coming out of a lake next to a fairway. It so startled her that she fell down and began to scream, certain that she was about to be attacked. But she was not attacked at all. Instead, the alligator walked up to her and rubbed itself against her legs, then turned upside down as if asking to have its ample belly scratched. The woman got up and ran, her peculiar story soon making the national news. There was no plan to remove the alligator from the pond, the article went on, as it was considered a pet by the membership of the club.

In a strained voice, Dad called out, "News of Albert, Elsie! *News of Albert!*"

There was no reply but when I walked into the kitchen, I discovered my mom, who was washing the dishes at the time, looking through the window into the darkness as if she were looking a million miles away.

Then she put down the plate she was washing, slowly wiped her hands on her apron, and walked into the living room, where my dad was sitting in his easy chair with the newspaper in his lap. She held out her hand and he handed her the paper. She read it and then did the most astonishing thing. Never one to show much affection toward him, she sat on Dad's lap and hugged him. "Thank you," she said. And to my further astonishment, for the one and only time in the history of my life and his, I saw my father bury his face in my mother's hair and weep.

A Further Postscript

IN OCTOBER 2009, MY MOTHER LAY ON HER DEATHBED, clearly disappointed. She was ninety-seven years old and had hoped to live to be one hundred but, based on her doctor's candid report and the fact that her second son was uncharacteristically hovering about, she knew she probably wasn't going to make it. To cheer her up, I told her I would drive her over to the beach, an offer I thought for certain she'd at least entertain. After all, it was her love for the sand and salt air and the sea of the South Carolina coast that had caused her to decamp from landlocked West Virginia many years before. But her response was a firm no. "I don't want to go to the beach," she said. "I'm done with the beach. I don't need it anymore."

My father had been gone by then for two decades, the coal dust in his lungs finally taking him only a few years after he had left Coalwood and joined Mom at the beach. They seemed to have a good life there, although I understood very well that Dad was only there because he felt he owed it to his wife after the years she'd spent in Coalwood.

I pulled up a chair and held my mother's hand. It felt so fragile that I thought if I squeezed it too hard the bones inside would turn to powder.

They had once been a working woman's hands, strong enough to snatch me up by the nape of my neck when I was pulling one of my usual childhood pranks and swat me a few. Now, as her life ebbed, her body was turning to fine crystal that the mildest distress could shatter. When she said she didn't want to go to the beach, I knew she was truly on her way out.

Her bed had been moved into the living room of her house so the hospice workers would have room to work around her. They needn't have bothered. She had no need of them. Before long, she lapsed into a state that was neither here nor there and neither now nor then. She talked to her long-dead brothers, Charlie and Ken and Robert and Joe, and to her mother and father. She even talked to Victor, the brother who had died of fever when he was but a child. And, of course, she talked to her cats and her dogs, who had departed the world so many years before, and her late, much lamented pet fox Parkyacarcass, and her beloved squirrel Chipper. I was told by her caretakers she really enjoyed talking to the fellow named Albert, whoever he was. I smiled and said, "I'm not surprised."

The hospice workers also said they never heard her talk to her husband. I told them I wasn't surprised about that, either, that I thought they managed to say everything they wanted to say to each other while he was alive.

As her days ticked down, Mom sometimes held both her hands toward the ceiling as if she were holding something. When a nurse pushed them down, she put them back up. "I'm reading," she explained. After she finished her book, she lowered her arms on her own. She was, I believed, writing and reading her own book. She had always wanted to be a writer.

On a visit I suspected would be my last, I was sitting beside her when her breathing slowed and became shallow. I thought this was the last but then she opened her eyes and looked at me. "Those stories about Albert," she said, "they were fun to tell."

"I probably learned more about Dad in those stories than anything else," I said. "But, Mom, what *really* happened?"

She took a deep breath, then accomplished a small shrug, her thin shoulders barely moving against the white sheets. "We drove to Florida and let Albert go at a golf course near where Uncle Aubrey lived, then drove home."

"What about all the other things you said you and Dad did?"

"We did them all," she said in a voice I had to strain to hear, "even when we didn't."

I held her hand, feeling the warmth of it gradually turning cold, and believed, really believed, and as I believed, I heard a sound that sounded like someone or something very far away saying, *Yeah-yeah-yeah*. It was a happy sound. "Hello, Albert," I said into the forever that seemed to be opening up for the frail woman on the bed. "Get ready for her. Your mom is coming home."

Acknowledgments

COALWOOD, WEST VIRGINIA, WAS BUILT TO MINE COAL but strong families ended up as its most important product. I was lucky to be part of one of those families headed up by two very interesting people, Homer and Elsie Lavender Hickam. I am indebted to them for raising me and seeing to my education and also providing the stories that comprise this book.

The story of Albert's journey wouldn't have been written without the encouragement of Frank Weimann, my marvelous literary agent. When I proposed the idea to him, I fully expected him to say that it was crazy. Instead, he immediately said it was a story I needed to tell and for me to get right on it.

Albert's story also wouldn't have been told without the support of Kate Nintzel, my wonderful editor at William Morrow. She made it "her book," and much of the novel is the result of her insights and suggestions as she guided me through its creation. When Kate had other obligations, editor Margaux Weisman was always there to help me and Albert along.

ACKNOWLEDGMENTS

I am now lucky to be part of another strong family and that is the one at William Morrow. At the risk of leaving someone out, I want to thank publishers Liate Stehlik and Lynn Grady for their kind and generous support. Also thanks go out to Jennifer Hart (group marketing director), Kaitlin Harri (marketing), Kaitlyn Kennedy (publicist), Juliette Shapland (international sales), Adam Johnson (cover art), Virginia Stanley (academic and library marketing), Tricia Wygal (production editor), and everyone at this great literary house.

Thanks also to my wife, Linda Terry Hickam, who is my first reader and always has great insights. She even found a life-like stuffed toy alligator for us to carry around in our car so I could get an idea of what Albert in the back seat was like. She didn't provide a rooster because she said she didn't understand why he was on the journey. Neither do I but as long as he did, I guess that's all that matters.

Photographs Pertaining to the Journey

CARRYING ALBERT HOME IS A FAMILY EPIC, WHICH MEANS it's a blend of fact and fiction, evolved from stories told by my parents, both of whom were West Virginians and knew how to make their tales tall as the hills that surrounded them on all sides. Still, there are clues as to what was real and what wasn't in the photographs my mother kept that were discovered in a number of cardboard boxes after she passed away.

When I finished writing this book, my editor, the wonderful Kate Nintzel, asked me to look for any photos that might have something to do with the journey. I hauled out Mom's boxes to see what was there. Unhappily, in most of the photos, Mom didn't think it was necessary to identify the people who were in them. This isn't a criticism. We're all guilty of keeping photos that other folks wouldn't understand without an attached description. Still, it was frustrating as I went through the old pictures she thought were important enough to keep for decades. Photograph after photograph, the eyes of people, young and old, stared back at me, saying, in effect, *I was important to your mother but you don't know why, when, or where.* Some I could identify, such as my grandparents and my uncles and aunts and so forth, but not my uncle Victor, who died long before I was born. Fortunately, his photos were one of the few Mom identified.

In *Albert*, I have Elsie talking about Victor, who, it's clear, she still thinks about a great deal and whose death has profoundly affected her. Still, I was surprised at the number of pictures of this tragic little coal camp boy she had saved. Just as I wrote, I think she never stopped mourning him. During the few times she spoke of Victor to me, she said she thought Victor would have been a writer. Why she thought that, I don't know. Some people, looking at those old pictures, think Victor and I look something alike. Maybe, somehow, Mom positioned me to fulfill the hopes and dreams she had had for her brother. If so, I'm glad she lived long enough to see me become an author of many books. Of all the things I did in my life, I am certain she was most thrilled by my success as a writer.

One of my hopes during my archaeology photo dig was to find an image of Albert. When I found pictures of Mom's other peculiar pets, such as her fox Parkyacarcass and Chipper her squirrel, I was encouraged. Sadly, however, no images of the alligator turned up. A tantalizing clue to his existence, however, was revealed when I found a photo taken at the company house where my parents lived in the 1930s and 1940s. In it, a cat (or it might be Parkyacarcass) can be seen drinking from a concrete pond. The coal company, which owned the house and the yard, was not given to installing ponds for its coal miners. In fact, the installation of such a permanent and expensive addition in the yard of a company house would have been considered foolish. After all, company houses were assigned to miners only for the duration of employment. So what was the pressing need for such a pond? When I grew up in the same company house, I knew that pond very well, although Mom had prettied it up with plants. Even though I didn't understand it at the time, she called it the alligator pond. It was only when she began to tell me the story of Albert's journey that I understood why.

Continuing my photographic excavation through Mom's old boxes, I came across a number of pictures that show her in Orlando with various friends and her Uncle Aubrey. In them, she is radiant, fresh, and happy, very much different from the frustrated and often acerbic woman I knew in Coalwood and described in my memoirs *Rocket Boys* (aka *October Sky*), *The Coalwood Way*, and *Sky of Stone*. I think she forever yearned for those carefree days in Orlando when once she had danced with a funny, charming, long-legged boy.

Of the photos I found of my dad as a young man, his facial expressions indicate a thoughtful, serious fellow quite similar to the older Homer I knew. Over the years and in other books, I have struggled to figure out who he really was and what motivated him to become the man he became, tough and relentless to others while patient and deferential to his often difficult wife. Certainly, he took on the challenges presented to him over his lifetime with all the strength and intelligence he could muster. One of those challenges, most certainly, and to the end of his days, was Elsie Gardner Lavender.

Although Mom and Dad never mentioned they had brought along a camera on the journey, two photos turned up that might have been taken during the events chronicled in this novel. One of them of Elsie is marked on the back "KW Garden, 1935." Could it be her in Hemingway's Key West garden? It would have certainly been like Pauline Hemingway, a pleasant and kind woman by all accounts, to send it to her. Another is marked "SSprngs," which shows a young Homer holding a pith helmet beside what might be a glass-bottom boat. Was this in Silver Springs, Florida, during the journey? And is that the reptile wrangler's helmet? There's no way to know. All I can say is I believe all the images shown in this section had something to do with the time when Albert was carried home, and love, that strange and marvelous emotion, was left to endure in the hearts of Homer and Elsie Hickam.

Elsie, fresh off the bus from West Virginia after graduating from high school, poses in Orlando, Florida, where she went to live with her rich Uncle Aubrey. Soon she would meet Buddy Ebsen and fall in love.

Homer, in a photo marked "SSprngs" on the back, is beside what is possibly a glass-bottom boat at Silver Springs, Florida. Is this evidence he and Elsie were really in a movie being filmed there? Note he is holding a pith helmet. Did it belong to the reptile wrangler?

Elsie, in a fancy dress sitting on the running board of a fancy car. This was in Orlando during her "Buddy" days. Soon Buddy would leave and she would go back to West Virginia and marry Homer.

Elsie, fresh and relaxed, lazes beside a lake near Orlando. She would long for those days for the rest of her life.

Elsie's "rich" Uncle Aubrey and an unidentified friend on a golf outing. He had some remaining funds even after the Great Depression, enough that he continued to play golf on posh courses in the Orlando area.

One of the few photos Elsie marked was this one of her "Uncle
Aubrey Bouldin." He was her mother's brother. This was apparently
taken on one of his few trips to see his sister as un-Floridian
mountains are in the background. He was a dapper dresser!

Another photo of Uncle Aubrey on a visit to his sister, Elsie's mother.
This photo was not in coal country but probably on a farm along the
way. It was on one of these trips that "rich" Uncle Aubrey offered
Elsie a chance to escape the coalfields and come live with him.

Victor Lee Lavender was Elsie's youngest brother who died when he was six years old from an unspecified fever, probably the flu that led quickly to pneumonia. She grieved for Victor all her days. It was her belief that he would have been a writer. For that reason, she was happy that her youngest son eventually became one.

Elsie Hickam, probably in the early 1930s in Orlando, Florida.
There she attended secretary school and worked in a diner.

Homer Hickam (senior), probably at high school graduation in 1929. His family apparently went all out for the photo, paying for colorization. His vivid blue eyes were what originally attracted Elsie to him.

This photo was marked "KW Garden 1935." Could this be Elsie in a garden on Key West, perhaps even at the Hemingway house?

Photo taken in Coalwood, West Virginia, around 1949 of brothers Jim (left) and "Sonny" (Homer Jr.) Hickam. Jim is holding their new puppy. Behind them to the right is the pond that Elsie, their mother, called the "alligator pond." This is the pond her father built for her to hold Albert.

Photo taken in Coalwood, West Virginia, probably around 1940. The cat (or it might have been Elsie's fox) can be seen drinking from the "alligator pond." The house and yard belonged to the coal company, so Elsie's father installed it for her to hold Albert.

Elsie and her "rich" Uncle Aubrey in their happy days in Orlando. All too soon, Elsie would go back to West Virginia.

This photo, taken in the 1950s, is the house where Elsie and Homer Hickam lived when they had Albert in the 1930s. A former boardinghouse, the company turned it into a duplex, the one on the right the one occupied by the Hickams. The large plant along the fence line is the site of the pond built for the alligator. The company filled in the pond after Elsie and Homer moved to another Coalwood house.

Reading Group Questions

- Do you think the marriage of two young people like Elsie and Homer would last today?

- What is your opinion of Elsie and Homer? Did you like them both equally? Did you understand their motivations? How were they different?

- Did you like Albert? If so, what made him likable? Do you think a real alligator would act that way?

- Why do you think John Steinbeck and Ernest Hemingway have cameos in the novel? Did you like the way Hickam wrote about them?

- Although the novel states that the rooster's purpose in the story is not entirely understood, do you have an opinion about why he made the journey? Does he have a particular significance?

- Why do you think Buddy Ebsen sent Elsie the alligator?

- Did the novel make you want to put an alligator in a bathtub in the backseat of your car and go on a 1000-mile road trip? In these times, what do you think would happen if you did?

- Why do you think Huddie and Slick kept popping up in the novel?

- Why do you think Homer loved Elsie so much? What about her was lovable? Do you think Elsie loved Homer?

- Hickam says that in the process of writing the novel, he came to understand that the stories his parents told him about Albert were their 'witness and testimony to what is heaven's greatest and perhaps only true gift, that strange and marvelous emotion we inadequately call love.' Do you agree this was a love story?